2

D0498363

*The*
*Apprentice*
*Lover*

# The Apprentice Lover

## A NOVEL

## JAY PARINI

HarperCollins*Publishers*

HarperCollins books may be purchased for educational, business, or sales promotional use. For information, please write: Special Markets Department, HarperCollins Publishers Inc., 10 East 53rd Street, New York, NY 10022.

FIRST EDITION

*Designed by Lia Pelosi*

Printed on acid-free paper

Library of Congress Cataloging-in-Publication Data is available upon request.

ISBN 0-06-621071-2

02 03 04 05 06 ❖/RRD 10 9 8 7 6 5 4 3 2 1

*For Devon,*
*these and all other words*

*prologue*

Surprising even myself, I dropped out of Columbia during my last term, in 1970, just three months short of graduation, and went to live on Capri. I left behind my college friends, my parents, and everything familiar in an attempt to cut loose from the overfilled barge of my youth, which had become too heavy to drag. My departure was hard on everyone, especially me, but I had no choice—or that's how it seemed then.

It had been a terrible winter, and spring had so far been worse. I lay awake at night, disoriented, as if tumbling into a well, fading and falling. Alice with no Wonderland at the bottom of the hole. And nothing seemed to help: barbiturates, prayer, pot. The world, by day, was tinny and artificial, a 3-D movie watched from a seat in a darkened theater, looking in on life from outside, alternately depressed or anxious, always distracted, sure I would never live beyond the age of twenty-five. (Always a slight hypochondriac, I now read minor ailments—overgrown pimples, tension headaches—as signs of melanoma or brain cancer, thus giving my spiritual unease a convenient physical location.)

In calendar years, I was twenty-two, but emotionally I was younger. That winter and spring, I read a great deal, as usual, but everything seemed, overtly or covertly, about love or war, the two subjects that sat like deadweights on my chest. I marveled at the passion of Ovid in his love poems for Corinna, wondering what it might feel like to care so much about someone, full of a vaguely disembodied sexual longing that made me queasy at times, ill with dissatisfaction. I would have liked to make contact, physical and emotional, with some of the women at Columbia, but the effort seemed beyond me. On the subject of war, the rhetoric of Virgil struck me as verbiage, however stirring. I didn't care a feather about the fate of Rome or its empire. Caesar's Gallic wars were not mine. I'd had enough of wars, ancient and modern.

My only brother, Nicky, had been killed in Vietnam a few months before my departure. He died near Quang Tri, in winter, having volunteered for what his lieutenant in the obligatory letter to my parents called "a routine reconnaissance mission." He had stepped on a land mine, which meant you didn't get to see the body, or its remnants, when they shipped it home in a medically sealed bag. I can still see my poor father, standing bereft at the back of the church, shaking his head and fumbling with a rosary. Nicky had been dear to him, a son who had reflexively obeyed the call of his country, as he had, during the Second World War.

The steel casket was draped in a flag. They had played taps in the cemetery in Pittston, an honor guard standing by from the local VFW, where my father went most Saturday nights to play cards with old friends and fellow veterans, all of whom believed adamantly in the righteousness of the Vietnam War. "Nick was a real hero," the letter from the lieutenant had said, without elaboration, leaving the details (supplied by countless war movies) to our imaginations, which was probably just as well.

I knew something about Nicky's war and how it felt to him. He had taken to writing me letters from Vietnam—the first real communication with him that I'd ever had—and I knew exactly what he thought about this particular war. He hated it, and would have found the flag-draped casket deeply ironic. "This war is about nothing I understand or believe," he wrote. "The whole thing stinks. It's not just stupid, a well-intentioned adventure that somehow went wrong. It's fucking evil. And the worst evil is always one that follows from ignorance." Nicky had become a student of that ignorance, and took pleasure in going over the details with me.

Perversely, my brother's death guaranteed that my draft board, in Luzerne County, would let me alone. The members of that august body knew my father and grandfather well, and it was tacitly agreed that families should suffer only one death per nuclear unit in Vietnam. I would never be drafted, despite my low number in the national lottery. "You're free," my mother, in a hoarse ironic voice, had whispered as we passed beneath the leafless, iron-colored beech trees, walking away from Nicky's grave, which overlooked the Susquehanna River.

Free—a lovely word. Yet I felt less free than ever before. Nicky had been the one my father assumed would join the family company, Massolini Construction, founded by my grandfather and now managed by my father. Nicky was the one who was "good with his hands," and his death had interrupted that plan. In an ill-conceived moment, thinking it would comfort them, I told my parents I would return to Pittston myself, to work in the company, upon graduation from Columbia. They had been surprised, but pleased—even delighted. "Why not?" my father said, suppressing an outright smile. "We can use a good man, somebody with your brains. You're gonna run the company yourself pretty soon." My grandfather had simply kissed me on either cheek: the ultimate blessing.

My mother was quietly satisfied by this turn of events. "You're a good boy, Alex," she said. "We need you around here." Nicky was lost, but she would have me forever. This decision of mine made sense in Pittston, since everybody in the town already thought of me as my mother's son. And they were not far wrong. I loved her, and she loved me, and my father had never been quite allowed into the intimate circle that we drew around us. As a kid, I went shopping with my mother every Saturday afternoon, just the two of us, and we'd stop at Bellino's, a soda fountain in Wilkes-Barre, for milkshakes and hamburgers. We had picnics together by the river in late spring, under heavily scented cherry blossoms, and her pannier overflowed with things I loved: imported vanilla biscotti, parmesan and provolone cheese, sardines, and Genoa salami. In summer, she would take me into New York to see musicals on Broadway while my father and Nicky went to Yankee Stadium. All her aspirations had been put into one basket by the name Alexander Massolini.

Yet I bolted. Without bothering to explain—to my parents or myself— I abandoned the United States and Massolini Construction and my college career, taking an unlikely position in southern Italy as secretary to

Rupert Grant, the eminent Scottish writer, who had lived for the past decade in a villa on the island of Capri in the Bay of Naples. My parents (neither of whom had gone to college) were more confused than angered by this move. They had lost Nicky, and now I was disappearing into the unknown. To them (and both were Italian Americans) Capri was outer space. I might as well be sending myself into orbit, with no promise of return.

"All the money we put into your education," my mother said, sighing, "and this is what comes of it? You don't even get your degree? You don't even want a normal job?" She complained that I showed her and my father "no respect." She could never have imagined treating her own parents in such a way. ("It would have killed your grandmother, God bless her, and may she rest in peace.") *Respect*, my mother said, again and again. That was the essential filial act, and it was a word she dropped like a stone into our conversations, an incontrovertible truth. But I was tired of showing respect. What I needed now was something more difficult to demonstrate: self-respect.

The scene at the hotel in New York, on the night before I sailed on the S.S. *Genovese*, was more harrowing than I'd feared. My mother, whose heart was famously bad, could not pull herself together for the occasion. Her blood pressure, which my father had dutifully learned to take, approached life-threatening levels in these circumstances, and it wavered into dangerous territory that night. Palpitations ensued. You could see the thumping in her temples, her pulse like some native drumbeat in the jungles of New Guinea, manic and relentless.

"You got to calm yourself, Margarita," my father said. "The bottom number is over a hundred. Dr. Senna told me that's not okay. You're gonna get a stroke with that kind of number." We had worried relentlessly about her blood pressure ever since she had been taken to the hospital a couple of years before with dizziness and shortness of breath. "This is nothing cardiac," she maintained, with the medical equivalent of false modesty. "The doctor, he said, 'Mrs. Massolini, your heart is holding up fine. But you're not a young woman anymore.'" Her blood pressure, however, had to be brought under control. "You ever see what happens when you don't take the lid off the marinara?" she said. "Splat—

the sauce explodes over the wall." I had heard this before, and often imagined my mother splattered like tomato sauce on the walls, her eyeballs stuck there, staring.

"First Nicky leaves me, then you," my mother said, her baleful eyes fixed on me. What I heard was *How can you be doing this to me, the one who raised you?*

"Nicky is dead," I said, holding her gaze. "He didn't leave you, Mom. He's goddamn dead."

My father, a slight man in his mid-fifties, with a bright gold tooth that glinted when he smiled, stepped from the shadows and slapped me, a quick backhanded swipe that stung my cheek and brought tears to my eyes. This was the first and only time he ever hit me. Horrified, I pressed my back against the paisley wallpaper behind me, trembling. Briefly, I hated him. Not only because he had hit me, but because he had once again succumbed to my mother's whims, playing into her narcissism, her need to control the lives around her and make every figure in her gaze an extension of her own imagination and sensibility. He had failed me, now as before. He had not protected me from the perpetual warfare waged on my independence by my mother. She wanted to absorb me, and my father understood this, and he had been unwilling, or unable, to help. If anything, he had helped Nicky more—defending him against her, making excuses for his escapades, even admiring them. Not surprisingly, my studious character, my love of reading and writing, baffled and threatened him.

"Your mother hasn't suffered enough, is that it?" he asked, furious but already backing down emotionally. A man who prided himself on self-control, he could not contain his own trembling. Now his eyes glistened, and he sucked quick breaths. I thought he might faint.

Recognizing his weakness, I softened. "I'm sorry," I said. "I really didn't mean . . ."

"You didn't mean," he said, shaking his head. "The problem with you, Alex, is you don't mean. Sometimes, I swear, you don't think. A college boy, and you don't think about what you mean and what you don't mean." There was more sadness in his voice than anger, and I felt ashamed. Always, in my family, it was considered a failure, a mistake, for a male to show emotion, to lose his temper and lash out. Men controlled themselves. They managed to stifle emotions before they could root and grow into visible feelings.

My mother—a woman of two hundred and thirty pounds in her bare feet—collapsed on the bed, sobbing quietly. Her shiny black hair fanned out against the tangerine swirl of the bedspread. Her pulpy hands were tucked beneath the pillow, supporting her head. The hem of her red polka-dot dress, which had been a gift from me on her fiftieth birthday the year before, rode up to her thighs. I could not look at her. She had provoked a crisis, it had crested violently, and the denouement continued. The narrative pattern was familiar but no less painful.

My father stepped closer to me, face to face—a rare move for him. I was four inches taller, but still cowed by this compact, muscular man of few words and little in the way of formal education. His silences unnerved me. "You go to Italy if that's what you want to do," he said. "But you're breaking her heart. Look at her, Alex. And don't forget what you see."

How could I forget it? I'd been so close to my mother, and breaking her heart was the last thing on earth I wanted. I didn't want to break anything, but I had no choice—or believed I had no choice. To stay would have meant being overrun. My interest in literature, and my going to Columbia, had taken me rapidly along paths leading away from northeastern Pennylvania and home. Had I really attempted to take Nicky's place by going back, the results would ultimately have dismayed everyone. My expectations for myself, and my parents' vision of me, were deeply at odds.

Nicky was thirteen months older than me, and not a likely soldier. A delicate, intelligent child, prone to asthma attacks and ear infections, he made up for his frail start by taking karate lessons at the Catholic Youth Center in Scranton. The sport had "brought him out," as my father said, and he became a black belt at fourteen. This mastery of a violent art had borne some dark fruit, and twice he got himself expelled for kicking ass in the schoolyard. In senior high, he resisted every attempt to tame him, acting like a young Marlon Brando, appropriating all the hackneyed symbols of rebellious youth: T-shirts, Lucky Strikes, motorcycles. Nicky was smart enough, probably smarter than me, but he never did a stroke of work or paid attention in class. That he got into King's (a small Catholic college only a few miles away) had seemed a miracle—a tribute to my grandfather's influence in the community—but he dropped out during his sophomore year, worked briefly in a car parts store owned by a friend of the family, then enlisted in the army before the draft board could make its move. (My father, of course, roundly approved of Nicky's decision.) Fairly soon after basic training in North Carolina, he'd been shipped to Vietnam. Only a few months were left on his tour of duty when it suddenly and sadly ended.

My mother loved Nicky, but she had put her hopes on me. Second in my class at Scranton Prep—a good Jesuit high school—I'd turned down Georgetown for Columbia, and done well there, majoring in classics. My mother thought I might return to my old school in triumph, as a Latin teacher. "Father Gallucci keeps asking about you," she said, though I knew she was making this up. Gallucci hated me, ever since an infamous theology class where I questioned the Argument from Design, wondering why God, if he had designed the universe, had screwed up so badly. Gallucci's feral stare dissolved into a smirk. "Mr. Massolini," he said, "please tell the class exactly what God has 'screwed up' so badly." Without missing a beat, I had said, "Why, this school, Father. In an ideal universe, could this school exist?"

That flash of rebellion, for me, was rare. A good boy by training and inclination, I kept my head down and my mouth shut. But Gallucci, with his tight-assed spiritual smugness, brought out the worst—or the best—in me. It was implausible that he would have asked my mother about me, but she made up this kind of thing, trying to manipulate me. I had, however, become a serious student of her deceptions, and at some point in high school I determined she would not trap me, not ever again.

After a night of sobs that came like intermittent squalls (I slept in the adjacent double bed), my mother pulled herself together, accepting her defeat in this particular battle, although certain she would prevail in the general war. My father, too, had becalmed himself and sunk back into his old, submissive role. The next morning, he apologized at the breakfast table for hitting me. "Don't take it personal," he had said, over hash and eggs in a coffee shop on Sixth Avenue, near the hotel. "I kind of lost my temper last night, but I didn't mean anything by it." My father had indeed meant it, but this was no time to insist on truth-telling. He wanted to make up with me before my departure, and so did my mother. To separate on bad terms in these circumstances would have been horrific for everyone.

After a silent taxi ride along Eighth Avenue, we got off near the docks, overlooking the Hudson. My father, peering warily around at the street bums, helped me find a porter, and I disappeared into the crowd at Pier 49 after the briefest of good-byes—a peck on my mother's cheek, and a firm handshake from my father. (The hard calluses on his hand reminded me that his working life mattered to him more than anything that happened at home. He could be almost Napoleonic at work: directing large numbers of men and machines into action, attracting admiration, even adulation, from his employees.)

The *Genovese*, as my father had noted from dockside, was "not exactly the *Queen Mary*." It was "kind of crummy" as ocean liners went. This, in fact, would be its final transatlantic voyage, sailing from New York to Genoa in eight days . Nobody had troubled to scrape and repaint the hull in many years, and the general state of neglect showed. But I hardly cared. To get away was luxury enough.

On the aft deck, a small figure in the excited company of passengers, I pressed to the cold railing and waved the white handkerchief my father had stuffed into my pocket when he saw my tears. ("You're gonna do fine, Alex," he had whispered in my ear. "Everything is gonna be beautiful over there. You got a way about you I never had." He didn't really know how I would do, but he guessed it was his role, as father, to reassure me. But I knew, and he knew, that I was setting forth into a huge blank space—a world far from anything he or I had known.)

My parents, Vito and Margarita, who had loomed so large through my past two decades, dwindled as the strip of rubbery water between myself and them lengthened, stretched to a point of unbearable tension, then snapped. My stomach hardened, my intestines braiding themselves in knots, as I kept waving (pointlessly, since they couldn't see me now) and the boat passed the Statue of Liberty, which had welcomed my grandparents only five decades before. ("I can't tell you what she meant to me, that lady," my grandfather always said. "There's no words. After weeks at sea, she stood there like a giant. Everybody went down on their knees in the rain, on the wet deck, on their goddamn knees.")

It seemed ungrateful of me to reverse the journey my grandparents had made with such difficulty. My mother's parents, who were dead, had come from Liguria in 1908. My father's, who were still very much alive, set out from Naples in 1919. I had heard the story so many times from my paternal grandfather, about how packed the ship had been, with people taking turns sleeping in the tiny bunks, and everyone lice-ridden, seasick, and worse. They had abandoned their families—poor, illiterate, well-meaning people—and made their way across a vast, threatening sea. "It was bad weather all the way, and the weak ones died," he told me. He, of course (and that was the point of the story) was not among the weak ones.

If anything, my grandfather—Alessandro Massolini—was the strongest man I have ever known—a figure who dominated his only son, Vito, who had never really found his own way. Indeed, his stint in the Second World War had been the only period of his life when he had escaped his father's massive shadow.

Alessandro arrived in Luzerne County as a young man of twenty with nothing to his credit but an equally strong and recently acquired wife, Anna Rosa, whom he had married without the consent of her parents (because he was from the wilder, poorer south, she from the more respectable north). He had resisted the hard, ancestral voices that kept telling him he was really a peasant, and that he should not assume too much or reach too far. In the Old World, your caste was a given, an invisible stamp you wore on your forehead until death. Defiantly, Alessandro rose above his origins, conjuring Massolini Construction from a handful of tools and one employee—himself. It became the most visible company of its type in northeastern Pennsylvania. He erected schools and office buildings, hospitals, and strip malls from Carbondale and Honesdale to Nanticoke and Pottsville. Many of the well-known buildings in Scranton and Wilkes-Barre had been his projects.

And there was I, in a family video rewinding, being sucked back to a geographical and spiritual place my grandparents had never remotely wanted to revisit. "What happened a long time ago is over," my grandfather said, resolutely, whenever I tried to pry loose memories of the Old Country. "This country is about what's gonna happen next, not what did. What did doesn't interest nobody around here."

I had my own memories to deal with, too. That I could never go back to Pennsylvania and live out Nicky's life for him was clear; Columbia had made that impossible. Yet college life itself had become unbearable, a path to a preordained, professional future that felt like a heavy weight I had not yet tried to lift. I could not go forward or backward. What I needed was a fresh landscape, and the blank check of time unmeasured by parental or institutional expectations. I wanted a canvas where I could paint myself into the picture, adding or subtracting traits at will, a place where I had no former history from which I had to be absolved. And so I was sailing to Italy.

They say you can't remember pain, but I do. I remember exactly what it felt like to step from one life into another, self-consciously. To stand for hours on the deck of that old ship, in wind and rain, searching the eastern skyline and waiting, with an almost intolerable sense of anticipation, for the first glimmer of a fresh continent, its shadow on the faint blue horizon gradually becoming substance. For better or worse, strong personal winds drove me, and I had all sails open.

# PART ONE

*sic transit*

*one*

___

Somewhere between Amalfi and Capri, the sea turned indigo, depth piling on depth. The transition startled, and I imagined myself falling overboard, losing myself in the inky swirl. It seemed I had lost so much already, and what I had to gain was uncertain: the faint amber glow of an island in the distance, a possible mentor, a sense of myself as a writer, and some agency in a world where I was unable to control what happened to me. But these ambitions were hazy, clear only in the retrospective lens of three decades. What I really felt was a vague tingle in my stomach, a generalized fear of the unknown that mingled with a greedy anticipation, a feeling of windows flung open to experience.

I spoke Italian poorly, the little I knew having been gleaned from conversations with my paternal grandparents, and they spoke with such a thick Neapolitan accent that I could hardly make myself understood in Rome, where I'd spent my first two weeks upon arrival. But I was a quick study, and with Latin spread beneath me like a safety net, I could fall only so far. My vocabulary grew with extravagant speed, spreading vines along an invisible trellis of syntax buried deep in my psyche. I listened intently to fellow passengers on the train from Rome to Salerno, and spoke in isolated bursts of colloquial phrases to fellow passengers on the bus to Amalfi, which I always wanted to see. By the time I boarded the ferry in Amalfi, I could—if I limited myself to occasional phrases—pass myself off as a young, if somewhat laconic, Italian.

The Capri ferry in 1970 (unlike the current hydrofoil) was a bulky trawler, its straking painted bright Mediterranean blue, with red trim on windows and rails. Each morning it began its journey in the glaucous port city of Salerno, where my father had landed with General Mark Clark's Fifth Army during the invasion of Italy in 1943. For reasons of his own, he rarely discussed the war, though it had consumed five years of his life. The Battle of Salerno, a famously bloody conflict in which he had been among the first to come ashore, was even less frequently mentioned, although once, on a camping trip in the Poconos long ago, I'd managed to pry loose a fair account of this experience. It was as though he'd been waiting for years to tell someone about Salerno. Oddly enough, he almost never mentioned it again after that. "I don't remember more than I told you already," he would say, when prodded, shutting the door to that conversation.

I had hoped to spend time in Salerno, walking the beach where my father had landed and trying to imagine my way back into his boots. As a child, I often thought of it, and considered him a hero. But some impediment blocked the pursuit now; I found myself averting my eyes from the waterfront as I hurried from the train station to a bus stop. That war was over, with its anguish and euphoria and mixed allegiances. I could not visualize it, except for the endless sentimental films seen mostly on late-night TV. One day I might face that beach in Salerno, but not at this time. I refused to become a tourist in my father's past, resetting my compass for Capri, whose vivid, light-drenched image beckoned—a war-free zone if one ever existed. (Even my father had no will to revisit Salerno, rejecting an offer that once came from the VFW—a package tour for veterans of the Italian campaign. "Once in Salerno was enough," he said, with unusual passion, "and I don't care if the beach is lined with dancing girls. They can have it.")

It seemed that, somehow, I shared his disinclination to face Salerno. It might have been painful to stand there, where he had landed and (I assumed) lost so many friends. It would certainly have brought feelings about Nicky to the surface, and I was trying hard to get over them. I wanted to push the past year out of my head. To forget Nicky, the war in Vietnam, and the turmoil of my last few months at Columbia, when every assignment had seemed irrelevant, an abrasion. I wanted the freedom to read only what I felt compelled to read, and to write what absorbed me. I didn't want anyone judging me, grading me, wondering if "everything was all right." Everything was not all right, and I was here in Italy to shift the stage. To begin again, free of that past, discarding old selves.

Eager to see the Amalfi Drive, I had taken a bus northward along the zigzag road, with its steep western slope to the sea. The pinkish tile roofs of villas were barely visible from the road, although glimpses of their opulence fed my imagination. An elderly man beside me on the bus—a retired postal worker, as I quickly learned—served as de facto guide, explaining that the Mafia liked this coast above all others, and had pumped lots of money into those villas. "You should see their boats," he said. "The worse the criminal, the bigger the boat."

There was barely room for one small vehicle on the road, but the massive blue SITA bus hurtled forward, swaying, the driver blasting his two-tone horn before each hairpin curve to warn oncoming drivers that certain death lay ahead if they didn't immediately scuttle into any available space. The drop on the left, over sharp amethyst-toothed rocks or steep lemon groves, was brutal, but I reassured myself that the driver had traveled countless times along this road before. It reassured me that everyone else on the bus was unconcerned; indeed, the man in the seat in front of me had fallen asleep, his head limply attached to his neck, rolling left and right as we rounded bends.

In Amalfi itself, a town that climbed on its knees from the harbor and busy *centro* to a ruined monastery whose Greekish columns lent to the whole scene a classical touch, I splurged, spending the night at the Luna, a white-washed hotel with a cloistered courtyard and fine views of the coast. As I learned from a guidebook, Richard Wagner had lived at the Luna for a period, writing *Parsifal* on its sun-bleached terrace, so I could not resist the allure. (That Ibsen had spent some dismal winter months writing *A Doll's House* in the same hotel interested me less. I was too young to appreciate Ibsen.)

Though not wealthy, I had enough in my reserves to tide me over rather comfortably. My grandfather was bankrolling me to the hilt. Nonno and I had always been close, and when he heard I wanted to live in Italy, he opened his substantial wallet like an accordian. "Alessandro," he said, lowering his voice to an ethnic rumble, "I'm behind you all the way. You're smarter than Nicky ever was, *il povero*. Brains like you got don't come on a platter." He put four thousand into an account for me, saying another four would be lodged there whenever I signaled. "After that," he warned, with a kiss on my forehead, "you are on your own, *figlio mio*."

What he said was only partially true. I was smarter than Nicky in one way: I hadn't got myself killed in Vietnam. Apart from that, I wasn't sure what smart meant, apart from an ability to suck up to teachers and get the necessary grades. But I took Nonno's money. If this was what "family" meant to an Italian-American grandfather, so be it. I was indeed part of the family, and partook of its good fortune. The arrangement suited me fine. Had his name been Jones or Smith instead of Massolini, I'd have probably gotten a fond farewell shake and a kick in my skinny ass.

I promised Nonno that when I became a successful writer I would pay him back, but he just waved his hand, a familiar gesture that had waved off endless attempts at gratitude over the years. "I don't want your money," he said. "You can sign your book for me, *basta*." Then he said, "And it better be a good book if it's got my name on the cover." We shared a name, more or less: Alessandro Massolini. But I was Alex Massolini. More American than Italian—that had been the intention of my parents. "You can't get ahead in this country with a handle like Alessandro," my father said. "Even DiMaggio was Joe, not Giuseppe. Marilyn Monroe would never have married a guy called Giuseppe." But Alex Massolini was close enough for Nonno. So the book had better be a good one.

I sat in the ship's bar, reading one of the handful of books I carried with me, an English translation of Rilke's *Letters to a Young Poet*. An English teacher of mine at Columbia had recommended it, and I'd been grazing contentedly in its pages for the past week. In his third letter to his correspondent, written near Pisa on April 23, 1903, Rilke had warned against reading literary criticism. "Such things are either partisan views, petrified and grown senseless in their lifeless induration, or they are clever quibblings in which today one view wins and tomorrow the opposite." In contrast, "works of art are of an infinite loneliness." He recommended solitude. *"Everything* is gestation," he said, "and then bringing forth. To let each impression and each germ of feeling come to completion wholly in itself, in the dark, in the inexpressible, the unconscious, beyond the reach of one's own intelligence, and await with deep humility and patience the birth-hour of a new clarity." I wanted to achieve these clarities, and to learn the patience to let them gather. Only then would I write something worthy of my grandfather's name.

Since arriving in Italy, I had seen countless replicas of Nonno—wizened old men with faces like baked mud flats, and white hair sprouting from their ears and noses. A small army of dozing *nonni* could be found in piazzas from Calabria to Trieste, an empty glass of wine on the table beside them. They slumped in buses or strolled the tortuous streets of villages they knew well enough to sleepwalk without fear of getting lost. Indeed, the ferry to Capri boasted several exact replicas of the type, including one of the waiters in the ship's bar: a grizzly, hump-backed Amalfitano called Andrea (virtually every male in Amalfi is called Andrea, after the patron saint of sailors). He served me a frothy cappuccino, his hand shaking so badly that much of it spilled into the saucer.

"Where are you going, *ragazz'*?"

"Capri," I said, pouring the spilled milk from the saucer back into the cup. I was a little offended by his assuming I was *un ragazzo.*

"We also stop at Positano."

"Well, I'm going to Capri," I said, feeling good about my Italian, which held up decently so long as I didn't venture beyond the simplest of conversations.

"You are a tourist?"

"Not exactly."

"But what will you do there?" he wondered, his nostrils opening with the interrogation.

I considered explaining to him about my secretarial job on Capri, but I guessed it would lead me into linguistic corners I could not easily back out of. I tried to pretend that the notebook on the table was drawing my attention. But this only inflamed his curiosity.

"What are you writing, *signore?*"

"A poem," I said.

"Ah, we have many fine poets in Italy. You know Dante—*La Divina Commedia?*" He launched into an incomprehensible but highly dramatic recitation from the epic, clipping off the final syllables (thus ruining the rhymes) in the manner of most southern Italians. His performance brought much of the activity around us to a halt, and when he was finished, a birdlike woman in a black dress began to clap.

I listened with a distracted amazement. Would anyone but a college professor in America be able to recite verbatim from a similar text? Did we have a similar text? *Song of Myself*, perhaps?

The recitation finished, he said, "So, tell me. Do you know Capri? The Blue Grotto? The Matromania Cave?" His bushy white eyebrows lifted, and they would not settle into place again until I answered.

I shook my head. The only Blue Grotto I knew was a cheap spaghetti joint near the Columbia campus.

"This is paradise, Capri. They come from all over the world to see it, even China. It is what we call a legend." While he extolled the virtues of Capri—the pure air, the remorselessly brilliant sunshine, the intriguing people—I finished the cappuccino, feigning interest in his monologue. I had been in this situation with my grandfather many times, so it felt familiar. One had to appear attentive enough not to hurt the speaker's feelings, but not so attentive that elaboration was provoked.

"You will excuse me," I said, when he paused to light a cigarette. I left him shifting from foot to foot as I gathered my things, joining a cluster of tourists, mostly Germans and Swedes, on the foredeck. How else to escape his conversation?

The sight of the breaking coastline was enough to silence idle chatter as a fine mist dampened our faces but didn't obscure our vision. Cove upon cove opened for us, with whole towns wedged precariously into the cliffs. It was the season for lemons, like bright bulbs in trees that were wrapped in black mesh to keep the fruit from spilling. Occasionally, a villa of substantial size and opulence appeared, clinging like a swallow's nest to the cliff. Based on what I gleaned from overheard conversations, the coast teemed with famous movie producers, industrial magnates, and Mafiosi. "Carlo Ponti lives there, the film producer," one of them said, pointing to a sculpted mansion on a jut of land between clashing rocks. I had never heard of Carlo Ponti, but I was still impressed.

On the other side of the ferry, in the open sea that bent to the earth's curve, fishing boats could be seen in the distance, trolling with nets designed to catch the cascades of dime-size clams that were popular on the coast, usually cooked in olive oil and garlic and served with spaghetti. Toward the northwest, a bank of dark clouds appeared without warning, a fierce line marking off blue sky from black. The sea, as if newly alert to a shift in atmosphere, became choppier, the bow parsing the waves more severely. Loud squawking gulls that had trailed us all the way from Amalfi like an elaborate kite continued to buck and weave, devouring whatever morsels were churned up by the ferry's wake. (I thought of a gorgeous phrase from Yeats: "That dolphin-torn, that gong-tormented sea." But what on earth *was* a gong-tormented sea?)

At first, I wasn't aware that somebody was talking to me. My own thoughts were just too loud, and the voice beside me found it difficult to compete. (This had often been a problem: the outside world failing to compete with my own highly nuanced, occasionally overwrought, inner voice.)

"You haven't heard me!"

"What was that?"

A slender young man stood beside me, spitting into my face as he spoke. "I said, where are you from in America? Am I to presume?"

He was fair, with milky skin and a face like an ax-blade that poked from the hood of a wine-red sweatshirt. A thickly accented English nested in that thin, rather nasal, voice. His eyes were large and compelling, and they invaded my foggy presense like search lamps.

"Are you Italian?" I asked.

"French is my original," he said, confidently. "I am born near Lyon."

"Ah, Lyon," I said, nodding as if I knew it. "I'm an American, yes. How could you tell?"

"Your shoes," he said, his fingers tugging at a cornsilk beard. His long hair was dirty blond and unwashed, tucked into the hood but just visible. He smelled of dirty jeans, travel, and cheap *pensione*.

I was self-conscious about my leather hiking boots. One did not see Italians in hiking boots, it was true. Not, I suppose, unless they were actually hiking.

"I am oppose to Vietnam War," the Frenchman declared, though nothing prior in our conversation could possibly have drawn the remark. "I am disliking to this colonial war. We were there, you comprehend. My uncle, he was fighting there—an officer in Indochine. A very long and bad war we had, and now you are repeating our misfortune."

Ever so briefly, I had pushed Vietnam from my head, and it upset me to have it unexpectedly invoked. I steadied myself by holding the railing. "It's a very bad war," I said. "I agree with you." I said nothing about Nicky, of course. Since coming to Italy, I had not mentioned Nicky to anyone, although the subject of Vietnam had arisen several times in Rome, and I'd had an unpleasant argument on the train to Salerno with an American businessman, a veteran of Korea, who argued (without a trace of irony) that if we didn't fight what he called "the Marxist-Leninist rampage" in Southeast Asia, "on their own ground," we'd soon be fighting them in California. (I coyly suggested that Berkeley already had more Marxist-Leninists per capita than any city in Southeast Asia.)

In the weeks that had passed since I left New York, I'd done a lot of quiet thinking about Nicky and me. I wasn't exactly sure what part his death played in my dropping out of Columbia, but it had amplified feelings already in abundance. Alienation—as a concept that I sometimes used to explain myself to myself—seemed hackneyed and false; but I had certainly lost interest in "achievement," as such; performing in the theater of my parents' imagination no longer felt compelling. What I wanted seemed more urgent than ratification by some abstract institution. The world as I found it sickened me with its cruelty, its shameless inhumanity and lack of compassion.

After a long silence, during which the Frenchman appeared to think about what I'd just said, he spoke again. "Now I'm going to Capri, for tourism. Maybe more. Who can say? You will be long there, I wonder?"

"I plan to stay," I said, savoring the oddity of such a statement.

His mouse-colored eyebrows, like a drawbridge, lifted. "This is surprising, that you will stay there. You are a student, no? I see you with your
books in the bar."

"Not any longer." I explained that I had dropped out of Columbia. One
day, I said, I would collect a few credits somewhere and get my diploma.
(At my mother's insistence, I had gotten a note from the dean of students
saying I had left in good standing and could resume my studies whenever
it suited me. Yet it amazed me how little I cared about the actual degree—
though I would have been the first person in my family to acquire one, as
my mother frequently noted. "You just wanna be a working man, like your
father?" she would say, often in his presence. "I don't think so, Alex.
You're gonna work with your brains, not your hands.")

He studied me as though I were a painting. "You are like me," he
intoned, at last. "I am without discipline, a student at the Sorbonne. We
have had many riots there, before last year. A small revolution in the
streets. You have heard something of this, I'm not to doubt."

I had. The student revolt had furnished world headlines, inspiring
many in the States and elsewhere. Though Columbia had had its own,
highly publicized, rioting, it had always seemed to me parochial by comparison, vaguely parodic. It's one thing to take over a university administration building, quite another to shut down the Latin Quarter.
Moreover, the French workers had apparently been sympathetic to the
student revolt, joining forces with them at the barricades; our protests
were, if anything, despised by the men in hard hats. Certainly my
father—like most of the men who worked for him at Massolini Construction—had been deeply upset by the protests. I had kept from him
my own lame participation in several marches and "teach-ins."

"My name is Patrice LaRue," the Frenchman said. "I am philosophy."

"A student of philosophy?"

He offered a sidelong smile that reminded me shockingly of Nicky,
who grinned like that whenever he said something ridiculous. "And you,
mister? What do you study?"

"I majored in classics—Latin, mostly. A little Greek."

"Ah, Virgil and Homer. I have read these, but in French." He seemed to
drift briefly into reveries of ancient times. "And what do you make in Italy?"

"I have a job on Capri," I said, hoping that answered his question. "I'll be working as secretary for a writer who lives there, Rupert Grant." Because English was not his language, I found myself hitting every syllable like a tambourine, letting it resonate.

"I have heard of Rupert," he said. "A Scottishman, no?"

"That's right."

"He is very popular in France. I have read only one book of Rupert, about Ulysses. You know this story?"

"*Siren Call,*" I said. "It's probably his best known work."

"His best work?"

"Best *known.*" I preferred at least half a dozen of his other novels, and thought even more highly of his poetry and essays, although I doubted Patrice would know about these. "I'll answer letters for him, type manuscripts, that sort of thing. I'm not quite sure what the job entails."

"You are so lucky man," said Patrice. "I have dreamed to have such a position. In France, the writer wants to do everything himself and he trusts no one."

Patrice must have been twenty or more, but he appeared younger, a hipless adolescent. The shoulder-length hair, which he parted in the middle, gave him a feminine aspect. He pulled a cigarette from the pocket in his sweatshirt and offered me one. "I will stay for as long as possible on Capri," he explained. "But I do not have so much money. If I may find a job, I will be so lucky as well."

"Are you dropping out of the Sorbonne?"

"Drop in, drop out. We are not so strict in France. We come and go." He explained that after having enrolled in the university, one simply attended lectures. They were given in vast halls, and nobody took attendance or monitored your progress. "When you are ready to take the exams, you do it," he said. "In France, the result is everything, the process . . ." He made a derisive, slicing gesture with his right hand.

"And how is readiness for exams determined?"

"By the mind," he said, putting a finger to his temple and twisting it, somewhat ominously. "It is self-knowledge. I will know when I am ready for this."

I envied his Gallic self-confidence. There was a firmness about the

French that seemed part of their heritage. They assumed a certain great-ness in the world, as the heirs of Napoleon, Hugo, and Sartre. (I had recently come upon a lovely remark by Jean Cocteau: "Victor Hugo was a madman who thought he was Victor Hugo.") One could hardly imagine culturally dominant figures like Hugo or Jean-Paul Sartre in England or the United States; they would make no sense in either place.

In 1970, to be young and French seemed the ideal combination of attributes. By comparison, young Italians—at least those I'd met in Rome—appeared feckless and groping, overly tied to familial expecta-tions and obligations.

"So, please tell me," said Patrice, "where you will stay in Capri? With the Scottishman?"

"On his property," I said, as vaguely as possible, suspecting that Patrice might want to throw himself upon my hospitality. Grant had writ-ten that I would "have use of a small cottage at the bottom of the gar-den," but he would probably not appreciate it if I arrived with an entourage.

"Ah, this will be so interesting, to live with a man of creativity." Patrice looked at me longingly. "*Moi*, I will find a *pensione*. They are not so expensive there, I am said, but in Paris . . ." He clucked his tongue and shook his head.

I remembered the loaf of bread and slab of gorgonzola I had bought in Amalfi that morning and stuffed into my knapsack. "Have you eaten, Patrice?"

His baleful look amused me.

"So please," I said, speaking English as though I were translating from another tongue, "you must join me. I have bread and cheese."

We climbed the narrow, metal steps to the top deck, near the bow, and sat on a bench together to share my little parcel of food. The crennela-tions of the shoreline on the starboard side of the ferry held our gaze as we ate: a gorgeous spectacle that seemed to defeat verbalization. In the distance, one could see the russet outline of Li Galli, a series of rocks that lay just off Positano. The largest of these, Isola Lunga, amounted to an island, with a few houses carved into its stony shoulders.

"It's beautiful," I said.

"Yes, but too much beautiful," Patrice responded. "They should make a law against it, this . . . abundance." He smeared the soft gorgonzola on his bread with a thin, greasy finger. "When you see something like this, it steals from you the possibility to imagine for yourself."

I objected, but said nothing, not wishing to involve myself in a discussion of aesthetics. I had observed seductive views before, but this was different, and would take time to absorb.

Luckily, for me, I had time. If I lived frugally, I had enough money to sustain me comfortably for a year or two. And I had this job, which I'd magically summoned by writing a letter to Grant on a whim. Having read a recent volume of his essays on poetics, I sent a few of my own feeble efforts, a handful of sonnets, vaguely reminiscent of Wordsworth, in care of the Villa Clio, Capri, having noted this address at the end of his preface. I mentioned, in passing, that I had decided to drop out of Columbia and planned to visit Italy, where I hoped to scout for work. He replied at once, praising my poems and, to my amazement, offering a job. "There is not much in the way of financial gain to be had," he said, "but we have accommodation that might suit a young man in your situation, and there is plenty of bread and wine at our table." I wrote quickly to accept the offer, suggesting an arrival date at the end of April. Neither of us ever mentioned how long the appointment might last, but this didn't worry me. Life, at twenty-two, was infinite, open-ended, and beyond such petty calculation.

"We are bobbing like the cork," said Patrice, licking the gorgonzola from his fingers as a shadow suddenly fell across the deck. The winds had suddenly picked up so fiercely that the ferry began to dip and roll. Others on deck rushed for the most convenient railings, while Patrice and I held to our seats. "I don't like a storm at sea," he added. "You are often struck with lightning in these circumstance." He had barely finished the sentence when the rain, in lukewarm horizontal sheets, swept over the port railing, chasing us inside.

Patrice and I settled at a small table bolted to the floor near the door. Next to us, an obese Arab woman in a caftan was puking into a brown bag while her tiny husband, unshaven, massaged her shoulders and whispered comforting words. The beautiful, almond-eyed children of an Italian couple pointed at her, imitating the puking noises and giggling.

Loudly, their mother scolded them, explaining that to tease sick people was to make *una brutta figura*. A man in a brown linen suit and Borsalino stood by the bar, singing an unfamiliar aria in a deep baritone.

"It is the carnival of life, this boat," Patrice said, gesturing pompously. "Do you like Puccini, by the way?"

"I've never really listened to him," I said.

Patrice appeared wounded by my admission. "You must acquaint him," he said, as neutrally as possible. It would not have done to scold someone who had recently provided bread and gorgonzola. "Opera is the height of art, mixing the elements of literature with music and visuality."

I nodded, suppressing a smile and making a mental note to remember *visuality*. Patrice redeemed himself, however, when he went to the bar and reappeared at my elbow with a glass of grappa. "This will prevent you from getting sick," he said. "The more you drink, the more you will prevent."

Grappa is a pure form of alcohol, best drunk late at night, after a bottle of wine and lots of food. Nevertheless, its medicinal effects in the current situation were easy to anticipate. One might still get sick, but it wouldn't matter. I downed the glass, as instructed by Patrice, in one throat-inflaming gulp. My spirits, as if summoned from backstage to the proscenium, brightened.

"Now you are well," he said, waving his hand over my head. "Everything will improve, believe it so."

He had barely spoken when the sun came pillaring through the clouds. The rain, as if switched off at the source like a shower, ceased, and the sea fell calm—and darker than before. We hurried back on deck in time to see, in the near distance, the sheer limestone cliffs on the northeast tip of Capri, a geographical feature made ominous by the Roman emperor Tiberius, who had those who disagreed with him tossed from the heights of Il Salto ("The Leap") onto the boulder-broken shingle below. Soon the Faraglioni could be seen, too: a series of vertical rocks thrusting upward like ancient ruins.

"You see, Tiberio enjoyed to live in exile here, on Capri, because there is no hidden harbor. The enemy, they can't approach without being seen. Very nice and safe, if you are crazy dictator."

As I knew from a course on Roman history, the man who inherited the empire from Augustus had perhaps the hardest act in history to follow. Born in the fourth decade before Christ, he died in A.D. 37, nearly eighty years old. By this time he ruled most of the known world from a tiny island in the Mediterranean—a dazzling feat of political ventriloquism. The survivor of endless plots and conspiracies, he had even managed to outwit and subdue the powerful and popular Sejanus, his younger rival and most obvious successor.

Tiberius baffled everyone when he abandoned Rome, the center of the empire, for a self-imposed exile on Capri, in A.D. 26. As recounted by Tacitus and Suetonius—both suspect as historians but excellent as storytellers—he lapsed into a life of sybaritic madness. He was egomaniacal, sexually twisted as well as omnivorous, riven by fits of jealousy that maddened those around him, including one of his closest friends, the renowned jurist Cocceius Nerva, who committed suicide by slowly starving himself to death before the emperor's eyes simply to protest his extravagance and moral degeneracy. I thought this would make a wonderful novella, or perhaps a play, and determined to write it one day.

Although I hadn't written much prose yet, the idea of historical fiction appealed to me, and I looked forward to discussing the subject with Grant, who had already written a dozen historical novels that had changed the nature of a genre once dismissed by critics as the domain of second-rate writers. Fearless and wildly erudite, Grant had roamed the corridors of history from ancient Greece to Elizabethan England and, most recently, had published *Dying Above His Means*, a novel about the twilight years of Oscar Wilde, that period when (after the prison years in Reading) he retreated to the Continent with Lord Alfred "Bosie" Douglas, his impossible young lover (and the original cause of his imprisonment).

"There are two harbors, but only one really," Patrice explained as we rounded the Punta del Capo, heading straight into the wide-flung arms of the Marina Grande, whose docks were crammed with sailing yachts and cruisers. "This is the big harbor," he announced, gesturing to signify bigness. "She is the north side. The small harbor is on the other side. Nobody ever arrives there, in Marina Piccola, though Lenin did, when he visited Capri—before the revolution, of course. In 1908, I think. He came to see his friend, Maxim Gorky, another revolutionist. Lenin was used to arriving in unexpected ways."

When I asked Patrice how he happened to know so much about Capri, he waved dismissively. "I have read the guidebooks. You understand, my memory is wonderful. She is my chief asset." He sighed, as if suddenly recalling something, then added: "I have suffered much pain from this asset, I admit to you. One must forget to be happy. I have too much inside that is unforgotten, and the load feels so heavy on me."

It was easier to trust Patrice than to question what he said, so I put myself temporarily into his hands. He rhapsodized in fractured English about the heights of Anacapri, the windswept, dolomitic presence of Mount Solaro, the haunting aura of the Matromania Cave, and the peculiar light show known as the Blue Grotto. "You will see this for yourself," he said, "these things I describe." That he had never actually been to Capri himself was passed over lightly.

My pulse quickened as the ferry approached the Marina Grande, with its winter forest of sailboat masts visible in the docks on one side. A dozen or so smaller vessels crossed our path like water-spiders, and there was a general din of seagulls, who flocked and fed lustily on scraps that seemed to pour from a range of vessels. Our ferry struck the concrete landing forcibly, then settled into an eerie stillness, followed by cries of *Ecco! Finalmente!*

Patrice hugged me, as though by arrival in Capri we'd accomplished something. "I am so happy here," he said.

"Me, too," I replied. And it was true. For the first time in what felt like months of unease, despair, and disaffection, I felt something akin to happiness.

*two*

———

We shared a taxi ride from the
Marina Grande in a snub-nosed Fiat convertible painted a color never
found in nature, a gaudy chartreuse. Ignazio, the driver, gave Patrice the
name of a boardinghouse in the via Sopramonte where the mere mention
of his name would produce a sizable *sconto*. "You pay less than half with
my name," Ignazio boasted. As I soon learned, everyone on the island
had a cousin in business somewhere and was eager to secure for you what
they called a "special price." Apparently nothing on Capri was ever sold
at retail except to naive day-trippers, who poured onto the island in vul-
gar quantities in July and August, but in late April formed only a steady
trickle—the human equivalent of a light spring rain.

Patrice asked me to meet him for a drink that evening at the Bar
Tiberio, a small café-bar in the Piazza Umberto I, known by its candy-
striped awnings and glass-and-bamboo tables. Its interior had been
carved from the crypt of the handsome baroque church, Santo Stefano,
that rose above a small flight of steps and gave obliquely onto the square.
I assumed that whatever happened at the Grants, I could slip away
briefly, and Patrice was eager to have an account of my first meeting with
*lo scrittore*, as the Capresi called Rupert Grant.

It was not hard to find the Villa Clio, but I had acquired the self-
defeating habit of ignoring directions. Guarding against myself, I bought
a map from a vendor in the piazzetta, then followed a winding footpath

toward the Villa Jovis, the finest of the twelve imperial villas on Capri. Along the way, I passed a patchwork of barrel-roofed houses, most of them bleached blue or faded Pompeiian red, the typical colors of southern Italy. At an unsigned crossroads, I veered off sharply toward the via Tragara—a footpath with a distant view of the Marina Piccola below, with steep terraces ledging above it. The whitewashed houses tumbled like dice, split a hundred ways as they scattered down the hillside.

Following instructions, I turned right at a small chapel, the Santa Maria de la Croce, then right again at an unmarked stone path leading to the sea. Medlars, mulberries, and almond trees caught my attention, although I wasn't yet aware of their names. I would only slowly learn them, and that was part of my education on Capri. It was also something I owed to Grant, who insisted on naming all botanical things with absolute specificity. "Never say tree," he told me, "say lemon tree, carob tree, mimosa." The air, stirred by a light breeze, smelled of eucalyptus, familiar from a visit I'd made to California the previous year (in futile pursuit of a Barnard coed with long blond hair and a guitar). The breeze itself, so fresh and warm, gave me a good feeling about Capri. I felt easy there, however far from home in reality.

A wrought iron gate marked the Villa Clio. (The name of the villa had been removed to keep away tourists, who might hesitate to ring an anonymous bell in the idle hope of rousing Rupert Grant.) I pressed the button just below a speaker in the white stucco wall. "*Avanti!*" crackled a female voice in the steel mesh. A buzzer sounded, and I pushed the gate. It opened with a groan onto a dirt path, which I followed past beds of unfamiliar yellow flowers. I paused briefly to shelter from the sun in a small loggia, then continued down a path toward the villa: a whitewashed structure that was smaller than I had imagined, although it was built into the cliff and seemed to exist on several levels. Like most houses on Capri, it affected a rustic, ancient look—simple and secure, with clean curves and fresh lines, an architectural style pioneered by Edwin Cerio, a local entrepreneur and architect, in the twenties.

I approached the house slowly, savoring my first view. I knew that, in the weeks and months ahead, familiarity would make the house invisible; one takes the most beautiful visions for granted, after a while. The green wooden shutters that hung on all windows were closed—not uncommon in the early afternoons of southern Italy, when the Mediterranean sun commands the scene with blunt, obliterating power.

My knock was answered by a solid, fresh, and chestnut-eyed young Capresa with straight black hair cut across her forehead like a crow's black wing; she opened the door slowly and bowed, calling me *professore* as her eyes dipped to the floor. The black, downy hair on her arms and upper lip gave her a distinctly Moorish aspect. Her name was Maria Pia, and she came from a family whose women had, for generations, been servants to foreign residents. In a few decades, she would grow amply into the role of *massàia,* one of those diligent, earthy Capresi women who live close to the island, with its indistinct shifting seasons, attentive to the parish gossip, committed to agricultural routines that people much like her family and friends had taken for granted for centuries.

"*Venga qui, professore,*" she said, urging me to follow.

I was not a professor, of course, but I nodded gratefully, following her into the large front hall. As I soon discovered, any foreigner in southern Italy with the slightest claims upon gentility and education was called *professore* or *dottore.*

"*Molti italiani abitano in America, professore,*" she said, her dialect so extreme I could only guess at what she meant. Something about Italians living in America.

I nodded and said, rather stupidly, "*Sì, sì.*"

She led me into a long and narrow room with vaulted ceilings, whitewashed walls, and sofas that hovered in place under their white cotton dust wraps. The floor shone with luminous white tiles, known locally as *le riggiole;* common in Neapolitan homes and public buildings, they were fired individually, two inches thick, with a faint roseate glow that made them appear translucent, as though the soil below were leaking through. Borders of green foliage crept around the margins of each tile, so that the effect was not monolithic against the whitewashed walls, where vaguely modern paintings were hung. They were obviously by the same artist, with nude figures (mostly male) grappling in various sexual positions, late Picasso in manner (but not content), unabashedly imitative. I was left to stare at the largest of these, which hung over a sofa. The figure in this painting—an androgynous creature with three eyes and two navels—was being attacked (or fondled) by several grotesque, equally androgynous figures who were noticeably smaller.

I found myself uneasy amidst these paintings. Were they meant to suggest something about the household I was soon to join?

"Do you like Picasso?"

I turned to see a tall, gaunt woman in her early forties. "This is a Picasso?"

"They're by a friend here, Peter Duncan-Jones. Quite a brilliant painter, in my view. Rupert doesn't agree, but he knows nothing about art. Peter thinks he's Picasso, so I call him Picky. Why not? Everything is make-believe on Capri."

I held out my hand. "I'm Alex."

"I assumed as much," she said, kissing me politely on either cheek.

She was beautiful in her way, extremely thin, breastless and boyish, her cheeks gathering a mass of shadows. Her voice was what the British call "plummy," the words neatly clipped at the margins, like an Oxford quad. Her brittleness, mingling with a sophisticated air, was deeply in contrast to Maria Pia's aura of peasant innocence.

"It's lovely here," I said, glancing around the room, my eye resting on a clay sculpture of an erect penis that adorned the coffee table. Another product from the imagination of Peter Duncan-Jones, as I later learned.

"We like our little house," she said. The word "house" as she pronounced it vaguely rhymed with the word "nice."

The house was not, as I learned, so little. The exterior of the Villa Clio was deceptive, suggesting compactness and limit where neither quality was inherent. It had been built in the late twenties by a wealthy English lord in pursuit of *la dolce vita*. Every decade had seen additions or modifications, and seven bedrooms were tucked away. Connected to the house by a cyprus allée of some thirty yards was Grant's study, which had been fashioned from the remains of an old stone barn.

"You are quite attractive," Vera said, lighting a cigarette and raising her fine, penciled eyebrows. "Rupert will enjoy that."

Exactly why Rupert should care about my looks puzzled me, but I was mostly flattered. In truth, I was not conspicuously attractive. Just shy of six feet, with a scholar's tendency to stoop, I considered myself average in appearance. My brown hair—which I had taken to parting in the middle—was fairly long and straight; I had dark brown eyes and a nose that arched slightly: a faint tribute to my paternal grandparents where that nasal arch could still be found in abundance. Acne had never been a problem, and I was blessed with smooth skin that tanned easily and acquired, by summer's end, a kind of nut-brown tint. Having played a good deal of tennis and basketball in the past decade, I was not unfit, but the glimmering physique that follows from regular, strenuous exercise had never seemed worth the effort.

Vera Grant, however, had bestowed on me one of her highest forms of praise, though I wasn't aware of this until later. She took me instantly into her graces, accepting me as a person of equal sophistication, although this was far from the reality. From my view, I had never met anyone quite like her. An edge of irony sharpened every remark that fell from her lips, making her seem dangerous. Her eyes were catlike: gray, with flecks of green and amber. Her fineness appealed to me—the wrists twiglike, the narrowness of her chest making her seem more fragile than she was, as if a hard wind might snap her in two. But her character was such that the delicate frame served as a decoy; she was not easily bruised, emotionally or physically. Her stamina, as everyone on the island knew, inspired awe in those around her. She could drink most guests under the table at dinner, then hike to the top of Mount Solaro the next morning without flinching. Empires were built by women like her.

"Is Mr. Grant here?" I asked.

"Darling, you must call us by our Christian names, Rupert and Vera. Capri is very informal." She crossed her legs to reveal her thighs. "He's swimming," she said. "He always swims after lunch. The rest of the island goes to bed, but he goes swimming."

"Mad dogs and Englishmen?" I said.

"Indeed, though he's a Scot."

I soon discovered that Rupert was no slouch when it came to siestas. He was a master of the *sonnolino*, which he considered the secret of his legendary endurance, reflected in a ceaseless flow of poems, translations, novels, and essays. His work schedule did not vary, except when he trav-

eled: he worked every morning from seven until midday, taking naps—
ten- or twenty-minute naps—whenever he came to an impasse in composition that would not yield to his usual headlong thrust.

"My real work is done when I'm asleep," he told me. By checking out
of his conscious existence, he could get the "little elves," as he called
them, to work for him again. "I like the Buddhist notion about work," he
said, "the idea that if you hit a log in the appropriate place, it splits easily. You must not work against the grain." I would fill my notebook with
these aphorisms (which ranged from the brilliant to the mundane) in the
coming months, and they would inform my own work—and work
habits—for decades. My friends in later years would mock me for beginning sentences with, "As Rupert Grant once said . . ."

Vera asked Maria Pia to bring us tea and commanded me to sit beside
her on the largest sofa, clasping a huge pillow to her breast as though it
were a life raft. For what seemed an uncomfortably long period, she just
stared at me, studying my features.

"How long have you lived here, Vera?"

She started a fresh cigarette, though the previous one was barely finished. After taking a long draw, she blew the smoke away from my face,
settling in for an explanation. "We began coming here—to Italy, not
Capri—in the fifties. The *nineteen* fifties. You won't remember them, as
you were just a lad. It was a marvelous time to live in Rome. Rupert used
to have an apartment near the Piazza Navona. He knew everyone:
Moravia, Pasolini, Elsa Morante, Fellini. But everyone died on him, or
left the city, or got bored. He got bored, too, I suppose. This villa came
on the market nine years ago. It was something of a ruin, so we could
afford it." (With more than a little help from her father, as I was told by
several of their gossipy friends.)

"It must have been a good place to raise children," I said. Grant had
mentioned in his second letter confirming my appointment that he had
two children, Nigel and Nicola, both in their mid-teens.

Vera brightened. "My little darlings," she said. "They were born in
Rome, but this is home." She looked into the distance. "They're at
school in England. Nigel's at Charterhouse. Nicola's at Cheltenham. She
fancies herself a painter." She looked at her nails, which needed atten-

tion. "You'll meet them in July, if you stay." She handed me a photograph in which the children appeared quite young, perhaps ten and twelve. "They're larger now, but just as beautiful. We've been lucky. Adolescence has a way of killing beautiful children, doesn't it? They come up all spots and big noses."

I was still trying to digest her remark about my staying. Was it meant to warn me? To threaten? Perhaps she was merely being realistic. Grant had said nothing about the length of my tenure, but I assumed that both sides would have to assent for the position to continue beyond a certain point. Just now, I wanted nothing more than to live there forever, in a place where everything I'd been through up to this day simply didn't matter. On Capri, I was free of Pittston, of my parents, of the social and academic pressures that had soured me on Columbia. Although I couldn't have verbalized this at the time, I planned to reinvent myself at the Villa Clio, to become a worldly and cultured person. To start over again, on my own terms.

I studied the room, its physical details, like a student preparing for exams. The dark wooden tables were crammed with family pictures in silver frames. I could see half a dozen transformations of Vera from childhood through the present; in one, she was a young girl in a bathing suit on the beach somewhere—the French or Italian Riviera, I guessed. Elsewhere, she was bowing before Queen Elizabeth, a debutante of about sixteen in a long formal gown. In another, she was half hidden in a crowd where all the women wore huge, preposterous hats of the kind that English women of a certain class wear at weddings. In yet another, she sat on a large horse, dressed impeccably for the hunt. Her wedding photo with Rupert was prominently positioned: a county wedding, probably in Surrey or Sussex or some such place. One could hear the bong of ancient bells in the church tower, which (according to Vera, on another day) "had been built by the Normans." Grant was in tails, wearing a top hat, and Vera looked improbably young. I recognized W. H. Auden among the crowd of well wishers and felt a slight chill. Auden was, of all living poets, the one I most admired, having memorized perhaps a dozen of his poems. I had read, and heavily underlined, his essays in *The Dyer's Hand*.

I wanted to know exactly what these people knew, expecting everything around me—the bric-a-brac, the wall coverings and gilt-framed mirrors, the faux-modern art—to become a part of my own mental furniture. My own ignorance and lack of worldliness felt unacceptable to me. But I could certainly overcome them. I didn't have to remain ignorant, naive, and gauche—all traits that seemed, at this moment, to describe me to myself.

The tea arrived on a trolley, wheeled in by Maria Pia. When I caught her eye, she turned away quickly, embarrassed or offended.

"The Italians don't like tea," Vera said, pouring from a blue-veined china pot into hand-painted mugs, adding milk and sugar without asking how I liked it. "They think it's only for bad tummies. I had to teach them how to make it properly."

I sipped the tea and inclined toward her, enchanted by the accent and manner. My experience of English people was limited to one or two examples. Mostly from reading fiction, I had in my head an anthology of virtues and vices I considered "typically English." Vera had a passion for gardening, which seemed perfectly in keeping. But she was also the author of several well-known cookbooks, including *The Feast of Italy*. This seemed defiantly unBritish.

Vera was twenty years younger than Grant, who had been married before, but all memory of that earlier union had been erased. Even Grant's older children, two married daughters (roughly the age of Vera herself), were never mentioned—I would only learn about them from Grant's entry in *Who's Who*.

"I can see we're going to be good friends," Vera said.

I agreed, relieved to know that my own warm feelings were reciprocated, although her enthusiasm puzzled me. I had hardly declared anything of myself.

"What you must realize is that not everyone around here is necessarily honest," she said. "People lie all the time on Capri."

"We Americans are not so bad at lying," I said. I was thinking about the Gulf of Tonkin Resolution, but kept this to myself. The Vietnam War would probably not be debated at the Villa Clio; indeed, the Trojan War seemed a more likely topic in these surroundings. "What about the Italians?"

"Who cares?" she said.

I was relieved that Maria Pia had withdrawn to the kitchen, though I guessed (rightly) that she didn't speak much English. It would take some time to get used to Vera's patronizing attitude toward the Italians, whom she considered mere children, barely capable of looking after themselves.

"I fear I've shocked you," she said. Her gaze opened, admitting me to a sense of intimacy. "The Italians are very sweet, but they're deceitful. They will steal a plum from your pocket while you're sleeping, then attempt to sell it to you when you wake up."

Maria Pia emerged from the kitchen with a tray of semisweet rolls glazed with vanilla icing, a specialty of Capri. I took one and thanked her.

"Do you like her?" Vera wondered.

As Maria Pia hovered beside me, the question seemed inappropriate, at best. "In what sense?"

"Would you like to have her—you know—in bed?"

I blushed, extracting a broad smile from Vera.

"You needn't worry," she said. "She doesn't speak English."

"It wasn't that, I —"

"I'm sorry, I've embarrassed you. Wicked old Vera, I must hold my tongue. We've become silly on this island. Say any bloody thing that comes into our heads. It's a matter of our isolation. We're cut off, you see."

"I like it when people say what they think."

"Then you'll enjoy yourself hugely." She sipped her tea and stared ahead.

"Rupert mentioned a cottage in the garden," I said.

"It's a shed, really. Used to be his study. Not very warm in winter, I'm afraid. A bit damp. But it's getting warmer now, with spring and all that. You'll be comfortable enough. There's a bed, a table for work, and some chairs. Mimo was supposed to give you a sofa, but he's unreliable."

"Mimo?"

"The gardener who cannot garden. The island is full of such people: the plumber who cannot plumb, the painter who cannot paint, and so forth."

The way Vera leaped from topic to topic, like a bird from branch to branch, would have unnerved me, but my mother's mind worked in a similar way, so I was used to disjunctive thinking. I waded bravely into her thought stream: "So Mimo works for you?"

"Only in theory, like the other servants. Nobody really works around here, but we support their families. It's the island way—a form of feudalism."

I could sense Maria Pia hovering behind me, still holding the tray of rolls.

"This opportunity comes at the right time for me," I said.

"How very American," she said.

"I'm sorry."

"Never apologize, darling. Let that be your first lesson in proper self-regard. Other lessons will follow." She leaned close to me, taking my hand. I could smell tobacco on her breath, but it was not disagreeable. "I will promise you only one thing: I will tell you the truth, if and when it matters. Do you understand?"

For reasons unfathomable to myself, I trusted her and nodded.

"That's super," she said, with the faintest glimmer of a smile. "We're going to be such good friends, Alex. I shall teach you to cook, and perhaps one day we'll open a little trattoria. Wouldn't that be fun?"

# *three*

—————

My new home was a stone cottage with shutters on the windows, a blue door with a screen, and a flat roof made of terra-cotta tiles. It stood, as promised, at the bottom of the garden, not far beyond the dark-blue swimming pool (painted to reflect light in the manner of the Blue Grotto), and surrounded by cyprus trees that stood like centurions, their spears high. The flower beds on the seaward side of the house teemed with Vera's handiwork, although only a few were in bloom. "Gaillardia, dianthus, fuchsia, agapanthis, iris, and tritoma," she explained, with a schoolmarm's delight in precision. "They'll emerge in due course. One by one."

Mimo hovered in the middle distance, a shovel in hand. Like an old crow, he appeared to sink into his own black shadow, unshaven, dressed in dark clothes with a filthy cap on his head. I waved at him, but he didn't acknowledge me.

"Pay no attention to Mimo," Vera warned. "He's not quite right in the head. A mule, I believe."

"A mule?"

"Kicked in the head. Ages ago."

With that, she left me to myself, saying that if I wanted a swim I could join Rupert at the beach or use the pool, which they had repainted and filled only the week before. It would not be hard to find her husband at the beach, she assured me, pointing in the direction of the sea. "The water is chilly," she added, "but then, so is Rupert."

I saw her pass the window as I settled, dazed, on the bed. Vera was unlike anyone I'd ever met, and the atmosphere at the Villa Clio was both intriguing and a little scary. But I was willing and eager to put my doubts on hold. I had taken the plunge, and I would swim.

The cottage was tiny, but everything I could wish for was here: a double bed (made up, in the Italian style, of twin beds pushed together), a side table with a lamp for reading, an oak dresser missing several knobs, and a three-legged table by the window with two cane chairs. There was a fireplace, a bookshelf, a dilapidated wing chair, and a small refrigerator that had already been supplied with fresh milk and butter. A sink and small stove in one corner were a gesture in the direction of self-sufficiency, and I found coffee and sugar in the cupboards, plus a crusty loaf of bread and a bag of semisweet Italian breakfast biscuits. The bathroom, created from what had recently been a feeding trough for swine, was small but serviceable, with a toilet and shower. Vera had explained that I should make my own breakfast, but that lunch and dinner would be taken with them, in the dining room. Rupert, she warned me, considered these meals an important part of life at the Villa Clio.

The first thing I did was put my letters from Nicky in the bottom drawer of the dresser. A manila envelope held the dozen letters from Vietnam that had become my secret hoard of pain, and a source of inspiration. I did not want anyone to know about the letters or Nicky. A large part of my life now was about forgetting, and I would become expert in the craft. Nevertheless, I often felt Nicky beside me, in broad daylight, watching. We met directly in my dreams, talking in ways never possible when he was alive. I wanted to put things right and make amends for my silly and cruel disregard for his intelligence and capabilities.

My mother had marked him from early childhood as the lesser son, the one who would eventually cause trouble. In contrast, my father had been protective of Nicky, who was, like him, not an intellectual but "good with his hands." When he went to Vietnam, my father had felt reassured, as if his years of standing by his son had been justified by this act of courage and patriotism.

I tended to side with my mother. For years I shook my head whenever Nicky misbehaved, which was often. The more obnoxious and agitated he became, the calmer I grew. His blackness only whitened my white-ness. I had tried to argue with him, to explain that he was his own worst enemy, but he resisted me as he resisted my parents. Though I was the younger sibling, he defined himself against me; if I was getting good grades, he would get bad ones. If I went to catechism with enthusiasm, he played hooky, describing himself from the age of thirteen as an athe-ist, much to my mother's horror. My quietness and tendency toward self-reflection only enhanced his chatty shallowness. That he demolished two cars by the age of seventeen surprised no one. He smoked cigarettes, drank with abandon, swore, and (as we learned after the fact) talked his pregnant girlfriend into an abortion during their senior year in high school. (Nicky could talk a mouse into hunting cats.)

"Disturbed" was the word my mother used to describe my brother: one of those bland euphemisms families employ to disguise unnamable anguish and fear. Pegged by her as a child who would "come to no good," his death in Vietnam had struck her as a logical development. Unfortu-nately, Nicky put more stock in my mother's opinion of him than in my father's. On some level, he believed there was nowhere for him to go, and had found a way to confirm a path of pathlessness by dying in a pointless war. ("Goddamn gooks live on both sides of the DMZ," he wrote on arrival in Saigon, "and I can't explain to you why we plant our flag for one and not the other.")

Having unpacked my few belongings, I undressed. There was some-thing luxurious, after travel, about stripping and stretching out on a per-fectly made bed. On my back, naked, I let my first impressions of the cottage assemble slowly, aware that these would undergo many revisions. No place ever appears the same after you have lived there for a week or so. After several months, the size of a room seems to increase with expe-riences that overlap, erasing (imperfectly) all previous ones, creating a palimpsest of sorts that invariably deepens and grows more complex.

The afternoon light had acquired a powdery aspect, a dust of gold that lay thinly on every surface in the room. The breeze puffed through an open window on the seaward side, riffling the pages of my notebook, which lay open on the table. Already I was eager to scribble in my jour-nal. I had decided before coming here to keep a strict account of my time at the Villa Clio, thinking that one day it would come in handy. (The possibility that one day I might write a biography of Rupert Grant had not escaped me, but I pushed the notion into the background. I did not want to think of my life as "research.")

Eventually, I put on my bathing suit and sat by the bookshelf in the shabby wing chair with springs pushing through the faded fabric. Other people's books were always more interesting than one's own, and I was curious about what volumes Rupert Grant would keep here. I guessed any books that meant anything to him would be in his study, but even his spillover interested me. A handful of thrillers by John Buchan and Nevil Shute abutted mysteries by Georges Simenon and Nicholas Blake. A tattered copy of *Death in Venice* wedged between two miscellaneous leather volumes of Gibbon's *Decline and Fall of the Roman Empire*. *A Shropshire Lad* tilted against volumes by Cecil Day-Lewis and John Betjeman. On the bottom shelf were two novels by Hugh Walpole and *Old Calabria* by Norman Douglas. It worried me that I had not read one of these books, and that some were completely unfamiliar.

Feeling ignorant and slightly afraid of meeting Rupert Grant for the first time, I trekked down the path to the sea through a grove of olive trees to a bare knoll, where marram grass stirred in a dry wind from the north. The air, though bright, was cool. (I had not imagined swimming until May or June.) The beach was visible below, a rocky stretch of shingle whose whitish-gray pebbles could have, from that height, been mistaken for cockles.

Just off the path, to the left, was a sheer limestone cliff, and I guessed the view from there would be especially dramatic. Though never comfortable with heights, I pushed through scrub to the edge. The vertical drop was about a hundred feet, and below were black rocks, their sharp blades poking through a swirl of surf. My head spun, as I suddenly envisioned myself pitching forward, falling helplessly, then smashing on the rocks. There was no easy way to die, but this would be horrible. I backed away to the main trail, gazing into the middle distance, feeling weak as I stumbled down the zigzag path.

Rupert Grant stood in the water below, a milky surf swirling around his thighs. Well over six feet, he stooped slightly as he walked, but not like an old man; he was more like an English schoolboy, gangly and awkward. As I reached the headland, the details of his physiognomy assembled. The white hair had been the first thing that caught my eye as he walked toward me, moving with what seemed like a fierce yet highly controlled natural energy. He was tanned, though the skin on his chest was peeling badly, with the pigment washed out in small albino patches. The lines in his face, growing more visible as I approached, were deep, and the high cheekbones raised a spidery swirl of veins breaking close to the surface. His cheeks, when I got close, were pinkly veined: a result of heavy smoking. His eyes were slate gray, fallen from a younger blue.

"Ah, you're Lorenzo," he said. His deep voice had the slight rustle of a Scottish accent.

"I'm Alex."

"I prefer Lorenzo. Will that do?"

"I don't mind," I said, faintly.

"Good. It would be awkward if you did." He saw I was not smiling, and that I looked away. "It's more jolly this way. You have to invent yourself anyway, what? Adam in the garden, when he named the beasts, was the first artist. Old story. So it goes. We're all pale ancestors." He rubbed his chest with a red towel, flaking off skin. "I'm falling apart. Sixty-three tomorrow, so you're just in time. We're having a little *festa*, party on the beach. Good wine, I'm told. Roasting a pig, too. You're a pig-lover, no?"

I nodded, vaguely. His rapid-fire speech and odd linguistic mannerisms made the conversation difficult to follow. It also had the effect of distancing us.

"You'll meet everyone," he said. "The whole bloody island is coming. Vera's idea, not mine. By nature, I'm a recluse."

"Your wife suggested I should call you Rupert."

"Ah, she found you first. Clever girl."

"We had a cup of tea."

"No matter. You will like Vera. I do."

It seemed peculiar that he should say this about his own wife. Then again, marriage, from what I could tell at my limited vantage, seemed not always to improve relationships. My own parents, I was beginning to think, might well have found better mates. My father's natural aggressiveness had been turned inward, giving him ulcers and stripping him of that grainy individuality one values in people. My mother had been prompted, by his self-annihilation, to assert herself unduly. She became a dragon folded in the gate of our house.

"Are you settled?"

"Yes," I said, "I like the cottage."

"It will do. Unless you expand."

"Excuse me?"

"Add on. People on Capri are always adding on: friends, cats, lovers, ghosts."

"I don't intend to add on."

"Good chap. I don't mind occasional guests, but I can't feed the multitudes. I'm not rich, you see. My novels don't sell. Or most of them don't." The furrows of his brow deepened. "Do you know Bonano, your countryman? Never sells under a hundred thousand copies. Ridiculous man."

"I've never read one," I said, to the relief of my new employer.

What I knew of Dominick Bonano came from a profile I'd skimmed in a recent copy of *Esquire*. He was the author of fat potboilers sold mostly in airports, invariably bound in lurid jackets. One of them—*The Last Limo on Staten Island*—had achieved some fame as a movie, though I'd somehow missed it. Bonano lived in style in Anacapri in a many-level villa that had formerly belonged to a German industrialist. As I discovered, Grant had a mild obsession with Bonano, though they were far from genuine rivals. Nobody took Bonano's multigenerational sagas about Mafia families seriously, though he earned millions in royalties and movie options.

"You've had secretaries before?"

"Several. Good chaps, mostly. One of them was a thief, but we fixed that." His eyes seemed to glaze over, as if he were suddenly lost in thought. It would become a familiar shift: Grant losing contact with the present, slipping into a parallel universe. I would have to learn to bide my time while he journeyed to wherever. As suddenly as he would disappear, he'd return, usually drawing his hand across his face to reconnect with the moment. "As you know, I have two girls," he said, "research assistants. Nice girls, Holly and Marisa. You'll like them." He explained that Holly had come from England about six months before me. "She's quite

talented," he said, "writing a novel when she's not working for me."
Marisa he described as "an Italian girl, who wants to become a journalist." She had been with him for about two months. "The kind of work I
do requires research, of course. Facts, as we say. But I'm not a slave to
them. You have to take possession of facts. They're never true until you
make them true." He shook his head like a dog that has just stepped
from the water. "Wilde once said that the English are always degrading
truths into facts. I try not to do that. Then again, I'm Scots, what?"

I wanted to respond gaily. To make an impression, to show I was intelligent, well-read, sympathetic, and to suggest that his work interested to
me greatly. But I found myself mute, my tongue thick with anxiety. I did
not really understand why he needed so many research assistants, and
wondered about Holly and Marisa. An evasiveness in Grant's descrip-
tions of them puzzled me.

"We'll have bundles of time to chat," he said. "Perhaps I can teach you
something. One never knows."

I had no doubt that many lessons lay ahead, and this appealed to me.
I'd had fantasies about mentors—strong father-figures who could explain
the world to me and set me straight. I had eagerly sought them out, with
small success. There was a teacher at Columbia, Professor Justin
Lorimer, who offered a course in Roman poetry that I took during my
sophomore year. He had focused on me attentively, and I found the quality of thought in my papers improving under his critical gaze. But I
wanted more from him that he could give me, and he seemed uncomfortable when I began to stop by his office without anything specific in
mind. Once, he said he was "in the midst of something," and began to
read in my presence.

In retrospect, I suppose this yearning for mentors had something to do
with my own father's remoteness, although this sort of speculation didn't
interest me at the time. All I knew was that Rupert Grant immediately
inspired in me feelings of longing. He represented a world I desperately
wanted to possess myself. I wanted his counsel and help, his guidance.
Mostly, I wanted his approval.

"Try the water, lad. It's tolerable," he said. "But be careful. There's an
undertow. People don't realize . . ."

"I'm a pretty good swimmer," I said.

"Even so," Grant said, with an ominous glance at the sea. "I'll say no more." He shook water from his left ear, hitting himself on the other ear with the heel of his palm. "When you've had enough, come to my study. We'll have a cup of tea."

I could see that teatime came often at the Villa Clio, and that I would have to acquire a taste for the ritual as much as the substance itself. As I discovered, the British do not so much travel as transport their ways to better climates.

I stepped blithely into the water, and could see at once what Grant meant by an undertow. A weaker swimmer might easily be tugged under. I lost my footing at one point, stumbling, having to fight the current as I began to swim. I cut through the worst of it with strong overhand strokes as invisible paws tugged at me, trying to drag me down. When a wave caught me off-guard, crosswise, I swallowed a mouthful of salty water, and began to retch. For a moment, I thought I might actually drown. Only by intense focus was I able to churn forward, ignoring my discomfort, my fear, and a sense of disorientation. Only when I got about half a mile from shore, where the currents were deep, did I feel at ease again, treading water, with my back to the horizon.

The island was impressive from that vantage: pink-amber in the late afternoon light, the Faraglioni—rocks like raised, geologic fists—sheer on my right, and the presiding peak of Mount Solaro high above on the left, wreathed in cloud. The hillside was dotted with white villas and expensive hotels, all neatly buried in the carefully tended landscape. Expensive yachts flying international flags—Monaco, France, Liechtenstein, Belgium—moored in the bay of the Piccola Marina, while half a dozen fishing boats stalled in my peripheral vision.

I could just see the tiny figure of Rupert Grant, arms akimbo, on the beach. His abrupt, determined, elusive manner had taken me by surprise, and I foresaw that life at the Villa Clio would not be simple or straightforward. If I had thought it would be, this was merely a function of my own foolishness or wishful thinking. One inevitably tries to look ahead, imagining in detail the physical and emotional landscape that lies in wait, but these attempts are vain. Life at the Villa Clio was beyond anything I might have constructed in my head. The actual Vera Grant, I feared, was more aggressive and complicated than my hypothetical Vera, whom I knew only from a photograph on the jacket of a brightly illustrated cookbook I had seen at Rizzoli, in New York, before leaving. Rupert was less penetrable than I imagined, from his essays, he might be; there was something northern and inaccessible there, a granite quality, a self-protectiveness. But I cautioned myself to draw no conclusions. "Expect nothing, and you will always be pleasantly surprised," my grandfather often said, translating an old Neapolitan saying. It seemed, under these circumstances, like excellent advice.

*four*
___

I lay awake that night, thinking about a letter from Nicky, written within a week of his arrival in Saigon.

*Dear Asshole,*

*Arrived Saigon. Not what I expected, but what the hell can anybody expect anywhere?*

*You'd never know there was a war on. Taxi cabs running up and down the streets, lots of restaurants, people sitting on the sidewalks, drinking beer, making jokes. Looks kind of happy to me. And if it weren't for the occasional Army jeep, you'd say, shit, this is vacationland.*

*Just waiting and watching, scratching and snoring. That's the problem with this war, they tell me. Gotta make it happen, so says my friend Eddie Sloane, another asshole like you (he dropped out of a college somewhere in Iowa). I better do something before I lose my fucking mind.*

*Lots of girls and cheap, too, I'm told. Beautiful, in their weird yellow way, with long legs and skinny necks. Fuck like bunnies. If you're lucky your dick won't swell up like one of Dad's big zucchinis and drop off. (Remember those zucchinis? Big motherfuckers, weren't they? He used to come into the kitchen with them in September and scare the shit out of Mom, waving a big one around. "Put that goddamn thing away," she'd say.)*

*Dad isn't the kind of guy who normally waves his club. You aren't either.*

*Nice and quiet types. Peaceful and easy. Mom likes that, huh? I guess I scare her, since I'm never nice and not very quiet, except when stoned. Booze still sends me screaming through the streets, so I got to be careful. Pot is more peaceful, right? I mean, you don't feel like killing somebody after a good joint. You don't mind so much if they take you down. We all gotta die sometime.*

*Excuse my rambling. If I don't sound exceptionally intelligent, blame the weather. I've got a good excuse, believe me. It's so fucking hot day and night, your brain gets like a piece of chocolate left on the dashboard in mid-August. Like a wet piece of shit. So you say things you wouldn't say to anybody back home, and you talk bullshit all night because you can't sleep and don't want to, in case you don't wake up. Eddie and I talk all the time. Iowa is nowhere, I tell him. Back in Pennsylvania we pronounce it O-hi-o.*

*We tell stories when we can't sleep, trading them like you and I used to trade baseball cards. He knew everything there was in just a few nights about all of us. About Mom's fat ass and Dad's big empty tasteless zucchini and your humongous fucking classical brain and literary presumptions. Is that the word? I'm no fucking writer, but I know what I like.*

*PFC Fucking Massolini. Who's that? I got another month or so here, they tell me, in Saigon. Then up country we go, over the river and through the woods. Can't wait. Proud to serve. Mr. Rawhide himself, with my M-16, gas-operated, ready to rock. Got twenty rounds in the magazine. Thing weighs 8.2, not including the strap. And not including the fucking grenade launchers they're hoping to teach me to launch, which means you're also stuck with ten or so extra rounds of ammo. A lot to hump and haul through mosquito swamps and elephant grass when you've got jungle rot and wanna scratch and dust your balls with DDT.*

*Eddie's part Indian, he claims, so they made him the medicine man. (We call him Sitting Bullshit.) Bastard's gonna haul bandages, iodine, plasma, morphine, tape, hypodermics, all that glassy, gooey, spooky shit. Save your fucking life in the right (or wrong) situation, so he's got to haul it. The walking drugstore.*

*Speaking of humping, you still got your cherry? I hear those girls in the Ivy League are pretty damn tight-assed, all talk and no action. A hand-job in the library stacks if you're lucky. Come out here, and get laid in style. There's a whole street in Saigon, Ding Dong Avenue, they call it. Stopped by last night. You'd love it, man—regular shopping mall for tits and ass. Take your pick, honey. You stand in the lobby and point, then the Momma unites you in the elevator, till death do you part. The bitch takes you upstairs, saying things with a shit-eating grin like "Americans big money" and "U.S. soldier good man in*

*bed." Nice bathtubs, where she scrubs your nuts and prick. Big beds, mirrors
on the ceiling so if you're into that kind of kinky shit you can watch yourself
hump (if you're on your back). Or maybe she can watch you hump. They seem
to like it, the fucking, though you can't tell shit from their Shinola. I can't anyway, but what did I ever know?*

*Dad got all emotional and told me the night I left that he learned something
in The War, but he never said what. Started to say something about Italy. About
Salerno. But the words didn't come easy and he just quit talking. Like whatever he learned over there wasn't worth saying or was too deep to spit it out. I
don't honestly think I'll learn a fucking thing in Nam. Don't believe there's anything much to pick up here except the crabs.*

*"Is there a God?" Eddie keeps asking me—it's like the biggest question in
Iowa, he claims. "If so, how did he think up all this shit? How did he come up
with Nam?" Maybe he's a demonic genius, I said to him. Maybe he's bored. This
whole fucking mess happened because there's nothing on TV up there in heaven,
and you can't lay an angel.*

*I told Eddie he should ask you the biggies, and that there's more to you than
meets the eye. Underneath it all, you got some balls. I believe that. You come on
quiet at first, but then somebody bangs up against your wall, and you squeal.*

*By the way, if Uncle Sam Wants You, take my advice. Give Uncle the big fin-
ger. No good is coming out of this war, that's for sure. Whatever Dad says, he's
wrong. He's "so proud of me," he writes. Mom writes nothing, though she sends
clippings from the* Wilkes-Barre Record. *Just the sort of info I really want to
know, like who in my high school class got knocked up and had to ring the wedding bells. Not me, I tell you. I'm not going home, not to Luzerne County.
That's history. It's funny how clear you can see things from a distance. I recommend it, though you might think of Paris, not Saigon, as about the right sort
of distance. You think about home in ways you never could when it's right
around the corner, or in your face.*

*I could have chucked it, the war thing. Gone to Canada like Buzz Mooney
or shattered my pinkie toe with a jackhammer like Benny Dixon's cousin from
Nanticoke. Some days I think I should have pinched the doctor's butt at the
physical or just walked into the exam with a real hard-on and started jerking
off on the spot. Guys do that kind of shit, and it works. But I made a decision.
Just do it. Go to the fucking war.*

*Sometimes you just got to do something. Whatever it is, you got to make it
happen, goddamn it. Make it happen. You do what you got to do, Asshole. And
you do it well.*

*Hey, enough philosophy for one letter. War turns you philosophical, they say. Eddie claims there is more philosophy in this platoon per square inch than at Harvard and Yale, and I swear he's right. You should hear some of this shit. If you're lucky, maybe I'll pass along some of the good stuff, and maybe some-day it will mean something to you. Then again, maybe it won't.*

*So write me, Asshole, when you can take a minute off from slapping your dick around. I don't know why I'd like to hear from you, since you're a prick and always were, but I would.*

*Your Big Bro in Lotus Land,*
*Nicky*

## *five*

Maria Pia pointed in the direction of Grant's study. "He is expecting you," she said, in the local *dialetto*. Given her tone and expression, she might well have said, "He will cut off your prick if you disturb him, but be my guest."

I knocked softly.

"Indeed," he shouted.

*Indeed?* I leaned close to the door, then knocked again.

"Lorenzo, I'm waiting."

He was slumped in a leather chair, wearing his wire-rimmed reading glasses. *La Stampa* was open on his lap, and a glass of neat whiskey lay half drunk on the table beside him. His white, voluminous hair stood up like a coxcomb, complemented by frothy eyebrows that seemed to move independently of each other. "So you like to swim," he said. "I didn't wait for you to come ashore."

I felt guilty. "Were you expecting me sooner?"

"Yes," he said, "but no matter. I will get Maria Pia to bring us tea, unless you'd rather whiskey?"

"Tea is fine."

"Good. Sit down."

While he was gone, I scanned the room. The wooden desk was a trestle table that faced out from the wall, smothered in scraps of paper. A fountain pen lay beside a pot of India ink, and I remembered that the two letters he'd sent me were elegantly scripted, not sloppily typed or scratched in ballpoint. A dagger—unsheathed—glimmered beside the inkpot; it had a carved ivory handle. On the opposite wall were marks in a wooden board, the signs of target practice.

There was a colorful map of the ancient world beside the board, and floor-to-ceiling bookcases on the other walls that supported an extremely old set of the *Encyclopedia Britannica*; below it, the New York edition of Henry James vied for attention with a handsome set of Balzac in purple cloth bindings. Odd volumes of the Temple Shakespeare scattered among other books. One shelf was devoted to Italian novelists and poets, most of them fairly recent: Eugenio Montale, Ignazio Silone, Elsa Morante, Carlo Levi. Moravia was there in abundance. Gore Vidal's *Julian* nestled beside *I, Claudius*. There was a nice run of Graham Greene in what looked like first editions. (As I soon learned, most of them were signed by Greene, who had spent a part of each year in Anacapri since 1948.) *Brideshead Revisited* was there, too, with a faded spine.

"What ho," Grant said, entering with a tray in his hands. It would take some time for me to get used to this affection for Edwardian phrases, like odd snatches from P. G. Wodehouse. "We can get down to it," he said, taking his seat. "Can you take dictation?"

"Not in shorthand," I said.

"No matter. I'll dictate slowly. You can write slowly."

I nodded.

"Of course, you'll type my letters and manuscripts." He looked at me nervously. "You do type?"

"Yes."

"Americans are good typists," he said, "but that's where it ends. Nothing of real interest in your literature." He poured my tea through a strainer. "I take that back. Nothing of interest since Henry James. Do you like James?"

"I've only read *The Turn of the Screw*."

He sighed. "We have our work cut out for us, don't we?" After handing me the cup, he found a paperback of *The Europeans*, which he put on the tea tray. "Read this first, it's early James. Easy to follow. We'll move slowly. Eventually, you'll be ready for the good stuff. *The Wings of the Dove* is best, I suspect."

"Why not start there?"

"You would crumble. It takes time to get used to his methods, the periphrasis . . . Trust me, Alex. I've been through this before with Americans. They're brought up on Hemingway. Very destructive influence, Hemingway. Baby talk."

Patriotic reflexes I had not known about sent an unfamiliar tingle through my body. "You don't like Hemingway?"

"He was a silly man, a minor figure. There is one decent book of stories, the first, I think—some lovely things there. Nick Adams and so on. After that, it's mostly bluster." He settled back into his chair, balancing the tea on his lap. "Faulkner is better, I suppose, but he's an acquired taste. I've never acquired it."

"I like Fitzgerald," I said. I actually loved Fitzgerald, but didn't want to overstate the case. Whole paragraphs from *The Great Gatsby* lingered in my head like poems.

"Pretty writing," he said, dismissively. "Americans like pretty writing. Joseph Hergesheimer, James Branch Cabell, Fitzgerald."

I didn't dare ask who were Hergesheimer and Cabell, but I got the point. "What about our poets?"

"*Our* poets?"

I ignored his baiting. "Eliot, for example? Or Frost?"

A bemused look crossed his face.

"Whitman? Or Emily Dickinson?"

"Eliot, yes. I used to see him in London—a remarkable ear: *Dry the pool, dry concrete, brown edged.* That's it. Excellent critic, too. Who could resist *The Sacred Wood*? Frost was a decent poet, but I can only take him in small doses. And the shorter the poem, the better. Whitman I admire, in bits and pieces, and Dickinson, yes. Monotonous, perhaps, but memorably so."

"*The Sacred Wood?*"

"Eliot's essays—the early ones! Good God, man." Disgusted, he plucked a copy of that slim volume from a shelf behind his desk and piled it on top of *The Europeans*. "Read 'Tradition and the Individual Talent.' It puts paid to most criticism written since. You can ignore the book reviews. He tends to fuss a bit."

"What about Auden?" I said.

"He's English, no matter what he claims."

"You and he were friends at Oxford?"

"We were contemporaries. But I was at Magdalen, so we met only in passing. We got to know each other later." He slumped in his chair. "Everyone knew that he was the important poet, even before he published anything. Stephen printed his first poems on a small press. I still have my copy."

"Stephen?"

"Spender," he said, exasperated. "Stephen is not a poet, but he looks the part. Rather dreamy, Stephen. They pay him huge sums in America to play the great bard. Someone has to do it, I suppose."

I told him I admired Auden, and he told me "Wystan" and his companion, Chester, had once owned a house on Ischia, a neighboring island. "He might turn up this summer. There is such a rumor afloat."

"I'd like to meet him," I said.

Of course Grant knew many of the people he mentioned, but I felt a mingling of awe and suspicion whenever he dropped luminous names, as he often did. How had he managed to befriend so many poets, novelists, philosophers, historians, journalists, film directors, and actors? Was Britain such a small world that, as he once claimed, after a while you knew everyone?

Now Grant told me about a novel he planned to write in the coming year. It would be set on Capri, mostly in the present, with excursions into various centuries. "The island is full of wonderful stories and characters," he said. When I told him that I hoped to learn more about Tiberius, he lit up. "I've been asked to translate *Lives of the Twelve Caesars*. You read Latin, what? At Harvard?"

"Columbia. Yes, but my Latin is not wonderful."

"No matter. Suetonius is straightforward." He popped up again, finding a copy of Suetonius, which he put in my lap. "Translate the chapter on Tiberius. I've got a good Latin dictionary if you need one. Will do you some good, and help me. I'll correct your prose."

I was mildly put off by this expression. How would he "correct" my prose? But I said nothing, and would try, for a while, to keep with the program as laid out by him.

"Suetonius is unreliable, as history, but he's fun," Grant said. "Smutty in places, though he stops short of pornography. Knew how to keep a reader's attention." He finished the whiskey in a gulp and wiped his lips with the back of his rough hand. "The emperor trained small boys—*pisciculi* is the word he used, I believe—to frolic between his thighs when he went swimming. They would nibble at his cock. Eventually, he commandeered infants from local families—liked their sucking reflex. Rather disgusting, don't you think?"

"Yes," I said, unambiguously. He did not, I feared, consider the emperor's behavior disgusting enough.

"Had a painting in his bedroom, old Tibby—Atalanta sucking off Meleager. Very sexy. Loved it, apparently." He lapsed briefly into silence, staring blankly ahead—a habit of conversation that would become familiar but never comfortable. "It was pathetic, I suppose. Came to a bad end, Tibby—at least in the version of him put forward by Suetonius. Died cranky, unfulfilled, and much loathed. One dislikes lust in old men, don't you think?"

"I've never thought about it."

"You will," he said. "Have you read St. Augustine's *Confessions*?"

For once, I had. It had been required reading in a course I'd taken during my freshman year.

"Good boy. Think of Tiberius as Augustine without the conversion. Burning in lust. Horrid spectacle." Grant went around to his desk, taking some pages from a brown folder. "Here's your first official task, a little job of typing. Something I did for an American travel magazine," he said. "I do prose for money. It's like breeding dogs so that I can afford to keep a few cockatoos." He contemplated this simile for a moment. "Poetry has no market value. That's why I prefer it." He handed me the pile. "See what you can make of this. Double spaced, please. Wide margins."

I took the pages from him, seeing they would pose a challenge. Sentences were crossed out, rewritten above, then crossed out again, with arrows and balloons in every available margin. "When will you need this?"

"Two, three days. No hurry. We don't hurry around here."

Without knocking, an olive-skinned girl of about twenty in tight, faded jeans and a pink T-shirt walked in. She wore leather sandals that showed off her bright red toenails. That she was aware of her unusual beauty was evident from the way she swept her brown hair, casually, from her forehead. But there was also something dark and sulky about her, as though she had swallowed a purple thunderhead. She curled into his lap, draping an arm around his shoulders.

"Mind the tea," Grant said.

She kissed his eyebrows, lightly. I didn't know quite where to put my eyes. I had seen plenty of adolescent displays like this at Columbia, but usually after long, beery parties in darkened dormitory lounges.

"This is Marisa," he said. "Surname, Lauro: Marisa Lauro. A poem in its own right."

I nodded slightly in her direction.

"Marisa does research for me," Grant said. "Very bright girl, this. She's digging up stories for me about Capri, aren't you, dear?"

I waited for Marisa to speak, but she didn't. Her makeup was thick—the lipstick redder than red, and her eyes like water at the bottom of deep wells of eye shadow. She wore large gold earrings, and the smell of cologne permeated the room. Her jeans were way too tight.

Grant folded his hands around her narrow waist, and her head slumped onto his shoulder. She seemed in need of comfort, and I felt like an intruder. I stood to leave.

"You needn't disappear, Lorenzo. We won't fuck in front of you. Promise."

I hoped that my face registered nothing. "I've made arrangements to meet a friend in the piazzetta," I said.

"What? Already got a friend in the piazzetta?"

"I met him on the ferry. A student at the Sorbonne."

"Is he French?"

"Yes."

"Marvelous. Invite him to my party—tomorrow, at six, on the beach."

"Really?"

"Why not? Is he beautiful or intelligent? Either will do."

Marisa was finally aroused to speech. "What a silly man you are,

Rupert," she said, her English heavily accented. "Don't say things like this. You embarrass him."

"He's a student of philosophy," I said, riding over her remark.

"A beautiful philosopher," Grant said, "how excellent. One always prefers beauty to intelligence in a philosopher, since philosophy is nonsense anyway, especially French philosophy. Tell him to join us. He needn't dress."

Even before I was gone, Grant had begun to kiss Marisa, pulling her toward him with his large hands. From the corner of my eye, I saw her knees lift as she swiveled to face him.

I closed the door and ran.

## *six*

That night, in the dining room, I met Holly Hampton, Grant's English assistant, for the first time. She was elegant in a distinctly English way (although her mother was from Philadelphia), with pure but understated features. Her blond hair was silky, parted in the middle, and cut just above her shoulders. She wore a simple white dress with a high neckline. Our eyes rarely met, but I found myself excited by her presence, and wishing I could study her face at leisure.

To welcome me, Vera had made one of her favorite dinners: tagliatelle al prosciutto for the first course, or *primo*, then salt cod alla romana, served with long green beans marinated in olive oil and garlic. This was followed by a cheese tart covered in pine nuts and raisins—crostata di ricotta. The wine, from Grant's cellar, was Bianco del Vesuvio—"a whorish little vino," he said, filling glasses around the table, "but suitable for us, I fear." He obviously relished the position of *arbiter bibendi*.

Grant introduced me as "a Latin scholar fresh from the New World."

"My brother is a Latinist," said Holly. "At Balliol."

"That's an Oxford college, Lorenzo," Grant said, when I didn't respond at once.

"I know," I said.

"Sorry, old boy. That ignorant look of yours rather deceived me."

A grandfather clock stood against one wall, ticking loudly.

"Please, Rupert," said Vera. "It's his first night."

"He's a strong chap," Grant said. "And we're already friends, aren't we?" His nostrils appeared to flare.

"*Malefico,*" said Marisa, clucking her tongue.

"Oh, do speak English, Marisa," Grant told her. He turned to me. "She spent a year in Liverpool, and she's perfectly fluent."

"I hope you'll like us when you get to know us," said Vera, tentatively.

"For God's sake, Vera, let it go," said Grant, with a detectable slur in his phrasing. I guessed that he had been drinking since our meeting in his study.

"Rupert is drunk," said Holly. "He's not always so frightful."

Maria Pia and a delicate-looking young man called Alfredo, a cousin of hers, were serving the first course. There was nothing elegant about their presentation as they dropped the plates before each person at the table with a clatter.

Grant leaped from his seat, moving around the table, putting his arms on Holly's shoulders. "She is my prize," he said. "I believe she will be a fine novelist one day."

I noticed that Marisa blanched, looking down.

Holly shook off Grant. "I'm writing my first novel, and so are a billion other people."

"I'm a fairly reliable reader," said Grant, "and I like what I see." He kissed her on the back of the head.

"I must be not good," said Marisa. "You have never told me anything of this kind, Rupert."

"How could I, since I've read almost nothing of yours? Unlike most reviewers, I insist on reading a work before judging it."

Vera quickly poured herself a second glass of wine, agitated by her husband's performance.

"Our new friend, Lorenzo, is himself a poet," Grant announced. "Why don't you recite something? Acquaint us all with your work." He folded his arms, as if waiting for my recital to begin.

I said, "I'm not much of a poet."

"But you sent me poems. I rather liked them."

"I don't remember any," I said.

"Dementia, what? Brain cells washed away by alcohol? I sympathize."

"I just never bothered to memorize them," I said. "They're not good enough."

"Oh, dear," he said.

"Do sit down, Rupert," Vera said, looking sternly at her husband.

"Shut up, Vera. You're becoming a bore," he said. I had never heard that word carry so much negative weight.

Walking slowly around the table, he glared at each of us in turn, eventually taking a seat. Munching a piece of bread, he told us that he'd heard from a producer at the BBC that morning that one of his novels, *Siren Call*, was being considered for a serial. "There will be money in it," he said, "especially if I get to do the scripts."

"These projects never pan out," Vera said, dampening the flame of his enthusiasm. "Or they take decades to materialize."

"You're always so refreshing, Vera," said Grant. "It's no wonder I love you."

"I fear Alex will get the wrong impression of us," she said. "We don't always carry on like this."

"I have an idea," said Grant.

"Shall I alert the press?" Vera quipped.

Grant ignored her. "There's a marvelous game," he said, "a way to introduce us properly to our new friend, Lorenzo d'America." He wiped breadcrumbs from his mouth, as everyone waited. "Let's assume it's my turn. My dear wife must state the *least* likely thing that could be said about me. Go ahead, Vera. What would no rational person in the galaxy ever say about me?"

"Rupert Grant has no idea how clever he is," she said, without hesitation.

"Bravo!" He clapped his hands, then turned to Holly.

"I'm not much for games," she said.

"Do be a sport," Vera said. "We used to play this game at school."

Holly put a finger to her lips, thinking. "Rupert Grant," she said deliberately, "always lays his cards on the table."

"Very nice," said Grant.

Marisa didn't have to be prodded. "Mister Grant," she intoned, "does not care too much what people says about him."

"A dagger, dear girl, an absolute dagger," he said. "I must work to correct this misapprehension on your part. You see, Alex, the game has many positive aspects. It's better than psychotherapy." He gestured toward Vera. "The focus will now shift to my wife of many years, and I shall go first." He wrinkled his nose, in deep thought. "Vera Grant does not have a jealous bone in her body."

"How ludicrous," said Vera. "He's reversing the game."

"I stand corrected," said Grant.

Holly did not wait a moment. "Vera Grant should employ a cook. The food at the Villa Clio is rubbish."

Grant was expressionless. "You're clever, Holly, but I detect a lack of wit in that response. It does not speak well of an Oxford graduate."

"You take your games too seriously," said Holly.

"Poetry is a game," I said.

"A game of knowledge," said Grant. "That's Wystan's formulation, I believe."

"How literary we are," said Vera. "I really should have invited the press."

Marisa said, "Vera does not care what he makes, her husband."

"I should hope not," said Grant. "I do whatever I please."

"Bollocks," said Vera.

Grant sighed. "As you see, this is a game of knowledge, too. But humankind cannot bear very much reality."

I recognized the last line as a quotation, but could not locate the source.

"Marisa Lauro is a serious journalist," said Grant, portentously.

"Marisa Lauro doesn't care what people say about her," said Holly, glaring at Grant.

"Marisa Lauro paints her toenails only to please herself," said Vera.

"Every girl is painting her toenails except Holly," said Marisa. "I am not so intelligent as these," she said to me. "I am sorry for my confession. But you will not tolerate me for long. I am going to bed." She rose and left the room, her pasta course untouched.

No one spoke till she was gone.

"Tetchy girl," said Grant, reaching for her glass of wine, which he gulped.

"She's very sensitive, Rupert," his wife said. "I wish you'd be more careful."

"Life is too short for that," he said. "Truth is all that matters."

"I'd have voted for Beauty," she said.

Grant turned to Holly. "It's your turn, I suspect. We aren't letting you off the hook."

"I'm tired of this game," Vera said.

"Come on, darling. Play up, play ball, and play the game," said Grant. This was, I supposed, another quotation.

"All right," said Vera. "Holly Hampton is perfectly transparent. What you see is what you get." A permanent-looking smirk formed on her lips.

"But one sees so little," said Grant. "Or, perhaps, one sees so much. I'm not sure."

"Let's say that I'm a mystery," said Holly, "even to my myself."

"We like you as you are, my dear," said Grant. "Make no adjustments for our sake." He tapped his fingers on the table, formulating a line. "Holly Hampton is desperately in love with Rupert Grant," he said, suppressing a grin.

"I do love you, Rupert," she said, flatly. "Why else would I sleep with you?"

Vera's smirk vanished.

"What about you, Lorenzo?" Grant wondered. "We don't really know you, but if we did, what would we never say about you?"

I didn't hesitate. "Alex Massolini is a hard sell," I said.

Vera crinkled her brow. "You're a pushover in a shoe shop, is that what you're telling us?"

"He's what Americans call a wimp," said Holly.

"I see," said Grant. "Lorenzo will be good fun for all of us, what? Gullibility an endearing flaw. But we shall do our best to correct it, I daresay."

## *seven*

---

I was late for Grant's party, and could see from the cliff above the beach that tables had been laid end to end, and that a crowd had already gathered, most of them forming a circle around Grant.

Being shy, I admired those who were not. And Rupert Grant was blessed in this regard, having a robust outwardness that would have been trying had it not been modified by a Scots wryness and general British sense of cool. He stood with a drink in hand, in the midst of some amusing anecdote. His white hair, a Pentecostal flame, leaped above his head. Shoeless, he wore a long-sleeved, flowing, chalky blue shirt, in the style of a Russian mujik. The girls, as he called them, were at either side, his attendant muses, beautiful and subdued, while Vera wandered at the edge of the crowd, by herself. The scene made my stomach clench.

That her husband diverted himself with younger women right under her nose could not have made her life easy. I had searched her face for signs of anxiety or resentment, expecting a great deal of repressed anger; but little presented itself, apart from the occasional sly or cutting remark. Looking back, I wonder how I managed to navigate this situation. Certainly I wanted to fit in, and suppressed any complicated feelings about the Grant marriage, accepting their arrangement as simply a fact of life. I told myself that worldly people didn't trouble themselves with such things as conventional morality. Everything I'd been led to believe about love and marriage was put on hold as I strode forward into this brave old world.

Though Grant was close now, my attention was absorbed by Holly Hampton. She tossed her head back, laughing, reacting strongly to Grant's witticisms. To me, she seemed entirely beautiful in a boyish way. Just the outline of her body intrigued me: the odd, quirky angle of her hips, the way her head cocked slightly to one side as she listened. Her wrists dangled, and she had a quick smile and distinctive laugh. I liked the deep part in her hair, which revealed a lovely white strip of scalp.

Occasionally one can tell a lot about someone on brief acquaintance, and this was true for me with Holly. It had not surprised me, for instance, when I learned that her mother was from Philadelphia's Main Line. (You didn't usually meet English girls called Holly.) But her education and upbringing had been wholly British. She was obviously the product an English public school, and her aloof manner had been perfected at Lady Margaret Hall, her Oxford college. Even the physical mannerisms were British and class-specific, as when she held her arms around herself as she stood back to listen with her head tilted to one side. There was an aura of composure and self-assurance that, at its worst, veered toward complacency. At its best, it was reassuring; Holly knew her place in the world, and the place of those around her.

"God, we're surrounded by Yanks," Grant said, having caught sight of me. He beckoned over a burly man of fifty with a salt-and-pepper beard, drawing me urgently toward him. "Dominick," he said, "this is my new assistant, Lorenzo. He's from New York."

"Pennsylvania," I said.

"Dom Bonano," the man said, holding out his hand. "Let me guess. You wanna be a writer."

I simply smiled.

Bonano pushed his large, irregular face ahead of him like a cart full of groceries, his nose only a few inches from mine. "I guessed it just by looking. I must be a genius or something." He blew his nose in a handkerchief. "Allergies, excuse me," he said. "This is the worst time of year for that, all the flowers. The island is lousy with flowers."

I felt desperate to get away from him, but there was no easy exit.

"What kind of stuff do you write?" he wondered.

"Poetry," I said. "I'm thinking of a novel."

"Thinking, huh? Listen up, Larry. Everybody wants to write a novel, but if it was so easy, everybody would do it. There would be five million new fucking novels on the shelf every year."

"Alex," I said. "My name is Alex."

"Alex what?"

"Massolini."

He brightened. "A paisano! Just what we need in Capri, more goddamn wops." He asked where my family came from—a habit common among Italian Americans, who are forever prodding in the dark of their past for signs of origin, aware that place and legitimacy are somehow connected.

"My father's parents came from Naples," I said. "My mother's were from Calabria."

"Naples is great," he said, "but it's run-down. Full of pickpockets and hustlers. Mine were from Palermo. The cousins love to come here, visit their *cugino Americano*. Christ, they love it." I had been slowly backing away from him, but he pushed close again, speaking in a low voice. "I hate to be the one to break the news, Al, but there's no point in writing novels. Nobody wants them. Not like when Hemingway was king, and when it was really something to write a novel. Not anymore." He sniffed again, rubbing his nose. "Not that I'm writing literature myself. I just tell a good story. There's always an audience for a whopping good tale." He seemed to be saying, *the critics seem to have forgotten that Dickens and Balzac were storytellers first and foremost.*

Bonano's face held my attention like a car wreck. The nose was mottled and bulbous. His black eyebrows would not lie down. The general manner reminded me of my Uncle Vinnie, my father's younger brother. The business he pursued had something to do "with electronics" (so he said). Although he maintained a large Victorian house in West Pittston, with a portico and magnificent view of the Susquehanna River, Vinnie spent most of his time on the road, in New York and Miami, where he stayed in suites at glitzy hotels. He bought a new Lincoln Continental, usually with a soft top and white leather seats, every other year. His wife, Gloria, would not be caught dead without a string of pearls around her neck. In winter, she draped herself in mink; summer, it was silk all the way. (Soon after I left Columbia, I got an unexpected call from my uncle. "You want to go into electronics," he said, "you call your Uncle Vinnie. I could use a smart boy like you.")

"You come over and see me soon," Bonano said. He scribbled his number on a piece of paper and pushed it into my shirt pocket. "You'd like my daughter, Toni. She's a college girl, Bryn Mawr."

"A good school," I said.

"You bet your ass. She's in psychology. Reads Freud all the time. Every time she opens her mouth, that stuff comes tumbling out. This complex and that complex. Oedipus and Electra. I hate that shit, but what do I know?" He looked around, as if afraid someone would overhear us. "Hey, she'll be here in a couple months."

I kept a neutral expression. As with Vinnie, you couldn't give a man like Bonano too much ground or he would eat you alive.

"You call me now. Promise?"

"I promise."

"Good boy, Al."

"Alex," I said.

"Got it," he said, then tapped me on the shoulder and walked away.

"He's death," said an English voice behind me. I turned to see the kindly face of a man in his sixties, lean and tan. "I don't know why Rupert invited him. The brotherhood of fiction, I assume."

"Rupert seems to like him," said Vera, appearing beside the Englishman. "You've met Peter, I see?"

"Not yet," I said.

"Peter Duncan-Jones," he said. There was a natural warmth about him that I liked at once.

"He's an admirer of yours," said Vera.

"Oh?"

"Your paintings—the ones at the villa," I fumbled for the rest of the sentence, "caught my eye."

"A good eye, I should say."

"Be careful," Vera cautioned him. "Alex is American. He'll think you are being serious."

"I am serious, darling. If I can't adore me, who will?"

"Indeed."

An old Etonian, Duncan-Jones wore a paisley cravat, a navy blazer, and white trousers with cuffs: the look typical of English stockbrokers on holiday. A family signet ring adorned the little finger on one hand, the mark of a gentleman.

"We call him Picky, for Picasso," Vera put in, repeating what she had told me before just to annoy him.

"*You* call me Picky," he said. "Nobody else on this planet finds that amusing, Vera." He turned toward me directly, and I felt worried about Vera. She seemed unable to get a purchase on the company. "You might like to see my studio, Alex," said Duncan-Jones, jotting his number on a matchbook and stuffing it into my shirt pocket. "It would be an honor." He explained that his companion, Jeremy, had gone to London for a few days, but he would also be glad to meet me. "Jeremy is a social butterfly," he said. "Flit, flit, flit."

That everyone craved my company puzzled me. I had accomplished nothing, and whatever charms I might possess were still hidden. Now and then I rose to my own defense, but I felt more acted upon than acting, afraid to make my wishes known. As I soon learned, however, *any* new resident on Capri attracted attention, at first. Once the honeymoon was over, they would leave you in peace, especially if they considered you the worst of all possible creatures, a bore.

Patrice leaned heavily on my shoulder, materializing like Ariel in Prospero's cell. I thought again how uncannily he resembled my brother: not just the smile, but the sharp face and pointed chin. They were both slender but somehow sturdy, rather androgynous, though Nicky had gone to great lengths to override this trait. He had been at various times a weight lifter, a karate expert, a motorcyclist, and a football player (briefly, during junior high—much to my father's delight). He would do anything to insist upon his manhood.

"I am not introduce," Patrice said, breaking my reverie.

"I didn't see you!"

"But I wasn't here, *mon ami*. When I come here, now you see me. Modern physics!"

Patrice, who had already drunk too much, giggled like a schoolboy.

"Who is your friend?" asked Duncan-Jones. Patrice had drawn his full attention. After the briefest introduction, I left him in the painter's avid care.

"He's such a chicken hawk," said Vera, "but I do love him."

"Are you all right?" I wondered.

"Why shouldn't I be?"

"You seemed a little sad."

She looked at me harshly, and I realized I had opened a box that she preferred to keep shut. Changing the subject, she seized my arm. Her agenda for me was powerful, and she used me to divert herself as we moved from Milanese publisher to Greek fabric designer to Russian countess, the names or titles mostly lost on my unsophisticated ears. Only Count Eddie von Bismarck, the grandson of Otto, left a dent in my memory—how could one forget *that* name? Ego was vividly on display everywhere as dusk settled and all heavenly and earthly bodies swelled. There were supernovas and falling stars, asteroids and moons; every major celestial object had a swirl of light around it, but the whole event most evidently reflected the pull of Rupert Grant, a mysterious field-force that attracted everyone who encountered him.

Suddenly Grant's voice rose above the crowd. "Vera! Where is Vera?"

The next thing I knew, she was racing toward him. The call of her husband was primal, and she clearly lived for his attention.

Marisa Lauro appeared at my elbow. "You are enjoy yourself?" she asked.

"It's fine," I said.

She eyed me carefully. "Vera, she likes you."

"I hope so." I could see she was a little drunk, and this seemed unappealing.

"But Rupert," she said, "he isn't so sure."

This surprised and unsettled me. Had Grant already formed a negative opinion of me? Had he actually communicated his dislike to Marisa?

The scenario was unlikely, and I suspected Marisa of playing some game with me.

"Don't let me worry you," she said. "I wasn't meaning that. You are very sweet to me."

I was eager to shift the subject. "What brought you to Capri?"

"As Rupert has told, I am a journalist," she said.

"Whom do you write for?"

"Nobody. This is my future, this career."

"I see."

Her blouse was too short, exposing a patch of bare belly. My eyes gravitated there, but Marisa seemed not to mind. That was, after all, the purpose of the blouse.

"We should be friends," she said, touching my arm.

I was relieved when a young Italian man with a gold chain around his neck called to Marisa.

"You must excuse," she said, rushing off.

In the distance, I noticed Holly walking in the direction of the Faraglioni. Emboldened by the wine, I followed, catching up with her around a bend. She sat on a rock looking out to sea, as in a painting. The vermilion light streaked from the sky into the water.

"What a sunset," I said.

She gulped, putting a hand over her throat. "You mustn't!"

"Mustn't?"

"You startled me."

"I'm sorry. May I join you?"

"It's a free country."

This wasn't exactly the welcome I hoped for, but I crouched beside her. "Do you like the party?"

"Quite a collection," she said. "The island attracts them."

"It attracted us."

"How terribly flattering."

"Will you stay here long?" I asked.

"On this rock?"

"On Capri."

"I have no plans," she said.

Every response she made closed a door, and I had to search for another entry. "You do research for him?" I asked, regretting the question before it had left my mouth.

Her look darkened. "You think I do nothing but fuck him, is that right?"

"I didn't mean—"

"You did," she interrupted. "To be frank, Rupert asks very little of me, professionally. I believe he likes my company."

I scampered onto safer ground. "So you were raised in England?"

"You make me sound like a heifer," she said. "But the answer is yes. My parents met at Oxford. He's a psychologist, at All Souls—that's a research college in Oxford." (As I learned from Vera, Sir Richard Hampton was the author of several important books on public policy and mental health.) "What about your parents?" she asked.

"My father runs a construction business. It was started by my grandfather, Alessandro."

"A patriarchy," she said.

"You should meet my mother before you make too many assumptions."

She seemed, for the first time, interested in something I had said, and asked about my poetry.

"I'm serious about it," I said carefully, "I want to write more poems, and better poems. For my own sake, really. I don't care if I ever publish them. I mean that."

"That sounds reasonable," she said.

"What about *your* novel?" I asked.

"I don't usually talk about it."

"Talk anyway."

She sighed. "You don't give up, do you?"

"It wouldn't be in character," I said.

This provoked the tiniest smile. "It's set on Capri," she said, "before the war. The Great War. That's one reason I came here."

"So you're doing research for yourself?"

She concurred, but her response was curt. She regarded me as a hopeless case, I could tell. "I had better get back," she said, shifting from the rock. "Rupert will miss me."

I walked beside her, letting the crash of the surf fill in for conversation.

Getting to know Holly was going to be difficult, but I felt a primitive urge to overcome that obstacle. I would not be brushed aside.

We rounded the point to see a bonfire, its flames billowing skyward. A number of shadowy figures danced around it, one of them banging a tambourine. Another stood at the side, playing a small accordion. The steep hillside above the beach had fallen into shadow, as had Mount Solaro—a brooding, almost invisible presence—more felt than seen. I found the scene strangely thrilling: the bonfire, the beach, the dancing. I had dropped mysteriously into a world so unlike anything in my previous experience that my nerves bristled with pleasure, electric.

Rupert Grant had joined the circle of dancers. I watched with interest as he raised his arms in the air like some parodic version of Zorba the Greek as Vera, seeming lonely, stood to one side, a drink in hand.

"What's your impression of Rupert?" Holly asked, with surprising bluntness.

"I hardly know him," I said. "But I've been reading him pretty intensely for the past month."

"Reading what?"

"The novels, some of the poetry." I felt defensive, as something in her tone suggested that she didn't believe me.

Holly persevered. "So what do you think?"

"He's good," I said, unambiguously.

"How good?"

"Compared to what?"

Sensing my discomfort, she pressed no further. "He's a remarkable man," she said, more to herself than to me. "One mustn't be too critical."

"I believe that," I said.

Impressionable at that age, when everything looked new and strange and freshly lit, I was ready to be convinced about any aspect of life, especially by Holly Hampton. Although many things suggested that life at the Villa Clio would not be easy, I intended to make my way in this particular world. As my brother put it: "You do what you got to do, Asshole. And you do it well."

# PART TWO

*gradus ad parnassum*

*one*
_____

Grant left the island for Rome in mid-May, taking Holly with him. He had some business there, and they would spend a few days at the Rafaele, a small, ivy-covered hotel hidden in a square behind the Piazza Navona. Marisa was left to lounge beside the pool, where she spent her time with a glass of wine in her hand, leafing through an Italian fashion magazine. She was supposedly writing a piece for a Roman newspaper on Capri—her first real assignment—but I had yet to see her doing much research. "I am thinking about it," she said to me, when I inquired about its progress over lunch. "When the article emerges, I will write it down."

I had seen her in tears more than once, and asked if anything was wrong. "My life is wrong," she said, rather melodramatically. I decided there was little I could do that would comfort her, so stayed away, unlike Vera, who grew especially attentive to Marisa with Holly gone. "I worry about the poor thing," she said. "Rupert doesn't take her seriously. I don't think he even likes her."

It occurred to me that Grant really didn't like women at all, but I didn't dare say this to Vera.

Grant had left me without a specific assignment. "Just get on with it, Lorenzo," he told me. *Get on with what?* I wanted to say, but didn't dare.

Vera told me that Grant had made few genuine friendships with other writers in Italy. He did admire Alberto Moravia—the uncrowned king of

Italian letters—and they would periodically exchange letters or phone calls. And when in Rome, he invariably called on Gore Vidal and his companion, Howard Austen, who lived grandly in a penthouse overlooking the Largo Argentina with their dog, Rat. "Gore is the only celebrity I can tolerate," Grant told me. "He has no morals. Morals are for those who can't think for themselves." Muriel Spark, an "English Tuscan," as Vera put it, turned up periodically for a day or two on Capri, although she considered southern Italy a foreign country and, according to Vera, "whined incessantly about the heat." Auden, once a close friend of her husband, rarely came to the island these days. "There is always a rivalry with Wystan, and Rupert dislikes competition," Vera said. Even Graham Greene, a legendary figure on Capri (though he rarely occupied Il Rosaio, his villa in Anacapri), had remained a passing acquaintance. "He went to a minor public school," Vera said. "And I find his books rather sour. There's nothing more depressing than an *English* Catholic."

I could not get a fix on Vera's attitude toward "the girls," though she referred in passing to her husband's "goatish little hobby." She had presumably come to an arrangement with him about their sexual life. In any case, she treated Holly and Marisa with respect, even affection—like fellow sufferers of an obscure disease.

Was the Grant arrangement what Patrice called a *mariage blanc*, a union without sexual content, a cover for their mutually independent lives? Or was this just a tony form of modern decadence? I knew about the Bloomsbury crowd, and Vera considered herself an heir of sorts to that sensibility. Her father, a wealthy entrepreneur who had come with his parents from Riga in flight from the Bolsheviks, had known Keynes at Cambridge, and Vera blithely referred to "Uncle Maynard" quite often. Her mother, from a famous county family, had also gone to Cambridge, and (as Vera said on more than one occasion) "once met Virginia Woolf at a party at Garsington," a manor house near Oxford where the Bloomsbury crowd often gathered under the supercilious gaze of Lady Ottoline Morrell.

I gradually pieced together Vera's personal history. After studying art history in England, she had spent a period in Florence at an expensive art school, where "the daughters of English gentlefolk apprenticed them-

selves to attractive older men in the pursuit of wisdom." It was in Florence, at the Villa Barbaresca, the neo-Palladian home of an English
baroness, that she met Grant, then in his early forties. He was recently
divorced, famous, and extremely eligible. The fact that he had barely
enough money to support the children of his previous marriage didn't
trouble her, as her parents had plenty and would be glad to supply her
and a suitable husband with all the necessities, even a villa on Capri if
that was their preference.

I hadn't, at first, been aware of Grant's social isolation, which was
largely self-imposed. Because my arrival in April coincided with his birthday, my first impression was misleading. I was, in fact, dazzled by the
company he and Vera managed to assemble on the beach that night. In a
fell swoop, my address book filled with local phone numbers and
addresses, and I had invitations to call at half a dozen villas. ("Who would
have guessed you would be popular?" Vera remarked, calling on me in
my cottage the next morning, bringing hot tea in a Thermos.) But I did
not immediately attempt to widen my circle.

I sensed that Grant wished for the Villa Clio to remain aloof, a place
where private fantasies were indulged, and where Art—his writing, Vera's
cooking and gardening—occurred unobstructed by anything but their
own demons. The dinner parties, plentiful in my first month on the
island, disguised a lack of genuine desire to mingle; Rupert and Vera
invited people to watch them, not to interact; the conviviality was, in
part, a facade, a means of structuring and confirming their isolation. By
late May, fewer and fewer guests crossed our threshold.

Holly and Marisa, in their different ways, had bought into Grant's
vision of privacy and self-indulgence, and together with Vera and the servants they formed a solar system of sorts, with Grant himself the super-
nova at the center, supplying the necessary heat and light. Vera was the
nearest planet, but a cold one, her atmosphere—layers of protective ice
and fog—difficult for ordinary human beings to fathom, although she had
sunlit clearings where great warmth and understanding could be found.
Maria Pia was a little moon, circling Vera, as was Mimo, who glowered
from the sidelines, a gardener who was more eyes than hands. Marisa and
Holly were equidistant from the star, although they managed to sustain

enough distance—emotional and physical—from each other to avoid clashing in their orbit around him. I was trying, anxiously, to find my place in this system.

Often I lingered in the cottage by myself, scribbling in my journal, writing home, rereading my brother's letters from Vietnam. He would have been a marvelous reporter, with his eye for the luminous detail. He often placed himself in situations of danger, and enjoyed talking about them with casual detachment. I caught glimpses of a brothel in Saigon, an opium den in a village, a night patrol in a remote province, where the threat of ambush made every step, every cracked branch underfoot or wild animal in the brush, a cause for panic. "There are eyes in the jungle," Nicky wrote, "eyes everywhere, and they're fucking malevolent. There are no kind eyes in Vietnam. It's all death here. Even the sex drips death like water in a dark cave."

I told no one about Nicky, fearing their pity. That would have been unbearable. It came as some relief that they remained oblivious to the outside world, where wars raged, people starved, dictators dictated, and vast sums of money passed among a few controlling hands. The Grants read few newspapers and never watched television. The Villa Clio, indeed, had no television set. "You can acquire only one station," Vera explained. "Nothing but bloody local stuff anyway. Telecapri is hardly a station at all. More like a peasant family feud."

Politics rarely arose in conversation, though the Grants were essentially Tories. They despised Harold Wilson and the Labour government, who in their opinion appealed to "the lowest common denominator" in British society. The TUC, the national trades union organization, was ridiculed as "a gang of hooligans" by Vera. Oddly enough, I found myself nodding in agreement when Grant and Vera bemoaned the "bogus socialist notion of equality." (Vera's Jewish grandfather had been dislodged from a position of prominence in Latvia by the Bolsheviks, although she was born in London and completely absorbed into the British upper-middle class.) At that time, I shared Grant's unequivocal belief in the superiority of the artist, in the privilege conferred by pure acts of imagination; I, too, disliked the "world of mass production" that was Grant's favorite bugaboo. His blithe assumptions about class unsettled me, though I dis-

missed my reservations as American gaucherie. At least he and Vera
never referred to the Vietnam War, which was probably of less interest to
them than the Boer War.

Complicating my situation at the Villa Clio were my feelings for Holly.
After our initial, botched, encounter on the beach, she remained wary of
me, or so I thought. She barely acknowledged any gestures of friendship
I put forward, as when I asked her to stop by the cottage one afternoon
for tea. English girls could hardly object to invitations to tea, could they?
"Yes, that would be nice," she had replied, "but not today. Another time,
perhaps." She seemed to suggest—or so I imagined—that no day would
be the right day.

Holly and Marisa, each driven by their own ambitions, got along surprisingly well under the circumstances. They often joined forces at the
dinner table, with Vera, to tease Grant (who seemed to luxuriate in this
teasing, which was a form of flattery). They shared a suite at the villa:
two small bedrooms in a separate wing, at the opposite end of where
Grant and Vera slept in a big yellow room with a view across the Marina
Piccola to the Punta di Mulo, with its ragged angostine cliffs. I wondered how sharing such close quarters was possible, given their rival-
rous connections to Grant. He seemed arbitrarily to pick one or the
other to serve as his "research assistant" for the day, and this involved
not only long sessions in his study but morning swims, walks, and
"naps." This was a form of what the behavioral psychologists called
intermittent reinforcement: the most vicious and powerful type of
reward, and one that turned laboratory mice into little neurotic fuzz
balls willing to perform any species-demeaning task for a drop of sugar
water.

In the early morning, I occasionally met Holly by the pool, where she
sat with the manuscript of her Capri novel on her lap—it had recently
topped a hundred pages, she said. When I asked to read some of it, she
refused. "Only when it's finished," she said. "I don't present work-in-
progress." The book was overly influenced, she claimed, by Evelyn
Waugh, whose work I'd never read. "You must, absolutely must, read
him," she insisted. I was lent a copy of A Handful of Dust, and found it
delicious as well as shocking. It also explained to me a good deal about

the world of upper class British society, which until my arrival at the Villa Clio had been largely unknown to me.

"You fancy Holly, don't you?" Vera asked, while her husband and Holly were still in Rome. We sat alone in the dining room, lingering over coffee one day after lunch.

"I suppose," I said.

"Rupert won't like that."

I feigned confusion, and this annoyed Vera.

"Rupert tells me that she's good at fellatio," she said. "You're familiar with the term, I presume."

Vera was disconcerting, without emotional boundaries, and willing to say anything that came into her head.

"I don't mind his girls," she said. "I wish you could believe that." Her intimate tone, the sense of trusting me with her private life, won me over. "You needn't worry about Rupert and Holly," she said. "She's nothing special, not to him. One of many in a long string of amusements. Seize the day, darling. Isn't that what you poets advise?"

"She isn't interested in me," I explained. "You see how she treats me."

"Like a poor, dumb booby," she said.

A poor, dumb booby.

"Poor baby!" Vera continued, "I've hurt your feelings."

"A little," I said.

"Have you made your sentiments clear to Holly?"

"Not really," I said. "I should just give up."

Vera sighed and put down her cup. "Are you queer, Alex?"

"What?"

"Queer. Patrice is queer, isn't he? I don't mind—the island is crawling with buggers."

I did not respond, flummoxed.

She studied me carefully. "About you, I'm uncertain. But it's bloody obvious that Patrice is queer."

"Not to me."

"You are not as alert as you might be."

That was understating the case. I began to wonder if I could possibly navigate the world of Capri, where every goal was obscured by the mes-

merizing light, refracted in a zillion ways. Motives were hidden or difficult to parse. *Lo pazzo d'isola*, as the locals called it, permeated everything, but it was worse at the Villa Clio. The island madness heaped
here, spoonful after spoonful like whipped cream, with nuts sprinkled
on top.

"Seize the day, Alex," Vera said, with false urgency. "Isn't that what
poets do?"

"With Holly?"

"Why not?" she asked. "It would not, of course, delight Rupert. But
who cares?"

ooooo

The month of my arrival remained the peak of contact between myself
and Rupert Grant, a period when he seemed determined to win me over.
I had tried to impress him, too, roughing out the Tiberius chapter for him
in four days by poring over a Latin dictionary well past midnight. Reading over my translation carefully, I decided it was not as rough as I'd first
imagined. The prose was clear, even fluent, with graceful flour-
ishes. I put the manuscript on his desk one afternoon with a barely
feigned modesty.

"Come, sit beside me," he said, lifting my typescript. There was a
scold in his voice, a slight edge of disapproval. "Let's see what you've
accomplished."

Warily, I pulled up a chair; he had a schoolmaster's way of lowering his
bushy eyebrows that made me highly self-conscious.

He donned his wire-rimmed glasses, his white hair like a waterfall in
reverse. His manner bordered on interrogation, yet his presence thrilled
me: he was an emotional and intellectual generator, and I wanted to
clamp my cables onto him, to let his power flow into me. For at least
twenty minutes he read to himself, occasionally mouthing a few words
sotto voce, leaving me to gaze around the room.

I found it impossible to sit near a bookcase without studying the titles,
alternately awed and depressed by the number of books I hadn't read. In
particular, I was drawn to Gibbon's *Decline and Fall of the Roman Empire*,

in twelve volumes, the maroon spines with gold lettering. Although I had studied Roman history at Columbia, I was hazy on the details, and made a vow to plow through Gibbon as soon as possible. The thought that Grant might quiz me about the emperors made me queasy. Before attempting this translation, I should have looked up what Gibbon had to say about Tiberius; it seemed unlikely that an emperor so esteemed by many had become a titan of self-indulgence—especially in the final years on Capri, when (to quote Suetonius) "having gained the license of privacy, he gave free rein at once to all the vices which he had for a long time barely concealed."

"Pay attention, Lorenzo," Grant said.

I leaned toward him, chastened, watching as he began to "correct" my work. Everywhere the fuzzy adjectives dissolved, absorbed into stronger nouns. "Adjectives are the writer's enemy," Grant said. "If you had got the right noun, you wouldn't need these bloody qualifiers." The same held with verbs, he said. I witnessed the blotting out of countless adverbs; often he transformed the verbs as well; thus "ran swiftly" became "sped." "You must find the right word," he said. "It needn't be fussy, just full-blooded. Let it carry all the freight it can." He quoted some lines from Eliot: " 'The common word exact without vulgarity, / The formal word precise but not pedantic.' That's the thing, what?"

With a thick horizontal line from his fountain pen he crossed out countless versions of the verb "to be." "What's all this *was, was, was?* Bad habit, Lorenzo." He urged me to use the active voice whenever possible. Thus, "Tiberius was somewhat held in check by the presence of Germanicus" became "The presence of Germanicus held Tiberius in check." "That 'somewhat' is foul," Grant scoffed. "You're equivocating. Resist the impulse." I watched as prose I had considered quite sophisticated and polished became tougher, grainier, more direct. He glanced at the manuscript, with his multiple erasures and corrections, and seemed to understand what I was feeling. "Look here," he said, "I'm not trying to change you, only to correct bad habits. There's a tune there, in your writing. I hear it, and that's a good sign. Every writer needs a tune."

I knew this, and was afraid of losing a tune that, however small, I had cultivated with some diligence.

"Revision won't kill the tune," he told me. "It actually brings out the tune. That's the point of it."

I said, "I'd like to show you one of my poems."

"By all means," he said. "But I won't spare your feelings. I've never known how to be tactful with young people about their work. It's why I gave up teaching. Spent a bloody awful year as Professor Grant, in Malaysia, just after the war. That was enough for me, thank you. Threw in the towel when a young lady threatened suicide because I challenged her scansion."

Many of Grant's more colorful anecdotes were invented, but they held one's attention. I assured him I wouldn't try to kill myself, no matter how ferocious his critique, but his warning frightened me; it would be some time before I dared to lay a poem on his desk. Nonetheless, I left his study that morning encouraged by the unexpected tutorial in composition—better than anything I'd encountered at Columbia. He was right about my prose. I vowed to bring him more to read in a few days, and I promised that the work would be tighter and stronger.

"Good lad," he said, dismissing me. Already his mind had turned to his own manuscript, the book on Capri, now gathering pages on his desk.

*two*

———

At the beginning of his second month in Vietnam, Nicky was shipped out of Saigon. "I don't want some patsy-ass assignment," he wrote. He wanted to get "out there, where it's happening, whatever it is. Like Saturday night back in Pittston. If you weren't out, you were a dickhead, a wussy who got no pussy. Like you, Alex. Always home on the weekends, your nose in a goddamn book, dick in hand."

*Dear Asshole,*

*I went and did it, yesterday. Not a month up here, and—you guessed it—I fucking killed a guy. Some poor bastard, and I didn't even mean to waste him. Was just sitting in a tree, minding my own business on the trail, thinking about nothing but pussy. Only half a mile from camp—playing lookout like we did as kids. We do it here all the time, taking turns on the trail near camp, keeping an eye open for the goddamn enemy. You just sit in a tree, M-16 on your lap. In daylight, you can read a book if you got a book you want to read. Or sit there and think about things. Or don't think about things.*

*You ever notice how, in the middle of some goddamn mess, everything seems so quiet? There is life, crumbling under your feet, and it's all smiles and kissy-kissy. Suddenly, wham. Reality sticks a finger in your eye. It's all over you, and over before you know what hit.*

*So there I was, sitting like a tree frog happy as shit, and this Commie walks out of nowhere. Black pajamas, sandals, Soviet weapons, the works, but all by his lonesome. Like he stumbled out of bed in the middle of the day, going down to take a piss in his pj's. A skinny little guy, walking along in a daze, kind of lost. I figured back in his village he was probably nothing special. A bike mechanic, maybe. The sort of guy who would bag groceries in Skettino's or pump gas at the Chevron. But what do I know? All I really know is I caught him top down. Put a hole in the back of his head that took away the whole fucking front part, ripped it right off, the face mask. Caught him again between the shoulder blades as he fell.*

*Half a dozen guys came running. Our guys, not their guys. We never found anybody else from their team in the vicinity. (He must have been on some private expedition, looking for butterflies. This place has these big white butterflies—like snowflakes in hell.) My team, they were ready to mow, man. I mean, Micky Donato's a big guy, and he came running ahead of everyone, spraying bullets from an M-60, his goddamn machine gun. Eddie was behind him, Eddie Sloane, the Iowa guy, my cornpone half-Injun friend, with his medical kit and a .45 caliber pistol, waving it overhead like the Lone Ranger and Tonto in one uniform. Then comes Jimbo Samuels, Black Jimbo, a skinny black kid from the Bronx, lugging his stoner, one of the those big motherfucker guns, and Fink O'Malley and Buzz Baxter. They were big-eyed, scared, excited as shit. Fink especially.*

*I don't know how he got to be called Fink, but it's how he introduced himself. O'Malley is from Boston, and he keeps a Red Sox pennant rolled up in his knapsack, for luck. A mixed-up bastard if I ever saw one, a walking medicine chest, with dope and tranquilizers, uppers and downers, inners and outers. He's got creams, too: for jock itch and toe rot, for blisters and boils. American skin wasn't made for jungles. Buzz is, well, another story. A bear of very little brain. Doesn't say peep to nobody, but he likes comic books—Spider-Man, Batman, Superman. One day he's gonna fly away, they say. Surprise everybody and fly away from this fucked-up shithole of a country.*

*Yes, they all agreed, the motherfucker was dead. Fucking eliminated. So we dug a hole and shoved him into it. It was too close to camp to just let the shredded wheat rot on the trail, which is usually what happens here. I mean, you don't go around packaging the goods, burying them. And they don't come with choppers and body bags and flags and shit, like we do. We pick off ten guys, they say, for every one of us they get. Which is good arithmetic, unless you're on the short end of the equation, which I don't intend to be.*

*You can only get so much from scenery, but I got to say, the scenery here is something else, especially in the highlands. I was telling Eddie it's like the*

*Poconos only with palm trees and kamikaze mosquitoes. Vines and bamboos, all that Tarzan shit. I was thinking of Tarzan when that poor bastard in the black pj's walked under my perch and got himself blasted on the old bean.*

*Fink said, Jeezus Christ, you shredded the poor fucker. They couldn't even sell him for body parts—unless all you wanted was the odd toe or finger. It was real weird to look at him, the way his face was pretty much pulped. You hit a guy from above like that, with several good shots, and it takes away most of the cheekbones, the nose, even the upper lip. The skull was like a jack-o'-lantern, only more fucked up. Bigger and blacker holes. Jeezus is right, I said. You nailed that one, Finko.*

*Nam is one nightmare hunting trip. No wonder I keep remembering those trips in the Poconos, with you and me and Dad, with Sam Barzini and Joey the Jock and Little Nino with the fat lip. Just last night I was telling Eddie about when you got your first deer, and how you didn't want to look at it. Dad got moral and macho, and he said that if you're gonna kill something, you gotta take responsibility. Spoken like an hombre. But then you started to cry, and he felt like a piece of shit and gave you my fucking chocolate bar. Mine! The nice part was when we got home nobody said a thing to Mom, and there was this amazing thing we suddenly had in common.*

*One of the few good things I can say for this adventure is that we're doing something together, me and Eddie and Mickey, Jim, Fink, Buzz. A good thing or bad thing, it doesn't matter. It's a team effort, and that brings a good feeling.*

*But that bastard I shot. What do I do about him? Do I take some responsibility here? Weren't no fucking deer, Eddie Sloane said. But you should have seen the guy, so messed up you couldn't take your eyes off him. While we were digging a pit the bastard got covered in ants like a piece of candy in summer on our sidewalk, but worse. I mean swarming. We tossed the fucker in the hole, covered him over, not very deep—just enough to keep the smell away and to satisfy ourselves that we'd done the right thing. Planted him, maybe a couple of feet under. It probably wasn't necessary, Mickey Donato said. You let anything just lay there by itself, uncovered, and it's history in maybe a day or two. The rotting time is fast-forward in the jungle.*

*Last night, I got thinking about being nowhere. Dying ain't so bad, I figured. We're all atoms, huh? Death is just a rearrangement of matter. It's just another way of putting the same old thing. And it probably doesn't hurt, not after the first couple of seconds, if you're lucky.*

*I don't know yet how bad it's going to be down the next few months or how often I'll get time to write. Lots of S & D coming up, which means you walk around in the bush with your dick out, looking for trouble. Really ingenious. You'd think somebody in Washington or Saigon would say, Hey, why don't we get ourselves a strategy? But there's no hope for that. It's not like any thought went into this war.*

*The thing is, I don't feel like a soldier yet, even though I killed this guy. I don't feel anything, which is creepy. I was sorry for the bastard, of course. He's got a past, a family, a neighborhood that knew his habits. There was a picture in his pocket, but I couldn't tell what it was or who. Boy or girl. Lover, friend, mother. I put it back where it came from, figuring I'd done enough to disturb his course through this particular universe.*

*Jeezus, there was something beautiful about that kid, with shiny black hair that fit him like a helmet, and his beardless chin. Not a hair on his goddamn chest—at least where it wasn't blown away. Like maybe I killed a kid, I said. Lieutenant Jack Waller, a prick under most circumstances, with a loose belly and a bald head, he said, Hey, it's war, so what did you expect, a fucking tea party? It's war, all right, I answered, but a kid's a fucking kid. He's got a mother, a history. Waller just shook his head. You must be Catholic, he said.*

*I hate to admit this, but I started crying. Weird, huh? I never cried back home, not once that I can remember. But Eddie took my arm, and he said, Sit. Sit your ass down. Here, have a drink. He had Jack Daniels—one of those miniature bottles you get on airlines that somebody must have slipped him. So I drank it. He said, Don't take it so hard, there's a lot more where this came from. A shitload more.*

*He meant death, of course. Not whiskey.*

*Maybe you've heard enough for one letter, Asshole. Sorry for the ramble. I hope it's okay to spill all this shit. From your letters, I can tell you're curious as a dog around a pile of new shit, so I don't feel guilty rambling on like I do, passing time. Write me again, and soon.*

> *From Nam, with kisses,*
> *Nicky*

## *three*

In heading to Rome, Grant left a vacuum. At meals, it was just me, Vera, and Marisa, though I sometimes asked Patrice to join us. Vera liked his amiable, diffuse nature, his ramshackle ways, and found him a waiter's job at the Quisisana, the fanciest hotel on the island. She had somehow persuaded Andrea Milone, the manager, that it would be sensible to have a French waiter. Americans generally preferred a French waiter to an Italian one, she explained; furthermore, the combination of a French waiter with Italian food was irresistible. Signore Milone found Vera's arguments *"un po pazzo,"* but he needed waiters of any national persuasion; high season—June through August—loomed, and Patrice claimed to have experience in a Parisian bistro.

The day after Grant left, I wandered into his study, hoping to absorb the atmosphere in an unobstructed way by sitting at his desk and imagining what it would be like to *be* Rupert Grant. Behind his amber eyes I imagined a vast consciousness—a landscape of hidden valleys, abrupt mountain ranges, tumbling seas. Reading his work with fierce attention, as I had done since arriving at the Villa Clio, I'd become more, not less, interested in the man behind the witty, eccentrically learned essays, the history-obsessed novels, and the passionate but formally restrained poems, most of which concerned some aspect of love. What I liked was how suggestive he could be: there was infinitely more on the page than met the eye, and I found myself scribbling in the margins, prompted to further thoughts by his thoughts. I became envious of his deftness, the shrewd felicity of his phrasing, the vast range of reference.

On the other hand, he seemed bland much of the time in person, reluctant to play the part of the artist-genius. He cautioned me against "reading too much into things," as he might say. Even Vera warned me that he was "not as interesting in person as on paper," suggesting that "only frauds are." She said that Grant's success as a writer had been the result of extremely hard work. "He is working all the time," she said, "even when he's playing. That's the only way it's possible."

I didn't begrudge Grant his success as a writer, but I'd become jealous of his relationship with Holly. Was she, like me, overly impressed by his achievements? This alone didn't justify her erotic attachment to him, which I sensed but couldn't understand. Physical attraction, on her part, seemed impossible, as he was forty years her senior. It was all such a howling cliché: the goatish older artist and his nubile consorts. Wasn't Grant embarrassed by this scenario, the ridiculous tableau vivant, with Marisa and Holly sprawled at his feet by the pool? Wasn't Vera, with her charm and undiminished beauty, able to satisfy his needs? The greater question, for me, was why Holly would participate in this spectacle.

I sat in Grant's oak chair, sinking into his space. The globe on the left was well spun, a symbol of the author's scope; he had written about the ancient and medieval worlds with ease. Even the complications of the modern world had never daunted him. He appeared to have read, and remembered, everything—although he always said he knew far less than anyone would believe: "It's all smoke and mirrors," he said. "We're all half charlatan, even the best of us—as Auden once said." He often dangled the name of Auden before my ears, knowing how much I admired his work. (A volume of Auden's *Selected Poems* was on my bedtable, on "permanent loan" from Grant's study.)

The photographs on the desk surprised me by their studied conventionality: Vera in a sleek riding outfit, on horseback, smiling. The children, Nigel and Nicola, at the Marina Piccola, ankle-deep in water, both tall and blond, androgynous. In a small snapshot that had turned sepia with age, a much younger Grant sat in an English pub beside Auden, whose smooth face made him almost unrecognizable. In a larger one, on a rooftop in Rome, Grant and Gore Vidal stood beside an older, smaller man in rumpled clothes. Tennessee Williams? Christopher Isherwood?

The dagger beside the inkpot caught my attention. I had seen him fiddling with it, running a finger along the sharp blade. Once I had seen him hurl it, for no reason, across the room at the wooden board pinned to the wall beside the map. It had stuck tip-first in the wood. "A little trick I learned in school," Grant said. "In another life, I'd have been an assassin. Writers are all murderers in disguise, what?"

Murderers in disguise? I didn't understand. My idea of a writer was far different from this. To me, a writer was a healer, a builder, a creator. Not a destroyer. When I suggested as much to Grant, he shook his head sadly and clucked his tongue. "If you're really a writer, Lorenzo," he said, "you'll slay your next of kin first, and proceed from there. It's a bloody business. A bloody goddamn business."

I leaned over a gray folder marked "Poems, Unfinished." Opening it, I saw on top, in Grant's meticulous script, a brief poem or fragment:

> *Green eyes I love, and yellow hair,*
> *a hip that tilts into the sun:*
> *I should be driven to despair*
> *if she thought I was not the one.*

Not so good, I decided. Sentimental, plain without the kind of simplicity that is hard-won. The last line was ludicrous: "if she thought I was not the one." On the other hand, it was unfinished, a scrap of verse that might develop into something of interest. What upset me was the subject: Holly. It could not be a poem about anyone else: the green eyes, the yellow hair, the hip. The way her hips would shift to one side when she stood: that was part of her lovely awkwardness. I felt consumed by jealousy now. It is always dreadful when someone else desires exactly what you desire, sees exactly what you covet, appreciates its genuine but—as you dared to hope—unrevealed value. I wanted to be the only one in the world who "got" it, who understood why Holly was so appealing.

A further rush of unpleasant feelings overwhelmed me, a mixture of envy and resentment tinged with despair. I wanted Holly, not only physically, although certainly that. I thought of her in Rome with Grant at the moment, in a wide bed in some plush hotel room, unclothed; the image was painful, a brain blister in need of pricking. I wanted to lie beside her in that bed myself, to feel the length of her body, its contours and textures. I wanted to touch her hair, to brush her face with my fingers, to pull her as close as skin itself, breathing her breath, losing myself inside her. And I wanted her to know me. To see me. I wanted a deep intimacy that included friendship and erotic love, and I wanted to know her mind, to linger in the curls and twists of her consciousness, to see things through her eyes.

Though I didn't really know her yet, Holly represented something I had never had before, a kind of wisdom that—so far—I could only know by intuition. Her ironic sense of the world appealed to me, in part because it was without the tinge of contempt I often heard in Vera. My friends and relatives back home were definitely *not* ironic. They devoted themselves to surfaces. To accede to them, one had to spread an immense veil of ignorance over every object of perception, every scene and sentence. I did not want to live my life without irony, in that thinness of expression where only one dimension is acknowledged.

Suddenly I felt hands on my shoulders—caressing hands. Turning, I saw that it was Vera, and the intimacy of her gesture surprised more than alarmed me.

"You're snooping, aren't you?" she asked, whispering, close to my ear. "Naughty chap!"

"Just sitting here."

She kept massaging, squeezing the cords at either side of my neck, softening them. "You're tense, darling," she said. "You do need a good massage, don't you?"

I did, but this seemed like the wrong place and the wrong person. My muscles involuntarily stiffened, and I leaned forward away from her. This was, after all, the wife of my employer—a woman more than two decades older than me.

Her lips brushed my ear. "I won't bite," she said. "Relax."

I could not relax, but decided not to resist, letting Vera massage my neck and shoulders, digging and kneading with both hands. When finished, she leaned her cheek against my head, breathing into my hair. "I'll give you a better massage one day," she said, "if you like."

"I guess," I said.

"Tell me the truth," she said. "Are you a virgin?"

"No," I said. At least four women stood between me and my virginity, although I had yet to encounter either love or amorous continuity. I'd had four one-night stands, and during all but one I'd been seriously drunk or stoned. The names of my first three sexual partners were beyond retrieval, and the fourth I recalled only with pain—the whole thing had been her idea, not mine; the act itself had seemed less like lovemaking than hydraulics, and it left me with a wasted feeling. In general, the sexual revolution of the sixties, which had opened the door to ecstasy for so many of my friends in college, had remained only slightly ajar for me. Although my fantasy life was rich, I was poor in actual experience.

"You're lying, naughty boy," Vera said. "I can always tell when someone is lying, especially about sex. You're a virgin. It's printed on your forehead. In italics."

"I've had four lovers," I told her.

"Four! I take it back, then. You're a man of the world."

Her patronizing tone annoyed me, and I was about to complain when she planted a wet kiss on the back of my neck. I rose from the chair at once.

"I'm sorry if I interrupted you in the midst of profound thoughts. Have a seat, if you like. Read the great man's idiotic jottings. But I'm waiting for you in the kitchen when you're finished. Today you will learn how to make polenta. Now *that* is important."

She left me standing there, disappearing through the door in her white diaphanous shift, more like a young girl than a mature woman: unpredictable, willful. I realized that, in spite of myself, I was attracted to her, and found the idea of a full body massage by those fingers an appealing one. But I knew enough to resist, aware that life at the Villa Clio would become only more and more complicated, my heart rooting in soil where nothing good could issue from that attachment.

*four*

"She wanted to rub your back, and this cracks up your nerves?" Patrice asked when I told him about what had happened in the study with Vera. "I am not understanding."

"It was weird," I said. "She's old enough to be my mother."

This was technically true, although a universe stood between Vera Grant and my actual mother, who made the Oedipus complex a ludicrous formulation.

"It is wonderful, when they rub your back," Patrice said. "I am in heaven with this, but it's too seldom."

"Is nobody rubbing your back these days?"

"I don't tell you my private acts. I tell you very little, Alexi."

He had taken to calling me Alexi for reasons known only to himself. Everyone took liberties with my name, assuming I would accept, even delight in, any form of recognition, however skewed. But I said nothing about it. It was always easier to hold my tongue.

Patrice had taken a day off for us to visit the Blue Grotto together. It was one of the few major landmarks of Capri that had escaped our scrutiny. In previous weeks, we had picked over stones at most of the twelve ruined villas of Tiberius and picnicked in the mossy purple coolness of the Matromania Cave, where "bizarre and unnatural rituals have been performed over many centuries," as Grant explained with relish.

The village of Anacapri had become familiar, with its whitewashed maze of shops and houses, its intersecting footpaths lined with rosy bricks and overhung with vines. We'd hiked to the peak of Mount Solaro, with its vertical prospect of the Marina Piccola and the Tragara (the Villa Clio like a brilliant white dot in the distance). The cone of Ischia in the middle distance had grown as accustomed as the Faraglioni, which gave the illusion of following us wherever we went, visible from various points on the island. Patrice was fond of giving lectures, and I knew he'd have prepared a mini-lecture about the Blue Grotto, confecting a hodgepodge of facts and myths lifted from guidebooks and odd conversations.

"Giovanni will take us in the boat to this grotto," Patrice explained. "I know you will like Giovanni because he is wonderful man, with eloquence of his limbs. He is thinking of so much, but you wouldn't guess it. His *fàccia*, she is impassivity itself." How could I argue with that, or understand it? As usual, Patrice put himself in charge of my education, working to ensure that my opinions didn't vary from his.

Giovanni proved easy to like, though I could not visualize the "eloquence of his limbs." He had inherited from his grandfather an old-fashioned motor launch that he used to circumnavigate the island several times a day with tourists in the high season. "He speaks English but not so well," said Patrice, the pot calling the kettle. In keeping with many Capresi in the tourist trade, Giovanni had a firm command of a minuscule vocabulary. Like so many on the island, he could provide a monologue about the primary tourist sites, complete with names and dates, but if you asked him a direct question, his expression froze. "I am not so much English," he would say.

Patrice had settled well into life on Capri. He was now established in what amounted to a garden shed annexed to the parish house of a colorful priest, Father Aurelio. The church itself, Santa Caterina, stood nearby: a pink-washed chapel that could seat perhaps thirty worshippers at a time. It nestled in a grove of tall cedars just off the Tragara, unobtrusive except when a bell clanged in its campanile to mark the hour.

I had seen Father Aurelio before, his white cassock flowing as he crossed the piazzetta. He seemed perpetually hurried, as if racing to administer the last rites to some expiring parishioner. I had been told, by

Patrice, that Aurelio was a published poet, and that his work was "in the tradition of Rilke," who had lived on Capri in 1906 in a small house in the garden of the Moorish-style Villa Discopoli, not fifty yards down the path. (Aurelio was, in fact, a translator of Rilke's poetry, although his translations had only been published locally, in Naples.)

"You will meet Father Aurelio later," Patrice said in a hushed tone meant to convey his awe and respect for the literary cleric. "I told him you are poetic, too."

"That's an exaggeration," I said. "I can hardly call myself a poet. I've written very little, and published nothing." An unexceptional poem against the Vietnam War—written just a few months before Nicky was killed—had appeared in my college literary magazine, prompting an invitation from SDS to join its ranks. (This supposedly well-organized league of student radicals had somehow lost track of the fact that I had been a member for the previous fifteen months.) But that surely did not count. I was, at best, an aspiring poet, an ephebe.

"It is your youth that prevents you as a poet," Patrice said, with lofty incoherence. "Achievement will follow."

His blithe confidence in me, based on nothing, was less than reassuring. I had begun to feel fraudulent and unaccomplished, especially beside Rupert Grant, whose pen rarely paused during waking hours. "The secret of writing a novel," he said when I confessed my feelings of intimidation, "is steady attention. You must focus, Lorenzo. Let everything, all the petty distractions, dissolve—pay attention only to what gathers before you—on the page." When I asked him about a remedy for writer's block, he said wryly: "Lower your standards."

Nothing gathered before me except life itself, which I found distracting beyond what Grant could imagine. I was desperate for the kind of physical affection that had eluded me so far. Ardent sex with a woman I loved seemed a far, impossible shore. Worse yet, a channel of icy waters seemed to stand between me and that dream of landfall. Holly now occupied that place in my fantasy life, and I convinced myself that she and I would eventually sail away together. We would live in England, perhaps, and have several children and a thatched cottage. Our books would both achieve a surprising level of popularity for works of remarkable complexity and depth. Whenever possible, I hovered beside her on the grounds of the Villa Clio, but could not connect. Most of the words that passed between us were perfunctory or functional: "Would you pass the salt, please?" or "Has the rain stopped?"

I loved her particular scent. Until now, it had never quite occurred to me that each human being exuded a distinct smell, as idiosyncratic as a fingerprint. In Holly's case, it was a maddeningly erotic smell, and the slightest whiff edged me toward despair. Once, in Grant's study, while she was working at a desk in the corner, I bent over her shoulder and pretended to read what she had written. But I could not read the words. I could only fill my lungs with the smell of her, imagining what it might be like to bathe in, linger over, suck in, devour, and become that fragrance myself.

I tried to explain my situation to Patrice, looking for the relief that comes from sharing these agonies, but he was unsympathetic. "This Holly, she belong to Rupert Grant," he said, "and you, too, belong to him. Change your mind, or trouble will arrive, and you will not be happy." As usual, Patrice appeared to speak with the wisdom of the ages, as though he'd seen it all before. "I am feeling your anger to Grant," he said. "You have competition there. Only this is dangerous. Believe me."

"I don't think so," I said.

"But I am so sure," he said.

Giovanni waited at the Marina Grande, lounging on the aft deck of his boat in a canvas chair. He was a wiry young man, walnut-skinned, with hair that fit like a black skullcap. His eyes were cobalt blue: an oddity, given the skin and hair. His gaze moved rapidly from me to Patrice, with facial tics that suggested an underlying anxiety. We spoke Italian with him, though Patrice and I were confined to a simple vocabulary and a tight, rubbery coat of syntax that shed complexity like rain. As we *put-putted* in the motor launch toward the famous grotto, we listened to his canned speech—a recitation that, during the high season, he repeated dozens of times each day.

As Giovanni explained, the cave had been known to the Romans, who lined its ledges with statues. Local fishermen were aware of its existence for centuries, but its reputation traveled beyond Capri when two young

Germans, both of them painters, swam into the cave in the summer of 1826. Amazed by their discovery, they returned the next day with a cauldron of pitch, which they lit to view the interior. The flames spun light off the sandy white bottom, and the silvery-blue water became a strange and living thing that swung from side to side. The walls shimmered, blue-vermilion. The presence of an altar and marble figures against the far back wall of the cave added to the sense of radical enchantment, and the myth of the Blue Grotto was born—at least in Giovanni's account.

"Tacitus," he intoned, switching to English in a voice suitable for a loudspeaker, "was the largest Roman historian. He inform us that Tiberio would take the small boys and girls to the Blue Grotto, where he engage in sexual practices. Afterward, he would strangle them." Giovanni gestured dramatically, as if wringing the neck of a chicken.

Patrice gasped. "I have not heard of this," he said, "the strangulation. Such bad news!"

From the research I'd been doing for Grant, I knew that what Tacitus wrote about Tiberius had long been in question. He'd been scorned, by Napoleon no less, as "a detractor of humanity." While twenty or so lines about the emperor's late orgies enlivened the *Annals*, they were also typical of what Roman audiences expected to hear about a tyrannical ruler by a writer of this rhetorical school. Tacitus baldly contradicted himself elsewhere in the same narrative, calling Tiberius "a man admirable in character whom his people held in great esteem." When Suetonius later drew on this material for his own inflammatory passages, he introduced them by saying "they are scarcely fit to be told and still less to be believed." Well before the appearance of the *Annals*—written eight decades after the emperor's death—accounts of his life by his contemporaries never mentioned any scandalous behavior. Philo, for example, claimed that Tiberius lived a "clean and pious life on Capri, an example to all." Even Plutarch, that severe advocate of conventional morality, wrote of the old emperor's "dignified solitude during the last years of his life." That could not have included the strangling of small children whom he had just molested.

Suetonius nevertheless adored all disreputable bits about the emperors, though his carelessness undermined his accounts. (Professor Lorimer once reminded my class at Columbia of Quintilian's observation that "a liar must own a wonderful memory.") Suetonius, when he wrote about Caligula, mentioned that the younger man had to "hide from the stern and moral gaze of Tiberius by disguising himself in a wig." Would a young man need to hide from the gaze of a pervert and child molester-cum-strangler? Even Juvenal, a lover of scandal, wrote breathlessly about the "tranquil old age of Tiberius, who lived on Capri surrounded by learned friends and astronomers." So what could one believe? How was it possible to sort through the distortions of history? Wasn't history itself a kind of fiction?

These questions rumbled through my head as I listened to Giovanni's monologue, but I kept silent. He was obviously pleased with himself, and he—and Patrice, too—might have misconstrued any qualifications I offered. ("Do not be interrupting when he make his speeches," Patrice had warned me. "He is too sensitive.")

We rounded a point, anchoring in purple water beneath a large, over-hanging bluff encrusted with seagulls. The water itself was strangely qui-escent, too smooth for its own good. Giovanni gestured toward an entrance in the cliff wall that looked no more than a few feet high. "You swim into that tunnel," he said, in Italian, explaining that he himself did-n't like to swim. "Only if necessary do I swim," he added, lighting a cig-arette. "I hate the water so much, I should have been a fisherman. They *really* hate the water."

Patrice and I slipped into our bathing suits.

"You are good with swimming, no?" Patrice asked me, nervously. He looked pathetic in his suit, so thin and wan, like a hipless adolescent.

I assured him that he had nothing to worry about on my behalf, and we launched ourselves from the port side of the boat, falling backward over the rail. I noticed that Patrice held his nose when he jumped, and that he swam with his head high, like a dog.

Although it was mid-May, the water felt chilly on this side of the island, more so than on the Piccola Marina side, with its southerly expo-sure. I swam steadily toward the tunnel, using an overhand crawl, assum-ing that Patrice followed in my wake. After a surprisingly brief passage through the tunnel, I found myself afloat in a vast tub of light, the water like a large jewel, many-faceted, a cool wet fire. Shadows played off the roof and walls of the cave, and I whooped, thrilling when my cry was quick to bound and rebound, glancing off the grotto's countless angles. Several minutes passed before I realized that Patrice had not appeared in the cave beside me. At first, I felt more puzzled than frightened. It had, after all, been a short swim from the boat to the entrance of the grotto through calm water.

I shouted, "Patrice! Patrice!" The name tripled in size, pinging off the walls. Getting no response, I swam back toward the entrance, my head above water, searching. I recalled some giddiness in his laughter when we talked about swimming into the grotto, and understood that now as fear. I can't say how long I looked for him, but it seemed like a painfully long time. Two minutes? Maybe ten?

I discovered him at the entrance to the tunnel itself. Still vaguely thrashing, he was a foot beneath the surface, but sinking. I plunged, grabbing his hair with my left hand, pulling him up. He tried to fight me off, but it was all gesture, a self-destructive instinct I could not fathom. Having been trained as a lifeguard, I had no problem in getting him to a ledge at the side of the tunnel. Weak as a whippet, he did not resist after that initial flourish.

"I am drowning," he said, water dribbling from his lips, in a reedy voice as we sat on the narrow ledge.

I pounded him between the shoulder blades to facilitate breathing. "You *were* drowning."

Patrice eventually pressed his back to the wall, sucking in slow breaths. "You have saved me, Alexi," he said, hoarsely. "I owe my life to you."

"You scared the shit out of me."

"I am your servant," he said.

The severe disjunction between what he probably meant and what he actually said forced a grin from me. I claimed (falsely) that I had merely assisted him. "Just a hand," I said, "I gave you a hand."

"He is not just giving a hand," Patrice said. "I owe my life to your marvelous swimming."

Unsurprisingly, he had lost all curiosity about the grotto, so we abandoned the site, swimming back to the boat, with Patrice preceding me by a few yards. At one point he rested in the water, putting a hand on my shoulder for support, telling me again that I "was the hero of his life." Back on deck, he explained to Giovanni that our exploration of the Blue Grotto would have to wait until he had regained his confidence in the water. "I am without courage," he said. "The water have defeated me."

We docked in a cove nearby, then climbed a flight of stone stairs to an olive grove, where Giovanni reached into a cloth bag he had carried and produced fruit and cheese with a vaguely cool bottle of white Corvo, a dry Sicilian wine. Patrice was mute, still traumatized by the episode in the grotto; he sat with his back against a rock, devouring a hunk of cheese, with a bank of wildflowers above his head: blue lobelia, clusters of blood-bright amaryllis. He seemed Pre-Raphaelite, a pale and insubstantial figure painted by Rossetti. Both Giovanni and I studied him intensely, savoring the food and wine, saying nothing. It was as though a brush with mortality had whetted our appetites, sharpened our senses to a point of painful acuteness.

*five*
———

Luigi Aurelio, the good father, was all beneficent angel as he heard from Patrice the details of his ordeal by water. "I am nearly drown, except for this man, my poet-friend," Patrice said, nodding toward me.

The priest's almond eyes turned toward me, then swung back to Patrice. "Only our Savior, he can walk on water," he said, in heavily accented English. "You must see, the grotto is marvelous, but not if you are dead. The dead cannot appreciate these splendors. We have a duty, a *duty*, to absorb them before passing on. God was careful to provide every delight."

I was no theologian, but this sounded heretical to me. Nevertheless, I took to Aurelio, who welcomed us in the tiny kitchen of his three-room house. He seemed an incarnation of Rilke, so gentle and wise—a genuine father. I watched him with fascination as he moved around the room, light as cloud scud as he knocked over the sugar bowl or scattered biscuits onto the floor: the bland, ever-present vanilla biscuits that Italians like to eat for breakfast. His talk was frothy and good-humored, dashed with allusions to Dante, Guido Cavalcanti, Giuseppe Parini, and other Italian poets I knew only by reputation. Rilke, in his own translation, was never far from his tongue. "He is the poet's poet, Alexi," he said to me, having picked up this name from Patrice. "Tell me, do you know *Sonnets to Orpheus?*"

I did not, so was treated to long, obscure quotations in Italian. I nodded my approval, hoping he would not question my comprehension. When I told him how much I admired *Letters to a Young Poet*, he drew the volume (in English, acquired during a stay in England, he explained) from the shelf and opened to the fourth letter, written from Worpswede, near Bremen. He read aloud, sonorously: "If you will cling to nature, to the simple things in nature, the tiny things one scarcely sees, and that so unexpectedly multiply beyond measure; if you have this love of insignificant things and seek them out, as one who serves, to win the confidence of what seems inconsiderable—then everything in your life will grow easier, more coherent, and somehow more acceptable." Aurelio then treated us to a sermonette about the love of nature, and how being on Capri one experiences the true glory of the world. "My church is in the woods, on the beach," he said. "I go there for meeting God."

I told Father Aurelio that many American poets were deeply affected by the natural world, and he grew excited.

"You must recite one of your own poems, Alessandro!" he said. "I'm so curious."

"They aren't finished," I said.

"I adore the fragments."

I shook my head. "Not mine, you wouldn't."

Aurelio led us into the garden, where the afternoon light was yellow as it played over a hedge of pale marguerites. The dirt of the garden was pinkish brown, and the air smelled of eucalyptus, a faintly metallic odor, like old pewter.

"Rilke is so correct," the priest said. "Nature is our teacher. If you stand still, and if you listen close to her, you will learn everything you need to know about eternity. She has never failed us, and you will not find her unfaithful." He looked toward one corner of the garden and recited some favorite lines from Montale, another of his touchstones. The lines rolled mellifluously from his tongue:

> *In te m'appare un'ultima corolla*
> *di cenere leggera che non dura*
> *ma sfioccata precipita.*

He translated the passage for me along these lines: "I can see in you a sundown crown of ashes that refuses to linger, that falls apart and crumbles." Aurelio added, with dramatic finality: "We are nothingness."

"That's a big word," I said, hiding a degree of cynicism. I had never found abstractions particularly moving.

"Are you a Catholic, Alexi? You must be Catholic."

"Yes, of course," I said. It didn't seem worth explaining to him that I had lapsed in my faith since going to college, although Nicky's death had brought me face to face with the terrible fact of human finitude, and I had recently begun to reconsider the question of religion. It seemed impossible that human beings had evolved from chaos, or that the imagination—so limitless and thrilling—died when the body crumbled.

"Is your Rupert a Protestant?"

"I don't think so," I said. I simply guessed that Grant was an atheist, recalling that he'd once said, at the dinner table, that people who used the word God in their conversation made him ill. It puzzled me that a poet could not believe in the realm of the spirit, which realized itself in "the world of ten thousand things," as the Buddhists described it. But what about my beliefs? Father Aurelio certainly took my Catholicism more seriously than I did, and I chose not to disabuse him.

"You will say your confessions with me, tomorrow at noon," he said. "And you will attend my mass on Sunday."

Confessions? Mass? Saying no was probably my least favorite activity in the universe. "If you were a woman," my father once joked, "you'd be pregnant all the time."

Patrice, as usual, cut to the quick: "I do not believe in his mumbo-jumbo. I am raised Catholic, too, but what sense is there in this creed? But you, Alex, are different story. I said when I first saw you, he is such an American, and they are full of belief in everything."

ooooo

That night we had dinner with Father Aurelio at the Trattoria da Maria above the via Krupp near the Piccola Marina, devouring large bowls of spaghetti alla vongole, followed by a local white fish, spigola, grilled over a wood fire by Maria herself, a large woman with muscular arms and a toothless smile. Below the stone patio with trellised roses and trailing geraniums, the sea was visible, spangled with the gold light of early evening. We polished off two icy bottles of Tiberio without the slightest hesitation, egged on by Aurelio. Normally a light eater and drinker, Patrice, emboldened by his miraculous lease on life, was voracious. We finished the meal with the complimentary bottle of grappa that the padrone by custom put on every table after serving a big meal.

I followed Patrice back to the converted garden shed he called home, saying good night to Father Aurelio at his door.

"And don't forget your confessions tomorrow—at noon," he said, waving a finger at me, with a wry smile on the large red lips that bloomed, a pulpy flower, in the dark foliage of his beard.

"You can expect me," I said.

The shed itself was not unpleasant or dirty, just cramped. In the dim light of several candles the room seemed cozy and benevolent. And the longer you remained inside its walls, the larger it seemed. "She seem to grow with familiarity," Patrice mused. "I am notice this always."

"I could use a drink," I said.

Patrice agreed, uncorking a warm bottle of Tiberio. "This is special, 1966. I am said a good year for this wine." I'd actually had enough alcohol already, but my appetite was aflame, and I was willing to ignore the wine's temperature. In certain moods, drink calls to drink, and the world becomes expansively liquid. Patrice set the bottle on a rickety table and filled two mugs. After we'd drunk perhaps half the bottle, he lit a bowl of hash. "I have conned this from a boy at the hotel," he explained. "It is Morocco. Very pleasant."

I said nothing as I took the pipe. Hash was unfamiliar to me, an exotic cousin of the usual pot I'd smoked in the States. We sat cross-legged on the floor, and half a dozen scented candles flickered in a semicircle around us. Smelling of cinnamon, the candle fumes blended nicely with the hash, which seemed abrasive, though I didn't complain. The high came quickly, piggybacking on the alcoholic euphoria already in place, and I liked the combined effect.

"You have saved my life, Alexi, and I owe you mine," Patrice said,

seeming to enjoy the grand gesture. He would have made a good character in a medieval romance by Sir Walter Scott, full of high sentence and
portentousness. "Nothing you ask of me is impossible. *Rien.*"

"We must defeat the English when they invade our borders," I said,
imagining myself as Robert the Bruce.

"I will walk to the moon for you."

"You're stoned," I said.

"No, Alexi. My sincerity must not be doubted."

I reassured him of my gratitude for his gratitude. It began to annoy me
that he kept referring to the incident in the Blue Grotto. I would not have
let anyone drown, friend or enemy, if I could help it. (I had not been an
Eagle Scout for nothing.) If anything, saving Patrice this afternoon
seemed insignificant, a feat of mere physicality and pure animal instinct.

There was a time, long ago at Lake Winona in the Poconos, that kept
rushing back to me. A present and palpable vision, not a dream. Nicky and
I had gone fishing in a wooden canoe my father bought for us soon after
we acquired the lakeside cottage. The night had been unseasonably cold
(I think this happened in November, but I can't be sure), and the water
was chilly, with a mist rising off the lake at dawn as we rounded the point
beyond our cottage and settled into a cove to fish. Stupidly, I managed to
flip the canoe by reaching for bait. The tackle box scattered in a hundred
bits and pieces, and the rods sank quickly. And so did I. I was eight, and
had been swimming for several years, but a combination of things—the
unexpected flipping of the canoe, the loss of my rod, the inability to kick
because I wore rubber boots, and the frigid water—unraveled my composure. I must have gone down two or three times before I felt Nicky's hand
in my hair. He dragged me confidently to shore, boots and all.

I never thanked Nicky. If anything, I treated him badly for having
demonstrated his physical superiority, complaining to my mother when I
got a cold that it was Nicky's fault. He had, I said, insisted on fishing,
when it was obviously too cold. We never spoke about this incident, not
until Nicky wrote to me from Vietnam. "Asshole," he said, "you remember when you tipped the fucking canoe and then blamed me for everything, even though I saved your lousy can? I lost a brand-new tackle box
and two good rods, and Dad had to fetch the canoe. And then Mom rode

my case for a month, saying I should look out for you. Jesus Christ Almighty."

I suppose it was out of rage and resentment that Nicky became a howling James Dean cliché: the kid who sought and found trouble in the usual places. That he managed to do reasonably well at King's, a respectable local college, had not registered with anyone but my father—who consistently found something to praise in Nicky. My mother simply ignored Nicky's successes, being so awed by my golden performances that anything with fewer karats and less gloss seemed irrelevant. Nicky glowed only after a six-pack of Rolling Rock; he smoked unfiltered Camels, snapped his gum at the most irritating moments, and hung around with monosyllabic guys on motorcycles with girlfriends in matching leather jackets. My mother derided all of this, never losing the chance for a subtle put-down. In retrospect, it amazes me that Nicky didn't explode, though maybe he did.

"It is good, no—the hashish?" Patrice wondered, exhaling. "My mind, she fizzes."

"*Aussi moi, mon ami. J'aime beaucoup hashish. Je suis tres content e plus haute que le ciel,*" I said. My fractured French—spoken with a self-conscious American twang—always amused him, and I enjoyed launching forward onto these weak limbs of language, tumbling into a grammatical abyss, forcing winces from Patrice.

"You don't like it when Vera, she massage you, yes?" Patrice loomed into view, transfigured by the candlelight. I could swear I saw a halo around his head, but it must have been a weird refraction.

"What was that?"

"Vera, when she rub your neck. You told me this story about what she did. It was no fun for you," he said.

I could finally cut through the haze of mangled syntax and hashish.

"Do you like her?" he asked.

"I don't dislike her."

"I think you like her very much, Alexi."

"Okay, I like her fine. But it's not relevant, since she is somebody's wife, and she could be my mother." The edge of anger in my voice took me by surprise.

"I would like to give you the massage myself, but it would displease you, I'm afraid. But I am very good at this, the Swedish massage." Patrice was deeply stoned, his eyes glassy. His face was uncannily like Nicky's— though my brother's face was hard to recall. He did not photograph well, and the picture I kept in my wallet only vaguely resembled him, flattening the features so that he seemed broader and blander of visage. I guessed that Patrice, too, would lose something in photographic reproduction.

Before I could confirm or deny anything, Patrice came around behind me. He began to knead my shoulders, his hands surprisingly strong. I tensed—as I had with Vera. I wasn't comfortable with this form of intimacy, and the fact that Patrice was a man rattled me as well.

"Be soft, my goodness," he said, "you are very stiff for me tonight."

The hashish felt like a safety net spread out below me, an emotional cushion. I relaxed, taking a long draft from the pipe as he worked. The smoke fit my lungs tightly. Holding my breath, I let the chemicals mix with my blood, sensing a pleasantly silken numbness in my outer limbs. My head was predictably light, though I wasn't dizzy. I felt wonderfully clear-eyed. And I soon began to enjoy the mastering hands of Patrice as they worked the fibers of my neck and shoulders, then traveled toward the middle of my back, fingers leaping from vertebra to vertebra like stones in a stream.

"You must lie on the bed so I continue," he said. "I will perform the best massage you have imagine."

With my shirt off, I lay down on my stomach on the bed, my face to the left, toward the wall. Patrice sat beside me, out of view, working with unrepressed fury, folding and unfolding muscles, digging and kneading, finding crevices that I had not realized were part of my anatomy. A knot of nerves would harden, then relax, as if summoned only to be banished. He played with nimble fingers, seeking and finding a kind of sensual music—odd fifths and hauntingly diminished chords, tonic and subtonic combinations that drew emotions from me I had not confronted directly before. When he rubbed my feet, I found myself quietly weeping. Was it thoughts of Nicky that were released? Some lines from his letter came floating into my head: "Dying ain't so bad," he wrote. "We're all atoms, huh? Death is just a rearrangement of matter. It's just another way of putting the same old thing." Under the controlling hands of Patrice, I felt the separation of spirit and matter occur—the strands gently untwined, my soul lifted and laid clear as the flesh was isolated and calmed.

Patrice would have liked to complete, sexually, the experience he'd set in motion that night. I understood that, but held back, refusing to let myself surrender in that way, even when he straddled me to get better leverage as he massaged my shoulders. The weight of him, the pressure of his body lengthening against my own, was overpowering and affecting, but I kept a hand firmly on my internal rudder, intent upon steering this skiff (which could easily get out of control) in ways that would not torment me in the morning.

"Go to sleep, *ami*," he said. "You are tired, I see that. You must dream now."

Trusting him enough to let myself go, I floated away on a dark swell of exhaustion, entering a dream as one enters a warm bath, relaxing into the contours of a phantasmagorical world that seemed only a brief step from where my hash-filtered mind had been in the last couple of hours anyway. Like a child in some magical library, I wandered from volume to volume. I kept meeting Father Aurelio in these books. He kept inviting me to the confessional, and I went. I confessed to all sorts of sins, real and imagined. And I was forgiven. Over and over.

Throughout the night I was vaguely aware of Patrice beside me: the musty smell, the tight skin and unwashed hair, the smoky breath. It was soothing, as when Nicky and I, as children, would sleep in the same bed on special nights, when our parents were out of town or, unforgettably, on the nights before Christmas. When I woke just before dawn, I realized I had an arm around Patrice's waist, but was not upset because we were friends after all. We were very good friends.

*six*

———

Father, I have sinned.

Tell me, son. What have you done?

It's of a sexual nature.

Be explicit, please. Remember, it's God you are talking to, not me.

I've been fucking goats, Father.

Goats are bad. I mean, for fucking. Anything else?

I have not loved my neighbors as myself.

On Capri? You've neglected your neighbors? The place is crawling with neighbors. Not like it used to be. I remember the old days, when—

Father?

Yes, my son?

You're ignoring me. I have sinned.

Tell me, child. What have you done?

I've abused myself.

Masturbation . . .

No, I've been killing people, stealing things, and so forth. My neighbor's wife, I fucked her and her goats as well.

Masturbation is worse.

It is?

Theoretically. That's the one thing I remember from seminary.

You masturbated in seminary?

No, I was taught never to masturbate. It comes between you and God.

God really cares?

Very much so, my child. He cares about all His creations.

I am wicked, Father.

Nonsense. I mean, we're all wicked.

Even you?

I'm a priest. What do you expect?

I want absolution.

That's hard.

I thought the confessional was ideal for that sort of thing.

Only if you believe.

You think I don't?

I know it. That goat thing. And the neighbor's wife. The killing, the thieving.

I was only kidding.

You shouldn't have done that. I believed you.

You're gullible.

I'm a priest.

Now *you're* kidding. Are you kidding?

Forget it.

If I hurt your feelings, Father—

I said, forget it. I'm going to absolve you. Go home, child, and lead a clean life. Say ten Our Fathers.

What about Hail Mary?

Do what I tell you.

Thank you, Father.

Good man. In the name of the Father, the Son, and the Holy Ghost, your sins are forgiven. Go with God.

Amen.

Amen.

*seven*

—————

I kept hitting roadblocks with my own writing—failures of nerve, mostly—and was incapable of finishing anything. One morning, sitting in the piazzetta beneath the candy-striped awning of a favorite café, I wrote a long story about two young men (closely modeled on Patrice and myself); they were both reading Sartre's monumental work *Being and Nothingness* and their conversation was meant to represent two opposing philosophical camps. That afternoon, in Grant's study, I asked him if it were possible to hold a reader's attention for a dozen pages or so with a detailed conversation about Sartre's philosophy. He did not hesitate with his reply: "Only if the two chaps are sitting in a railway car," he said, "and the reader knows there is a bomb under the seat."

I had, of course, no metaphorical bomb under the seat, and I put the story in a drawer. Writing became a dreaded activity most days, but I could always read with pleasure, and it pleased me to read the novels and poems of Rupert Grant while living beside him. He had been generous with his books. "Take whatever you want," he said. "Just put it back when you've done." I burrowed my way through the novels I'd not yet read, and lingered in his *Collected Poems: 1930–1968*. The poems, in particular, gained weight and resonance by having Grant's actual voice in my head, its Scottish whimsicality, with a mandarin pause at certain points in the delivery. My original respect for Grant, as a writer, enlarged, bordering on naked hero worship by the end of June. This expansion coincided with a continuing disillusion with the man himself.

As a poet, he had come of age in the heyday of Georgian verse, with its simple lines, regular meters, and a sentimental view of nature. But even his early work had a tinge of modernity, as in "Ancient Lovers," a lyric from his undergraduate days:

> *Day by dream the summer long*
> *I loved you, ancient lover, when*
> *As young as apples, green and gold,*
> *We huddled by a windy fen.*
>
> *And when the season turned again.*
> *A world of shaken tinsel fell*
> *Like orange rain. We burned the leaves*
> *Yet learned from these our lives were frail.*
>
> *The winter came, and years; through hail*
> *Of time I loved you fervently*
> *And never lingered, looked behind.*
> *We met each season earnestly.*
>
> *And now I love you urgently,*
> *For spring has come with empty hands*
> *To ancient lovers, soon to sleep*
> *Forever under quilting sands.*

One could see the influence of Yeats there, of course—early Yeats, in particular, whose young apples would certainly have been "green and gold." That "windy fen" seemed straight from the *Georgian Anthology*, and the sentimentality of the last stanza had roots in the Victorian age. But "day by dream," that odd sleight of mind, anticipated the work of

Dylan Thomas. The transition from "earnestly" to "urgently," however, was pure Auden.

I asked him about this one afternoon when I found him under a tattered straw hat that, with the large sunglasses, obscured his face to such a degree that I only knew it was him by the angle of his sloping shoulders and the rough, dark hands. He sat beneath his favorite lemon tree, in a folding chair, with a book spread on his lap. I seemed to wake him from a dream, and repeated the question about Auden. Had that early poem been influenced by Auden?

"Auden? Hadn't heard of him when I wrote that poem," he said, "but tell me something, Lorenzo. Did you try to fuck my wife when I was away?"

Flabbergasted, I denied that any such thing had happened.

"Just checking," he said. "I gather she likes you. No harm done, if you had. Free love, and so forth."

"Well, I didn't."

"Don't go moral on me. You're a young chap. Young chaps like to fuck, don't they?"

"When they can."

"That's it. You've had your opportunity. You muffed it."

I was feeling more than a little frustrated now. "We never talk about poetry," I said.

"Literary chitchat, is that what you're after?" He took off his sunglasses, and I saw that I had annoyed him. "You and Holly are alike, you know. Always want a lesson in literary history. Marisa's easier there. She wants nothing that is not absolutely phallic."

"She seems lonely," I said.

"A sulky girl." He used his hand to shade his eyes from the sun. "I don't mind that, as long as she does her work."

I had yet to notice that Marisa did much of anything, despite her ambitions as a journalist. She apparently spent time for Grant at the Cerio library, near the piazzetta, digging up tidbits about Capri for his novel, though I had difficulty visualizing this. Her bedroom, I had noticed on my one visit there, was littered with fashion magazines, and she was often seen carrying one or two. Holly, by contrast, worked hard, but focused exclusively on her own manuscript, which became heavier each week. As far as I knew, she did no research for Grant whatsoever.

"I know you admire Holly," Grant said, "but I should tread softly. She thinks you're silly."

Silly? "I'm afraid I interrupted you," I said, failing to conceal my annoyance.

"I was reading." He held up the book. "Tony Powell, *From a View to a Kill*. Magnificent." I scrutinized the spine. He pronounced Powell to rhyme with Lowell. "I recommend Powell—the early ones, in particular. He's gone a bit soft lately. They call him the English Proust, but that's a compliment to neither England nor Proust."

"I'm sorry I disturbed you," I said, having had my anger somewhat deflected.

"For Chrissake, don't keep saying you are sorry. It makes *you* sorry when you say that."

I could think of no response.

"Lorenzo, dear boy," he said, managing to get some affection into his voice. "Go to your cottage. Type my manuscript, or read, or wank, or write something of your own. I'll pick over it, if that's what you want."

The whole conversation was too confusing, too troubling, and I couldn't digest the large lump Grant had put into my emotional stomach. Tactfully, he ignored my distress, putting on his sunglasses as a way of dismissing me. His head dipped forward, into the book, and his finger moved down the page to locate the exact place where he had left off.

I went back to the cottage, determined to go my own way. I didn't need his literary conversation or counsel. The fact that he'd known so many writers, that he knew so much about the craft of writing, was an accident of personal history. I would make my own history, independent of him, and not be reduced to a mere satellite in his universe, a minor moon revolving around his planet. The Sun King could go fuck himself.

## eight

Late one afternoon, toward the end of May, I came upon Holly and Marisa on the beach. They sat beside each other in low canvas chairs, an empty bottle of wine between them, and their glasses tipped in the sand. Except for meals, I rarely found them together, and was surprised to see them here. (My assumptions about their rivalry—which existed more in my head than in reality—were hard to disrupt.)

"Swimming?" I asked, kneeling beside them.

"My head is," said Holly. She wore a two-piece suit that exposed a slender, pale belly.

Marisa leaned toward me, her dark hair falling forward across her eyes. "The sea is too cold," she said. "I am not so British. They can swim in the ice!"

"Has he been mean to you?" asked Holly.

I looked at her blankly.

"Rupert is a wicked old man," she said. "He says he offended you. You wanted a tutorial, and he refused."

"I wasn't offended," I said, though my voice betrayed my feelings. "And I wasn't looking for a tutorial."

"He should be punish," said Marisa. Her toenails shimmered like cherries.

"He's a bear of very little brain," Holly said. "Pay no attention to him."

I sat on the pebbles beside them, leaning back with my weight on my wrists, staring at the sea—a bronze shield of light, with a sailboat stalled on the horizon. "He doesn't know it, but I'm learning a lot from him," I said.

Marisa raised her eyebrows. "For me, I am learning nothing," she said. "My work is a disaster."

"You're not working hard enough," Holly told her.

"So I am," she said, thrusting her jaw forward. "It's my concentration that is broken."

I was surprised by this adamantine aspect of Marisa, a hardness and self-conscious assertion of herself. Before this, she had struck me as pouty and distracted, a purely sensual creature. Like Grant, I had thought of her, and Holly as well, as physical more than spiritual beings, and my shallowness upset me.

Suddenly Rupert Grant stepped from the water, not twenty yards away, shaking his head to clear his ears. He was already as tanned as most lifeguards in July, although his skin was leathery and dry. The flabbiness in his stomach suggested that he'd once been much heavier.

"The great white god himself," Holly said, as he walked toward us on the pebbles, stepping carefully.

"I see my little class has gathered," he said, wiping his face with a towel. I could see the blue veins in his legs bulging—the skin translucent in places. There was a yellow fungus growing in his toes.

"We're at your feet," said Holly.

"I hope you're taking care of Lorenzo, what? He requires some shep-herding," Grant said.

"I'm happy to do it," said Marisa.

Grant leaned toward me. "Be careful, she bites. I've got the wounds to prove it."

"I'm not as edible as I look," I said.

"Nonsense," said Grant. "You're perfectly delicious. Like a sweet from one of Vera's cookbooks."

"I'm going to swim," I said, racing toward the cool, metallic surf. I needed to cleanse myself, to clarify the muddy waters sloshing about my brain. I still believed the Villa Clio was a good place for me, and that I would improve as a writer in the presence of a master. And I was still fascinated by the world that Grant, like Prospero, summoned from the air around him. Yet the seeds of disquiet had been planted in the past weeks, and I was afraid they would soon mature into towering, unwelcome plants.

# nine

I sat one evening with Peter Duncan-Jones on the terrace of his villa, Casa di Fiori—a damp, narrow house that hid behind an artfully arranged garden. ("It's a tedious little place," Vera had confided to me, "but the terrace is charming. Peter often paints on the terrace.") Peter and I had just finished a cool bottle of Lacrimae Christi ("the tears of Christ"). A fan of light swept over the terrace, with the sun slipping into the sea below, setting the water ablaze.

"You mustn't mind Rupie," said Peter, in response to my account of a conversation with Grant that had particularly upset me. "It's got nothing to do with you. He's a haunted house."

"He had a very bad war," said Jeremy, his companion.

"Nonsense," said Peter. "He had no war at all. He had a commission of sorts, but worked for the information office in London. One of those lucky bloody sods who was too young for the first war and too old for the second."

"I was referring to his first marriage," said Jeremy.

The villa perched just above the Belvedere Cannone, overlooking the via Krupp and the Marina Piccola. It was, as Peter admitted, a "poky little villa," but he had no money to speak of. His paintings rarely sold, "except to tourists from Arkansas or Nebraska," who bought them for decoration, not for art's sake. Jeremy, on the other hand, had made some money in London real estate, so they lived in modest comfort. (Jeremy spent most of his time cooking, showing all the signs of having mastered the art: a bloated stomach and a series of receding chins. Even the fat around his knees jiggled.)

I visited Peter now and then, mostly for consolation. He was unfailingly kind and willing to listen and advise. He could seem facetious and facile—the perfect model of the English dilettante—but that was only a mask he wore in public. I found him more subtle and pleasant than he wanted to appear. He was not his own best advocate.

His relationship to the Villa Clio was complex. Grant genuinely respected him as a person (not as a painter), and Vera genuinely respected him as a painter (not as a person). Between them, they formed a coherent, and humane, response to a man who gained a good deal of self-respect from his association, as he put it, "with the Grant circle."

"Rupert doesn't actually realize how famous he is," I said.

"Oh, darling, he does," Peter replied, taking a long drag from his cigarette, holding the pinkie finger with his family's signet ring apart from the rest of his hand. He often wore a paisley smoking jacket around the house, as if expecting Noel Coward for drinks. "Rupie likes being famous, but he doesn't like people recognizing him or fawning. It's a quandary, you see. Fame without any of the benefits of fame."

Jeremy brought us each a little plate of what looked like green-speckled dumplings.

"Rabaton alessandrini," he said. "Ask Vera about them. It's her recipe."

As I later discovered, they were easy to make: you churned stale bread and Swiss chard through a food mill, added some herbs, eggs, ricotta, and parmesan, then shaped the rabaton into palm-size balls and dropped them into boiling vegetable broth. When they rose to the surface (as with tortellini), they were done, so you rescued them, sprinkled them with grated cheese, glazed them with butter, then served them warm.

"You're an angry young man, Alex," Peter said, seizing the wheel of our conversation rather abruptly and steering into a thicket.

"Me?"

"I'm only saying this because I've taken a liking to you. Otherwise, I'd never be so honest. Usually, it doesn't pay, does it? I mean, who needs it?"

"I never thought of myself as angry."

Jeremy, his mouth obscenely full, leaped in: "I'm to blame, dear," he confessed. "Just the other night I said to Peter, something is wrong with the boy. I think he's depressed. And Peter mentioned that Vera had noticed it, too."

"That's true," said Peter. "Vera has seen you sulking and brooding. Young Hamlet, she calls you."

I wondered to what degree this was true. Did I sulk and brood? In my own sense of things, my mood had dramatically improved since setting foot on Capri. Before leaving the U.S., I had felt lethally unhappy. In any case, it irked me to think that others were speculating on my mental health. As far as I could tell, I was calm, even-tempered, accommodating. I reminded myself less of Hamlet than Polonius, as described in Eliot's *Prufrock*: "Deferential, glad to be of use, / Politic, cautious, and meticulous." The quotation now filled me with self-loathing.

"Is it the girl?" Peter asked. "Girls will do this to red-blooded boys like yourself."

"Holly?"

"Marisa, actually," he answered, surprised. "I gather you fancy Marisa."

"I do, but I prefer Holly."

"Or Patrice?" Jeremy smiled coyly. "Now he's my type—those hard buns."

"Alex is not musical," Peter said. "Are you musical, Alex? I don't think so."

They both looked at me intently.

"It's an old-fashioned term for queer," Peter explained.

"Not really," I said.

"I see, you're not sure." It was not a question from Peter but a statement. "Nobody is ever sure. But at your age, they are especially unsure."

"I'm sure," Jeremy said. "I've never really understood the *point* of women."

The fact was I didn't want to discuss any of this. "Why are you both grilling me?" I asked, putting down my plate of rabaton. "This place is fucking insane."

"Our little casa?" Jeremy asked, with mock horror.

"This island," I said, rising to my feet. "Nobody seems to realize there's a war going on. A fucking war!"

Peter and Jeremy looked at me as if I were mad.

"Vietnam!" I shouted.

After an awkward moment of silence, Peter said, tentatively, "You're a liberal, is that it?" His detached manner, which implied superiority rooted in self-control, infuriated me. It was as though he were discussing a specimen in a museum, holding my heart in sterile pincers to examine its slimy workings.

I would not let go. "Don't either of you read the papers? This is a god-damn brutal and idiotic war. We're killing people every day, including women and children. American men are dying as we speak."

"Dying for what?" Jeremy asked, raising a supercilious eyebrow.

I hurled my glass at the terra-cotta floor.

"Do be calm," Peter said to me, though glaring at Jeremy.

"Maybe I don't want be calm when people are dying."

"It's been going on for a long time," Peter said. "Wars, rumors of wars. It's a by-product of empire. When I was a child, the British did this sort of thing. Now it's your turn."

"This war is no rumor."

"We're not on opposite sides or anything," Peter said. "I consider Richard Nixon a piggie-wiggie."

"We liked LBJ even less," added Jeremy. "That accent. Appalling. He apparently would interview reporters while sitting on the loo."

I could see there was no point in extending this particular conversation. Both Peter and Jeremy meant well, but they had not come crashing up against the Vietnam War as I had. They had not lost a brother, a home, a whole imagined future. They didn't know that everything had changed for me. That I could hardly write to my parents, they were so bitter about my leaving. That I dreamed about Nicky night after night and fought to keep him from dominating my waking thoughts. Nicky my friend and enemy, my adviser, my sounding board, the butt of my jokes, and the only one who would ever actually *get* most of them. We had, between us, formed a kind of whole, as in Plato's parable; it occurred to me now that I might spend a lifetime searching for the other part.

# PART THREE

*amo, amas, amat*

*one*
___

$A$s Nicky's tour of duty lengthened, his letters from Vietnam became more reflective, even philosophical. This was, for me, an unfamiliar aspect of my brother, who had never seemed terribly inward or prone to self-scrutiny. At home, he was too busy defending himself against all comers, on guard most of the time, striking attitudes, ready to parry each blow that came with an equally strong countermeasure. That I had dismissed him as dumb or crude, even to his face, upset me. I should have realized that brothers, as the old Neapolitan saying goes, are versions of each other.

But I had reasons for behaving badly. Nicky could resort, when threatened, to violence as a way of showing me who was in control. From an early age, he knocked me around, often "accidentally" inflicting a bruise. (I still bore a scar above my right eye, just below the hairline, where a rock opened a slice that required several stitches. Nicky, of course, swore he'd aimed well over my head, but similar incidents happened again and again.) By posing a physical threat, he attempted to control me, and it worked fairly well for most of our years together. If he wanted something, he took it, and all I could do was call him names, complain to my parents, or take subversive, retaliatory measures. By my early teens, I'd become practiced in the terrible art of passive aggression.

Apart from occasional attacks, Nicky was not typically mean or selfish;

his generosity was even surprising, given the position he'd been stuffed
into by my mother. I suspect he considered himself unwanted, except by
the unwashed, pimpled, foul-mouthed creeps from Wilkes-Barre and
Nanticoke whom he considered his friends. What held them together
was devotion to six-packs of beer and harsh, unfiltered cigarettes, which
they often wore in the sleeves of their T-shirts. If the rest of us wore
scented aftershaves, Nicky and Company, as I called them, appeared
to bathe in the mechanical fluids that kept their various engines
purring.

"That son of mine, Nicky, he can't do anything right," my mother was
often overheard to say on the telephone. (She spent a good portion of
each day on the phone with her friends from the St. Ann's Circle, a group
of parish women who met once a month for bingo and traveled in a group
to Scranton every summer to make a Novena.)

"Nicky's gonna be fine," my father would counter, flashing a shy
smile that revealed a gold tooth in front—a peculiar deformity that
always embarrassed me in public. (Why did no one else have a father
with a gold tooth? Where, I used to wonder, did one even get a gold
tooth?)

Around our house, it had been Cain and Abel to the hilt. I only began
to view Nicky in a different light when, in his letters from Vietnam, I
heard an unexpected note of clarity and grace, a kind of hip articulate-
ness that must have been buried there all the time, waiting to emerge.
In the moral forcing house of war, my brother matured at breakneck
speed, and could hardly contain himself in writing to me, putting on a
self-performance that surprised and dazzled me. There was still the
edge of superiority that all older brothers have, although in Nicky's case
he felt so inferior to me, intellectually, that it dulled that edge. I found
in those letters a brother I hadn't known, a friend and confidant, and
looked forward to his return from the war, believing we could repair the
damage done before; I felt sure that a long and fruitful brotherhood lay
before us.

One letter, in particular, changed my sense of him definitively. It was
written from a camp near Quang Tri, the area where he spent the last
three months of his life, mostly on recognizance missions, although he

was also involved in Search and Destroy—a tactic peculiarly suited to the madness of Vietnam. "You just walk through the jungle looking for trouble, waiting to be ambushed," as Nicky said. "It's maybe the scariest damn thing that any human being can do. Every snap, crackle, and pop in the jungle drives you nutty. And what is a jungle except snap, crackle, and pop?" The wonder is that anyone came back alive from those excursions.

*Dear Asshole,*

*Here I am, deep in shit, and not even worried. Isn't that a bitch? I mean, if I didn't know there was somebody waiting to blow my head away, I'd say I was on vacation—a tourist, taking in the sights, on some fucking safari.*

*Nam is many things to many people, but it's also a place for philosophy, let me tell you. I spent some pretty intense nights talking with Eddie and the guys, and we got farther than Friar Makowski ever got in that class I took at King's: Philosophy 101.* What is True? *he used to ask us. In Vietnam, you don't ask that question. Nothing is true in Southeast Asia. It's made up, start to finish. The reasons for the war are not true reasons. Maybe there are no true reasons. And the politicians from Nixon on down are lying to the public. That's what politicians do. They lie to the public and to the generals who lie to the lieutenants who lie to the sergeants who lie to us: that's the real Domino Effect.*

*The mission is everything, they tell us. But I'm no missionary, and that's a problem here. I don't see that I've got a mission to kill some poor skinny bastards who think it's cool to run around in black pajamas or live in rat-infested tunnels for months on end. It's their country, isn't it? I mean, they are free to kill each other if they like. But even they don't seem to know what the people of Vietnam really want. I can't even keep the gooks straight in my head: VC, Minh, NVR, Chinks. South or North Vietnam, they say, makes about as much sense as South Rhode Island and North Rhode Island. Truth begins with the line between North and South, somebody in Washington, D.C., said. But who drew that line? Who is making up stories to justify their actions?*

*It's not that I'm against stories. Around here, we tell stories all the time, invent them and pretend they're true. If they make us feel good, they are called* True. *If they scare the shit out of us, we yell* Liar!

*Some true things are pretty obvious. Like the finale of Buzz Baxter, a nice dumb fucker who went to take a piss in the shade of a palm tree and stepped on a booby trap, then bang, and that's it for Buzz—an arm here, a foot there. The ground was so thick with vines and shit, it took us two hours to cut an LZ for the chopper. We should have planted him there, the bits and pieces we could find. When the chopper was gone, taking most of him to Paradise, we found a glob of something dangling from another tree. That's his fucking nuts, Mickey Donato said. His nuts are hanging on the tree. A nut tree, he called it. A funny guy, Mickey. But I think it really* was *the bastard's nuts in a little bag of skin, bloody and mushy, a million sperm probably still alive and swimming around and wondering what the fuck hit them. Fink, the medic, shimmied up and scraped the glob into a plastic bag, and we buried it. "Nuts to nuts, ashes to ashes," Mickey said, crossing himself. Now that made sense. Was too fucking true. The truest thing I'd heard in a long time around here.*

*Now the question of Good—another Biggie that Friar Makowski liked to rumble—is maybe harder than the question of True, if you want my opinion (which you don't but will get anyway, since I've got all afternoon to sit here and can't think of anything better to do but write this stuff). True is just the flipside of False; they are Siamese twins playing Ring Around the Rosie. But it doesn't work quite so easy with Good. Or maybe it does. Come to think of it, it does. You probably can't have good without bad. Or peace without war. I have seen both of these famous opposites here, and they are the same when you dig deeper. Good and Evil. Peace and War. Nicky and Alex.*

*After Buzz got blown away, it was so damn quiet. I swear it had been raining, but the rain seemed to catch midway between the clouds and the ground. Even the jungle noises stopped—the click of bamboo, and the billion trillion bugs who run their little machines at the same time, night and day. It was so god-awful still. And the expression on the dead bastard's face, now that was true. His eyes wide open, looking at or maybe through the disaster, the complete fucking ruins around him. But what am I trying to say about the Good? A dead young man is not good. You can't say that and continue to make sense. But why would it matter in the long run? Is death so different from life that we have to make such a fuss about the distinction?*

*In war, you have life and death rubbed under your nose in a way that doesn't happen so much in civilian life. Everything is set up to make us believe we're gonna live forever. But the fact is sooner or later, we're all gonna die. Buzz Baxter was sooner. I'm at least gonna die later than him. Now that's true, and it's beyond repudiation, though whether it's good or bad I can't say.*

*For weird reasons—hey, maybe you don't find them so weird, who knows?—I don't want to die before I figure out some of this stuff. It would be nice to get a few answers to the Big Questions, just in case. Maybe I'd rather sit in the sun with a bottle of beer between my knees. But what choice do I got? When you see guys go down every day, you scratch your head and wonder what the point is.*

*Any suggestions, professor, and you know where to reach me. You don't get me here, try c/o Ho Chi Minh.*

*Your very own,*
*Socrates*

## *two*

---

I'd been given a part of Grant's work-in-progress about Capri to type, and I couldn't get some pages about Tiberius out of my head. The emperor had been haunting me since I'd translated the passage from Suetonius. If the excesses described by Tacitus and Suetonius were even partially true, it wasn't far-fetched that his friend, Cocceius Nerva, the eminent jurist, should feel moved to starve himself to death in protest. The sexual politics on Capri under this Lord of Misrule must have been unbearable at close range.

It was bad enough at the Villa Clio. I disliked the way Grant played Marisa and Holly off each other with a kind of sly malice, flattering them when necessary, fanning their desire for his attention as needed, chiding or ignoring—always to satisfy a private whim. I took notes, mentally. (It seemed foolish to write down anything along these lines—there was always the threat of something being read by the wrong eyes.) There he was, Rupert Grant, an experienced lover of the old school behaving in ways I considered despicable; yet on some level I envied his success. Marisa, Holly, and Vera were appealing creatures, each in their distinctive ways. And they doted on him, vying for his attention, willing to submit to his whims.

It could be muggy in June, and after five hours of typing, I often went to the beach. These watery escapes had become habitual, and I would go out a long way by myself, absorbed—a consciousness afloat, detached from the shoreline world. In fact, I had always gone to water for an escape, not only from the heat. I recalled hot summers in Pennsylvania, when the air stuck to your skin like cellophane and the birds were too exhausted to stir, sitting on the telephone wires in serial array, stunned. High humidity invariably provoked histrionics from my mother, who would sizzle and scream; my father would come home late from work, muttering under his breath. "Nothing but heat lightning," he'd say.

He avoided her when he could, rising early, leaving the house in his Ford pickup for a construction site at six-thirty. Nicky got up next, frying things that left a fatty stench or slopping milk and Wheaties over the waxy cloth that covered the kitchen table. The "Breakfast of Champions" appealed to his self-image as a teenager, and he ate heartily and drank endless mugs of Tang, an artificial drink full of vitamin C. Soon after breakfast, he would pump iron on the back porch, trying to inflate himself. A lurid poster of the famed muscle-builder Joe Weider hung in his bedroom.

My mother objected to Nicky's bodybuilding fervor. "That's a sport for queers," she would say. "Queers are weight lifters. They want to show off their muscles, their big bulges." She never failed to serve up an example as evidence for the prosecution. "Maria Malfieri's son, Rudy. Now there's a pansy if I ever saw one! He's a hairdresser in Wilkes-Barre. A good one, they say—gives a good perm. But my God, the muscles!" This kind of remark would infuriate Nicky, who invented ingenious ways to spite her, like posting pictures of famous weight lifters on the refrigerator or refusing to eat dinner (her cooking was sacred to her, the magical source of her power) while he skipped rope ostentatiously on the back porch, the *thump thump thump* reverberating in the kitchen while we ate silently at the table. Occasionally he sat in the kitchen while she cooked, cranking a dumbbell, "working on his pecs," as he put it.

My mother rose late, coming downstairs with her hair in a net, her velour housecoat barely concealing her girth. Like a tree, she added rings every year; they gathered around the waist and beneath her chin. (My grandfather Alessandro once shook his head wistfully when he saw her straining to pry her body from a car: "*Spamponata*," he said, meaning "a blown rose.") By the time I reached high school, she had accumulated two hundred and twenty pounds—a weight at which she claimed to "feel just about right," although the burden on her knees had begun to cause pain. The doctors warned her that she was a ticking time bomb, a heart attack waiting to happen, especially with her high blood pressure, but this only gave her ammunition. "I might as well have another helping, since I'll be dead soon," she would say at family meals, rather casually, as if commenting on the weather. One could hear, beneath this, the unspoken refrain: *And you'll be sorry you didn't treat me better!*

My relationship with my father was different. He was, in his way, a decent fellow who never quite understood the terms of his marriage. He had lived in the shadow of my grandfather, the head of the family, for so long that he had never quite found a voice of his own. He had gravitated toward Nicky for obvious reasons; for one, Nicky was "good with his hands," and they could spend hours together hunched over a motor in the garage on weekends, fiddling with a carburetor or replacing a fuel pump. And Nicky had, from an early age, showed an interest in hunting and fishing. Although my bookishness puzzled my father, he never discouraged me. "Read," he would say, discovering me on the back porch in a hammock, a book on my lap. "It's a good habit." And one that he had never himself acquired.

I avoided both my parents whenever I could, skipping breakfast and slipping away to the river. The Susquehanna was silty and soft, lukewarm from July through early September. There was an isolated landing, half a mile from the Exeter Anthracite Company, which had long ceased operations but whose ghostly buildings—abandoned breakers and rusted machines—had never been razed. It was lovely there, and you could dive from the rocks if you kept it shallow. Sometimes I'd swim to the other side, under the bleached cliffs of Camel's Ledge (as beautiful and menacing as Il Salto, with its desperate sheer sides below the Villa Jovis). Or I'd float on my back to the Coxton Bridge, its iron lacework a monument to the industrial age, which had its own peculiar grace notes. In the water, I felt free and selfless—a creaturely creature. Water was another element, wholly unlike my house, my family, and the stifling air surrounding them. All expectations dissolved in the swift current.

That feeling of wanting to escape gripped me as I picked my way along the dirt path beside the flowering broom, a bank of bright yellow, going down to the beach below the Villa Clio. What I needed was a good rinse in the sea. But Grant had beaten me to the punch, as usual. I saw him down there, lying beside Holly on the sharp pebbles: she with her top off, her breasts bare to the sun, white against the deep tan around them; they glistened as she rubbed them with tanning oil, the nipples taut. I watched greedily, guiltily. Grant in his sling bathing suit sat next to her, under his straw hat, in sunglasses, reading aloud, his voice inaudible but filling the air. He gestured with one hand, and Holly shuddered with laughter, bending to kiss him—a brief, filial kiss. He put down his book and touched her face, letting his fingers walk across her cheeks and forehead. Then they kissed deeply, lingering in each other's mouths and arms, tumbling onto the blanket. I looked away.

"Naughty boy!"

I startled, turning to face Marisa, who had crept up behind me unawares.

"You are the Peeping Lorenzo," she said. Her accent was thick and sultry.

"I was going to swim, but—"

"They were practically fuck, so you didn't want to disturb them," she said.

"Something like that."

"Are you still pining to hold her?"

"I'm not pining," I said.

"You are. And she's annoyed from it."

Her expression amused me. Marisa may have learned colloquial English during her time in England, adding to it lately at the Villa Clio, but she was still Neapolitan in her cadences, in the way she hung words together. She had merely placed little English cars on the crazy, looping roads of her Italian syntax.

"I don't see why she would be annoyed," I said.

"And who wouldn't be so annoy?" she replied. "You hang around her like the dog-puppy. You wag your tail for her. 'Bowwow. Please, could I have a bone, miss?'" Marisa meant to sound derisive, but a note of compassion softened her remark. I was perhaps more pathetic than objectionable.

"Everyone finds me amusing," I said. "I should have gone into show business."

"I hope you're not so serious." She put a finger on my lower lip, tipping my head toward her breasts. "Do you find me beautiful, Lorenzo?"

"I do."

"I'm so glad for this. It would be unpleasant if you thought I was ugly. In Italy, it is not good to be ugly. Beauty is considered your duty, a morality."

"You are definitely not ugly."

"Oh, good. I am relief. So let's swim in the pool together," she said. "Nobody's ever use it so much, but I love this pool. Don't you think so?"

I followed, under her spell. At poolside, the travertine tiles glistened but were cool beneath our feet; the pool itself was absolutely still, a piece of fallen sky. The air smelled strongly of cyprus.

*"Guarda! Scorpione!"* Marisa cried, pointing at a small scorpion, which seemed paralyzed by the sun. "She is very poison."

I stepped on the insect firmly with a bare foot, as I had seen Grant do—what he called "the old snuff-step." According to him, if you crushed it quickly it couldn't sting you. The exoskeleton collapsed under the ball of my foot, and the juices ran. I said, *"Basta, così."*

"What a brave boy, Lorenzo!" Marisa said. Then she lay belly down on a lounge chair, leaving just enough room for me to sit beside her. "Now you put the oil on me, you hero."

"You like to tease me."

"Do what you are told," she said. "I have given you a simple request."

I obeyed happily, massaging the oil into her neck and shoulders. The scented liquid seemed to vie with nature for olfactory dominance, and nature was losing. My fingers trembled as I rubbed the substance into the small of her back. Ever so slightly, she lifted her hips. A glorious move. I sucked in my breath. It had been, it seemed, such a long time since I had been this close to anyone.

"You are very beautiful," I said.

"You have meant this?"

"Absolutely."

Marisa turned toward me, with a timid smile. "I will visit you tonight, no?"

"What?"

"I will come to your cottage. Eleven o'clock?"

"My cottage?"

"Yes, I will make the visit. I am like the village doctor, going house to house."

I quivered inside. Could she really be saying this? "Eleven is fine," I said. "It's more than fine. I'm very happy." My own language seemed to conform to hers: childlike and straightforward, almost naked.

"Bravo," she said, as though I'd just put forward a tremendous performance of some kind.

I couldn't believe I'd invited her, or that she had suggested it. It seemed wrong to interfere with Rupert Grant's sexual arrangements, whatever they were. I owed him a certain loyalty, as his secretary. He had given me his trust, and I felt awkward about betraying him. On the other hand, I wanted something for myself, not nothing. I'd had enough of nothing in the past few months, and the sexual strain had become unendurable. Had I not seen him ignore or spurn Marisa on several recent occasions, I would have felt less inclined to accept her invitation. I found her alluring, though my attention had fallen mostly on Holly. Marisa had certainly sought my gaze at the table, in the garden, in the study. And once, in the piazzetta, she had briefly grasped my hand and squeezed it. I had squeezed it back, offering a slight smile. But there had been no explicit encouragement from me.

A shadowy figure loomed in the garden, near a tall cyprus. It was Mimo, who often seemed to hover like a black crow sunk in his own darkness, his wings pulled back. Standing with a rake in his hands, motionless, he watched us closely. His eyes hung there in space, small fiery black eyes, inhuman. I scowled back, but this had no effect whatsoever. He was leering at Marisa, and hardly noticed my presence.

"Mimo is fascinated," I said.

She sat up and glared at him, forcing him to turn away. "He lurks everywhere," she said to me. "*Una brutta figura*. I hate these men who are lurkers."

Hearing this, I wondered if Holly considered me a lurker. I had surely done more than my share of lurking since my arrival on Capri. Though moving on a higher social plane, I was no better than Mimo, a figure in the shadows, the lascivious outsider, hiding in plain view, making *una brutta figura*. Even at Columbia, I had lingered on the edge of my small circle, not quite fitting in, observing the behavior of my friends with a cynical detachment that disguised nothing more than fear. In my final year, I lived off-campus in an apartment with several male friends, each of whom spent most of his time smoking dope or plotting the next stage of the revolution. I had been dragged to political meetings and antiwar rallies, held picket signs, and sat on the steps of administration buildings. I had marched on Washington and poured red paint (to signify blood) on the walls of the Department of Justice. But none of this activity had engaged me fully. I was still struggling to move beyond a fierce solitude that made all social contact seem unreal. As the war grew increasingly insane, under Nixon, I found myself disoriented, unable to think, obsessing over my brother. I finally broke away, unable to bear the clamor inside and outside a moment longer.

As they would, my problems had followed me to Capri. I had been stalled, passive, and frustrated since my arrival, and it was now time to do something aggressive and positive, to "make it happen," as Nicky said in one letter. "Whatever it is, you just got to make it happen, goddamn it. Make it happen."

Now Marisa—lanky, oiled, athletic—plunged into the water, shattering the calm surface of the pool with a shallow dive, taking the length of it without needing an extra breath. The Capri light seemed to waver, swinging through the pool, turquoise. I watched her shadow in the water, slithering forward, sleek. When her head finally split the water, she flung back a swaddling of black hair: "Come in, Lorenzo! Don't be so lazy! She is warm!" She kicked across the pool on her back, each splash retilting the light.

I watched her, waiting until she drew herself from the water, loose-limbed and slippery-skinned. She smoothed the wet, black hair behind her head. To myself, I quoted a favorite line from Catullus: *"Vivamus, mea Lesbea, atque amemus."* ("Come, my Lesbea, let us live and love.")

Now she walked toward me, her feet printing the travertine tiles. Yes, I said, I would be Lorenzo. I would be whomever, whatever, it took to make this happen, even if I jeopardized everything with Rupert Grant. It was time to live and love.

# *three*

That evening I had been invited to
the villa of Dominick Bonano in Anacapri. It was my second visit to the
Villa Vecchia, meaning "old house," though it was fairly new, built in the
fifties by a wealthy German manufacturer of bathroom fixtures. "The
guy made the best goddamn toilet seats in Germany," Bonano told me,
showing me around the house in May. Standing in the doorway of one
bathroom, he said, with his usual eloquence, "This is the best place in
Capri to take a crap."

I liked the way the Villa Vecchia had been built on many levels to
accommodate the ragged, sloping hillside, with several terraces overlooking Punta Tresete and the Tyrrhenian Sea. In the distance, Vesuvius
was faintly visible, an exhausted legend wreathed in scarlet haze, a
reminder that no life is without the threat of unforeseen and violent era-
sure. The cone of Ischia rose between Capri and the mainland: an island
that, in my mind, belonged to Auden, who had owned a house there.

Bonano was a self-centered but amiable raconteur, highly intelligent
despite his raw manner. He delighted in stories of village life in Anacapri.
My first night with him over dinner he explained that the liveliest pro-
cession of the year took place on the Feast of Saint Anthony. The local
bands, in uniforms with gold lace on their shoulders harking back to the
Bourbon kings of Naples, would huff and puff, threading the town's narrow streets *a tempo di màrcia*. "In the old days," he said, "everybody in
Anacapri would get up at four in the morning. After a series of masses in

the cathedral came the big parade at noon. *La processione!* Kids dressed up like angels flew by, then came the *Figlie di Maria*—skinny-legged, angelic girls in white robes and blue veils." But his favorites were the old ladies, "*bizzocche*, black dresses and veils, these old prunes who never lost their cherries. They stayed true to their first love, Alex—Jesus Christ."

It relaxed me to hear Bonano talk. So like my Uncle Vinnie, I kept thinking. Crude but funny, with a bemused slant on the world. Nothing got too serious around Vinnie or Dom. They surfed the world, finding just the right waves, holding their balance. If they toppled into the sea, they got up and shrugged it off. *C'est la vie.* Got back up on their boards and caught the next wave. Even Bonano's wife, Rose, was familiar—a version of Vinnie's Gloria. A plumpish woman with mounds of platinum hair teased (in sixties style) to a dome, Rose liked to call attention to her origins in the American southwest, near Albuquerque, by draping herself in turquoise and silver. Heavy earrings tugged at each lobe, and she clanged as she walked, with several bracelets rattling on each arm. Her father, Vera told me, had made a fortune in movie theaters, owning (as Bonano claimed) "half the movie theaters in Nevada, Wyoming, and New Mexico." Now her brother Rocco ran the chain, though Rose scooped a sizable yearly profit from the company.

Not that she needed it. Bonano was himself a millionaire several times over. He frequently hit the national best-seller lists with his mob family sagas. They were big books, often running to six or seven hundred pages. "You don't wanna read them in bed," he quipped, "since they might drop on your chest and smother you." Three of them had been made into movies, and one—*The Last Limo on Staten Island*—had pulled in several Oscars, including Best Actor for Anthony Quinn as Carlo Mobilio, *capo di capi* of the Mazzino crime family. "It's not Lit," Bonano told me, during my initial dinner at the Villa Vecchia, "but neither is it shit. Look at the best-seller list sometime—there's a lot of good writers on the lists, for a few weeks anyway. Mailer and Vidal, for example. Or that Roth guy, who wrote the Portnoy book—the one about jerking off into a piece of liver. Not my idea of literature, but the critics went nuts for it." He called the critics "a bunch of assholes who identify with the kind of guy who enjoys jerking off into somebody else's liver."

Bonano despised the "U" crowd, as he called them: writers who lived and taught in universities and colleges. "They're bums, mostly, and they've screwed up everything. Their books are about nothing. Writing about writing, for God's sake! Who gives a shit about that? A novel has to tell a goddamn story." He argued that plot was central to good fiction. "Why do you think Dickens and Balzac pulled in the big numbers? They were the kings, Alex. They invented the whole goddamn form. We're still feeding at their trough. And those college writers who want to play around with the form—hey, it's a free country—but they will screw it up. Pretty soon we're gonna lose the readers. One reader lost is gone for good. It's TV all the way from there, and the programs ain't gonna interest Jean-Paul Sartre."

I couldn't really argue with him, not having a vast acquaintance with the "U" writers he mentioned. Like him, I admired Graham Greene, as did everyone on Capri. "He's the best, the cream of the cream," Bonano maintained, slapping the table. "You don't compete with Graham when it comes to storytelling. You just tip your hat to the gentleman. It's called professional respect." He added, "The guy sure knows about spies. He was one himself in Africa, during the war."

I asked if he saw much of Greene, hoping I might catch a glimpse of the novelist myself. Bonano shook his head sadly. "*Il Maestro*, he seems to spend more time in France these days, somewhere on the Riviera. Got himself a girlfriend there, I'm told. A French lady. But once or twice in the summer, you'll see him in the piazzetta. You want to meet him, I'll arrange it. He's a pretty friendly guy, for an Englishman, though you'd never guess it from his books."

"They're depressing," said Rose. "What's that one about Mexico, with the priest who drinks?"

"*The Power and the Glory*," I said.

"I like that one," Bonano said. "The way I see it, I'm a good Catholic and so forth, but I don't go around in a cold sweat about heaven or hell. You can tell Graham is a convert. They're always the guys who take up the collection."

Somehow I wasn't surprised to hear that the Bonanos owned an apartment in Manhattan, on East 77th, overlooking Central Park. "You can't live on Capri all year or you go stir-crazy," Bonano explained. "Every-body gets into your pocket. It's a small place. But we're here half of the year—March to October. Those are the good months." He told me, again, that I would like his daughter. "She's your type," he said.

So there I was, revisiting the Villa Vecchia, ready to meet my destiny in the shape of Toni Bonano. I fought off a queasy feeling, guessing that she would not especially please the eye—the fruit can't fall too far from the tree—and that I would regret having agreed to this encounter. No girl likes to meet a guy anointed by her parents, and Toni would already have been made wary by their enthusiasm. On the other hand, given her parents, it seemed likely that she had grown accustomed to their match-making. They had not been shy about pushing us together, so I imagined this was not the first time she had been tossed into the company of a cho-sen suitor.

The actual Toni Bonano confounded my expectations.

"So why did you drop out of Columbia?" was her first question, popped within seconds of my meeting her. "I mean, you were so close to graduation. It doesn't add up."

"It's a long story," I said, "and it doesn't make sense anyway. Just something I did."

"You're impulsive?"

"I guess."

We had been left to our own devices on the terrace while her parents "finished the dinner," as if two local cooks weren't up to their elbows in pots in the kitchen.

Toni was a solidly built but striking young woman, taller than both her parents, from whom nature had cleverly and benevolently picked and chosen features, taking the slight arch in her father's nose and her mother's appealing high cheekbones. Her enthusiasm for track-and-field had served her well; in fact, the long hours of racing around gravel tracks in empty stadiums had slimmed and sculpted what might, under less benign conditions, have become a hefty body. That she was big-boned was not in question, but she carried herself gracefully. The Dalton School in New York and Bryn Mawr had worked their class magic, and Toni shared none of her parents' crudeness. Yet she had held on to their unaffected warmth and energy, and her eyes—large chestnut eyes beneath blond-streaked hair—fixed me in their gaze.

"You ask a lot of questions," I said.

"I'm a nosy person," she responded. "I hope you don't mind if I ask a lot of questions."

I shook my head. "Feel free. But I might lie."

She tipped her head slightly to one side. "You want to be a writer, so you're probably nosy, too."

"I'm curious about things."

"That's a euphemism. You're nosy—just like me."

I grinned, finding her superbly pleasant.

"And shy, too?" she asked.

"Only in the company of others," I said.

She passed over my little joke. "I don't meet so many shy people. The places I live—you know, you don't find them so much in the academic world. There are lots of neurotics around, and people who can't communicate. Navel-gazers. But that's different. The people I meet are usually passive-aggressive, and that's pretty boring."

I felt my ears burning. Without knowing it, Toni had exposed raw emotional flesh. Yet I liked it that she had no fear of stepping on sensitive ground, and found something fresh and direct about her lack of pretense. After the confusing social scene at the Villa Clio, this atmosphere felt liberating. Its distinctly American qualities appealed to me as well. Americans often presented themselves as frank and friendly, available for immediate contact, although these contacts were rarely—were not intended to be—lasting or deep. I had noticed at Columbia that guys in my dorm acted like your oldest friend within minutes of first meeting them; yet only a few relationships developed beyond the initial warm flush. America was, in the end, a lonely country, full of bluff and cheerful creatures who didn't really know what to say to each other after the first flurry of superficial bonhomie.

"Daddy likes you," Toni said. "Mom does, too." She lit a Marlboro, offering me one first, which I refused. Tobacco had never interested me.

"I'm glad," I said, aware that they hardly knew me. "I like them, so it's mutual."

"They're fish out of water here. Fortunately for them, they haven't noticed."

"But you like Capri, don't you? I mean, it's so beautiful."

"I could never live here, not permanently. But it's fun to visit. What a bizarre bunch." A conspiratorial look crossed her face. "The Grants, for example. Is that going okay?"

"It's all right."

"So you don't like them. I guessed as much."

"They're pretty interesting," I said. "There's a lot going on."

"Rupert's too domineering."

"What writer isn't?"

"Daddy."

"I don't know him well enough to say."

She stepped neatly around this subject. "I've known Rupert since I was a little girl."

There was a long pause. "He's eccentric," I said.

"That's way too generous. Only on Capri would his lifestyle make any sense."

"You think it makes sense here?"

"He's always had girls around him. They're his Muses, or so he claims. Daddy thinks he would prefer boys anyway—the Brits all do." She ran a hand through her lovely hair. "I wonder how Vera copes."

"Pretty well," I said.

"It's called repression."

"Ah, I forgot. You're a psychology major."

"Daddy told you?"

"The first time I met him."

"And what else has he told you about me?"

"Only good things."

She took a long drag on her cigarette, then exhaled. "Have you read Norman O. Brown?"

"He's just a name to me."

"Have a look into *Life Against Death*. It's a totally new look at Freud. He argues that we should take Freud seriously. That would mean getting rid of repression altogether. Bizarre, I know—but it follows."

"Maybe we need repression. Maybe things would fall apart without it."

Toni grew animated, having guided the talk onto familiar ground. "That's what Freud suggests in *Civilization and Its Discontents*. Or seems to. But if you look closer, he's arguing for more than that. Repression has fucked us up. We need it, for sure. But enough is enough. We're repressing each other all the time, in personal and larger ways—like in Vietnam. Who needs that? That's Thanatos, death."

"More Eros, huh?"

"Lots more," she said.

I said, "Freud would have adored Rupert Grant."

"That's just old-fashioned British licentiousness. Not the same thing as genuine polymorphous perversity. A counterfeit version, maybe."

In walked Rose Bonano, ablaze in a loose red shift with golden spangles. Her lipstick was reddish brown, unnatural, but the same color as her fingernails and toenails, which poked through her leather sandals. She carried a plastic tray that teemed with antipasto goodies: slices of local sausage, chunks of parmesan, and gray-green olives in tiny white bowls. "You guys are having a brainy talk, I see. You better eat."

"We were discussing Freud," I said.

"Hey, she's a psychology major," said Bonano, appearing on the terrace with a bottle of wine in one hand—a rosé from Ravello. He leaned on his daughter's shoulder. "She's gorgeous, right? And smart!"

Rose lowered her eyebrows, and I suspected it would be no fun to get on her wrong side.

Bonano feigned a guilty look. "Okay, honey. I'll behave. No bragging about my only child. So what if she's a genius and happens to look like a movie star?"

"Do your best to ignore Daddy," said Toni.

Bonano beamed. "Why not? Join the crowd."

We settled in for a jolly evening. The Bonano clan treated me like family, asking about Massolini Construction, my parents and grandparents, my Italian roots. I summoned a few family stories—most of them about my grandfather and namesake—but never mentioned Nicky. Although I never quite lied, I gave the impression I was an only child—like Toni. When the conversation shifted to Vietnam and the national lottery, I pretended my number was so high I could never be drafted. To my relief, everyone at the Villa Vecchia opposed the war. Indeed, Bonano had signed a major petition against the bombing of Cambodia that appeared in the *New York Times*. "I'm not a protester," he said, "but this thing in Asia, it's out of control. Nixon is crazy. Why bomb Cambodia anyway? What have they done? It's going to make everything worse, believe me. Stir up the hornets. Watch what happens there—a nice little country, and kaboom—up in smoke." He talked about Cambodian and Laotian politics with no apparent strain, reaching back easily in time to the fifties and before. I was surprised, and duly chastened, by this knowledge of Southeast Asian history. It was too easy to dismiss a man like Dom Bonano because of his manner and appearance.

Throughout dinner, which took its usual Italian time, I was conscious of the ticking clock. Marisa might be taking a bath now, thinking about me, planning to visit the cottage. The prospect of lying beside her was strange but thrilling. I felt buoyed by the wine, by the friendly conversation and genuine interest turned toward me. In gratitude, I complimented Rose on the food, assuming that she was responsible for the menu, though aware she hadn't personally prepared each item.

"I see you've been in the kitchen with Vera," she said. "Be careful. She'll want you to start a trattoria with her. She even asked *me*, and I hate cooking."

I explained that I loved the time spent in the kitchen with Vera, who had entered dozens of her best recipes into my journal. Only that afternoon she had lectured me on cotechino, a pork sausage roll that you covered with prosciutto and served with a rich, onion-flavored gravy. She described it as "the culinary equivalent of good sex."

"You'll remember the recipes long after you've forgotten Rupert's poems," Rose said, only a touch facetiously.

At ten-thirty, my anxiety peaked. Marisa would appear at my cottage in half an hour, and I needed at least that much time to get back to the Villa Clio. If I weren't home when she called, Marisa would be disappointed and angry. She was perfectly capable of rage, as I recalled from an afternoon when she and Grant, for reasons unknown to me, staged a shouting match of operatic proportions. The darker side of Marisa—her temper, plus a brooding quality that bordered on depression—was often apparent, and I didn't relish contact with it.

"You like cognac?" Bonano wondered, hovering behind me with an ornate bottle. "This stuff will knock your socks off."

"Don't get him drunk, Daddy," Toni said.

"Hey, he can handle it. I've heard about those fraternity parties. Am I right, Alex, or what?" Bonano poured the brown-gold liquid into a snifter the size of a giant soap bubble, then drew it slowly under my nose. "Ambrosia of the gods," he said.

I had waited long enough to make any decision about my departure entirely moot. I would never get home on time. Taxi service was sketchy at this hour, and no buses ran after ten. I consoled myself by thinking Marisa would probably not have come anyway. Why jeopardize her own position at the Villa Clio and her relationship with Grant? Indeed, why would I jeopardize mine? While nothing explicit had been said, I understood perfectly well that both Marisa and Holly belonged to him.

I had glimpsed the extremes to which Grant could go when pushed. Once, after reading a profile of himself in an Italian newspaper, he lunged with a letter opener, gouging a huge hole in his antique desk. (I was standing beside him, breathless, hoping my chest would not seem like another appropriate target—since I had pointed out the article.) Another time he flung a book across the room at Marisa, who had been sulking. She sulked at the slightest provocation, so it puzzled me that this particular sulk had drawn his wrath. Thus far, I'd been spared the full brunt of his fury, though I didn't doubt my turn would come. "It's only a matter of time," Vera said one morning, in the garden, as we trimmed a rosebush. "He'll bite your head off. Then you'll squawk around the room for a while." After a pause, she added, "Then you'll expire."

Had it been Holly waiting for me at the cottage, I would have abandoned the Villa Vecchia long before; but Marisa did not have quite that pull for me. I felt attraction, but no compulsion. It would be pleasant to sleep with her, but that was all. As I drank Bonano's peppery cognac, its vapors stinging my nostrils, I realized it made no sense to pursue the Marisa business. An affair with her would shrink my chances with Holly even further, and it could hardly improve my relations with Grant. In general, life at the Villa Clio would instantly become more complicated and nuanced. I didn't think I could stand more nuance and complication.

"Here you go," said Bonano, putting on the table before me a signed copy of *The Last Limo on Staten Island*. "First edition," he said. "My hair wasn't so gray," he added, pointing to the author photograph.

I fingered the neon-colored dust jacket, which featured a stretch Caddy (1959, jet black, with gigantic fins) parked beneath the portico of a Greek Revival mansion. "Thanks," I said, "but you didn't have—"

"He's got two hundred copies in the basement," Rose cut in. "We're never gonna get rid of them before they go moldy. Take all you want."

Bonano sighed. "Thanks, Rose."

I read the inscription. *To my fellow writer and paisano, Alex. Forget the fancy stuff! Tell good stories!*

"I'm glad to have this," I said. "If I can think of any good stories, I'll tell them."

"Why don't we let the children alone?" Rose muttered, sotto voce, to her husband.

"Yeah," he said, "sure. Good idea. Help yourself to more cognac, guys."

After another drink, I followed Toni to the pool for a midnight swim. "There are bathing suits in the poolhouse," she said, pointing to a tiny building at one end of the garden. "Help yourself."

I did so, and when I emerged, she was already in the water, having slipped into a bikini herself while I was changing.

"It's not bad," she said. "Come in."

I leaped, clumsily, splashing her. We treaded water for a few minutes, head tilted back. A billion stars sprinkled over us, and I quoted some lines from Gerard Manley Hopkins: "Look at the stars! look, look up at the skies! / O look at all the fire-folk sitting in the air!"

"You wrote that?"

"I wish," I said. "A Victorian priest wrote that, a Jesuit."

"Sounds like a Jesi," she said, lifting herself to the side of the pool. "Are you religious?"

"Gnostic," I said.

"What's that?"

"My own thing."

"Cool," she said, lifting herself from the pool.

I watched her closely, taking in everything.

Her body fit naturally with the setting—a garden sculpted from the wild, tamed by travertine and tile, illumined by recessed lighting that seemed to caress this little world's cunningly wrought surfaces: bushes shaved into perfect globes against the background of umbrella pines and camellias, a maze of paths with stone benches set artfully beneath woven canopies of vine. Toni might have been a marble statue—so smooth and molded, the lines classically drawn, idealized beyond the point of eroticism, which seems oddly and perversely to depend on error, visual mischance, a touch of formlessness.

"Do you like my body?" she asked.

"I do."

She responded by diving into the water again, flipping onto her belly before she jackknifed and plunged to the bottom. I was still treading water, watching her form as it shattered into angles and shapes like a Cubist painting. Her head broke the water only a foot in front of me.

I reached to touch her hair.

"We can meet another night," she said, ducking away from me. "Daddy is waiting up for me. He always does for a week or so when I come home. Then I become Old News."

I told her I could meet again whenever it was convenient. My schedule at the Villa Clio was flexible. I had no plans, no obvious commitments. Indeed, I could see no direction whatsoever in my life. I merely stumbled from moment to moment, day to day, person to person. Though not unpleasant, it was the next best thing to chaos.

We dressed quickly, then she walked me to the gate, where we kissed politely, a peck on the lips.

"Call me," she said. "I get bored here."

"I will."

Stumbling to the piazza of Anacapri over crooked paving stones, I wondered if Toni Bonano would become a friend or a lover. It was impossible to tell, but either possibility was fine. In truth, I needed a friend more than a lover, a reference point outside the crazy circle of the Villa Clio. I needed someone to say, *Alex, they're all nuts. Remember, they're all nuts.*

## *four*

The clock in the tower of San Michele la Croce gonged twelve times as I made my way home, having crossed from one side of the island to the other by taxi. By now, I recognized many faces in the piazzetta, a mix of resident foreigners and locals who could be found, in some combination, on any night of the summer under one of the colorful awnings, a glass of grappa or espresso on the table before them, a cigarette in hand. Capri came alive at night, and even small children (always dressed to the nines) were allowed to parade with their parents, *fare un giro*, making "a circle" in society at late hours that, to an American, reeked of child abuse. I caught sight of Patrice, transfixed in conversation with Giovanni at the opposite end of the square. To avoid them, I ducked into a side alley, hurrying along the Tragara, back to the Villa Clio.

Moonlight bathed the grounds, turning the lawns ghostly; every blade of grass seemed distinct, otherwordly in the phosphorescent glow. I stood for a moment in the moon's full light, transfixed. Beside me, Vera's flowers shone colorless, white as stone. All the bedroom lights were out—the Grants retired each night quite early—but I found my way easily to the cottage by following the pale gravel path.

In those days I slept naked, especially on hot nights. Without bothering to turn on a lamp—the moonlight was more than sufficient, pouring through windowpanes onto the tiled floor—I began undressing on my way to bed, dropping bits and pieces behind me: a sweaty shirt, shoes and socks, a pair of jeans, my boxers. The cool sheets of the bed would feel welcoming. Built of stone, the cottage always retained a certain musty coolness, and a fragrant cross-breeze swept between the open windows, never failing to create obliging conditions for sleep.

I realized, before I hit the bed, that I was not alone.

"You have been late, no? And drinking!"

"Marisa?"

"I have waited too long for you. You make me so angry, Lorenzo. We have made arrangements, no?"

"I'm sorry, I—"

"Don't argue it. You have been to the bar, I can smell. The men in Naples are like this when they go to the bar." She draped her arms around my neck, pulling me toward her breasts. Like me, she wore nothing.

I resisted, slightly.

"You don't like my body?"

"No, I do. I like it very much."

"So be here," she said. "It is a very short life."

I could hear Nicky in my head, urging me on. "Just do it," he was saying. Yes, Nicky, I said. Yes.

Our bodies lengthened beneath the sheets and the world was soon all skin, teeth clattering as we kissed, clicking like ice cubes in a glass. I tasted the tobacco on her breath, but it was not unpleasant. Her arms circled me, and she pressed close, rocking against me with her hips, now undulating with quick, sharp pelvic thrusts. I was startled by the length of her, the sense that her body seemed to extend in every direction for a thousand miles. Her long black hair was wonderfully thick and rich, and she had recently washed it—the shampoo was fresh and clean. I took long, slow breaths.

"Make love with me," she said, her voice hoarse.

I said nothing, but followed her instructions, sinking into my first full sexual experience in many months, savoring the liquor of her body. I drank her in, loving the soft fuzz of her pubic hair, the moist brush of skin and tongue. When I finally came into her, she was wide beneath me, her legs as open as I could possibly have wished for. She was wet and warm.

I floated out to sea on this raft of pleasure, forgetting everything that had ever happened in my life, ignoring everything to come.

Afterward, Marisa sat up in bed and lit a cigarette while I lay half asleep beside her, too exhausted to contemplate anything so rational as a consequence. I had been completely in thrall to instinct, and didn't mind at all. The experience had felt absolute, unmediated, and commonplace in the best way. Before long I fell asleep, my arm across her stomach. A deep and apparently dreamless sleep overwhelmed me, as if the unconscious were going to let me off the hook for once. When I woke, soon after dawn, I noticed that she had gone, and that the moon, too, had fallen across the sky, dragging with it the whole night sky.

I sat in bed with Rilke's letters, fumbling for a passage in the seventh letter that I recalled dimly and wanted to reread. "For one being to love another," he wrote to young Kappus, "that is perhaps the most difficult task of all, the ultimate and last test and proof, the work for which all other work is mere preparation. For this reason young people, who are beginners in everything, cannot yet know love: they have to learn it." I underlined that passage, knowing I had a great deal to learn about this subject. "But young people err so often and so grievously in this," Rilke continued, "they (in whose nature it lies to have no patience) fling themselves at each other, when love takes possession of them, scatter themselves, just as they are, in all their untidiness, disorder, confusion."

That morning, more than ever, my life was just those things: untidiness, disorder, and confusion.

## *five*

For days I wandered around the Villa Clio in a state of dread, certain that the ax would fall. In one scenario, I imagined Rupert Grant appearing at the door of my cottage, blowsy-faced with whiskey, his eyes watering. He would tell me how much I had hurt him, accusing me of betrayal. I would be asked to pack my bags at once. In another vision, I saw him sending Vera in his place. She would come with sad eyes, and speak softly, and tell me that under the circumstances I should probably consider blah blah blah. In the worst scenario, Grant would burst into my cottage in a rage, a pistol in hand, demanding satisfaction. But nothing of the sort happened.

Instead, I remained in my cottage or strolled the gardens of the villa in a confused daze. One morning, I sat on the cliff overlooking the bay below the Villa Clio, listening to the sea grind its teeth below. Falling from great heights had always been a recurrent nightmare, and this particular cliff seemed to beckon. I went there to confront my fear, hoping to tame something inside of myself. I sat on the edge, dangling my feet, as if tempting fate. With a feeling of triumph, I walked away, having temporarily mastered some dark impulse toward self-destruction.

I had wondered about Vera's reaction to the news, which I assumed would reach her—there were few secrets at the Villa Clio—but she was blithely unchanged. At one point, she mentioned that Marisa came from a "rough background" in Naples, and described her father as "a violent lout" who abused his daughter. But that was it.

The response of Grant had worried me the most; Marisa was, after all, "his" girl. To my relief, he seemed warmer than ever toward me, asking to see my latest poems. "Don't be shy, Lorenzo," he said. "I'd be delighted to see what you're doing." When I told him there were no latest poems, he instructed me to write some. "Write about whatever concerns you," he said. "A poem is a shared burden." He put a large hand on my shoulder, saying that I had done a good job of typing his manuscripts and answering his letters. He wanted me to take on more responsibilities soon—perhaps to dig into the Suetonius translation again. He suggested that I might get equal billing on the title page as cotranslator.

I was flabbergasted. Perhaps he was relieved that I had made love to Marisa? It was obvious that Grant favored Holly, but his exclusion of Marisa in the past month had begun to upset the rhythms of the household. Vera had commented, wryly, that Marisa had been neglected of late, and that her "mooning about" would send everyone around the bend. "You're a great man," she said to Grant in the kitchen one afternoon, when it was just the three of us, "but I don't believe you've kept our darling Marisa satisfied."

Vera raised the subject again only a few days after I'd made love to Marisa. We were having a glass of wine on the terrace behind the kitchen when Vera said, "I've seen the girl pouting by the pool. It's ridiculous."

"Perhaps Alex will lend a hand?" Grant said, bemused. "Won't you take the girl to the piazzetta for a drink? A good chance to practice your Italian."

"Alex has other fish to fry," Vera said. "His prospects have apparently improved."

"Tell all," Grant said, as if I were not present.

"Miss Bonano is intrigued by her compatriot."

"Ah, the Italian American connection!"

I shook my head in disbelief. They could simply not resist this kind of ironic banter, at my expense. And I was an easy target.

"Toni is quite attractive," Vera said. "One could surely do worse."

"One has," Grant said.

The ubiquitous British "one" lodged at the center of so many sentences at the Villa Clio, deflecting scrutiny, enhancing the already thick air of unreality. "One" was never to blame, and "one" rarely offered apologies.

That Vera knew about my exploits in Anacapri startled me. I'd had only one conversation with Toni since meeting her at the Villa Vecchia, although we had made plans to have a picnic on Mount Solaro on the coming weekend.

Vera understood my confusion. "I had lunch at Da Gemma with Rose yesterday," she said, referring to a popular local restaurant. "She mentioned that you and Toni had got on rather well. Apparently the girl is smitten."

"I doubt it," I said.

"Everyone is smitten with Alex," Grant said.

"Indeed," added Vera.

"Toni and I got along well enough," I said.

"I don't know why," said Vera, "but I have a distinct feeling about this. Mamma Grant has a wonderful sense of intuition. Famous all over the island."

"Vera hears wedding bells," Grant said. "I rather think he's having himself a good time. I don't mind. A young man's fancy, and so forth, what?" Grant winked at me. It was reassuring but odd. He seemed to like a sense of male camaraderie. I had slept with Marisa, and he knew it and didn't seem to care. He also imagined—or so I guessed—that I had, or would soon, sleep with Toni. This wasn't bad, since it meant I was not serious about Marisa, which would have made things complicated. He was probably relieved that my attention had wandered away from Holly. She was his focus, emotionally. His interests might shift in time, but at present she compelled his attention, and he didn't want competition from me.

Unfortunately, Holly held my attention, too. I was consumed by thoughts of her, and found myself writing her name in my journal, over and over. Just to spell the name gave a kind of secret pleasure. I treasured all glimpses of her, especially if I caught her unawares: sitting by the pool, with her ankles crossed, or reading beneath an ilex in the garden. Large feelings of tenderness toward her welled up in me as I watched her. She seemed wholly self-absorbed at times, lost in some daydream of god-knows-what. I wished I could get inside her, not just inside her skin but inside her mind. I wanted to live at the center of her experience. She represented a kind of sophistication that I could only envy.

For me, most cultural knowledge had come through the pages of books; but Holly had been taken through the great museums of the world by her parents. She talked off-handedly of visiting the Prado, the Louvre, the Hermitage. She had been to operas in Paris and Milan, in London and New York. She could join in when Grant, in a moment of boozy inspiration, launched into an aria from Puccini or Verdi. She knew the names of the mythic characters in Wagner's cyclical extravaganzas, and she could be found listening to Beethoven's late quartets, which she knew intimately. By her bedside—I had crept into that room more than once, my heart pounding in my throat—she kept novels in French and Italian. Her only lapse in taste, as far as I could tell, was a volume of poetry by Kahlil Gibran. (I kept asking to see her own novel, but she refused. "I don't believe in showing things till they're ready. My drafts are frightfully rough," she said.)

I summoned courage and typed one of the few poems that I considered finished from my journals and left it on Grant's desk. It was, obliquely, a love poem for Holly. Everything I wrote came out that way, yet this one at least had the virtues of concealment, with the feelings that lay beneath it subdued by form. (I recalled a line from Emily Dickinson: "After great pain a formal feeling comes.")

Grant asked me to come to see him for morning coffee, another ritual imported from Britain. He usually had coffee with either Holly or Marisa, although Marisa had not recently been invited. I had supposed that Grant and I would be alone, but found myself sitting beside him with Holly working at a side table in one corner of the study.

"Don't mind her," Grant said.

"I don't," I said, rather feebly.

But I did mind. I minded a great deal, given the subject of the poem, and my feelings about Holly. I had somehow wandered, naked, onto a public stage, and the audience was primed for a good laugh. I could feel the blood rising in my cheeks, my ears hot and prickly.

I watched Grant as he ran his finger down the page, as if reminding himself of the poem. Spidery red lines filled the whites of his eyes, and his finger trembled: a sign that he'd been drinking too much the night before. "I'll say it aloud, Lorenzo. It's often useful to hear a poem. The words, they take on another aspect. The flaws often emerge. One tends to miss them when reading to oneself . . . skip over them. What?"

He read slowly, giving each word its due weight, lingering at the end of each line, though my enjambment at several points begged for the sense to spill over onto the next one. There was a Celtic lilt in his voice that actually enhanced them, lifted them in unexpected places.

> *I wander alone beside the sea at dawn,*
> *half wondering if I am real or not;*
> *reality eludes me. I've been brought*
> *by simple despair to this uncertainty.*
>
> *Whatever it is that I must look upon*
> *seems false, as I feel false. Propinquity*
> *means nothing as I walk beside the sea;*
> *its glassy surf seems far away, unreal.*
>
> *I wonder what I'd feel if I could meet*
> *that whirling darkness, deep below blue deep.*
> *I wonder if she would remember me*
> *years hence, if I should fall, if I should keep*
> *a rendezvous with what I cannot see.*
> *I wonder at my own obliquity.*

"It's rather a sonnet," he said, after a longish pause during which I noticed that Holly had acquired a bemused look as she pretended to work. "Fourteen lines, in any case. But a mere fourteen lines does not a sonnet make."

"What does it make?"

"A poem of fourteen lines."

"It's in iambic pentameter."

"More or less. I don't recognize the rhyme scheme."

"I invented it."

"Ah."

"Wasn't it Ezra Pound who suggested that a rhyme should occur only when necessary?"

"Pound was a fool, dear boy."

"It's only a rough draft."

"And not so bad. Don't mean to sound dismissive. Bits and pieces I admire. Propinquity / obliquity. Clever. If I understood the last line, I might consider it marvelous."

"What confuses you?"

"I can't imagine a young man wondering at his own obliquity. What would that entail?"

"Who am I? That sort of thing."

"Ah. The question of identity."

Holly laughed, then suppressed her laugh.

"I don't mean to hurt your feelings," Grant said.

"He does, too," said Holly.

Grant gave her a sharp look, then smiled—a pike's sidelong smile. "The opening lines trouble me," he said. "The speaker half wondering if he's real or not. Not believable, that. Somewhat adolescent, what?"

I saw it was jejune. I did, however, have an unreal sense of myself at times. I could not quite locate the center that everyone talks about, the vaunted and overly analyzed Self. As Proust once suggested, we each have a thousand selves locked inside us. Any one might emerge at a given moment. But how could one say this without sounding idiotic, facile, or immature? My poem was all those things.

Grant recognized my discomfort. "I do like the business of the sea appearing unreal. That's better. And the way you use propinquity here— as I said, that's nice."

Nice. I hated that word, and it surely made no sense in this context. How could one's use of a word like propinquity ever seem "nice"? (That I had borrowed propinquity from one of his earlier poems apparently had not occurred to him. If it did, he appeared not to mind.)

"Yet 'deep below blue deep' is my favorite bit. You resisted the temptation to say 'depth below blue depth.'"

"That would have been too obvious," I said.

"Exactly. And I rather admire the rendezvous business. Too bad everything collapses in the last line."

I saw what he meant, and it was painful. My talents were terribly limited, and would remain so—at least, that was my immediate feeling in response to Grant's critique. I felt terribly exposed.

"I must say," he said, "there's a facility here. One mustn't dismiss that. It's rare enough, God knows."

I knew what he meant, and this pleased me. I didn't find it especially difficult to churn out lines of passable pentameter. Perhaps sheer quantity would in due course yield excellent work?

"But, dear boy, you mustn't let your facility run away with you," he said. "A poet has to have amazing verbal facility. That's a donnée, something we assume. The hard spiritual work has no shortcuts, unfortunately. In the end, you can't write beyond what you are. Largeness of spirit, a complex range of emotions, a well-stocked mind, ferocious discipline—well, these are necessary. And more as well." He appeared to look inwardly, with despair. "Much more. There are no end of requirements. And after this, one wants a further thing. *Fortuna*."

"Dumb-ass luck," I said.

He smiled. "It helps to be born in the right place and time. Elizabethan England was a fair start for Shakespeare. I rather envy Eliot, you know. Coming when he did, after so much Victorian fog. So many vapors in the air that wanted clearing." He put a hand on my thigh, affectionately. "Try another on me soon."

"Thanks," I said. "I've got some poems in my journals. Very rough."

"A poem is never finished, only abandoned."

"I like that."

"Valéry," he said.

I looked vacant.

"Paul Valéry. Decent poet, but a better critic. A friend of Gide's." He straightened his back, he often did this before entering what I thought of as his lecture mode. "I have a copy of *Eupalinos* somewhere. I'll lend it to you—dramatic poem. Rather fine in its peculiar way. Socrates is a character, and he argues, mistakenly, that the work of creation is more important than the work of self-knowledge. Wrong way around, as I said. Bloody cart before the horse."

Holly and I were fixed on him, even transfixed, and he understood that he had attention. Like a bulb caught in a surge of current, he brightened, momentarily, then lapsed into the usual glow.

"Sorry, chaps. Must get to work," he said. "Capri calls."

He referred to the subject of the novel underway. He was making progress, as Holly and I well knew. Lately, reams of handwritten manuscript had landed on my desk—I guessed I was typing fifty pages a week, although a good deal of this was revision. I was astonished by the productivity of this man, who got to his study most days before I was awake, and who often returned to his study in the evenings, after dinner—even after several glasses of wine. He was driven by forces I could only just comprehend. (I once heard him say, "I'm chased out of bed every morning by a pack of hungry wolves, but they haven't caught me yet.")

"It's absurd," Vera said, one day, when I mentioned how hard Grant seemed to be working. "He's working harder now than before. It's the age, I suspect. Time's chariot and so forth."

"Wingéd chariot," I said.

She wisely ignored my pedantry. "He has some absolute in mind—always whoring after it. He considers himself a failure, you see. Hasn't quite matched his potential."

"He's human."

"My God," she said, in a feigned hush. "Don't let him hear you say that. He doesn't know."

I went back to the cottage to rework my poem about Holly and draw a few more of Grant's ink-scrawled pages into the deceptive clarity of type. My mind, though, was on our dinner at the Villa Clio that night. It was not the food that interested me—though Vera had already gone into high gear in the kitchen. The Grants were expecting dinner guests: Gore Vidal and Howard Austen. Graham Greene had arrived in Anacapri a couple of days before—the news had drifted through the piazzetta, and he'd been invited, too. The news had been delivered casually, by Vera. "Gore is coming tonight," she said, when I helped Maria Pia bring the remains of morning coffee into the kitchen. "Howard will be here, too. They're staying with the Bismarcks. Graham will join us."

"Graham?" I asked, in near disbelief.

"Yes, Graham, as in Greene."

Gore and Howard and Graham. It seemed a long way from Uncle Vinnie and Aunt Gloria.

*six*

———

In 1948, Graham Greene bought a small villa in Anacapri, Il Rosaio, with royalties that had been frozen in Europe during the war. Yet the island had never been a permanent home; the idea of permanence itself held no appeal for him. He was a perpetual foreigner, a man on whom art and architecture—culture, in the usual sense—were lost. What engaged him most were politics and people, especially those with a revolutionary and leftist tinge. By nature, he was an outsider, a spy, an itinerant. He had often traveled to exotic and dangerous places—Sierra Leone, Haiti, Mexico, the Congo, Vietnam. And he had managed to capture the atmospheres of these famously corrupt and decaying countries in his fiction.

I was no expert, but I'd fingered many of his novels in bookstores, skimming pages, noting titles and subjects. I'd only read with care *The Quiet American* and *The Heart of the Matter*, both of which I admired, with reservations. I expressed these to Vera as I worked beside her in the kitchen, stuffing prunes into a pork roast. (This would be the main course—arrosto di maiale alle prugne, one of her fail-safe recipes: "You don't try something new when you have guests," she said. "If you must poison someone, poison your family.")

"I'm not a critic," she said, regarding Greene. "But you might enjoy *Stamboul Train*. That's Graham at his best—light and breezy, a bit irreverent. A conventional thriller, but well done. Not the pompous Graham of *The Power and the Glory*. I've never understood that Catholic business. If he's a Catholic, I'm an aboriginal." She tucked a row of prunes under the bone, laying them end to end like stones edging a garden plot. "Rupert prefers *The Comedians*. It's the one about Haiti, and the trouble there. The movie was horrid . . . that dreadful Elizabeth Taylor. I don't know what Americans see in her."

I felt uneasy whenever Vera fell into this chattering mood, which often seized her in the kitchen. Her opinions were, in general, quite interesting, but she lacked faith in them. Her bold assertions seemed hollow and ungrounded.

"You won't get much out of Graham, I'm afraid. He's not very talkative."

"What about Vidal?" I asked.

"Gore? He is marvelous. Howard, too. Everyone loves Howard."

"Do you like his novels?"

"Of course," she said, wiping her forehead with a slippery palm. "I haven't read them all—he's very prolific. I suppose he's at his best when it comes to history. He should have been an ancient Roman. Maybe he is."

"Is what?"

"A visitor, I mean, from the past. He can't live in the States. They can't tell when he's joking and when he's serious. It drives him mad." She recommended *Julian* as his best novel, and *Burr* after that. "I adore the essays, too," she said. "He's the only amusing American I've ever read. The only *intentionally* amusing American."

Vidal had arrived a couple of days earlier, from Rome, with Howard Austen, his companion of two decades. They were staying in an imposing house overlooking the Marina Grande with Vidal's old friend, Mona Williams, a wealthy American from Kentucky who had married various wealthy men and was now attached to Eddie von Bismarck, a grandson of the famous German chancellor. ("You've met Eddie," Vera said. "He's queer as a coot. Their marriage has none of the usual features—they rather like each other, for example. It's a kind of formalized friendship. Admirable in its way.")

Greene had recently arrived from southern France, where he now spent much of the year in the company of a French woman called Yvonne, who rarely came with him to Capri. "Graham hates being coupled with anyone," Vera said. "In any case, he still has a wife back in Oxfordshire. Poor old dear." I wondered if he spent much time in England. "Good lord, no," she said. "England appalls him. The rain, the food, the people. He despises France, too. Capri is another matter. He likes it well enough to visit, once or twice a year. But nowhere is home. He prefers it that way. Mysterious old Graham."

In the sitting room at about seven, I was introduced to Greene, Austen, and Vidal by Grant, who called me "his American assistant." Vera added that I had become a member of the family, adding that I wrote poetry.

"I used to write poetry," said Vidal. "Somehow the idea of having no readers was disconcerting." He glanced at me. "Voluntary readers, that is—not the sort of readers who get assigned a book in school." The novel, he suggested, was fading as fast as poetry had in the past decades. "I don't think anyone wants novels anymore, not even your novels, Rupert. Sorry to be the bearer of bad news."

Vidal was tall, physically imposing, with an angularly handsome face designed to grace magazine covers. Having once studied ballet, he retained something of the dancer's poised way of carrying himself, keeping his center of gravity in just the right place. This was quite the opposite of Greene, who had never lost his English schoolboy's slump. A lanky man in his sixties, with meticulously combed but thinning hair, he seemed to shy away from me when I shook his hand. His nose—the snout of a drinker—was blue-veined, fleshy, and rose-tinted.

I sat next to Vidal, with Greene on the opposite side of the table beside Howard, a short, barrel-chested man with a Bronx accent and a warm, outgoing manner. He smoked an American cigarette, blowing the smoke away from the table. Marisa had been seated at my other side, while Holly was next to Greene. She looked ethereal in a pale blue dress that would have suited a nun; it swept below her knees, with her blond hair freshly washed and shampoo scented. Greene was entranced by her, and it was difficult for Grant to get his attention, although he made several attempts.

Maria Pia, assisted by her cousin Alfredo, brought course after course to the table. An older man called Gabriele, in a white jacket, was employed to keep everyone's wineglass full, and he worked assiduously at this task, which in the case of Vidal and Greene was no small assignment. Bottle after bottle of Corvo was opened and emptied as we ate.

There was gossip about various local worthies, including the Bismarcks and Bonanos, all of whom both Vidal and Greene knew quite well. Grant talked more freely about his book on Capri than I'd ever seen him do before, describing the shape and content of the book. There was talk of the British Labour government, which Grant seemed to despise (much to the annoyance of both Vidal and Greene). Then, inevitably, the subject I most dreaded came around: Richard Nixon and the Vietnam War. Kent State was mentioned. Greene and Vidal joined forces against Grant, and appeared to silence him. They had trunkloads of facts stored in their formidable brains, and Grant had not troubled to find out much about the war. He unleashed a few lines about "the domino effect," but these were swept aside by Greene, who delighted in baiting Grant. I remained avowedly on the sidelines, praying that an angel would soon pass over the roof of the Villa Clio, bringing conversation on this uncomfortable subject to a halt.

Without warning, Vidal turned to me. "And why aren't you in Vietnam?" he asked, arching an eyebrow. "I would have thought you were about the right age for cannon fodder."

No question could have been less welcome, and I swiveled toward Vera.

"What an awful question," she said. "Leave the boy alone, Gore."

"He isn't in Vietnam because he's in Capri," said Grant, crushing a piece of bread into the sauce on his plate. "It's one of the laws of physics. If you're here, you can't be there."

"I liked Vietnam in the fifties," said Greene, intercepting Vidal. "Met Ho Chi Minh once, a sly little chap. Yellow toenails. Rather clever." He swept everyone's attention into a small bag. "Amusing, too. Spoke lovely French—the old boy studied in Paris. He arranged for me to fly over Hanoi in a small plane during the French war. There was rocket fire, and it grazed one wing, but I never really thought we'd go down. I wouldn't try it now. The North Vietnamese have extremely accurate ground-to-air missiles, I'm told. Russian-made. Quite deadly."

"You were never in a plane over Hanoi," said Vidal. "That must come from one of your books."

Greene relished this challenge. "Nonsense, Gore. I've been over Hanoi a number of times, in various aircraft. I quite liked Hanoi—some charming old colonial architecture. The Americans will see to that, I suppose."

"Did you visit the opium dens?" Vidal asked.

Greene nodded. "And the brothels. I'd go back in a second."

"Tell Mr. Nixon. He's looking for a few good men. Put you right up front with the infantry."

"I'd be fighting for the other side, I'm afraid."

"No wonder they never gave you the Nobel, Graham," Grant observed.

"I don't want their bloody prize."

"Neither do I," said Vidal. "I already belong to the Diner's Club."

"Richard Nixon is a butcher," said Greene, still obsessing over Vidal's previous remark. "He belongs in a meat factory, not the Oval Office."

"Gore knows a lot about meat factories," said Austen, lighting another cigarette. A gold chain glistened on his neck.

"Be quiet, Howard."

"Fuck you," said Austen, smiling.

Grant shifted uneasily, stretching his back. "I can see no reason to object to this intervention on the part of your country, Lorenzo," he said, looking directly at me. "Someone has to stand up for something. It's a bloody awful world."

"Pax Americana, is that it?" Greene said. He chewed and talked at the same time. "You sound more and more like Kipling, Rupert. If you're not careful, they will appoint you Poet Laureate. No one has survived that fate, and that includes Tennyson."

"Tennyson bores me, but I don't mind Kipling," said Vidal. "*The Man Who Would Be King*—now that's a story I wish I'd written."

"I was talking to Rupert," said Greene.

Grant sipped his wine before talking—a way of controlling the pace of the conversation. "Grew up on Kipling," he said, side-stepping Greene. "First writer I ever really knew. Still go back to the early stories, *Plain Tales from the Hills*. Swift, clean, sturdy."

"I like the *Just So Stories*," said Holly.

"Me, too," said Greene, "but Kipling was a jingo, nonetheless. Rather an embarrassment at the end. The belief in empire, and so forth. A thing of the past, even then. Only America seems bent on acquiring one now. Shopping around for jewels to place in their crown. Talk about falling dominoes."

Grant was shaking his head. "You've been hoodwinked, Graham," he said. "You don't mean to tell me that the Americans actually want to control Vietnam? Why would anyone bother? It's a wretched place. No oil, no precious metals—not that I'm aware of."

"Empire is like any other lust," said Vidal. "After a while, any body will do."

"Not mine," said Austen.

"I rather admire Nixon," Grant said, playing the devil's advocate.

"So do I," said Vidal. "One rarely sees vice on this scale. It's inspiring. Only a great nation can support such maliciousness."

"Unpatriotic Gore," Vera put in.

"In fact, I'm quite patriotic," Vidal insisted. "Why else write about my country at such length?"

"They seem to have forgotten their history," Greene said.

Howard Austen was shaking his head. "The schools gave up a long time ago."

"The United States of Amnesia," said Vidal, who launched into a short history of the empire, beginning with the Louisiana Purchase and moving up through the acquisition of the Philippines. "It's an invisible empire now," he said. "We leverage the world with a dollar bill."

"People prefer it like that," said Austen. "You get the benefits of empire without having to exercise direct control. No cops running around with American flags on their helmets."

Holly, Marisa, and I watched the spectacle in silence, intimidated, with Vidal quipping away, with Greene making grand statements, with

Grant reflexively taking the opposing side. I hadn't thought of Grant as having reactionary politics, or any politics; but that evening he seemed a cross between Kipling and Churchill. At first, I'd been alarmed by the superior tone of the table. Then I realized that nobody here would go to the wall for an argument. One could say outrageous things in this company, testing them on the air, propositionally.

Vidal, in particular, seemed eager to try out various ideas, seeing how they would play in intelligent company. There was a solid core of belief there—a sense that America had betrayed its original democratic impulses, and that it had become a sham democracy, where only the rich have a say. All politicians, he claimed, were "bought men, controlled by their owners." He disparaged the two-party system: "We have only one party, the party of business. It has two wings, Republican and Democratic."

I waded in, gingerly. "It's still a fairly classless society."

Vidal laughed. "You don't really believe that?"

I did. The fact that I, for example, was the grandson of Italian immigrants on both sides meant something to me. I could not quite reconcile my own story with Vidal's appealing and ear-catching formulations.

"One day, you'll see that the Bank, as I call it, controls everything."

"I don't believe in conspiracy theories," I said.

Greene was smiling broadly. "Good chap," he said. "You mustn't let Gore badger you."

"He's a bully," said Austen fondly, lighting a cigarette.

"I grew up in Washington," Vidal said. "My grandfather was a senator. I've seen how the system works, and it's not pretty."

"You should run for office," said Vera.

"He has," Austen told her. "He lost."

"If I had won, it would have been a waste of my time."

"I thought, briefly, of standing for parliament," said Greene. "But Gore is right. It's the Beaverbrooks of the world who have their hands on the levers. I would have got lost in the system. Digested, rather."

"That would have been fun to watch," said Grant. "Like a rat going down the length of a snake."

"In the end," said Greene, "they shit you out."

Grant frowned. He didn't like the use of words like "shit" at the table, and later told me that Greene had never outgrown this adolescent streak. "Tell us your view of Vietnam, Lorenzo. You never answered Gore's perfectly fine question. Why didn't you go to Vietnam? Might they still come after you?"

I could hear the grandfather clock against the wall, with its slow fat tick. Maria Pia, in a black dress with white lace at the collar, was standing opposite, staring at me, aware—though she spoke no English—that I'd been put on the spot. The faces around me bobbed, unreal, in peculiar elongations of time. I was there and nowhere, vaguely aware of having drunk too much already—a glass of wine in the kitchen, and several more during the meal. I had eaten almost nothing, too excited by the company to care about feeding. Hunger seemed petty compared to the matters at hand and my wish to seize every conversational morsel.

Grant would not let me off the hook. "Perhaps you've already been to Vietnam? It's an odd system, isn't it? The typical tour of duty is what, a year or so?"

"A year," I said.

"So have you been there?" Austen asked me.

"My brother, Nicky, was in Vietnam," I said, moving from word to word carefully as one might step across a stream from wobbly stone to stone. I drew a big breath now. "He was killed."

Vera gasped.

Greene, too, looked very concerned. "How long ago did this happen?"

"Last winter," I said. "He was on a recognizance mission." I reached anxiously for water. "He stepped on a land mine."

"Bad luck," said Grant.

"That's one way of putting it," I said.

I had managed to acquire, for the first time, Holly's complete attention. Her eyes grew wide and glistened.

The table was frozen, and I found it unbearable. Rising, I excused myself. I rushed through the kitchen into the garden, trembling, and sat under an umbrella pine. It was sundown, and my eyes settled on a cloud of ferns, artfully untended. Below me, the sea moved through shelves of opaline translucence.

"Are you all right?"

I turned to see Holly beside me.

"Yes, thanks."

"I'm sorry about your brother," she said. "I had no idea."

"I shouldn't have mentioned it. Ruined the dinner party."

"No, you did the right thing. It brought the discussion, well—back to basics."

"We are basics."

"Yes, but you've been—closer—than most. Closer to the war, I mean."

"Nobody ever mentions the war here. Have you noticed?"

"It's not their war."

"Or yours."

"I'm part American," she said. "I feel some responsibility."

"Responsibility is good," I said, unable to conceal my annoyance.

While I was glad for Holly's attention, I could not suppress my anger. She had not, until this evening, showed more than a slight interest in my history. Now that she knew about my loss, I seemed interesting to her.

"One thing troubles me, Alex," she said, ignoring my irritation. "That time with Rupert, in his study. When he read and discussed your poem when I was present. It upset me afterward."

"It's a rotten poem."

"That's not my point. He just shouldn't have done that. It was cruel."

"I'm getting used to him."

"Everyone does, and that's a problem. He goes scot-free."

"He's a Scot," I said, making a feeble joke. "And he's a gifted man."

"What nonsense."

"You once thought him remarkable. I remember you saying it, after the birthday party."

"Everyone's remarkable, once you get to know them."

"I guess you are American," I said. "That sounds very democratic."

"I don't like to see Rupert treading on people, treating them like disposable objects."

I couldn't understand her turning on Rupert like this. "You and he are still friends, huh?"

"Of course," she said. "But I'm under no illusions."

She fell short of saying that I was under illusions, though I was. I had innocently apprenticed myself to him, and while part of me resisted, I still wanted to believe that, as an artist, he only did what was necessary in order to accomplish his work. If that meant cannibalizing the people around him, so be it.

A strong breeze lifted Holly's hair and riffled her dress, which in the evening light was diaphanous. Though angry, I still wanted to embrace her.

"Were you and your brother close?" she wondered.

"It was complicated," I said, not elaborating. I thought about what he wrote in that letter: "You probably can't have good without bad. Or peace without war. I have seen both of these famous opposites here, and they are the same when you dig deeper. Good and Evil. Peace and War. Nicky and Alex."

"I'm so sorry," she said, putting a hand on my shoulder. "If you ever want to talk about this, I'd be glad to listen."

"Thanks," I said. I wanted badly to kiss her, but refrained. It would have been unseemly.

Over Holly's shoulder, I noticed the shadow of a person beside a large hedge, barely distinguishable from the massive shadow of the bush itself. At first, I thought it must be Mimo. He had a way of making himself part of any scene like this. But I quickly realized it wasn't Mimo. It was Marisa, her hair like a black curtain, which she swept from her brow. When our eyes met, she pulled back into the shade, behind the bush, and I could for a moment imagine I had not seen her, and that life would be simple in the days to come. That was not, of course, a possibility. Not anywhere near the Villa Clio.

# PART FOUR

*ars longa*

*one*

———

It was early morning, the only time of day in July when I found it really comfortable to sit outside with a book. The sun sat like a red boulder on the eastern horizon, a warning that a hot day lay ahead. The sea was streaked with violet, still relatively cool. I leaned back on my cane chair under the lemon tree where Grant sat in the late afternoon. Like him, I wore a floppy straw hat, a castoff that Vera had given me.

I was reading *Love's Body*, the volume of provocative aphorisms arranged and recast by Norman O. Brown, the neo-Freudian guru-philosopher from Santa Cruz. Toni Bonano had lent it to me over lunch in the piazzetta the day before. Skeptical at first, I read it slowly, finding Toni's judgment sound. It was an exhilarating book, knitting a vast array of learning into a challenging, and provocative, pattern. I reread the opening lines: "Freud's myth of the rebellion of the sons against the father in the primal, prehistoric horde is not a historical explanation of origins, but a supra-historical archetype; eternally recurrent; a myth; an old, old story."

My own story preoccupied me now, but it was not so old. My situation had, in the past few weeks, changed dramatically. I had come to the island alone, uncertain, and full of turmoil that I could not quite manage. Despite having lived away from home for several years, I remained naive. ("A virgin," as Vera said, "in all but body.") Now three women—Holly,

Marisa, and Toni—occupied my thoughts in various ways. And there was Patrice, who continued to pine after me, sighing wistfully in my presence (though his affair with Giovanni had helped relieve the intensity of that situation).

Toni and I had met several times, yet I still didn't know where the relationship was going. She mentioned, during our picnic on Mount Solaro, that she'd been "seeing" someone "at home," meaning New York City. His name was Jason, and he was an architecture student at Yale. (A badly herniated disk had kept him out of the army, she explained.) Her parents, for one reason or another, were not so keen on Jason. (Dominick considered him a snob.) Toni herself was undecided. "You have to trust your instincts," I said, enjoying the aura of generosity and good sense created by such a statement. I was simultaneously relieved to hear that she had a boyfriend and reassured that it was not an irrevocable commitment. We were, for the moment, "just friends," but I wondered if this might change, knowing that friendships between men and women often deepened into something more intimate.

The situation with Marisa was more complicated. She had become more difficult than ever, sitting silently through meals, avoiding me in the garden or, more unnervingly, confronting me about my fickleness. "I am sad when thinking of you, Alessandro," she said, leaning into the window of my cottage one afternoon, her elbows on the sill. "You are so selfish all the time, thinking of only yourself."

She was right, though I refused to think of myself in those terms, and was always shocked when any notes were sounded not already in my tonal self-assessment. I had certain ideas about myself that were inviolable. I was nice. I was a good person. I meant well. At the very least, I did no harm. Yet somehow I had to reconcile Marisa's comment, which must have sprung from genuine feelings.

I pushed her from my mind, however. Holly remained the focus of my fantasies, the object I coveted, the one whose company I sought. I was hobbled by desire in her presence, transformed into a halting nincompoop. Needless to say, I envied Grant's access to her, and was angered by her attentions to him. What she saw in him, as a sexual partner, baffled me. He was an old and wrinkled man. There could surely be no gratification there? I understood that he provided a kind of mentorship for her as a writer, and when I realized that he was reading her manuscript one afternoon—I saw it on his desk, the margins full of comments and suggestions—I was, if anything, relieved. This made sense. But I still didn't understand the sexual angle, and Holly was not the sort of person with whom one could discuss such things.

One night, after everyone had gone to bed, I heard a splash in the pool while sitting in my cottage. Curiosity got the better of me, and I crouched behind a manicured privet hedge to spy on whomever. It was Holly swimming by herself. She floated on her belly in the water, doing what we used to call a dead man's float. I strained to get a better view of her, and my breath caught when I realized that she was naked. Her ass was lovely, white against the tanned lower back and sleek upper thighs. Her legs seemed impossibly long. When she flipped onto her back, her small breasts were white as well, poking through the water. Her blond hair fanned out around her head. I could see a tantalizing wedge of pubic hair.

I wanted her desperately, but my desire felt hopeless until the night of the dinner with Vidal and Greene, when Holly had seemed to revise her opinion of me. I was now a person to pity, someone to add to her collection of interesting types. Not a sexual partner, perhaps, but a person worthy of her attention. Whereas I had barely attracted her notice before, she now asked me questions, wondering what courses I had taken at Columbia, how I felt about the antiwar activities there, and what part I had played in them. (My SDS membership had clearly impressed her, though I neglected to say how inactive a member I had been.) She told me excitedly that she had once participated in a march on the American embassy in Grosvenor Square, and had almost been arrested. Her boyfriend at the time, a Rhodes Scholar from Connecticut whom she called Granger (presumably his first name), had actually spent a night in custody for kicking a bobby in the groin. ("Granger was a pacifist" she added, incongruously.)

Much to my discomfort, Vietnam became a subject of debate at the Villa Clio, especially with Vera and Holly, who prodded me with questions about the war, as though I must be an expert because my brother had been killed there. Grant, who continued to maintain that the war was a necessary evil—though he'd never known war at firsthand—sat stony-faced throughout our discussions or made sharp, ironic statements calculated to put us in our place.

Grant startled me that morning in the garden, approaching from behind while I was deep in *Love's Body*. I shuddered and looked up.

"It's bad luck about your brother," he said, squatting next to me. "I lost a brother in North Africa."

I raised my eyebrows.

"Nigel was an officer, under Monty. Rommel got him—anti-artillery fire."

I expressed sympathy but still felt embarrassed, having been caught under his special tree in one of his straw hats.

"It's a shitty thing to happen," he said.

That understatement would, two months ago, have enraged me; by now, I simply took his manner for granted. It was a tone upon which an empire had been constructed. No obstacle was too large, no defeat too numbing. Everything—even disaster—was taken for granted, viewed as part of a larger scheme that spelled eventual success. It was the same approach that had put Grant, after many setbacks, somewhere near the top of the heap of writers from his generation.

"What was his name, your brother?" Grant asked.

"Nick," I said.

"You were close?"

"Fairly," I said, not wishing to lay out the complications of our relationship.

"Bad luck," he repeated.

"War seems to increase the amount of bad luck people have," I said, unable to conceal some irritation. "Bad luck" seemed dismissive, although I understood that it played differently to British ears. On the other hand, I liked the fact that Grant was being friendly with me, aggressively so. He was showing genuine sympathy: a feature I had not found in abundance at the Villa Clio.

"You're doing a good job, Lorenzo," he said, his tone like that of a platoon leader singling out a particular soldier. "Just thought you might want to know that."

"Thanks."

"You don't intrude," he added. "One doesn't like intrusions."

"Thanks," I repeated.

"The last boy, Edgar—from Twickenham—he was no good at the typewriter. Made a lot of mistakes. Your copy is clean. No mistakes, grammar, and so forth."

I had actually hoped for more, but accepted this bantamweight and garbled praise without comment. Despite my complaints, there were many reasons to be grateful to Rupert Grant. He had broadened my scope, dropping books and suggestions into my lap. His work in "correcting" my drafts of the Suetonius had proved useful. My prose had become noticeably swifter, cleaner, and more sure-footed. The one thing that still languished was my poetry.

"Were you close to your brother?" I asked.

"Not so much," he said. "One hardly got to know one's family in those days. Sent to prep school in Sussex, far too early. Seven years old. Nigel went to a school in Hampshire."

From Vera, I had learned something of Rupert's family and childhood. His mother, from an English family who owned a large country house near Carlisle, had died when he was four, of liver cancer. His father, who never remarried, had been a successful lawyer in Edinburgh. That Grant retained a trace of Scots in his accent was a tribute to his fierce stubbornness: Scottish children sent to English public schools were not supposed to hang on to their burr. His first wife, whom he met in London during the war, had been the daughter of an English baronet. "Rupert was always climbing in those days," Vera said. Apparently it took exile on Capri—and the safety net of Vera's family fortune—to put him at ease, socially. "Even so," she said, "he doesn't really get around much. His life is really his work, as you've seen. It's a bit of a bore, for me. I should have married a lad." By this, I believe, she meant that she should have married someone who liked to go to parties.

Grant stood now, gradually unfolding upward, his knees cracking. "Bloody old knees," he said. He folded his arms and cleared his throat, suggesting that he had something further to say. His facial muscles twitched. As I knew, he often prefaced significant remarks with a slight reshuffling of the throat's mucous layers. The twitching meant that what he had to say was important but difficult. I helped him by shutting the book on my lap and saying nothing. That silence provided enough draft so that his words could be sucked out.

"I rather thought you should know that I've asked Marisa to leave."

"What?"

"Marisa will leave us. She hasn't worked out terribly well, her research. She's a lazy girl, as you will have noticed."

"She tries."

"Tries what? Her assignment was to find material on Capri. I sent her to the Cerio archives. But for what? She's done nothing. Spends most of her time by the pool. It's distracting for everyone."

"This is my fault," I said.

"Actually, Lorenzo, it has nothing to do with you."

"It does," I said. "We have made love."

Grant smiled. "Oh, dear," he said, feigning shock. "I assumed it was just fucking."

"I don't get it," I said.

"That doesn't surprise me. You're a young man, and you're an American. The combination is lethal."

"I'm not as stupid as you imagine."

"I don't imagine anything. You have done a good job for me. You are pleasant company, for the most part. And you don't intrude."

"Glad to be of service," I said, amazed that sleeping with one of his concubines did not count as an intrusion.

"Don't upset yourself over this, Lorenzo. Really, there is no point. I've made up my mind. But given your attachment to the girl, I thought you should hear it from me."

"Kind of you," I said.

Perhaps to comfort me, he said, with a biblical intonation, "This, too, shall pass."

I thought for a moment, then asked: "So when will she be going?"

"She and I have yet to discuss the details."

His lack of generosity toward Marisa upset me, and I was tempted to make a bold gesture and resign, believing that her precipitous loss of stature in Grant's eyes was closely related to her affair with me. I was also annoyed by his self-centeredness, his conviction that everyone was at his disposal.

"I'm not shoving her out the door," he added, seeing that I was upset.

"Marisa cares about you," I said.

He frowned. "She is a young and silly girl. You mustn't be sentimental, especially when it comes to girls."

"She likes it here."

"There's nothing for her on Capri," he said. "You don't know anything about her, Lorenzo. Her life is in Naples." He saw my eyes cloud over and grabbed my wrist. "You needn't worry. She will dazzle them in years to come. I recognize her abilities: she's quite clever in her way. This whole thing is my fault, not yours. I made the initial mistake by hiring her. I hadn't thought out the consequences."

With that, he left me alone under the tree, upset and uncertain. I had a terrible feeling about Marisa, and was not so sure about myself. Closing my eyes, I found myself thinking about Pennsylvania, juxtaposing Grant with my father. On the surface, the differences between them were beyond calculation. Grant was thoroughly cosmopolitan and seemed to have read every author since Homer. He had been to Oxford, and he knew everybody who was anybody from Auden to Alec Guinness and Noel Coward. He had been awarded the Queen's Medal for poetry, and (like any self-respecting bard) had refused the job of Poet Laureate. His name had recently been floated as a candidate for the Nobel Prize, but his conservative politics reduced the chances of his actually getting the award. My father, by contrast, had no formal education. He read nothing except the sports pages of the *Wilkes-Barre Record*. Beyond a small circle of builders in Luzerne and Lackawanna Counties, he knew few people. Yet my conversations with Grant and my father bore an eerie resemblance. In both cases, I felt that bridging the gap between them and me required a huge effort.

It was more difficult to think of my mother in relation to Vera. I didn't see the volatility in Vera that was my mother's stock-in-trade. Nor did she suffer from the insecurity that dogged my mother: an Achilles' heel inherited from her own mother, an immigrant from southern Italy who never adjusted to life in the New World, where the assumptions of peasant village life never quite applied. Yet Vera could, like my mother, be intrusive. She had prodded me about Toni Bonano, suggesting that we were ideally matched. "Don't make the mistake of reaching only for what you can't have," she said. "It's like in cooking. What's available—fresh and local—is always best." She claimed that Toni's mother adored me, and that Bonano himself found me extremely likable. "What's wrong with Toni?" Vera kept asking, as if anything were wrong with her.

It was obvious she thought I was queer, and that Patrice was my secret passion. "He's awfully dear," she would say, "but I shouldn't have thought him your type." She had nevertheless welcomed him to the Villa Clio with open arms, as if he *were* my boyfriend. It had recently infuriated me when she suggested I bring Patrice "as my date" to a party at the Bismarcks. "Eddie will understand," she said, slyly.

My mother never played games with me in the Vera manner. She preferred overt conflict, and would pit me against my brother or my father, often successfully. She appeared most contented when everyone swirled around her, snapping and bitching at each other. The faster we all spun, the calmer she became, as in the paradox of the wheel. Only Nicky seemed regularly disposed to shove a wrench into the spokes, bringing the whole display to a shrieking halt.

I rarely talked about my family in front of Grant, but once—prompted by Vera—I complained in his presence about my mother. "If it's not one thing, it's your mother," he said.

Slowly, I began to rethink Grant's witticism. Perhaps I was blaming my mother when the situation was more intricate that it appeared? My father had chosen to marry my mother for reasons of his own. He liked to appear the good guy, the gentleman; however, like everyone else in the world, he bore angers and resentments. He needed someone to carry these bad feelings for him, and my mother had proved an able vessel. She swarmed with grudges that might properly have been his, and was easily offended by his potential enemies. Even her eating seemed to keep him slim. ("Have another scoop of that ice cream," he would say, though the doctors had warned them both that her dietary habits could easily lead to an early death.) Her precarious health apparently balanced the scales in such a way that my father himself never missed a day of work in three decades due to illness.

My mother's letters arrived every week on Thursday or Friday, scribbled on blue U.S. airgrams, invariably folded in such a haphazard way that I could never open them without destroying some of the text. They began sweetly enough, but would soon degenerate into barely concealed accusations and complaints. She was "unwell" most of the time, alluding to her swollen feet, painful knees, breathlessness, high blood pressure, ringing ears, and palpitations. Nobody in the family took her problems seriously, though the doctors had warned her she might not have long to live. She herself (rather disingenuously) dismissed their concerns, saying that doctors had been predicting her demise for as long as she could remember. "If I live till you return from Italy," she wrote in early July, "I promise to bake your favorite cake: lemon poppyseed."

Apart from the fact that lemon poppyseed was actually *her* favorite cake, not mine, I disliked the veiled threat. If she were to die before I returned, I would feel guilty for the rest of my life. I might never recover from the sense of having killed my own mother. "The doctors say there is nothing I can do," she wrote. "I should probably try to lose a few pounds." A few pounds didn't begin to describe it. She needed to lose sixty or seventy pounds, and still she would seem obese to most people. What puzzled me was that one never saw her gorge herself, although she ate substantial meals (and her preferred foods were hugely high in fat) and nibbled constantly. She had been through the usual diets: the various high protein regimens, the grapefruit diet, the avocado diet, and so forth. They never worked because she ate whatever she pleased in addition to the special diet foods and supplements. To say that she ate between meals was misleading. She never wasn't eating. Her hand reached perpetually for something: nuts and candies, bits and pieces. She seemed to consume the world around her.

I addressed letters to my father and mother, aware that he might never read them. But I needed his presence in the greeting as a buffer, a way of making sure that my letters were not directly aimed at her. And I kept my revelations general. Often, I simply described various scenic spots on Capri and told of my excursions. I mentioned Patrice, in passing. I referred to Father Aurelio and mentioned that I had been to mass as well as confession. I talked about Vera's cooking, taking care to avoid over-praising her results. (That would only have been taken as criticism of my mother's cooking.) I wrote about Grant's obsessive writing habits and described his study in detail. Never once did I mention either Holly or Marisa; that would have made no sense, and only worried them. My first visits to the Bonano villa in Anacapri were elaborately chronicled, with close attention to the decor; again, I made no mention of their daughter.

Nor did I refer to Nicky in my letters home. Each of us in the family was grieving, but it seemed we could not help each other. We had failed Nicky in our separate ways, and there was no chance of repairing this now. Death was so frighteningly absolute, a high stony wall between the living and the dead that could not be crossed.

Nicky's funeral had been bizarrely impersonal, with that closed casket draped in a flag. The local VFW had sent a contingent of motley veter-ans to the cemetery, each of whom came to salute a war hero on that snowy morning in December, making assumptions about Nicky's atti-tude toward the war that I knew were false. As I knew from his letters, he did not think of himself as a hero, fighting for something called "free-dom." He often derided LBJ and the bureaucratic elite around him who had sent young Americans to intervene in a civil war they never them-selves understood. "One thing they don't seem to get," Nicky wrote, "was that the Chinese and the Vietnamese fucking *hate* each other." He also said, "the only dominoes falling around here are in the American bar-racks, where a bunch of bored guys got nothing better to do."

The priest at the funeral—a young fool recently attached to the parish—was annoyed by having to perform another ceremony so near to Christmas. His words of eulogy were generic, and he teetered on the brink of emotion only once, referring to the "great personal sacrifice that the Massolini family has made for freedom." I tried hard to suppress a grin, recalling Nicky's words in one letter: "Nobody in Nam thinks we're saving the world from anything. We know the truth, which is that powers above us and behind us push and pull. We're piss-ant pawns, moved about on this green jungle of a board. Looking for checkmate. So what if a few of us are lost in the game? It's only a fucking game."

One Sunday afternoon in late June, Grant and I took a walk together after lunch. On the way home, we stopped at the *cimitero acattolico,* where non-Catholic citizens of Capri, mostly foreigners, were buried. ("I shall lie here myself," he said, "and look forward to the day.") Among the many headstones that caught our attention was that bearing the sacred name of Norman Douglas, the novelist and natural historian who had lived most of his adult life on the island. Douglas had been a notorious pedophile, a sybarite who relished any form of sensual pleasure. He had also been a meticulous student of the region, and had devoted himself to the ecology of Capri, urging its preservation and planting countless trees over many decades. On a dark slab of *verde serpentino* marble that marked his grave were the words of Horace: *Omnes eodem cogimur.* We are all driven to the same place.

Thinking of Nicky, I had taken comfort in those words. A cold comfort, perhaps, but something that would sustain me in the days ahead, when I'd need every resource I could muster.

*two*

———

Marisa stood in the doorway of my cottage, wearing a large purple hat—the sort that English women wear to weddings—with a brim that shaded her face. She also wore dark glasses to hide what I assumed was the redness of her eyes.

I had rarely seen her in the past few days, as she avoided meals at the villa—a final affront to the Grants, for whom the dining table was a primary scene where their secular liturgy was enacted beneath a huge Neapolitan clock that ticked slowly and loudly. Nobody was going to kick her out, and it struck me as perfectly possible that Marisa might linger, awkwardly, for a month or two, just to make Grant's life miserable.

Now Marisa lurched toward me, smelling of wine. "Do I visit you again, Lorenzo? I will come tonight, if you say it. You have made love so nicely to me, I don't forget."

"I'd rather you didn't," I said.

"You have not found me sexy?" Her voice was plaintive, childlike, and her lips formed a kind of pout. "I have remember this night forever, you sexy man."

"I liked being with you, too," I said.

She shook her head. "Vera has told me the truth about you."

"And what's that?"

"You have love this Patrice, the French boy. Is this what you want? A boy to love?"

I suppressed a cynical smile. Could Vera have really stooped this low? It seemed unlikely.

Marisa persisted. "So you are sad that he has denied you. I can understand you on this. We have much in common."

"I don't want to sleep with Patrice."

"Or Toni, the American girl?"

"We are friends," I said, "and that's it."

"You are lying. I have seen you having lunch to her in the piazzetta. She is very beautiful, and I am not ignorant."

I just shook my head.

"Please, I am sorry about this, Lorenzo." She took off her sunglasses and wiped her eyes. "I have not been so easy to you, I understand. Forgive this."

I felt sad, but could not explain my feelings to her. I could not explain them to myself.

"You are beautiful, too," I said. I touched her cheek with my fingertips, as though she were a piece of marble statuary.

"Don't you touch me!" she said, slapping away my hand. "Don't you think to touch me again!"

She turned and walked away, a mystery. And I felt an ache inside, aware that I wanted her again. I thought of calling her back, saying, "Yes, please come tonight! I will be waiting for you!" But I knew my own heart well enough to understand that I would be faking a kind of affection I didn't own. That was the worst kind of lie, and it would have been cruel. What I had already done was cruel enough, and there was no point in compounding my crime.

*three*

———————

"You've hurt Marisa's feelings," said Holly, coming upon me in the garden late one afternoon. I was about to walk along the Pizzalungo—a wild scarp of land that swirled around Mount Tuoro, with its pine thickets and pink jagged rocks dominating the southeast region of Capri from the Grotta di Forca to the Grotta di Matromania.

"She told you that?"

"She said you were rude to her."

"I didn't mean anything."

"You didn't mean," she echoed, shaking her head. "You don't like her anymore? Is that it?"

"I like her fine," I said. It was an awkward admission. I certainly bore no ill feelings toward Marisa, but I didn't want her as a lover. That was preposterous, although I had behaved abominably, in a way that embarrassed me and frustrated her. "It's not that kind of relationship."

"What kind is that?"

I wondered if she was being coy. "We're not really lovers," I said.

"Lovers," she repeated, neutrally, as though adding to her vocabulary in a foreign language. In truth, I adored hearing her say that word, and wondered if it might ever be used to describe us.

"I'm going around the Pizzalungo," I said. "Would you like to come?"

"I suppose. Why not?"

"In another words, you have nothing better to do."

Holly gave me one of her quizzical looks, wrinkling her nose and draw-ing her eyes slightly together. I liked the way her eyebrows dipped toward the center. Her forehead was smooth and shiny, and her hairline formed a slight widow's peak—a feature that appealed to me immensely. "I'd actually like to take a walk with you, and it's not so complicated as you make out. You turn everything into a little drama, don't you?"

"Maybe I should write plays?"

Holly sighed. I could see that my self-obsession was boring, and I vowed to change. I must stop thinking about myself, about my writing, about the effect I was having on people. Life at the Villa Clio had worked its evil magic on me, and I was becoming someone I didn't like.

"Have you been to the Punta di Massullo?" she asked.

"I don't think so."

"There's a house there, the Villa Malaparte. You must see for your-self."

On the way, she told me about Curzio Malaparte, whose name was unfamiliar to me. The son of a wealthy Milanese mother and a German manufacturer, he had changed his name from Kurt Erik Suckert to Curzio Malaparte as a young man in his late twenties, in 1925. As a sol-dier in the First World War, he had proved himself as a warrior, winning a Croix de Guerre from the French government. He became a journalist, a newspaper editor, and a famous novelist, author of *Kaputt* and *La Pelle*. During the thirties, he formed a close friendship with Mussolini's daugh-ter, Galeazzo, who spent a good deal of time on Capri. While visiting her, he discovered the Punta di Massullo, a harshly beautiful promontory overlooking a small inlet. Malaparte bought the land from a farmer for the equivalent of a week's stay at the Quisisana, and used the influence of Il Duce's daughter to get permission to build there, despite local oppo-sition. He commissioned the modernist architect, Adalberto Libera to build the villa, but it was not completed until 1949, by which time the shape-shifting and opportunistic Malaparte had switched his allegiance from fascism to socialism, with a distinctly Maoist tinge.

We followed an obscure byway from the main path around the Pizza-lungo to the Punta di Massullo, at times climbing on all fours over steep rocks to get to the point itself. I was afraid of heights, and the sheer drop-off to the sea made me dizzy. I paused, leaning against a large oak.

"Are you all right?" Holly asked.

I liked her concern—a lot. "Yes," I said. "A little dizzy."

"Look," she said, pointing.

The bizarre villa, with its sharp, futuristic angles, was suddenly visible, large and unlike anything else on Capri. Steps swirled to a rooftop solarium with a white, saillike curve of brick. The villa was said, by its owner, to be "sad, harsh, and severe," like himself; it seemed wholly incongruous there, a piece of ultra-modernist sculpture dropped from the heavens and snagged on this ledge at a precarious angle. Its severity was thrilling and revolting at the same time.

"It's pure Malaparte," said Holly. "*Un po matto*, would you say?"

"I rather like it," I said. "Another of the sons of Tiberius."

"Worse, from what I've heard."

We approached the villa respectfully, as one might a pyramid, then climbed the steep stairs to the door. It opened with a slight push, the lock having obviously been broken.

"Maybe Curzio's home," I said.

Holly shivered. "Don't say things like that."

Inside, the bare living room (it had been stripped by looters at least a decade before we arrived) swept toward the southeast, with the Faraglioni visible through binocularlike windows. The sea below had by now acquired a coppery tint in the late afternoon light, which shone on the concrete floors. The walls glowed with a silvery hue, and there was green mold growing in vertical lines from floor to ceiling. The ceilings themselves were high, mottled with broken plaster. I could not imagine living in such a space.

Holly told me that guests at the Villa Malaparte included Jean Cocteau and Albert Camus, both of whom admired Malaparte's fiction. "Nobody lives here," she explained, "because of the will. When Malaparte died, in the late fifties, he left the house to the Chinese government. It was to become a retreat for Maoist writers. But the Italians contested the will, and it's still in limbo."

"I feel him," I said. "Malaparte's ghost. And it's not alien. He wasn't a bad man." Weirdly, I felt quite sure of that. Malaparte had been through many incarnations in one life, eventually finding his balance. The spirit of the house was calming.

"He died a Catholic," she said, "and a socialist."

I grunted approval. This information confirmed my sense of Malaparte. I could not have felt at ease with the ghost of a fascist. Then again, I wondered if it was Malaparte's opportunism that appealed to me. He apparently seized what opportunities lay before him, and shifted to accommodate himself to his surroundings, however threatening or complex.

Holly and I stood for a while at the round windows, watching a tanker in the distance as it cruised southward. I was startled by her hand, which had unobstrusively moved around my lower back. Her right thumb wedged in the back pocket of my jeans. In response, I let my left arm rise around her shoulder, tipping my head toward her. But this gesture only seemed to spook her, and she quickly removed her thumb, turning away from me awkwardly.

*Ora pro nobis, Malaparte,* I whispered to myself. *Ora pro nobis.*

*four*

Nigel and Nicola arrived on a blind-
ing-bright morning on the ferry from Naples, a girl of sixteen and a boy
of fifteen who looked shockingly alike. They were not twins, but nobody
could doubt they were products of the same union. Lanky as their parents, with sharp blue-gray eyes, they were indistinguishable from a distance. Nicola seemed not to have the slightest trace of female sexuality,
although close inspection revealed small breasts and slightly enlarged
hips. Nigel was like an arrow, straight and fledged with thick yellow hair
like that of his sister, worn long and parted in the middle. They both
wore khaki shorts, white shirts, and sandals without socks.

"Isn't it darling? They wish they were twins," said Vera, as they
approached. "But they're rather hard work."

More hard work, I thought. It relieved me to hear they would be gone
from the island in five weeks or so. Back to the Hundred Acre Wood.

The children were eager to see Grant, but they would have to wait
until lunch. As they understood, he would never break from his writing
until just before one. This was a boundary he kept resolutely in place,
though he hadn't seen his children for several months. I remarked on the
oddity of this to Vera, but she dismissed the idea that anything was
strange about it. "It's important for them to remember who he is," she
said. "It's part of who they are."

The fact that Nigel and Nicola looked alike faded quickly, since their
affects were entirely opposite. He was moody and ironic, casting his

scorn in random directions. Nicola radiated energy and optimism, and had brought a thick portfolio of art work recently completed, which she laid out for everyone to see—a dozen pastel watercolors of damp English gardens. There seemed always to be a cathedral spire in the distance.

Nicola's portfolio was discussed over lunch. Vera and Holly enthused over the pictures, while Nigel maintained that "nothing serious was ever conceived in watercolors." He admitted to a "certain restraint" in the pictures that he admired, but recommended that she "lose the spires." Grant—who hadn't seen the portfolio yet—merely grunted, although one could see that he adored Nicola when she kissed his broad forehead and called him Daddy. Marisa put in a rare appearance, sitting gloomily through lunch, then disappearing to her room afterward. ("On the bloody rag?" wondered Nigel.) Holly, who had befriended Nicola during their last school holiday, chatted amiably about the latest exhibition at the Tate, a retrospective on the career of Henry Moore. "I adore Moore," she said.

"I used to see a lot of Moore," said Grant. "What an unpleasant fellow."

This set the table aflame, and soon the conversation swirled around the question of what part character played in the quality of an artist's work. Holly was quite firm, saying that a painter's moral stature was evident in each brush stroke. Vera sided with her. I, impulsively, took the opposite side, arguing that Caravaggio, Titian, and Picasso were no paragons of personal virtue. I said that, where writers were concerned, there was less connection between the quality of the work and the artist. Joyce, for example, was self-centered and inconsiderate.

"Joyce was a minor figure," said Grant. "Were it not for American academics, he would have disappeared from sight ages ago."

"Oh, Daddy," said Nicola, with a scorn that reeked of admiration.

"Pater is right," said Nigel. "The Irish are always overrated."

Grant nevertheless approved of my argument. "The life and the work are not related," he said. "Or if they're related, it's in ways no critic could ever fathom."

Nicola interrupted him: "I think one sees the personality of an artist

in the line itself, the firmness of character. That's why I think Michelan-
gelo must have been a lovely man."

Nigel acquired a mocking expression. "A lovely man? I can't believe
I've come all the way from England to listen to this pseudy shit," he said,
the word "shit" rhyming with "kite." It was a peculiar affectation of his,
the distortion of certain key words so that he sounded hip. "Tell us the
local gossip, Mummy. Who is bonking who?"

"Whom, darling," said Vera. "Who is bonking whom?"

"Bonk?" I asked. The word was unfamiliar to me.

"It means fuck in your bloody language," said Nigel.

"Lorenzo is a civilized American," Grant explained.

"Is it possible?" wondered Nigel.

"You must ignore my son," Vera said to me. "He puts great store by his
sophistication, but he's just a schoolboy."

"Good for Mummy," Nicola said.

With a mildly scolding air, Vera cautioned: "Be nice to Alex, both of
you. We consider him part of the family."

"I'm always nice, Mater," said Nigel.

I had never experienced anything quite like the Grant children, with
their adult mannerisms and glorious looks. Young Nigel, in particular, was
ethereal, with classic English features, although his straight teeth were
anomalous in an English mouth. His nose was long and straight. His
voice had recently lowered, hovering uncertainly on the brink of maturity, and occasionally squeaking. He slouched a bit, forcing his shoulder
blades to poke through his T-shirt. His sandals exposed large toes, which
he tended to wiggle whenever he spoke.

Nicola was also straight-toothed and straight-nosed. Like her mother, she
was desperately thin, but strong. Without intention, she was sexy in a boyish, innocent way. There was something preternaturally wise in her steady
gaze: a sense of balance that, as I soon learned, was a kind of emotional
falsework put up, like scaffolding, while the building itself was under construction. It could not have been easy for a young girl, on the cusp of full
sexual maturity, to have a father like Grant, who slept casually with girls
who could easily be his own daughters, although I could not be sure exactly
how much the children knew about their father's intimate arrangements.

"Who are you sleeping with around here," Nigel suddenly asked me, over coffee.

"Be still, Niggy," his mother said.

"Infy! Infy!" he bellowed, pounding the table. This was apparently a bit of school slang that nobody else understood.

"He's very rude," Nicola said, "but his friends at Charterhouse are worse. That whole Carthusian lot should be taken into the woods and shot."

"I simply want to know who is bonking whom," Nigel said.

"I'm bonking nobody in this room," I said. "It's unpleasant, but true."

Holly looked at me briefly, then dipped her eyes. I detected a faint smile on her lips.

"Jolly well said, Lorenzo," Grant observed.

"I'm writing poems, Pater," Nigel said.

"Not homoerotic love poems, I hope? Carthusian speciality, that," Grant said. He was himself an Old Carthusian, and in *Play the Game*—a memoir of his schooldays—he'd confessed to a homoerotic attachment to a boy called Aleric, two years his junior. ("Now a cabinet minister," as he liked to say.)

"I'm hetero to the hilt, Pater," said Nigel. "It's an affliction, as you know."

"Good chap," he said.

Vera clapped her hands over her ears. "I don't need to listen to this. You're all mad, the lot of you."

Indeed, they were. I realized that the entire Grant clan, including Vera, was mad.

Now Maria Pia came into the dining room with an urgent expression. She whispered in Vera's ear, looking in my direction. There was apparently a telephone call for me from America, where by my calculations it was early in the morning, well before breakfast.

"Take it in the library," said Vera.

This was a peculiar time for anyone to attempt to reach me by phone, and I knew something was wrong. As yet, I had not received a single call from home, and it was unlike my parents to attempt such a thing unless there was an emergency.

## *three*

***

"Hello?"

"Is that you, Alex?"

"Dad! Is anything wrong?"

"How ya doin' over there, in Italy?"

"I'm fine. I just didn't expect to hear from you. Is something the matter?"

"I was trying to get through for some time. The operator, she didn't know from squat."

"The Italian phone company is terrible. And Capri is an island—it's like another country. The wires have to go under water from Naples."

"You don't sound too far away."

"Really?"

"Well, you do. There's like an echo or something. I keep hearing you twice."

"I *am* far away."

"Hey, tell me about it. I been there, remember? But that was a long time ago, thank God. I guess it's changed in the meantime. That's what they say."

"So what's going on, Dad?"

"I don't want to worry you or anything, being a long way from home like this."

"Just tell me what's going on, okay? Is Mom all right?"

"Not too bad, given the situation. It's her heart, Alex. The doctors aren't too happy about it."

"What's happened?"

"She hasn't been good these past couple weeks. This isn't like a sudden situation or anything. Don't jump the gun on me."

"Did she have a heart attack?"

"I wouldn't say that."

"You can tell me the truth, Dad. Is she dead or something?"

"Alex, please. Don't say that."

"You're making me nervous. It's like you never come to the point."

"She's not dead, I swear. That's not the problem."

"But she had a heart attack?"

"They think so."

"Who does?"

"The doctors. It's not so easy to tell."

"Where is she? In the hospital?"

"Intensity unit."

"Jesus. Should I fly home?"

"I asked Dr. Ciongoli. He said no. Tell him not to worry, he's a long way from home over there. It's just the arteries. I guess they ought to be pumping better or something. She has chest pain—runs right up her arms and down her fingers. And her breath is kind of short. As long as she don't get up . . ."

"That doesn't sound good."

"But she's definitely alive, Alex. They have medicine for that."

"I'm worried, Dad. This sounds dangerous."

"I didn't mean to call. But your mother thought . . ."

"She asked you to call, right?"

"She said, whatever you do, don't tell Alex."

"So you called?"

"You know Mom. She probably would have called herself, but they got tubes in her throat. She never complains, it's amazing. She's a good woman."

"Maybe I should come home, Dad."

"Don't be nuts. It's a long way, and it wouldn't make a damn bit of difference. She's got more doctors around her bed than I got bills to pay."

"I'm glad you called."

"Hey, I wanted you to know. Your mother and you are pretty close. You always were."

"Dad, I think I should come home."

"I said don't bother, and I meant it. If there's a serious problem, I'll call back."

"So it's under control? Is that what you're saying?"

"To tell you the truth, Alex, she looks pretty good. I mean, for a woman in intensity. I spoke to her on the phone a little while ago. She was hungry."

"That's a good sign."

"I agree. It's always better to be hungry. Especially in these situations."

"Yeah."

"So what about you? You eating okay? I mean, there's a lot of spicy food over there, I guess. I remember it from the war. I never had such heartburn."

"I'm eating fine, Dad. How are you?"

"Good, Alex. I'm good."

"That's great, Dad. So tell Mom I'm worried about her. I'll come home in a minute if there's any need. I could get a flight from Rome. They leave twice a day."

"Hey, no need. She said the same thing herself. Tell him to stay there, she said."

"She said that?"

"Yeah. He's learning a lot of stuff. That's what your mother said, Alex."

"She's right, Dad."

"Good, Alex. That's good, good. I hope you're doing your work for that guy, the writer."

"Rupert Grant. Yes, I'm working hard."

"Terrific. We want you to finish your degree, as you know. Not to bring up a sore subject."

"Sometime. Not right away."

"I know, I know. I don't understand what you did, Alex. The way you quit, with only a couple months before graduation. But hey, what do I know?"

"I love you, Dad."

"Yeah. Me, too. We love you."

"Thanks. So you'll let me know if anything changes. Either way."

"Sure, Alex. I'll let you know. So long."

"Yeah, so long. And thanks for the call."

"Bye, Alex."

"Bye, Dad. Bye."

*six*

---

*Dear Asshole,*

*Weather is here, wish you were beautiful.*

*How are things in the Ivy League? You thought I'd forgotten you, didn't you, sweetheart? Well, it's me. Up to my hips in elephant grass and flies like B-52s.*

*Let me tell you a story. Last week I was assigned to your basic listening-post operation, with half a dozen other bastards, all of us loaded for bear but hoping we don't find any. The idea behind this kind of operation is simple: hang around with your mouth shut, your radio turned on, just listening. Find out what kind of crap is going down up there, the captain told us. Captain Francis Fogg. That's not made up. Captain Francis Fucking Fogg.*

*So Fogg sent us over the river and through the woods. At twilight, I gotta say, it was something to behold, that river. Like pure red blood. It had been lousy to wade, but amazing to look at. Even Black Jimbo Samuels, who is no orator, made a little speech. "Ain't seen no scenery like this before, not nowhere," he said. "It kind of make you forget about the war." Mickey Donato shook his head. "I'm gonna write for a fucking brochure," he said.*

*We went into the woods to make ourselves invisible. Camouflage, head to toe, with all kinds of black shit on our faces and hands. ("I don't need that shit on my face," Black Jimbo said. "Just don't smile," said Waller. He also said, "I don't want to see nobody waving. I don't want to hear nobody farting. We are the woods, man. We are bamboo-brained, with hearts of palm." I liked that a lot. Bamboo-brained, with hearts of palm, and I told him he got an A from me, the professor.*

*After a while, we came to a place where the trail turned into a big woods, with a canopy of trees, and tiny flowers in the bush below. The area smelled mossy and damp. The usual jungle racket seemed to subside here, get absorbed into the tangle. And it was getting dark fast. That's when Waller said to spread out along the trail somewhere, go as far as you want to, and spend the night. All by yourself in the dark. No mommy or daddy, he said. No night lights but the fucking moon and stars. If you can see them, and rots of ruck. (Waller's eloquence was not something you could rely on.)*

*So I said to myself, given the usual level of noise and the fact that you spend most of your time in close quarters with guys who in real life you wouldn't probably give the time of day, I decided to go a long way out. Walk to fucking Laos.*

*After maybe three hours, I found a cool spot under a humongous tree of some kind—I don't know one tree from the next out here—then I zoomed into a kind of trance. Was too excited to sleep: the jungle is like caffeine, the way it turns up the volume in your head. But I got a good trance going, and I began to think about home. About returning a goddamn hero or something like that. I go to visit the old high school—walk in like a big shot. Look at me now, I say to them. But then I realize that Time has bit a chunk out of everybody's ass. Those still hanging on look like shit—Mr. Donatello, Miss Lupinksi, Mrs. Rider. They have forgot my name. The principal doesn't know me from squat. So there was never any point in going back. In trying to prove anything. Never any fucking point.*

*Maybe I learned something here, something like Dad learned in Salerno but kept pretty quiet about all these years, though he once said to me that everything changed for him after Salerno. He said it was the central fact of his life, more important than everything before and most things after. This was like the last thing he said to me that night before I left for boot camp—like some kind of secret between us. I asked him to explain what he meant, and he said, "You'll get it, I know that."*

*And you know what? He was right. I've come to a place inside myself here, a quiet place, that only gets clearer and quieter as it gets messier and noisier around me. Do you follow me, Bro???*

*In any case, I'm just lying there, having Deep Thoughts, such as those just transmitted, when the parade begins. I mean, The Parade! First I hear a few voices, and I want to shit my pants. Then I realize it's not just a few folks walking by in black pajamas, but the whole goddamn army of North Vietnam. The Commie Party of the Entire World. I mean, I must have fallen asleep beside the Ho Chi Minh Trail or something because I never saw so many soldiers—old men, medics, maniacs, gooks and geeks galore. I mean one after the fucking other, hoof and mouth, the whole fandango. And everybody's got a Russian automatic or some Chink weapon that could do serious damage if they pointed it your way and pulled the trigger. In the dark—and it was so damn dark—*

*they might have been carrying sticks. Maybe I had fallen into a time warp, I thought, and this was the army of Genghis Khan?*

*If I'd sneezed or coughed, they'd have gunned me down on the spot. Or cut my dick off. Who knows? They seemed both scary and pathetic at the same time. Just a bunch of guys trudging through the jungle at night, going nowhere at a slow pace, following the leader like a bunch of ants, filing along the trail.*

*I must have fallen asleep, I don't know. The trudging had got to me—all those geeks like a long insect with a million feet. I didn't know if I'd ever get back to Waller, Mickey, Eddie Sloane and Fink O'Malley and Black Jimbo. But I figured those guys were dealing with the same shit, too. They were squatting in trees or bushes, watching the big parade that came out of nowhere. Or maybe the whole shabang was some kind of dream? I'd smoked some amazing shit that day. Hanoi Hash. I wondered if I was seeing the Army of North Vietnam or just having my worst trip ever.*

*In the moonlight, everybody looked like a ghost. The black pajamas disappeared, and it was loose, ghostly heads bobbing in the air, not smiling, not talking. Just walking. The whole world on foot. Old men and young men, middle-age men, even some women. I saw every shape and form in front of me, and I thought I recognized a few. I'd seen them before, back in Pittston. On the streets in Wilkes-Barre. Seen them on the Little League field and in the Catholic Youth Center in Scranton.*

*Maybe it was just the worst fucking dream I'd ever had? Anyway, by morning they were gone. The trail was empty, and sunlight sparkled on the cobwebs in the brush, and drops of dew glistened. Poetic, huh? I sipped at my canteen, ate some rations—the chocolate first—and waited. I didn't want any nasty surprises. And when I finally headed back, retracing my steps through the jungle, I walked more carefully than before. Waller said he didn't think the area was mined, but what did he know? He'd also said we were alone out there. So I stepped careful onto the path, trying to avoid Toe Poppers and Bouncing Bettys. Followed the same path that the population of North Vietnam had followed, the whole goddamn country, the night before. It was kind of easy, getting in line behind the rest. Maybe it was their turn, in broad daylight, to take to the bushes, and to watch me.*

*I found the guys under a banyan tree or some fucking thing with big ugly leaves and gummy roots that stank like a hog's breath. O'Malley and Donato were playing cards and whispering, since this was a listening post. Like in church or something. Waller was writing a letter to his wife, Susie. We all knew about Susie. Black Jimbo was picking his toenails. I didn't see Eddie Sloane or anybody else.*

"*I'm glad you guys are okay,*" *I said.*

*They looked up like I was nuts. And when I mentioned the parade, they looked skeptical. Donato said, "I didn't see nothing." Waller shook his head, with a shit-eating grin. No, said Fink, there was nothing down here. You probably ate something bad, and it was working its charms. Maybe you smoked too much. Nobody had seen a goddamn thing, and I wasn't going to argue about it. I mean, who am I to insist?*

*Vision is like that, right? I mean, you see something, and it's fucking fantastic—scary, beautiful, damned, whatever—and you don't dare tell anybody else about it. You keep it to yourself because that's where it lives best. Down and fresh, the dearest thing you know.*

*But here I am I'm telling you, asshole. So keep it to yourself.*

*Socrates*

*seven*

---

**W**hy do we always feel like idiots when talking to our parents, whatever our age? The phone call from my father had stripped away any maturity that may have accrued during the past few months. Like a child, I stood there trembling in the library of the Villa Clio, surrounded by books, fine paintings, and elegant furniture, while my father talked in that plaintive, rough, generous, confused, uneducated, endearing voice. He could hardly imagine the world I'd fallen into, with its peculiar traditions and resonances, its particular values, most of which could not possibly compute in terms he'd ever understand.

It was not that my valley in Pennsylvania didn't have its own traditions, resonances, and values. I knew and even admired them, but I felt the contrast now, and it wasn't merely that I assumed that Capri was more sophisticated than Pennsylvania. It was, perhaps, in its way; but it wasn't this contrast that I found disquieting. I remained an American-style egalitarian, ready to denounce old Europe's autocratic, class-ridden tendencies. Yet I understood that the world of Rupert and Vera Grant, with its ironies and cultural depths, dazzled me nonetheless, making it difficult for me to imagine going home.

It amused me to think of Rupert and Vera transported suddenly to Pennsylvania, and forced to understand, sympathize with, and manipulate the elements of that world. Much would have puzzled and appalled them. The humor would have seemed crude, unfunny. The aesthetic values would have passed them by. On the other side, my parents would have found Capri just as alien, a corrupt and jaded island full of snobs and dissipated intellectuals. This was definitely *not* the Italy my grandparents recalled and sentimentalized.

My father, on the phone, had seemed unreal, remote, enervated. A dead man talking. I felt sorrow and pity for him, as I always had. Never conscious anger. Unlike many sons in history (if Freud and Norman O. Brown were right), I'd never rebelled against him directly, though I'd experienced the usual urges along these lines. The circumstances of my life had simply not afforded them a place to root, and so my rebellion had become oblique.

Hearing echoes of myself in the plastic receiver, I too had sounded strange and unfamiliar—a thin, disembodied voice. A thing I refused to acknowledge as my own. I had tried to become a different person on Capri, more worldly and independent, and to some extent I'd succeeded. But my father had tapped into and elicited an earlier version of myself— a person I wanted to forget: the dutiful son, a placating and innocent and narrowly selfish creature. Growing up, my goal in life had been to raise no hackles and trample no toes. And especially not my mother's toes or hackles.

The day after my father called, my mother was taken out of the intensive care unit. I was able to phone her in the hospital that next afternoon, and we talked politely, though briefly. (The idea of talking on the phone "long distance" always panicked my parents, with their Depression-era mentality. The idea of talking transatlantic was totally unimaginable, an act of suicidal extravagance.) "Don't even think of coming home, Alex," my mother said, hoarsely. "If anything happens to me, there's nothing you can do anyway. It's not your concern."

I never believed these unselfish assertions. They were made only half in earnest, and I could hear a countermanding voice behind them, saying: "If anything happens to me, it's all your fault. My illness was brought on by your departure, your selfishness, and your thoughtlessness. You'd better get your ass on that airplane, pronto!" Then again, she meant what she said on some level. Her better self struggled with her lesser, although it was an unequal contest.

Yet I sympathized with her situation. On the surface, who wouldn't? The woman had recently lost a son in the war, and her feelings of guilt— there are always guilt feelings where the dead are concerned—were probably exacerbated by having failed him as a mother. What children most need, a feeling of parental confidence in their ability to succeed in the world, had been withheld from Nicky. And this was largely her doing. She had chosen me over him.

I put down the phone in a confused state, wiping tears away. Whatever the reality behind my mother's illness, I realized I was not going home. I would attend my mother's funeral, should one arise. But I was not going home.

"Is everything all right?" Vera asked, entering the library with a pot of tea on a tray only moments after I had hung up. Her timing was eerily precise, as if she'd been hovering outside the door.

"I guess so," I said, wiping my eyes.

"You were able to speak with your mother?"

I nodded. "She seems okay. Out of intensive care. You can't tell with her. It's hard to know." I decided against giving Vera a detailed medical history of my mother, though I knew it by heart. Everything from the varicose veins to the angina pains and tingling hands. I used to call home from Scranton Prep at lunchtime to get the latest numbers on her blood pressure as though trying to get the score in the World Series.

Vera sat beside me on the leather sofa beneath a large painting by Peter Duncan-Jones: a version of Duchamp's *Nude Descending a Staircase*, only this nude was all man, and very well hung, the penis replicated in various colors and sizes. She put the tray on a marble coffee table, then set to work in her matronly English fashion: pouring the tea through a strainer into china cups, adding milk and sugar, stirring with a Lilliputian spoon. She put a chocolate biscuit in the saucer beside the cup, having noticed that I liked them.

"Here you are, darling," she said.

I balanced the saucer gingerly on my lap.

"You must be terribly worried," she said.

"I don't think she's going to die or anything like that," I replied. "She wants to frighten me, and to make me feel guilty."

"My mother is a bore, too," Vera said. "Only I've ceased to listen. One simply turns down the volume at a certain point."

There was a long pause, during which I gathered myself together. Vera was surprisingly good at dealing with these situations: cool and terribly practical in her approach to problems. The stiff, blue winds of British empiricism blew through the Villa Clio, despite its soft Mediterranean setting.

"How are the children adjusting?" I asked, moving the subject to more comfortable ground. "I'm enjoying their company."

"What a good liar you are," she said. "No matter—I appreciate the gesture."

I shifted nervously, having been caught out. "I like young people," I said.

She put a hand on my knee. "Nigel, as you know, fancies himself a poet. I was rather wondering if you might take him under your wing a bit."

"Of course," I said.

"That would be marvelous, thanks. You might read his poems and comment. Take him for a long walk. Play tennis. That sort of thing. He'd rather Rupert stepped forward, but that's not possible. Rupert has never really liked children." She lit a cigarette. "Are you writing poems?"

"Not so much," I said. "A few lines here and there. Nothing seems to stick."

"It's a difficult game. What I like about cooking is that you never get kitchen block. You can always slice and dice."

"You've been neglecting my education," I said. "I was learning a lot from you at one point."

"Let's have at it," she said. "I'm doing a cacciucco for dinner."

I'd never heard of this, and told her.

"A Tuscan soup," she explained, "filled with monkfish, dogfish, langoustines, shrimp, mussels. Quite easy, really, and it will dazzle them back in Transylvania."

I agreed, though even locating monkfish and dogfish in Pennsylvania would pose a challenge.

It occurred to me that I might help with Nicola, too. But Vera shook her head.

"She thinks you're a git," she said, in a low voice.

"And what's a git?"

"You know, someone who doesn't really know what he's about. A bit of a chump."

"Nicola barely knows me."

"Quite true. I told her you were just very American."

I felt queasy inside. Did everyone on this island see through me? Was I really so ridiculous?

"Poor little girl," Vera continued. "She met this dashing, older chap from Cambridge last summer, at the Marina Piccola. A Trinity man. Rugby blue and so forth. He invited her to May Ball or some such thing, then deflowered her."

"How do you know this?"

"Nicola suppresses nothing. Her letters are riveting."

"I'll bet."

"We don't mind," she said. "It's nice to know what's going on. As a parent, one can feel helpless."

"As a child, too," I said.

"But that's how it's supposed to work. A parent is—in theory—in charge. I have never felt any sense of control over either of my children. It's a bore, really."

"You'd admire my mother."

"A commanding presence?"

"General Patton in drag."

"I can't wait to meet her," Vera said, lighting a cigarette. "You know, I'm actually quite worried about Marisa. Something has gone terribly wrong."

"She has been fired," I said. "This probably annoys the hell out of her."

"Not true, I suspect. The actual job—if that's what one calls it— means nothing to her. And we haven't exactly run her out the house. Rupert made it clear that she's welcome to stay until she has sorted things out." She blew smoke away from me. "Perhaps you could help in some way."

"Me?"

"It's obvious that you've got a connection." She lifted one insinuating eyebrow.

"For God's sake, I slept with her once!"

"You must be awfully good in bed."

"I'm pathetic. I swear."

"I believe that," Vera said, putting out the cigarette, though it was barely smoked—a sign of anxiety. "I have this eerie feeling about her. She was walking in the garden last night. I saw her from the window and went down. I tried to talk to her, but she didn't even hear me. Then she started chattering, but it wasn't to me. It wasn't to anyone I could see. A bloody ghost or something."

I sighed, guessing she was right. All was not well in the world of Marisa Lauro, and I'd not helped her in the least.

# eight

I rose before six, as the sea below was just turning a milky silver, and the first bronze depths were only a hint on the horizon. In sneakers and gym shorts, wearing a sleeveless pink T-shirt from a tacky shop in the Camerelle, I went for a run along the Pizzalungo, taking a pine-scented footpath with staggering views of the Punta di Tragara. As always, I passed La Solitaria, a tiny villa on a cliff overlooking the Faraglioni. As Grant had told me on one of our walks, the house had been occupied by Compton Mackenzie, the prolific Scottish novelist, during the Great War, as Grant still called it. It was a pleasant spot, protected from the aggressive northern winds by Mount Tuoro, a prospect that rose behind it.

"I knew Mackenzie," said Grant, with a memorial sigh. "Met him in Edinburgh. He lived to be very old and mellow, but his fame had slipped away by then. Odd, how one can be among the most popular novelists in the world at forty, then invisible at eighty. *Sinister Street* was the one novel that every student in the twenties could be counted on to have read."

I sensed his discomfort, and said (the sentence after three decades still makes me cringe), "But you write for posterity."

"I write for myself, dear boy," he said. "Posterity isn't listening."

I often thought about the collection of characters who had made their home on Capri, many of whom were finding their way into the pages of Grant's latest book. Sexual outlaws, revolutionaries, artists, wealthy pleasure seekers. The population had, according to Mackenzie himself (whose books Grant had put in my hands), become less interesting after the Second World War, when it filled with "French artists who have won traveling scholarships, Dutch intellectuals, Scandinavian eccentrics, central Europeans flushed with self-determination, and of course pederasts and pathics of every nationality." That was the postwar harvest.

Things had apparently changed even more in the past decade. I had not, as yet, met any Dutch intellectuals or Scandinavian eccentrics, although the "pederasts and pathics" remained in force. The residents were mostly English, it seemed, with a few Germans dotted about the island—mostly in Anacapri. Patrice was the closest thing to a French artist on a traveling scholarship I'd encountered, although he lacked the artistic side as well as the scholarship.

Wealthy Italians from the mainland had also invaded Capri in recent years, building large and ugly villas on the opposite shore of the Marina Piccola from the Tragara. "They are mostly Milanese," Grant explained, with an air of mild contempt. "Just look at their houses. Their sense of beauty does not extend beyond the notion of a fat woman in bed." He claimed to have seen them pulling down old, wisteria-covered walls along the via Murlo and putting up iron railings "in the convulsive Munich style."

Over lunch with Toni in the piazzetta, I had repeated without attribution the remark about the fat woman, and she instantly detected its source. "You've picked up Grant's manner," she said. "He's always putting down the Milanese." That was the first I'd been aware of Grant's visible effect on me. It was, perhaps, inevitable that I would respond to such a strong personality, taking on his coloration. But I had fallen too heavily under his spell, and could see how many of his attitudes had become mine, for good or ill.

Now I ran by myself, savoring the isolation. I didn't want to be wholly absorbed by Capri and its crowd of "characters." Their frequently dismissive attitudes annoyed me, as did much else. Since the phone call from my father, I'd become sleepless and uncertain again—not much better than I'd been during the months after Nicky's death. I lay awake, thinking of my parents and their future without children. Family life, as they had grown accustomed to its shape and feel, had evaporated. Nicky was dead, and I was gone. For them, this meant a different sort of daily life from a continuation of their life together as just a couple—a phase of their life that my father occasionally referred to as "Life B.C.—Before Children." Like all children, I regarded this period in my parents' lives as a mythic age, when gods and monsters roamed the earth.

I could not imagine the existence that lay ahead for them, and I knew they couldn't either. My mother had no real work, having devoted herself to me and (less happily) Nicky. It seemed unlikely that she would now find a job: her weight made that impossible. And her bad heart didn't help. My father might give her a part-time desk job in the office of Massolini Construction, but even that seemed unlikely. She couldn't type, and the idea of her answering a phone boggled the mind.

My own future troubled me as well. Death—a subject I had managed to shove out of my head for several months, ever since arriving on Capri—began to loom strangely before me as I ran, a palpable, dark shadow that fell from every bright object on my path. If there was a God, he was surely demented, populating the world with creatures who could so clearly anticipate their own demise. ("The nice thing about death," my grandfather once said to me, paraphrasing a Neapolitan aphorism, "is that you only do it once.") With effort, I pushed these thoughts away. I was alive and healthy, strong and young. So be it, I told myself. There would be plenty of time for death.

At the end of my run, I stopped at Father Aurelio's chapel in the eucalyptus grove for early mass. I had done this several times in the past week, arriving in my sweat-drenched T-shirt, my skin glistening. I joined half a dozen prune-faced widows, in their black dresses and headscarves—the usual crowd. They sat impassively in different pews, hunched forward, fingering their rosaries, crossing themselves at the wrong times, but frequently, in perpetual mourning for Emilio or Ignazio or Luigi. After mass, they would stare at me as I left the chapel, crossing myself on the way out.

"It's not that they don't want you here," Father Aurelio told me one day. "It's that they've never seen before a young man who would come to mass in his underwear."

I felt cleansed and free, walking from the chapel's cool darkness into the blinding sun. Something like the grace of God seemed to alter my weight, and I ran home lighter on my feet, a spirit gliding on the world, aware of the vast kingdom of eternity represented, however obliquely, by the myriad forms of nature. By the time I rounded the point again, looking toward the Marina Piccola, the sun was too hot to bear, its brightness multiplied beyond calculation by the sea's million facets. But I turned my face upward, letting my cheeks and forehead burn.

As I ran, I thought of Nicky's words: "Vision is like that, right? I mean, you see something, and it's fucking fantastic—scary, beautiful, damned, whatever—and you don't dare tell anybody else about it. You keep it to yourself, because that's where it lives best. Down and fresh, the dearest thing you know."

ooooo

When I stepped into my cottage, the room was black and cool. My eyes would need several minutes to adjust, I realized, as I groped my way toward the bed. I would lie there for a while, letting lines of poetry gather in my head. Later, I might take a swim and sit on the beach with my journal. That was as good a place to write as any on Capri.

"Don't be so sweaty!"

"Marisa!" I said. "What are you doing here?"

"You have leave your door open, so I come in. You are not so happy that I am come?"

I couldn't believe that, once again, Marisa had found her way into my cottage, uninvited. She stood in a dark corner, almost invisible.

"I wasn't expecting you," I said.

"Don't be angry with me," she said, stepping toward me.

"I'm not," I said. "It's just that you startled me."

She came close, reaching for my face. "Your head, there is this mark, a scar. What has happened?"

"A long time ago," I said, "my brother hit me with a rock."

She seemed pensive, considering.

"I have no brother and no sister," she said, her eyes losing focus. The subject had touched some buried nerve. She kissed my lips, lightly.

A sexual encounter with Marisa was the last thing on my mind right now. I'd been running on the Pizzalungo, had been to mass, and the beginnings of a poem had begun to push its tendrilous shoulders through the soil of my unconscious. I wanted to water and care for that poem this morning, perhaps all day.

"Would you like a cup of tea?" I asked.

She sat on the bed and unbuttoned her blouse, exposing her breasts. "Forget this tea. Come to me, please, you Lorenzo. I am insisting."

Despite my disinclination, I could not easily resist the commands of a woman: that pattern had been established in early childhood. I moved beside her, onto the edge of the bed, inwardly determined to ignore her overtures. I must find some middle ground here, get into a genuine conversation. Perhaps we could go to the beach for a swim? Or have coffee in the piazzetta? Anything to ease myself over this hump.

"I don't mind you sweat," she said, reaching toward me and under my damp T-shirt. Her hand played lightly over the skin of my back, climbing the stairs of my vertebral column. Then she kneaded the soft skin just below my shoulder blades. "How do you like my rub?"

"It feels good," I said.

"You will make love," Marisa said. Her voice was husky and complex.

"I was going to write some poetry this morning," I said halfheartedly.

"I am your muse, then. Let me do this for you."

I had heard Rupert Grant on the subject of the female muse once too many times to find her suggestion in the least amusing. It was the loudest bee in Grant's bonnet. A crackpot theory of his that Vera lost no opportunity to deride. "He has left no idiotic stone unturned," she recently said as we washed clams in the kitchen, "and believes in moon goddesses and sun goddesses and God knows what else. Bloody wood nymphs and fuck-fairies. Anything to justify his randy streak, and to make it seem less juvenile."

Marisa put her tongue into my ear, but I jerked away. "You don't find me beautiful anymore," she said, rather mournfully. "I'm sorry."

"It's not that," I said. "You're as beautiful as ever. Even more so."

"You don't want me," she said.

"No, I really do."

As I said this, I realized it was true. The first time I'd seen Marisa, when she had leaped into Grant's lap and acted like a spoiled little girl, I had found her pretty enough, but her behavior made it difficult to appreciate her real beauty. (Girls who acted like kittens had always turned me off—I remembered such a girl at Columbia, during my freshman year, who would curl into my lap at parties. I ended the relationship before it ever began.) Marisa's style had never appealed to me. In the Italian manner, she used heavy layers of eye makeup and dowsed herself in cologne. Her earrings were too big and bright, and her jeans were excessively tight, as though applied with a spray gun. These superficial aspects of her presentation, though commonplace in Italy, grated on me. I preferred the wholesome simplicity of Holly, who wore neither makeup nor jewelry, not even earrings. She had no scent but her own, which I'd come to crave: a clean womanly smell that mingled with the faint aromas of shampoo. But this morning, Marisa seemed freer of makeup than usual, her hair gleaming. The only scent I could detect was definitely hers—a dark, thrilling odor that I recalled from the single night we'd spent together.

"I will leave you, Lorenzo," she said, rising, buttoning her blouse. "I have not come to annoy you, as I do. If you don't want me, I understand. I don't prefer this to happen if you are not pleased."

"It's not that," I said. "I wasn't expecting you."

Her face turned toward me, with tears glistening on her cheeks. Her lower lip trembled slightly.

"Don't cry," I said, reaching toward her.

Her head fell against my shoulder, and she seemed about to sob.

Unable to resist, I touched her chin with my fingertips, and she raised her face to mine. Her lips parted. And soon my tongue found her mouth, and her jaws loosened, and her tongue met mine in the deep waters of her mouth.

"Lie with me," I said.

"Are you sure?" Her voice was small and hesitant. "I don't want to. Not if you don't."

"I want to," I said, stripping off my shirt and lowering my gym shorts and underpants.

"Take off your shoes," she said, lying on her back to slip off her jeans. "I don't like to make love with the shoes on."

I obeyed. And within minutes, I was tangled on the bed with her, a swirl of sheets and wetness.

# PART FIVE

*vita brevis*

## one

Rains swept the island from the north one night in early August, with a rumbling of thunder that broke over the slopes of Mount Solaro and seemed to collect in the inlet below the Villa Clio. My cottage was damp and uncomfortable, the walls sweating, caught in the occasional gleam of lightning. I felt ill from having drunk too much wine the night before with Patrice, who'd been having a bad few weeks because Giovanni was under pressure from his family to marry the daughter of Capri's longtime *sindaco*, Luigi Mancini, who governed in the usual haphazard way of Italian politicians. "It is only the marriage of convenience," said Patrice, with mournful disgust. "There would be no sex here, and no love."

I was about to crawl into bed when I heard footsteps outside the door. I guessed it was Marisa by the urgency of her approach.

"Lorenzo! Is raining!" She rapped at the screen, her voice strained. "I am wet!"

That she waited for my invitation to enter surprised me. It was not like her.

"You are welcome," she said, incongruously, stepping into the room. Her T-shirt was soaked through, and the cotton material clung to her breasts like skin. "It is thunder, too," she added.

I had pleaded with her not to visit me again. While I enjoyed the sex, I found the relationship unsatisfying. It was, I believed, good for neither of us. Plucking up my courage, I explained in the gentlest terms that I didn't love her, so there was no point in continuing to sleep together. I said, without conviction, that I hoped we could remain friends.

We hunched at opposite sides of my three-legged table, like poker players, keeping our hands to ourselves. Her dark hair was tangled and damp.

"He is awful, your Rupert Grant," she said, with anger in her voice.

"So what's happened?"

"He told me I am stupid. *Stupido!*"

I couldn't imagine what Grant might have said to her, but it seemed unlikely that he'd called her stupid. His insults were usually indirect.

"I'm feeling too bad," she said. "I feel like killing myself."

Her melodramatic turn annoyed me, seeming operatic in a southern Italian way. "I'm sure he doesn't think you're stupid," I said, as thunder rumbled in the middle distance.

"Let me stay with you tonight. I have made nice love to you, Lorenzo. What is wrong with me?"

"I don't want that, Marisa," I said.

"You think I am stupid, too."

"I don't. You're very intelligent."

"You say so?"

"I do. But you should go home. To Naples. There is no point in hanging on."

"My father, he is worst than Rupert."

This was, from what I'd learned, an understatement. Vera had told me that her father had broken her jaw when she was eighteen—because she had spent the night with a boyfriend. I didn't even want to think about what that meant.

"There must be somewhere else you could go? Some relative? A friend?"

"I am nowhere," she said, her English dissolving fast.

"You will go nowhere?"

"My days are not so happy anymore. I was glad here, but that isn't true." I didn't like her expression, so lost, wild, and sad at the same time.

"You're going to be fine," I said, without confidence.

"I say good-bye to you, Lorenzo."

"We can talk tomorrow," I said. "You need some sleep."

"Maybe I will kill Rupert Grant."

I touched her forearm. "You shouldn't say things like that, Marisa."

"He doesn't deserve it."

I didn't know what "it" referred to, but I let the statement pass. The rain began to fall heavily outside my cottage, and I closed the big window overlooking the sea.

"You will give me a drink, no?"

I could hardly refuse her, and pulled a fresh bottle of grappa from the cupboard.

"I am always like your grappa," she said.

"Thank you."

She gulped her drink, then helped herself to a second. That, too, disappeared quickly. I told her to steady herself. "Your nerves are bad," I said, "I can tell."

"I am leaving you now," she said, rising on wobbly knees. She moved around the table and kissed me on the forehead. "I have like you so much. You are not the same as Rupert."

I heard her footsteps on the path, and the rain falling. For some reason, I kept thinking about her comment. I was certainly not like Rupert Grant. Nor did I want to be like him, not any longer.

*two*

———

I took Nigel with me one afternoon in early August to visit the house of Axel Munthe, the famous Swedish physician and author, who had made his presence felt on Capri for six decades, until his death in 1949. For much of his life, Munthe had a fashionable medical practice in Rome, where he lived in the Piazza di Spagna, in a house where Keats had once lived. But he had fallen in love with Capri in 1885, while recovering from exhaustion that was the result of his work in Naples during a devastating cholera epidemic. In 1890, he bought San Michele, a ruin built on the remains of a Roman villa in Anacapri. He restored it gradually, furnishing it with local antiques and ancient artifacts, among them a gleaming mask of white marble that was the handiwork of Phidias himself, the famous Athenian sculptor.

I loved San Michele, having been there twice before, once with Vera and another time with Toni Bonano. It was a memorable spot, still haunted by Dr. Munthe, who had left a print on every surface. His garden was a fine spot for a picnic, with steep views of the northern side of the island and Mount Solaro. As expected, Nigel was unimpressed.

"I don't see the point about San Michele," he said, shaking his head as he spoke, sweeping his hair into place. He was a beautiful boy, for sure. Patrice had found him "so ravishing" that he could hardly speak.

"It's a lovely house," I argued, "with lots of artwork inside. There's nothing like it on Capri."

"Our house is nicer."

"By modern standards," I said.

"Why bother with other standards?"

Once again, he stumped me. I found conversations with Nigel oddly disconcerting. He maintained an elegantly gloomy cool, despite the glittering life that fate had served on a platter before him.

"Munthe was a tedious old boffer," he said.

"How do you know?"

"Pater told me. A neurotic old boffer."

"But he had energy," I said.

"Americans admire energy, don't they?" He could barely conceal his contempt.

"Yes," I said.

"I find it boring, this cult of energy."

"Really?"

"Joie de vivre, that sort of thing. Tedious."

I had heard this line before, from Grant himself. He often made derisive remarks about joie de vivre, and never failed to disparage Picasso, whom he considered its leading avatar. "That little fool who wants everyone to think he's a genius," Grant said. "I used to see him clowning around the Riviera, playing the Great Man. Hurling bits of pottery across the room. Revolting."

"You were going to show me some of your poems," I said.

"I've changed my mind. They're rubbish."

"Don't be hard on yourself."

He looked at me with a kind of detached curiosity. "Do you always offer advice?"

I didn't want to patronize him, just because I was seven years his senior. In many ways, he'd experienced more of the world than I had. And he was obviously intelligent and articulate. Too articulate.

"I'm going to write a novel," Nigel told me. "A large and difficult novel."

"Good," I said, tentatively. Another budding novelist was just what the world required. "I hope to write one myself."

"Have you got a plot?"

"Nothing specific."

"I see," he said, turning sad eyes on me.

"Plot is important, you're right," I said. "The main thing is, you've got to tell a story."

"Stories are rubbish," he said. "For second-raters."

Once again, I could hear the echoes of his father. I came to him once with Dominick Bonano's line about telling stories, and he squashed my notion as though it were a cockroach. "Stories are nonsense," he said. "No good novelist depends on them. Narrative is the thing. It has to build in ways that 'story' doesn't take into consideration. *Death in Venice*, for example. That's it, what? The slow accretion of detail. The layered approach." He warned me about Bonano's theorizing, detecting at once the origin of my remark. "He's got something invested in stories because he has nothing else. He doesn't, for example, know much about language. Have you actually *read* him?"

At that point, I hadn't. But I soon dipped into *The Last Limo on Staten Island*. That it was not good was apparent from the first sentence: "A short, powerfully built man with metallic gray hair, Don Vincenzo was a man of character whose passionate nature led him alternately to perform acts of great generosity and terrible violence." What sort of character was that? Events in the narrative succeeded each other rapidly, but were undeveloped. The characters were thin, all well-defined types, and they rarely just spoke to each other; they "croaked" or "groaned" or "barked." The language suffered from countless clichés or near-misses. The sun was always "sparkling," and night often "fell with a thud." Bonano's Mafia thugs uniformly possessed a "grip of iron." Their women were "buxom," and they wore skirts that revealed "long, shapely legs." There were oddities of diction, too, as in: "Tony Bruticozzi always felt sad after coition."

"Are you still bonking Marisa?" Nigel asked.

"No," I said. I didn't elaborate. It would only have been used against me.

"She's a moody bitch," he said.

I tried not to respond in a way that he might interpret as approval for his remark. "She's been having a difficult time," I said. "I'm worried about her."

"Balls," he said. "Pater is giving her the boot."

"I know," I said.

"Last night, he told her to clear out."

I felt a peculiar chill in the pit of my stomach. "Last night?"

"I heard him telling Mater. He said, 'I've sent the bitch packing.'"

I was somehow not surprised. When I got back, I would go to comfort her. My own recent coolness toward her haunted me now. I listened to Nigel's chatter without really hearing him, feeling oddly disembodied, as though I could not keep my heart and head in the same physical space.

Nigel and I found a shady seat in one corner of the garden: white-walled, covered with morning glory and plumbago. The garden dropped northeastward in terraces, with a pergola above several water cisterns. We were protected from the sun by a great stone pine, which rustled in a throaty way in the slightest sea breeze. Maria Pia had packed a lunch for us—a loaf of bread with cheese and fruit. Nigel had subtly snagged a bot-tle of wine from his father's cellar, a mature Barolo that had probably been sequestered for a better occasion, and he uncorked it with guilty relish.

There were lots of visitors around us, mostly Germans and Americans, who seemed incapable of normal speech volumes. An oblong man in Bermuda shorts complained that Italy was "hotter than Cleveland, and without the air conditioning."

"Bloody day-trippers," said Nigel. "They ought to be shot."

"Dr. Munthe had them in mind when he rebuilt San Michele," I said. "He wanted a museum, with visitors." Vera had told me that Munthe had lived in a nearby tower, not in the villa itself. "He was an old fraud," she suggested, "a charlatan of a type that has always found Capri attractive. A lonely man, they say, and terribly insecure. He invented a character for himself—the eccentric, the lover of animals and birds, the connoisseur of ancient art and architecture. But look at San Michele. It's a monstrosity. A tourist attraction. It has nothing to do with the real beauty or architec-ture of the island."

I had read Dr. Munthe's well-known autobiography, *The Story of San Michele*, which in its day sold millions and made its author a wealthy man. Its author was charming, but shallow, determined to please the reader at

every turn. Truth was not important to him, only beauty. Reading it, I felt
I understood Munthe only too well, and that if I were not careful, I could
easily fall into that trap. I could turn myself into a "character," present-
ing a falsely buoyant self to the world. I could all too easily sacrifice truth
to beauty.

"You've been bonking Toni Bonano," said Nigel. "I know all about it,
not that it matters. I rather like it. She's quite pretty, in that hard American way."

"You're wrong, old man," I said. "Toni and I are friends. Nothing
more."

"A pity," he said. "What about Holly? Mater says you pine in her presence. Are you a piner?"

"I hope not."

"I don't pine. I don't like anyone well enough to pine for them."

"Have you got a girlfriend."

"Charterhouse is all boys, and mostly buggers," he said. "But I'm not
a bugger."

"No," I said. "I can see that."

"Nicola has a boyfriend."

"So I've heard."

"She's not a virgin, but I am."

"There will be plenty of time to remedy that."

"Pater's mad about girls. Mater calls it his 'little hobby.' I find it rather
disgusting."

I refrained from comment, hoping the remark would float away and
pop like a soapy bubble.

"It's not a secret," Nigel continued. "I realized quite a long time ago
that my father was corrupt in that way. A bit too lecherous for his own
good. But I've forgiven him. Mater doesn't mind. Super girl, don't you
think?"

"Your mother?"

"The estimable Vera."

"I like her."

"She says you're queer. Are you queer?"

"I don't think so."

"I told her that," he said. "You can always tell. They mince about, don't they. Mince, mince, mince."

"I try not to mince."

"You're very manly."

"Thank you."

I sighed, lying back in the grass. I found Nigel's conversation totally exhausting. He had no tact whatsoever, adopting a worldly tone at odds with his age and callowness. "He just chunters," his mother warned me. "Pay no attention to Nigel. Just nod agreeably. He will eventually stop."

"I heard about your brother," Nigel said.

I tried not to flinch.

"The Mater can't keep a secret."

"It's not a secret. My brother was killed in Vietnam."

"Bloody savages."

"Who?"

"The Americans."

It was not worth pursuing that line of argument with an English schoolboy whose grand pronouncements were like huge plants in thin soil. They could be toppled by the slightest winds of argument.

"Will you stay long, Lorenzo?"

"On Capri? I don't know," I said. "I have no plans."

"That's bang on," Nigel said. "Plans are evil."

After a blessed pause, he went on the offensive again. "Whatever attracts you to Holly? I don't get it. She has no breasts, no hips. I can't fathom her. There is something hugely missing."

"It's not about breasts and hips," I said.

"Pater adores her, too."

"I know."

"She's rather fill-in-the-blank. You have to guess what's there. Probably nothing is there."

"I do like her."

He clucked his disapproval. "I'd tread carefully there. Pater doesn't believe she has any romantic interest in you, or he'd be rotten. He would kill you, in fact."

"Your father?"

"He's frightfully erratic."

"Your father isn't erratic," I said.

"Oh, he is. But I don't mind. I really don't."

I could see he minded a great deal, as would any son. Indeed, I'd watched him vying with Holly for his father's attention, and failing. He'd been provoked into saying outrageous things at meals, simply to draw his father's wrath. (Angry attention was apparently better than none at all.)

Nigel swilled the rest of the wine straight from the bottle. "I don't like Italian wines," he said. "They're undistinguished."

"Really?"

"French wines are nicer."

"I'm not an expert," I said, hoping to wake a modicum of self-consciousness in Nigel, who plunged down any conversational road with abandon.

"I drink quite a lot at school," he said.

"Don't they mind?"

"They never find out. I can be quite discreet."

"Really?"

He looked as though I were speaking a language with no similarities to English. "When we get back," he said, in a vaguely conspiratorial tone, "I'll show you a couple of recent poems. They're rather disreputable."

"I don't object to that."

"Love poems, that sort of thing. You'll think I'm a wanker."

"I doubt it."

"Point is, I don't care what you think," he said. "I really don't."

I merely smiled. He seemed vulnerable now, so young and foolish. I wished I could do something to make him feel better, but that was beyond me, having all I could do to attend to myself at this point.

*three*

---

Chaos struck the following night.

Marisa had rarely been seen at the villa over the past week, and everyone knew that Grant had finally asked her to remove herself from the property.

"This slow-drip torture has to end," Vera said, as we were gathering empty plates for Maria Pia to take into the kitchen. Grant remained at the table, ignoring everyone, reading a newspaper while he finished a glass of brandy. Holly and the children were talking among themselves, planning a trip to the piazzetta for ice cream.

"Last week, I suggested that she go back to Naples," I said.

"A rotten idea."

"I know."

"You're full of rotten advice," she said. "You should become a psychiatrist. Americans are mad about them, aren't they? You could make a packet."

"We don't really have psychiatrists where I come from," I said. "And I don't want a packet of money."

"I keep forgetting that you're a poet."

Suddenly Mimo lunged into the dining room, his eyes wide. He looked as though he'd just seen the ghost of Garibaldi.

"*La signorina!*" he said. His mouth continued to move, but without words.

"What the bloody hell?" said Grant.

The room fell still. We all knew that he meant Marisa, and that something had happened.

Mimo motioned us to follow him, his large, dark hands clawing the air.

There was a mad race behind him, with Vera leading the flock. Holly and Nigel were just behind her, while Nicola and I trailed by half a dozen steps, rushing through the moist evening air, now tinged with woodsmoke. Grant, it seemed, was not going to run, but I caught a glimpse of him some twenty yards behind me, walking quickly, as we passed the swimming pool and turned toward the sea.

It was sundown, with the sea blood-bright as Mimo led us to the ledge I had dreamed about many times, our version of Il Salto, the leap. Before I got there I knew what it was.

"Dear God," said Vera, clutching my arm and teetering on the edge, looking down.

Marisa's body lay in a broken state below. Such a fall, or leap, could hardly be survived. The black swaddling of her hair, dandled by the surf, rose and fell, but she was otherwise motionless. I thought I could see blood in the water.

Grant approached us, out of breath. He looked a million years old as he peered over the ledge. "The silly girl," he said. "There was no need."

Holly looked once, then stepped backward. All life seemed to drain from her eyes.

"I'd say she was mad," said Nigel. "What do you say, Pater?"

Grant, to his credit, told his son to shut up.

Nicola began to weep, and her mother comforted her, guiding her back to the Villa Clio. There was no point in standing there, gaping.

"Call Ruggiero!" Grant called to Vera, who nodded. Ruggiero was the local commandante, a regular attendee at dinner parties on the island. It was always good to have the police on your side, especially if you were an alien resident.

Grant took me by the wrist. "Let's go down there. She might still be alive."

I was sick inside, wasted and confused. The world spun around me, a lazy Susan of colors and sounds. The voices I heard seemed unreal,

detached from their bodies. I myself felt detached: a floating consciousness that looked on this bizarre and tragic scene without understanding.
Involuntarily, I followed Grant down the rocky path.

It was apparent from thirty feet away that Marisa was dead, her brains
splattered on the rocks.

Mimo stood beside me, in tears, crossing himself every few minutes
and muttering what must have been a prayer. Nigel was chuntering on,
foolishly, about the possibility of murder.

"She didn't strike me as the jumping type," Nigel said. "I'll bet someone pushed her."

"The bloody girl dashed herself on the rocks," Grant said, bitterly.
"How very operatic of her."

I simply stared at Rupert, disbelieving. What a fucking asshole, I
thought. What a cruel, fucking bastard.

*four*

———

The news about Nicky's death had come from my father, who found me one night after dinner at my dorm. I was studying for an exam when there was a knock on my door. A call for me, I was told. The telephone hung from a wall at the end of the corridor, and everyone on the hall could hear your conversation, which meant that nobody's personal life was a secret. One quickly learned to speak in code.

"Hi, Alex, it's Dad," he had said in a constricted voice; I knew at once that something terrible had happened and assumed that my mother had taken a turn. She had been hospitalized in recent months on two occasions with what we thought were heart attacks, although the doctors had never pinned anything down. "It's not Mom," my father said. "I'm calling about Nicky."

"Is he okay?" I knew how absurd that was, but couldn't control it. I wanted, for a few seconds, to think all would be well, when I already knew the truth. This was the news I had dreaded for so long that the dread itself had become familiar, like an old, difficult, neurotic friend.

"Not so good," he said. There was an unnatural pause, while he collected himself. "It's pretty bad news I gotta tell you, son." My father began to cry—a quick, sharp sob he tried his best to stifle.

"Oh, God," I said.

"He's dead, Alex. Got killed over there, they said. Some kind of explosion." After more sobs, he added, "Your mother's pretty upset."

I could not speak. I don't remember much of anything after that, but several guys on my hall were soon standing around me. They seemed already to know that something had happened.

"I'm coming home right away," I said.

"That sounds good, Alex. You do that," he said. "I think your mother would appreciate it."

I remembered the painful numbness, like I'd been stung by a wasp in the heart. I felt it again that night, after Marisa's body was taken away by the police. The reality was unbearable, a fiery place where my mind could not settle for a moment. I sat at my three-legged table, drinking three glasses of grappa—finishing off the bottle that Marisa and I had started only a few nights before.

"Can I join you?" asked Vera, standing at the door.

"Sure."

"That's a decent bottle," she said, recognizing the local label, from Da Gemma, the restaurant.

"Yeah," I said, vaguely.

"Are you all right?"

"Me?"

"You, Alex. I'm worried about you."

"Why?"

"I know that you and Marisa, as it were, were close."

"As it were," I said.

"Don't play that game, please."

"Sorry."

"Look, I told you I'd always tell you the truth. So I'm telling you now. This is not your fault. Marisa was deeply unhappy. She had a horrid past."

"Her present wasn't so good, either."

"It's partly Rupert's fault, of course. But I wouldn't blame him. Not entirely. Marisa tried to kill herself before."

I looked up from my glass.

"It's true. She told me about it, soon after she moved in. I was able to talk to her, at first. Then she brought down a lead shield around her. I wished I knew how to help."

It didn't surprise me that she could not go further with Marisa. There was a dearth of empathy at the Villa Clio, although—in retrospect—it impresses me that Vera made this visit to the cottage. She knew more about me than I would have guessed at the time.

"I'm glad you came," I said.

"We're friends, eh?" She reached for my hands, and grasped them. "I was worried about you."

We sat for a while, saying nothing, then Vera left, kissing me lightly on the forehead.

"If you need something to help you sleep, I have some jolly efficient pills," she said.

"I'll be fine."

"Are you sure?"

I nodded, but doubted my words. I had felt a sadness creeping over me since moments after seeing Marisa at the bottom of that cliff, a long slow wave that seemed only to mount and mount, with no sign of cresting.

ooooo

In bed, I fell asleep, but it was not a pleasant sleep. I dreamed that Nicky came into the room. He had not, after all, really died. He had simply walked off into the jungle, eventually crossing the border into Laos. He had come to me for help.

"Nicky," I said.

"Hey, man. How you doing, asshole?"

"You're alive."

"What the fuck," he said.

"Do Mom and Dad know?"

He shook his head. "They're after me, Alex. I gotta hide."

"Who is after you?"

"I'm AWOL."

"The army doesn't know you're here?"

"They think I'm dead."

"But you're not."

"Hey, you're a fucking genius. You were always smarter than me, right?"

"I thought I was." Guilt overwhelmed me, and I began to cry.

"Stop that shit, okay? You're still an actor. You're an asshole, and that's why I call you an asshole. You know how fucking bad you were, man? You did everything you could to make me look bad. What fucking chance did I have?"

He was right, I knew.

"I ought to cut your fucking tongue out, you know that? That's what they did to assholes in Nam. They caught somebody who was telling lies, one of them little geeks, and they cut out his fucking tongue."

"I'm sorry, Nicky."

"You're sorry, huh?" He drew a blade from the sheath at his side. "Stick out your tongue, man. Stick it out or I'm gonna pull it out." He put a hand on my throat, digging his fingers into the soft skin.

"Don't, Nicky! Please!"

I woke as his muddy fingers touched my tongue, and I could taste the dirt of Vietnam. The acidic, harsh, and foreign soil.

Putting on a light, I found Nicky's final letter from Vietnam, which had arrived a week or more after we learned of his death. It was a consoling letter, though stained with death, and premonitions of death.

It began, as ever, with "Dear Asshole."

*I don't want to get you down or anything, but there's stuff going on that would make you sick. I mean, we go and fucking kill people around here like you and I used to shoot ducks in Exeter. Pop a few gooks, Fink says, when he's not too stoned to get out the words. Shit, he said yesterday, I ain't killed nobody in about a week. Articulate sonofabitch.*

*Still on vacation. I like the foggy mornings up here, in the mountains. Like the Poconos, without the dance bands. The whole platoon's up here, eighteen of us, on some special gig. I don't know what the fuck we're doing exactly, in a tactical sense, and Waller doesn't either. It's just S & D, boys. Find and fire. But I got the feeling there is some kind of mobilization, a master plan that we can't see from inside the trees. They don't tell us shit, Mickey Donato complained last night. That's just to keep us in our place. If we knew what they had planned for us, Westmoreland and the boys, we'd say No Fucking Way. Do it yourself. You don't see Nixon or any of those Washington wheels over here getting their hands wet.*

*DICK NIXON BEFORE NIXON DICKS YOU. That's the bumper sticker plastered on Eddie Sloane's medikit, though he didn't put it there, he says. Buzz did, he says, before Buzz got the Big Transfer. The damn thing's full of morphine, and I don't have to explain what that's for, do I? We try to keep Fink away from the box because he'd like nothing better than to get his hands on that shit. I've never seen a man swallow and smoke so much stuff and still hold a human conversation, if that's what you'd call it.*

*Waller spends a lot of time talking about Alabama and the farm. We hear about five little Wallers all in a row on Easter morning. It's like he's trying to get the story straight in his head before they blow it off. You wouldn't want your head detached with the story that's packed inside also in fucking shreds. Which is why I guess I spend so much time trying to put the pieces together. Not because I think they're gonna shoot me. They might, but I don't think that. I really do think I'm gonna come marching home with a Purple Star, man. With a little something to wear when I'm a stooped fucker at those parades on Armistice Day. I'll get drunk at the VFW and say, Shit, you guys never saw nothing unless you saw Nam.*

*The problem is, I got too many stories, too many fragments, and they never seem to add up. I go, Once Upon a Time, and there's no telling what I'll say after that. Take you and me, Alex. I can count maybe a dozen versions of our situation. I'm always the older brother, but in one version we're best of friends, in another we're at each other's throat. In one of them Mom is so goddamn nice and helpful and concerned, and Dad is like Chairman of the Board of Benevolence, teaching us to play ball and swim and do all that shit. And this is a true story. But there's another story, and it stinks. In that one, everybody (except Dad) thinks I'm a piece of shit and only you got brains. Only you are "college material." I'm just there, a kind of accident, an unfortunate case. Hardly even Italian.*

*You were a genuine certified bastard, Alex. Did you know that? You were always trying to make things a little worse for me than they really were. You pissed on me pretty bad. Maybe I deserved it, but maybe not. I was mad as hell at the way you just glided through everything. For me, it was a fucking obstacle course. But maybe the truth is that even without you I fucked up pretty wicked. Hey, I forgive you, okay? I'm telling you off, and absolving you. Ain't that the word? I absolve thee, Alex Massolini.*

*Enough of that shit. Most days in Nam there isn't time to run over old ground. There's new ground to cover, and lots of it. We usually split up in twos, like Noah's animals. So me and Eddie spend some time on the trail together.*

*We take turns staying awake, which is always the hard part. This time of year up in these hills it's foggy till about ten in the morning, and it's fog like you never saw in your life: thick, rolling sheets of white smoke. It blows through the trees. Like some fucking nightmare. You have to pinch yourself and say, This is real, man. It's no fucking dream. You don't want to forget for a second that this is real.*

*Like yesterday. Eddie was asleep, and I'd been awake all night. Then I heard something. Footsteps. No, I said. It's my imagination. I hear footsteps everywhere. But no, it was fucking footsteps, or a kind of slurp in the muddy path. Too careless for a soldier, I figured. But there he was, in a gap in the fog, a nice-looking guy, maybe seventeen, with an AK-47 just dangling from one hand, so casual. VC, grunt. Your basic gook. A big round face and black pajamas. Sandals and lousy haircut. The works.*

*I had straightened the pin on my grenade when I heard the steps, just in case, and now I tossed it in his direction. It wasn't that I disliked him or anything. I'm only a soldier, and this is war. As Waller says, You guys are not individuals. You are part of a machine that has a job to do. And you got to do what you're supposed to do, and when you're supposed to do it. Everybody performs his job and fewer guys get hurt. Mistakes cause wakes.*

*What the fuck? grumbles Eddie, waking to the pop. A kind of thud, not nearly so loud as you'd guess, and the echo seemed louder than the original pop. And then this gook tumbles, kind of slow motion, ass over heels. Face down in the mud. Eddie and I wait for ten or fifteen minutes, and there's not a peep out of him, so we figure he's dead. We walk over to the bastard and there's a hole in the back of his head big as a saucer. Let me tell you that what I saw in there gave me no confidence that God knew what the fuck he had in mind. We're all jerry-rigged. A mess of crossed connections.*

*One down, one million to go, said Eddie.*

*I was jumpy as hell about now. Where there's one gook, there's another. That's called Waller's Rule in this platoon, and it usually proves true. So we decided to lie low for a while, just wait till the fog rose, to see if we were alone or in downtown Hanoi.*

*We waited till afternoon, which drove me nuts because it was hot and crazy with mosquitoes like you never saw before, big motherfuckers who took a pint of blood in a single gulp. Because I'd been up for most of the night, I took a snooze about eleven, warning Eddie to wake me only if they were gonna shoot. You don't want to miss your own death, do you? And it happens around here. A couple of guys got wasted in their sleep last week. Never knew what hit them.*

*And, man, what a dream I had. It was like I was already gone. Just flying, over a humongous cloud, and suddenly it was Sunday dinner at home in Pittston, and we were all there. You had a wife, you bastard, and she was gorgeous as hell. A real brain, too. And some little kids were there, mine or yours. I couldn't tell. Dad was old, but nice to look at, like Nonno M, only with shaggy white hair and his tooth big and gold as ever. You looked pretty nice, in a tweed jacket. Even I had on some kind of suit myself, and it was maybe Christmas. And Mom was so soft and quiet, a little thinner. Not herself, but soft and quiet and thinner. And we were all together, and it was like the best dinner before us we ever saw. I don't know what you call that stuff, with lots of ragu and cheese. And lots of Dago Red from Nonno's cellar.*

*I'm writing this early in the morning, watching the shadows that keep moving. Pretty soon we'll get up, check our weapons, do all the stupid things we do before we head out. We'll be heading west, farther into the mountains. I'm just going to write this and put it into an envelope and address it. Weird to think that you'll be reading it, and it will be another day in my life and yours, and probably half of what I said here will sound like bullshit.*

*Anyway, we're heading back south in a couple of weeks, they say. Maybe to Saigon. Or the Delta. Rumors go around, and you can't believe what you hear. Funny how good you can feel, though, when you hear certain things, which is probably why we say them. To cheer ourselves up. To make it possible to put one foot in front of another without losing it.*

*Pretty soon (if you don't count too close) I'm going to Hawaii for a little surf and turf. R & R, with babes in bikinis on the beach. Kind of like your frat parties, only with real water and real girls. I'm just about there, in my dreams. You'll hear me on the wire. Hey, it's me, I'm gonna yell into the phone. Your old pal, college boy. And how ya doing?*

*Wait for that call, huh?*

*In any case, given my recent tendency to run off at the mouth, you'll be hearing from me. Hope life in the land of the free and brave is full of lollipops, and the girls are glad for your company. Keep swinging.*

> *Your own private*
> *Socrates*

"We keeping talking to cheer ourselves up. To make it possible to put one foot in front of another without losing it." You got that right, Nicky, I thought. And sometimes it doesn't matter what words we speak. Just the physical act of mouthing them relieves a pressure that otherwise might kill you. And so I talked my head off, circling the island like a hawk, descending here and there, plucking attention from friends like Patrice, Father Aurelio, and Peter Duncan-Jones. I had a long conversation with Holly about Marisa, sitting on a bench overlooking the Marina Piccola. She told me they had been "good friends, and never rivals." When I explained to her that I felt guilty, she looked at me severely. "Sheer egotism," she said. "Marisa never loved you, and you certainly didn't love her. She was depressed. Did you never see the marks on her wrists? They were mostly healed, but still visible. She was not well, not in her mind."

That evening, in Anacapri, I passed Il Rosaio, Graham Greene's villa, with its buff *intonaco* exterior and red shutters. I stood at the gate, looking into his garden. The walls ran with purple bougainvillea and ivy. There was a single light on, and I noticed the shadow of a man hunched over a desk. Greene was rumored to be still on Capri, working on a novel, although I hadn't seen him since the dinner party. I kept thinking that he, with his fund of experience, could help me, but I didn't dare call on him. Our connection was slight, and it wouldn't have made sense to spill my guts before him. It would surely have seemed absurd to a man like Greene, a symbol of worldly wisdom and British sangfroid.

What I needed was closure with Marisa. It surprised me that no memorial service was held on Capri. Her body was quickly removed to Naples by her family, and her belongings (in one massive trunk) followed by ferry a week or so later, carried to the Marina Grande on the back of an old mule led by Mimo. Two days after her death, I had glimpsed a man I assumed to be Marisa's father, a thickset Neapolitan with an unruly beard, scowling in the garden, making the necessary arrangements with Grant. He was not invited to lunch with the rest of us.

There had been no investigation of the suicide, although the local commandante had paid a formal visit to the Villa Clio, polishing off several cups of espresso, asking no hard questions. He apparently left satisfied that nothing untoward had occurred. The girl had been depressed, Vera told him. Grant agreed. They attested to her despondency in recent weeks, using words like *abbittimento* and *sconforto*. The commandante nodded sagaciously, using the word *depressione*. "*La povera ragazza*," he muttered to himself, shaking his head wistfully, observing that a distant cousin of his in Positano had once killed herself "for reasons of love." (The irrepressible Vera remarked: "There was certainly no love here.")

So I prowled the island, seeking consolation. I wanted to hear, over and again, that Marisa's death had nothing to do with me. The girl was disturbed, *scoraggiato*. She had many things in her life that contributed to her unhappiness, her *depressione*, and I was probably the least of them. If anything, I had lightened her load.

"Dear boy, you gave her something of a bolt hole," said Peter Duncan-Jones. He and Jeremy had, of course, forgiven my earlier outburst on Vietnam, putting it down to "bad nerves." ("I get them myself," Peter said.) His breezy manner was comforting, and he advised me to relax, suggesting that Capri was no place for a person who could not relax. He reminded me that the Quisisana Hotel derived its name from an old island saying that translates, roughly, "Here one finds health." "Do have another drink," he said, reflexively, filling my glass before I could object. A sharp cheerfulness never deserted him, and he remained unfailingly droll, often at the expense of good taste, as when he said, "Marisa might well have done something even less appealing. She might have lived."

I sought out Father Aurelio one morning after mass, inwardly doubting that the Church had anything useful to pull from its magic bag of wisdom. "You must believe that God has a plan," said Aurelio, in comfortingly formulaic Italian. "God will not abandon you. You must believe He is showing you something. He is saying, Alex, pay attention! Life is brief, but eternity goes on forever." In his usual eccentric way, he recommended that I study the *Duino Elegies* of Rilke. "This is Scripture! This is revelation!" he said. "The poets, they are the voice of God on earth. You must listen, Alex. There is a message for you in these pages." He handed me a copy of his own translation from the German, recently completed, in blurry typescript. "I am seeking a publisher," he said. "Perhaps Rupert Grant can assist me?"

Patrice, as ever, was willing to talk. I could count on him for sympathy and understanding, although his own problems with Giovanni distracted him. He could only listen for a brief time to my troubles without redirecting the subject back to himself and Giovanni. "He loves me, *il mio Giovanni*," he maintained, having acquired a melodramatic strain during his residence on Capri. "But he is pretending he doesn't love me. He is pretending that he like this girl, Lucia, who is too ugly and too fat. She has no sex for him, this girl. She is spoil. But Giovanni, and his family, they aspire to respectability! Respectability! This sounds much like some novel, no? Manzoni could write this! But where can she lead him, this girl? What is the purpose of this union? I will not go to the wedding, *alors!* Even if they invite me!"

One night, in his shed, I forced my despair on him directly, explaining that I had not slept well for days. Patrice flung his arms around me. "*Mon ami*, I love you so very *molto*," he said, in his unique blend of languages. "I love you as much as Giovanni, and I would take you away with me. I would take you tonight! But you wouldn't go."

These conversations invariably left me unsatisfied. My "bad nerves" grew worse. I felt empty and alone, my thoughts often returning to Marisa. I realized I had never really known her, and that I had not even tried to know her.

ooooo

Life at the Villa Clio continued as though nothing had happened. Marisa might well have gone to Naples to visit her family or taken another job on the island. It unnerved me that neither Grant nor Vera ever mentioned her at the table during the days immediately following her death. They seemed to talk aggressively of other things: the unusually "close" weather, upcoming visitors to Capri, or the latest literary gossip from Britain, which came via Sunday papers that arrived from London at the tobacconist's stand in the piazzetta on Wednesday afternoons. I said, rather bluntly, during dinner one evening: "Marisa seems to have disappeared without a trace."

My remark instantly provoked Grant. "You want to know about history, Lorenzo?" he said. "Well, Marisa is history. Put her from your mind."

Holly saw my distress and entered the fray on my side. "Alex is right," she said. "We shouldn't avoid the subject. That would be unhealthy."

Grant put down his knife and fork to sip a glass of Corvo. "Avoid?" he said, as if nibbling at the word to taste it. "I'm not avoiding anything, are you, Vera?"

"Marisa was a troubled girl," Vera said. "But let's not be morbid. Certain topics are bad for the digestion."

Holly wasn't going to drop the matter so easily. "Marisa was not a passerby who happened to tumble from a nearby cliff," she said. "She was a member of this household."

"Oh, do stop it," Vera said. Her attitude toward "the girls" always wavered, but now I heard in her voice a distinct note of hostility, not only toward the ghost of Marisa but toward Holly as well. Her husband's "little goatish hobby" had, after all, eroded her patience.

After a polite pause, Nigel spoke up. "Dead girls are disgusting," he said. "Did you see what happened to her head? Like a burst cantaloupe."

"Niggy, please," said Nicola.

"Yes, do be quiet," said Vera to her son.

"No, Mater, I shan't. I have every right to speak."

"Let the boy make a fool of himself," said Grant. "It's the only way he'll learn."

"To be like you?" asked Nicola.

"I say," said Grant, lifting his bushy eyebrows, "you're feeling Bolshie, what?"

Nigel grinned broadly. "Stroppy old Nicola."

"You're such a git," Nicola said.

"Bollocks," he said. "I've got every right—"

"Please, children!" Vera looked at them severely.

"They're not children," Grant said. "Don't infantalize them. They're almost adults, if I am not mistaken."

Holly stood, disgusted by the conversational turn. "You'll excuse me," she said.

"As you like," Grant called after her.

I watched Holly carry her plate into the kitchen. Not another word was said until she had left the villa, the door into the garden slapping behind her. Maria Pia hovered in the hallway, anxious. The fact that she didn't understand English probably increased her agitation.

"She's becoming a bore," said Grant.

Vera nodded, drawing her knife and fork together to one side of the plate to indicate that Maria Pia should clear it away.

"I must excuse myself as well," I said, rising.

"The exodus continues," Nigel intoned. "But not this little piggy!"

Vera looked at me slyly. "Crostata di ricotta?" She and I had worked together that morning on a ricotta tart, and she thought it would be difficult for me to pass it up.

"I'm not hungry," I said.

She looked away stiffly. "Suit yourself."

Grant shook his head, mockingly, then drilled a stare into my back as I left the room. His disdain was familiar; nevertheless I disliked the feeling it produced—a mixture of hostility and fear. I knew I could not remain on Capri, in his company, much longer.

ooooo

Mimo lurked in the garden, a black hunching form. There was something of Caliban about him: distraught, unhappy, ill-at-ease with his lot. He caught my eye and pointed toward the path to the beach. He seemed already to know I was chasing Holly, but how was that possible? In any case, I thanked him as I passed, although he simply withdrew into the shadow of a large umbrella pine.

I caught up with Holly not far from where Marisa had made her despairing leap. It was early evening, with the sea below phosphorescent, the surf quiet, the sky indistinguishable from the water itself. Holly sat on a bluff, with rocks tumbling below her in a kind of frozen avalanche. Her ankles were deep in marram grass, with thistles beside her, her hands folded in her lap. Had I been a painter, I'd have wanted to seize that image, to preserve it forever in all its intensity.

"He's become a parody of himself," Holly said, as soon as I fell within earshot. I guessed rightly that she referred to Grant.

"Nigel is worse," I said.

"He's just imitating his father," she said.

I agreed with a grumble, aware that I had myself been caught imitating him on more than one occasion. "It surprises me that Vera goes along with the program," I said. "She's more intelligent than that."

"It's not a matter of intelligence," Holly said. "She's powerless."

I didn't know how far I could tread along these lines. Obviously Holly had been party to the dynamic she now criticized, a willing participant in Grant's fantasy. She herself had played a huge part in making Vera's situation untenable. But I didn't want to press her about any of this. That would have been fatal to our relationship, such as it was. And as I had gotten everything wrong about Marisa, I didn't want to make the same mistake with Holly. What did I really know about her motivations?

"God, I want to get off this island," Holly said, tossing a stone to watch it tumble down the scree.

"To leave Capri?"

"This place is perverted."

"Why don't we go together?"

Holly turned to me, unmoved.

"We could just go somewhere else for a while," I said.

"Is that a proposition?"

I blushed. "No, I didn't mean—"

"You did mean."

"All right, I did."

"You're as bad as Rupert, aren't you?"

"I hope not."

"So do I," she said. "This is definitely not a proposition, but have you seen Paestum?"

I shook my head. I'd read about the Greek ruins at Paestum, but hadn't seen them. I'd hardly seen anything of Italy beyond Rome and parts of the Amalfi coast en route to Capri.

"I shall take you there," Holly said. "It might be good for both of us."

As we sat there, absorbed by the changing sky and sea, I hesitated to say anything more. For reasons beyond my understanding, Holly had invited me to travel with her to Paestum. Where this would take us, I couldn't tell, but was willing, even eager, to see.

A fog lay on the water most of the way to Salerno, but I didn't mind, sitting on the aft deck, my backpack stuffed with everything I would need for a week of travel. Holly, too, had a backpack—a battered "rucksack" that "had been her father's, in the army." She wore a pair of faded jeans, with a pink windbreaker over her T-shirt. She was reading Borges, the Argentine fabulist. In addition to Rilke—I felt isolated without it—I had brought *Love's Body*, a book you didn't read so much as reread, hoping to understand it better the second or third time around.

I had felt obliged to tell Grant that we would be gone for a few days. It was, in fact, a Thursday, so we could think of this as merely a long weekend. There had been no official work schedules at the Villa Clio, and I had been given assignments in a random fashion, then abandoned to my duties. Grant merely assumed I would accomplish my tasks in due course. In recent weeks, I'd been proofing articles for various English and American magazines: Grant churned these out at high speed, mostly because of his compulsive need to see his name in what he called "hard type." And there was also the compulsion to express his opinion on a range of matters, from the nature of love to the follies of the British Labour Party. "I can write about anything," he said, "as long as they don't wish for more than two thousand words. Above two thousand words, you have really to know what you're talking about."

Grant seemed only mildly surprised by the news that Holly and I were

going away for a few days. I had interrupted him in his study one morning, aware that he had probably been at his desk for several hours by the
time I knocked. He nodded, then asked if the proofs of an article des-
tined for *Encounter* were done. (I had finished those proofs several days
before and passed them back to him—a surprising lapse of memory for
Grant, who usually knew exactly where every project stood.)

I also told Vera about our excursion. Unpredictable as ever, she
seemed happy for me. "What a brilliant chap," she said.

I guessed (it was only a hunch) that she enjoyed the notion of rivalry
between Grant and me. If one assumed that Holly posed a threat to her
marriage, then it made further sense that she should want to see my
prospects with Holly improving. On the other hand, my notions about
marriage and relationships had been rerouted so many times in the past
four months that I hesitated to assume anything. Perhaps Vera was
merely being ironic?

I loved that foggy crossing, with the visual world diminished, and the
universe of sound and smell raised to a fine pitch. In particular, I liked
the way Holly's scent mingled with odors of diesel fuel that swept the
deck. The old ferry groaned and rattled, as though barely able to heave
its load of travelers—mostly tourists—from the Marina Grande to
Salerno, with stops at Positano and Amalfi.

We docked at the broken-down pier in Salerno at about four. The fog
had burned off, and the city itself glowed above the harbor, a panorama of
terraced buildings, their fading pink and biscuity facades soaked in late
afternoon light. It had become turgidly hot and humid, and we made our
way slowly toward the medieval Piazza Amendola, *il centro*. Along the via
Mercanti, a narrow close overhung with vine-strewn balconies and terraces, we found the Casa di Fiori. Holly had been to this *pensione* before
and assumed control, asking the elderly *padrone* for a large double room.
She emphasized the need for two beds, and he nodded conspiratorially.

We followed him up a damp stairwell with pocked walls and various
images of the Virgin Mary along the way. There was a lingering smell of
burned olive oil in the passageway outside our room, and I could hear a
man and woman arguing brutally in what sounded like German in the
adjacent room.

"*Due letti,*" the *padrone* said, leading us into the large, mustard-colored room, with a view of the street from an iron balcony. The toilet, he explained, was down the hall, but we had a sink to ourselves, and a real wardrobe. A bulb dangled from a fraying cord in the plaster ceiling. The two single beds were pushed together, forming a double bed. The *padrone* pounded on the wall to still the arguing couple. "*Tedesci,*" he said, as if to explain their bad behavior.

Holly and I had dinner in the piazza, under a striped awning. She was frank in her conversation, telling me stories of her childhood, her parents, her younger brother, still a student at Cambridge, and her previous love affairs. Again and again, she spoke of her father, whose superior wit and charm filled the entire family circle with a beneficent glow. He was gentle, but authoritative. Some described him as charismatic, although she doubted that such a term applied. He appeared frequently on BBC television, where his opinions on mental health were eagerly sought.

The only subject not discussed by us that evening was Rupert Grant, though I brimmed with unasked questions. Why had she put herself in such a situation? Did she love him? How did she really feel about Vera? What did she hope to gain from this interlude on Capri?

"Tell me about *your* father," she said.

In response, I explained that Salerno had peculiar resonance for me because of my father's participation in the invasion, which came near the end of September, in 1943. He had been twenty, a shade younger than I was now. It was his first experience of battle, although he'd been well prepared during a four-month training period in North Africa, where mock invasions had been meticulously staged. The army had constructed a fake town, like a Hollywood set, with wooden fronts and streets, high and low buildings. They went through all the motions, learning to leap out from cover, ready to fire; learning to expose as little as possible. They were lectured on the etiquette of occupation, too. Americans were not Germans, the officers said. They would not brutalize their victims.

My father had told me a little of this, and I had spent time in the Columbia library, reading accounts of the training, visualizing the Salerno landing itself. And now I was here. I was eating dinner, eating pasta, drinking wine, only hundreds of yards from where my father came ashore.

I told Holly that I once asked him if he thought that the Second World War was a necessary war, and he shook his head sadly. "You never know anything, as a soldier," he said. He'd never heard of Salerno before. He'd had no particular feelings about Hitler or the Italian fascists. What he understood was that everybody else was doing what he was doing, and there was a general agreement that the war needed fighting. He also knew that if he didn't go, he would have felt like a coward.

"How did he feel about your brother, and Vietnam?" Holly wondered.

I told her that my mother had opposed his going to Vietnam, but my father was largely silent on the subject, saying only that a man had to figure these things out for himself. He supported Nicky, and was proud of him. When I pressed him, he said that if we didn't defend ourselves in Southeast Asia, we'd have to defend ourselves in California.

I pointed out the weakness in that argument, of course. American interests were hardly threatened by a civil war in a remote part of the Asian world. The Chinese were not even friendly with the Vietnamese, so collusion wasn't the issue. If Vietnam fell, one did not expect the dominoes to continue falling. Our intervention could only have the effect of widening the war, destabilizing the region. Who knew what might happen in Cambodia, in Laos, in surrounding countries? We might truly antagonize the Chinese, forcing them to act more brutally than they otherwise might. I was just repeating the familiar arguments, having heard them so many times.

I knew that my brother's and my father's wars were unrelated, but I also understood that both were somehow connected to our primal urge to tear down the things around us—a feeling that overwhelms the child in the schoolyard who kicks over the block castle built by a friend, or built painstakingly by himself. I had firsthand knowledge of this urge. Indeed, there were days when I wanted nothing more than to bomb my own private Hanoi, to get rid of everything that annoyed, obstructed, or challenged me. I demanded an escalation of the emotional troops. I wanted to search and destroy anything that got in my way.

"Why don't we go to the beach now?" Holly asked, after we had finished our espresso.

"Not now," I said.

"You seem pensive," she said. "Is it your brother? What was his name again?"

"Nicky," I said.

"Were you just thinking about him?"

"A little," I said.

"You never talk about him."

"I guess."

"Were you terribly close?"

"Not really," I said. "I wasn't a very good brother."

She didn't press me, and I was grateful. She understood that if I'd wanted to talk about Nicky in any detail, I'd certainly have done so. She had opened a particular door, but I had refused to enter that room.

We got back to the *pensione* early, and Holly said she needed to sleep. I, too, felt exhausted by the events of the past week and wanted to sleep, and the idea of sleeping near Holly was enticing, even without the prospect of lovemaking. I sat in a chair, the single armchair in the room, and read while Holly changed into her nightgown. Before long, she had curled up on her side of the double bed and fallen asleep.

Eventually, I crawled into the cool sheets, taking care not to disturb her. I listened to the rhythmical flow of her breathing, and slowly absorbed the scent of her, now so familiar. I felt a great longing for her, a wish to lie naked beside her. But I was glad for what I had now, however meager. I had her company and good will, and I was about to fall asleep with her only a short distance from me. Close enough to touch, if I dared. But I didn't. She had clearly not invited me to reach across the slight divide between us. So I took care not to breach that gap. In fact, I rolled away from her to sleep, so that anyone looking down from above would have seen us as oddly Janus-faced: a single entity with opposing views of the world, and separate dreams.

ooooo

The circumstances of my sleep—in Salerno, with Holly beside me—made for an abrupt waking. I was at first disoriented, wondering where, and who, I was. But gradually the room dawned, and my situation clarified. I listened for a while to Holly's deep, slow breathing, then turned toward her. Her hair was splayed on the pillow, and her cheek puffed out in a childlike way. I worked hard to suppress the urge to pull her toward me, to kiss her eyelids and lips, her neck, her breasts. I wanted to lie beside her and absorb her, and be absorbed.

It was not quite dawn, but I couldn't lie there. So I dressed quietly and left, hoping to return before Holly was even awake. The beach at Salerno called, and what I'd been unwilling to confront some months before seemed possible now. The Allied landing area wasn't ten minutes by foot from the *pensione*, but I hurried, hoping to get there before the sun rose, as had my father, twenty-seven years before this morning, though he had approached from the water.

Having read so much about this phase of the war and the landing, I wanted to see the actual place, in appropriate light, and imagine the events that had altered my father's sense of the world. "Nothing was the same after Salerno," he said, when I pressed him on the subject. An inarticulate man, he could go no farther. But he'd gone far enough for me to comprehend the crucial nature of that experience in war.

The training in North Africa had probably not prepared him for what happened, for the reality of the invasion. How could it? He would have known that the bullets shooting over his head in ground training were aimed to miss. Lurching from building to building in the Hollywood-style set constructed for training purposes, he could only have felt ridiculous. The enemy was not there. This was cowboys-and-Indians, for adults. And one could only guess what it might feel like to face the fire itself, the onslaught of mortars and gunfire, grenades and rockets. To see one's friends wounded or dead. To face the fact of one's own possible obliteration.

Despite his usual reticence, stories about the war occasionally slipped from my father. Once while camping in the Poconos, he had seemed in a mood to talk, so I pressed for details. He remembered sleeping in a smelly pup tent in North Africa, and that he and his comrades had been so exhausted every night that a blizzard of mosquitoes had not damaged their sleep. All you wanted was sleep, he said, and nothing got between you and your dreams. Did he dream about the war, I wondered? No, he said, laughing at my stupid question. Not war. Like everybody else, he dreamed about home.

The preparations for the invasion had seemed, he said, interminable. The red-powdery roads were crammed with staff cars and trucks over-loaded with the thousand little and large things required of an army about to make a major invasion. Transports and amphibious landing crafts (called "ducks") of different shapes and sizes accumulated week by week in various North African ports. Huge freighters came with their bellies loaded, disgorging equipment. I used to have a book filled with pictures of tank-landing craft and troop-landing craft, with the barges that ran up beaches and deposited their goods, then scrambled back for more. (My father once pointed out, in a book of military aircraft, the kind of enemy fighters that had strafed the harbors in North Africa, and he noted the Beaufighters and P-38s that had fended them off. Once the Allies had gained control of the skies, they could prepare their fleets in peace.)

One night my father and his platoon began to move, entering the transport ships, moving together like cattle onto flat iron decks, their canteens full of water that smelled of disinfectant, huddled beside lumps of equipment. They had, by now, become used to living off C-rations, and each had in his knapsack a quantity of bland but energy-filled biscuits, canned cheeses, meats, and candy bars. Cigarettes were passed around the deck by nervous sergeants, and even those who had never smoked before took up the habit, their hands trembling. Nobody knew what would really happen, or could visualize the landing, or could know in his heart of hearts how he might react under enemy fire. That was the great question. Would you wilt, losing your mind altogether? Or would you find the tension bearable?

The convoy assembled and moved forward, flanked by destroyers. Overhead, silvery balloons floated in the sky, these artificial moons designed to keep the dive-bombers from attacking. The radios went silent as the sea grew louder and louder, as if roiled by the events that loomed. In each soldier's life, an invisible line would soon be crossed, a personal Rubicon. Life before action, and life after. That many of these men would die or go blind or lame was clear to everyone, but nobody talked about this. There were silly jokes about who looked scared and who didn't. There were obscene jokes, too. The more outrageously obscene the better. And the laughter felt good to many, and they could put from their minds for a few seconds the reality that lay before them. And then a shadow fell over the men, as the hugeness of the occasion became apparent. In this covering shade, each soldier encountered a solitude that, quite suddenly, he understood was his most precious and permanent possession, and he began to master the difficult language of silence.

Just before dawn, the rhythm of life abruptly shifted, and the troops disgorged into amphibious landing crafts. Before the men quite knew what was happening, the first great wave had begun to roll. The invasion of Italy was really underway. Into the pearl-haze of dawn, with nobody talking, and with the moon behind them, they poured themselves into action, becoming an army—a real army—at last.

I stood on the beach now, looking at a sea that ran in smooth, expansive waves without whitecaps. The sun was only beginning to rise, and it surprised me how easily I could see them approaching: my father and his comrades in the Fifth Army. The ducks massed on the horizon, arriving in droves, running up from the sea onto the broad, moon-whitened beach. Bulldozers worked frantically, pushing wet sand into mounds that became ramps for trucks to land on. An advance phalanx of specially-trained men were digging for mines on their bellies, clearing the way for troops and trucks and tanks.

I remember asking my father about the noise of battle. Was it loud? Was it bearable? He considered my question, then explained that if a shell burst within twenty feet of you, it was too loud to hear. But you could hear the popping sound of the .88s, fired from the nearby hills, and the machine guns rattling from the dunes. He remembered star shells lighting up the skies, and tracers that zipped across the beach. He heard a loud *whoosh* once, the explosion of a surf mine, and he saw a dozen or so bodies floating shoreward, but he never saw any blood. He was sure of that. He also remembered seeing a case of .50-caliber shells floating by him, the case gone green from contact with sea water. "It's funny," he said, "but it's only bits and pieces you remember, and it's never the important things. Not the worst things, either. Thank God you forget those."

It must have felt better to get onto firm land, where the men gained control of their movements. But quickly a new reality would have overwhelmed them, as they made their way on their bellies toward the city itself, over sand, with intermittent, deadly splashes of dirt and dust, as shells burst and the air thickened with smoke and the sharp smell of cordite. My father probably heard wounded men crying out, in pain so fresh and fierce that it quickly seemed remote, like somebody else's pain. I had experienced that only once, in infinitely less exaggerated circumstances, when an ax cut into my leg at summer camp, and I had to get thirty stitches. The real pain didn't come for hours, seeping in gradually. By the time the pain would have arrived for these soldiers, many would have died already or been dosed on morphine.

I once read an account of this invasion in a book of letters by soldiers to their friends and families. One of them described the stretcher-bearers, and how brave they were, carrying the dead or badly wounded to first-aid stations, the canvas of each stretcher soaked in gore. They remembered men walking through the fog of battle without arms, with an eyehole blasted away, an ear or chin removed. They saw men without legs, crawling. They saw things that nobody should ever have to see or remember—like children with their guts blown away or young men twitching in the sand, moments from death, begging for their mothers. Or dead mules in the road, their hash of furry intestines blackened by flies.

My knees weakened, and I knelt in the sand as the day brightened, with a red sun tinting the water. I believed I had seen something there, in Salerno. Heard and smelled it, even tasted it. And it would never leave me. It would become part of who I was, making it far more possible for me to connect to my father when I went home. He had been only nineteen when he went to war, and when he landed on Salerno, he was barely twenty. I'd never before quite understood what that meant. (As Napoleon once said, to understand a man deeply, you have to know where he was at the age of twenty.) The experience at Salerno would surely have framed his life in ways beyond calculation. It would have determined everything that came after.

I also realized, as I knelt there, that my feelings about Rupert Grant had shifted, however slightly. He acted like a general, but he had never known war, not as Nicky had, or my father. There was nothing wrong with this, of course. I myself had never experienced battle. But Grant's world was so purely aesthetic, a maze constructed to hide some mythical beast that frightened him. He had created a dazzling thing, employing his talents to the fullest, and yet those around him scarcely understood what he'd done, or what their part in his fantasy might be. On one hand, it was difficult not to admire a man with the power to summon a vision and declare it his. But there was a limit to this vision. I felt that I was only beginning to see through and around the construction.

## seven

Holly and I became better friends, but every attempt I made to shift the relationship in a more amorous direction was subtly rebuffed. When I reached for her hand in a restaurant, she let me hold it briefly, then withdrew. When I put my arm around her shoulder as we walked toward the bus station in Salerno, she managed to twist away from me. All conversational gambits designed to increase intimacy were resisted, and I would find myself in the lap of friendship once again. (I did my best to conceal my frustration, but it would break out insidiously, and I would quarrel with her about idiotic things, like where to eat or which bus to take.)

We left Salerno after lunch, sitting in the back of the blue SITA bus, which carried handfuls of passengers to villages along the coast. The sea was golden-pink in the August light, the beaches blowsy. Through the open window came the tinny smell of eucalyptus, ferried on a warm breeze. Having gotten up so early in Salerno, I felt ready for a siesta. But the presence of Holly kept me alert. I let my hand, at one point, stretch around her shoulders, resting above her neck; to my surprise, she put her head back on my forearm, closing her eyes. I felt no obligation to shift my position, and thrilled to the weight of her head against my bare arm.

Arriving in Paestum in late afternoon, we immediately found a *pensione* that overlooked its Doric temples, one of Italy's grandest remnants from the ancient world. The hotel was, fittingly, called the Magna Graecia, alluding to the ancient Greek empire that once included this part of Italy in its sweep. A spidery old woman in black led us to our room—a smaller version of the Salerno room, with twin beds pushed together. There was a faded portrait of the Virgin Mary above the headboard in a gilt frame, with a scrap of dry palm pushed through a loop in the hook that held it to the wall. The room had no toilet, but there was a makeshift shower in one corner, with a yellow plastic curtain that one drew around it. Through glass doors, the temples and the sea were perfectly framed.

"*Va bene?*" the old woman asked.

"*Sì, mille grazie,*" I said.

We left at once to see the temples. Paestum was, among all sites of interest in southern Italy, the most fascinating: Greek temples in astonishingly fine fettle, considering their ages. The site had been an ancient city of considerable opulence and grace, and it dated to the turn of the sixth century, B.C., when it was called Poseidonia. Eventually, in the third century, A.D., it became a Roman colony. What remained, after so many centuries, was a sequence of Doric columns, tall and symmetrical, with a slightly ruddy tint that tended, in the dust of late afternoon light, to turn orange.

The relative absence of tourists, even in summer, pleased us. A few Swedes were pouring over guidebooks, and some Germans took pictures of each other in the colonnade of the basilica, which had originally been a temple dedicated to Hera; but we had the prize all to ourselves, the Temple of Athena. Its bronze-tinted columns thrust at the sky, solid and straight, while a delicate cornice at the top of each formed a crown of sorts. The light fell slantwise from the west, and the columns replicated themselves in long shadows that crossed the courtyard, where lizards and scorpions scuttled among tufts of crabgrass.

Holly was lost in thought, leaning against one column, in a T-shirt like a white sail. I studied the outline of her body, wafer-thin. I was trembling inside, without access to words that could explain my feelings. Was this love? Or was I simply lusting after her? How did one separate these things—love and sex—or did it matter? I realized how little I knew of anything that mattered, and I was grateful to have Rilke back in my room, for comfort and wisdom. "Sex is difficult," he wrote bluntly to his young disciple. "If you only recognize this and manage, out of yourself, out of your own nature and ways, out of your own experience and childhood and strength to achieve a relation to sex wholly your own (not influenced by convention and custom), then you need no longer be afraid of losing yourself and becoming unworthy of your best possession."

I was beginning to understand a little of what Rilke meant as I thought about Holly. "In one creative thought a thousand forgotten nights of love revive," said the poet. I had not had those thousand nights of love, having experienced the strangeness of naked contact only a handful of times, most recently with Marisa. These nights had each been memorized, analyzed, and relived many times. Yet they were nothing in themselves, adding up to little but a flurry of sensations. Whatever the word "love" meant, it was not these nights. I had never really known the women I'd met in those wild stabs at sexual experience, and this saddened me.

Holly and I had dinner on a terrace overlooking the Greek ruins, and—for the first time—I began to make emotional contact with her. A full bottle of wine loosened the gates of inhibition, and I told her about my experience on the beach in Salerno. She responded by telling me about her father's experience as a prisoner of war in Burma. What a violent century it had been, we agreed, beginning with the Boer War, running through the tragedy of two massively destructive world wars, followed by an unbroken sequence of bloody regional wars from Korea to Vietnam. So many millions had been killed or maimed. So many people had been dislodged from homes, from beloved traditions. And for what?

"Capri is so unreal," I said.

"It's your life, Alex," she said. "Your life can't be unreal. That's illogical."

"I suppose I wanted something unreal."

"You're avoiding something, aren't you?" she asked.

My mind wandered, and I thought about Nicky, my parents, and the hectic and fragmentary years I'd spent at Columbia, trying to catch up—socially and intellectually—with my peers. My freshman roommate had graduated from Andover, and could never begin to comprehend the life I'd lived in Pittston, where only a few had ever been to Europe or read

Proust or heard about the Geneva Convention. I had managed, somehow, to ratchet up my levels of sophistication, and to pretend that I felt at ease with those around me. But I didn't. There had been a huge emotional fee attached to my recently acquired sophistication, and I was still paying it off, with interest.

Holly herself, I discovered, had come to Capri to sidestep things that troubled her. Much to my amazement, she described in some detail a "breakdown" of sorts during her final year at Lady Margaret Hall. In response, I told her about my last months at Columbia. Though different in context, these episodes had much in common: a sense of dislocation, an urgent wish for a change of environment. The more we talked, the less Holly seemed just a physical presence, and the more her soul became tangible. I thought of Tolstoy, who (in emulation of Buddhist monks) acquired the habit of bowing whenever he met people, acknowledging their separate, soulful presence, and I wanted to bow to Holly. Instead I reached across the table for her hand, and this time she didn't withdraw it.

After a glass of grappa, we paid the bill and returned to the Magna Graecia. It was late, but in the usual Italian fashion, the streets teemed with young children in fine clothes; they were taking in the evening with their parents, many of whom were no older than Holly or I. Teenage boys gunned their motorbikes, and girls in colorful blouses flirted with them behind dark eye shadow. Europop poured from the open bars. It was important for everyone to take a turn in the night air, *fare un giro*. This was Italy, after all, land of *la bella figura*.

From the balcony of our bedroom we could see the illumined columns of Athena's temple below us, ghostly in the chalk of moonlight. One could easily believe that centuries had not passed, and that holy rites of love might well be performed again on that sacred ground at any moment.

While I remained on the balcony, looking at the temples and the sea beyond, Holly slipped into bed. I soon followed, in boxers and T-shirt. Unobtrusively, I lay beside her, keeping my distance, expecting another night of sexual frustration, since the hand-holding in the restaurant had led nowhere, though I had stealthily draped an arm around her shoulder on the way back to the *pensione*. There was, it seemed, a line I could not cross. Vistas of friendship had widened, but physical love seemed far away, an impossible shore.

"*A domani,*" she said, her back against me.

"*A domani,* Holly."

"I'm awfully tired," she said, as if to explain her distance from me, and her position in the bed.

"It's the wine," I said. "I'm a little dizzy."

Leaning toward the weak lamp on my bed table, I read a few paragraphs from Rilke. "You are so young," he wrote to Kappus, "but I want to beg you, with all my soul, to be patient toward all that remains unsolved in your heart. Try, dear sir, to love the *questions themselves* that lie inside you like locked rooms or like books that are written in a foreign tongue." He urged, above everything, patience. "There is no measuring with time, no year matters, and ten years mean nothing. Being an artist means, not reckoning and counting, but ripening like the tree that does not force its sap but stands confident in the storms of spring without fear that after them may come no summer. It does come. But it comes only to the patient, who behave as though eternity lay before them, still and wide. I learn this daily, learn it with pain for which I am always grateful: *patience is everything!*"

Though I wanted everything to happen at once—poems, novels, love—I was beginning to understand Rilke's point. Truth glimmered off his pages. But soon I let the book fall onto the floor with a soft thud, switched off the light, and lay back on the pillow, closing my eyes in the room's half light, with street sounds churning behind the zebra slats of the shutters, which replicated themselves on the bedroom wall.

How much time elapsed, I can't recall. Ten minutes perhaps? In any case, Holly's voice—slightly husky, but soft—startled me.

"Are you awake, Alex?"

"Me?"

"Are you sleeping?"

I smiled. "Not any longer."

"I'm sorry."

"No, I was kidding. I'm awake."

"Oh, good," she said. She drew a long breath. "I don't know if you want this, but would you like to make love?"

"Sure," I said, as matter-of-factly as if she'd asked me if I might pass the pepper.

My heart was pounding in my throat and temples. We said nothing else, but I watched as—in the dim light—she lifted the nightgown over her head, so that I could see the outline of her small breasts, their upward tilt. She quickly turned toward me, moving as close as could be. I welcomed her, putting my arms around her shoulders, letting my face brush against the side of her head.

"I want you," I said.

The experience was like that which Rilke had described: "And those who come together in the night and are entwined in rocking delight do earnest work. They gather sweetness, depth, and strength for the song of some coming poet, who will arise to speak of ecstasies beyond telling."

I knew those ecstasies that night as we came together, again and again.

How unexpectedly the room filled with sunlight the next morning as I lay on the bed, on my stomach, and breezes drew across my buttocks and back. The air seemed light and pure. Holly stood at the open shutters, peering onto the terrace, still naked as well. I glanced at her, furtively, culling the perfection of her form. There was nothing to say that could possibly add to the experience, and we both seemed to understand that. Silence was, indeed, our best friend that morning, which I count among the sweetest mornings of my life.

## PART SIX

*gloria mundi*

*one*
———

The steamy air cleared in late September, when the island emptied of tourists, who returned to office towers in Milan, Paris, Geneva, Frankfurt, London, and Stockholm. The children of expatriate residents—including Nigel and Nicola—returned to schools in England and Switzerland. Adjusting to demand, the ferries began to cut back on their schedules, and Capri felt less besieged. One could get a table in the piazzetta, and the hotels began to whittle their staffs.

"I am soon dismissed," said Patrice, "but I hope not so. Signore Milone, he says, you are my most intelligent waiter. You can work through the winter season, even if we have no diners." Now that Giovanni was preoccupied with his intended, Patrice had time on his hands, and would appear at my cottage door in the late evening. Earlier in the summer, I might have discouraged these visits, but I needed him now— a receptive, sympathetic, and nonjudgmental ear.

That I'd not given thought to the consequences of my excursion to Paestum with Holly understates the case. I assumed that Rupert Grant, whose name was known to hundreds of thousands of readers around the world, couldn't care less what Holly and I had done. I imagined the social chemistry at the Villa Clio would adjust to our newly amorous relations, and that I could blithely continue as Grant's secretary. (Holly herself had admitted, in Salerno, that she and Grant were "not on their old terms of intimacy.")

What exactly would happen between me and Holly was not obvious to me. The morning after our night of love in Paestum, she grew inexplicably cooler. Over a sunny breakfast of coffee, oranges, and cornetti on the rooftop terrace of the Magna Graecia, she appeared unhappy and remote. When I suggested that she move into the cottage with me at the Villa Clio, she said this was "unrealistic." She warned me not to "make assumptions" about our relationship. When I made a cynical allusion to her and Grant, she suggested that I didn't understand her situation. "He has certain expectations," she said.

"He expects you to sleep with him," I said.

She shook her head. "I play a role in his life. It would be difficult to change that role and remain on the island."

"Are you afraid of him?"

"Of course not," she said.

"So explain," I said.

Her face hardened, and I knew that pressing her would yield nothing. Grant clearly exercised a power over her that I couldn't comprehend.

On the journey back to Capri, I tried to resume this conversation, but Holly resisted. The shadow of her British upbringing only darkened, enabling her to remain cool and sheltered in the midst of what seemed, to me, like an emotional storm. "Don't be so naive," she said, when I told her she had no future with Grant. "Don't assume anything. It's always a mistake to assume things about other people." When I seized her hand, she cringed, letting me hang on to it for a while, though obviously embarrassed by my need.

Back on the island, I attempted to follow the usual routines, but found this difficult. The situation between me and Holly and Grant was, of course, painful. And the attempt to erase Marisa from memory seemed willfully cruel. Whenever I raised her name, Vera frowned and Grant changed the subject. Even Holly refused to talk about her. "Don't be so morbid, Alex," she would say. "I feel as awful as you do. We were friends. But one mustn't dwell on such things." (Sadly, I realized how often a Calvinistic *mustn't* figured in her speech. Perhaps this was the appeal of Grant, whose speech was full of negative imperatives?) The topic drove a further wedge between us, giving that night on Paestum the status of a beautiful dream that one could not hope to repeat.

It didn't help that she behaved in Grant's presence as though nothing had happened between us. Jealousy peered over my shoulder, and I was convinced that he'd gotten his hooks back into Holly. But it made no sense. Was she simply impressed by his fame? Holly seemed too mature for that. I continued to wonder what drew her to the Villa Clio in the first place. Like me, she had originally approached Grant with a letter, having been given his address by a friend of her father's, who had known Grant at Oxford. She had sought a position as "research assistant," but it quickly developed into something more, Grant being Grant.

"He chooses very young and unthreatening girls," Peter Duncan-Jones told me. "Girls whose futures lie elsewhere. They're all in the business of creating a naughty past for their future fantasies about themselves." He rattled off the names of half a dozen other young women who had come and gone from the Villa Clio over the past decade: Susan, Miranda, Elise, Nicole. His wry companion, Jeremy, added a few other names: Gavin, Alphonse, Gennaro. (They both sighed at the mention of Gennaro.)

As usual, I sought out Vera for advice. Even at the worst of moments we had a visceral connection, and my need to talk now overwhelmed any sense of caution. I told her frankly about Salerno and Paestum, confessing my distress and confusion.

"You've become quite the chap," she said. "But I should warn you: Holly is not your type." Her catlike eyes glittered. "I should forget about her."

"I can't," I said.

"Dear boy, restraint," she said. "I really can't bear it when people talk like that, even when they are young and American."

The line about Americans was beginning to wear thin. "You English," I said, "you all think you're so fucking wise."

"You're upset," she said. "And I don't blame you. Rupert is a beast. He thinks he's doing it all for art, you see."

Vera had, it seemed, been bamboozled by her husband, who firmly believed that he invented all truth with the tip of his pen, if not his penis.

"Does Rupert love her?" I asked. That I could ask such a question of Vera Grant suggests a lack of focus on my part. I had given up trying to assess my audience.

"Love?" She tasted the word cautiously—like a piece of possibly spoiled meat from the fridge. "What is love?" The question echoed in all its sentimental amplitude.

"You're teasing me," I said.

"If you will insist on asking foolish questions, I will respond in kind." She reached for a cask of wine acquired from the local contadina. "Let's have a drink, shall we? I'm hot."

We sat in the alcove in the kitchen. It was unusual for us to drink so early in the day, but I welcomed it today. "I know that you dearly believe you love this girl," Vera said. "You've been mooning about for months, sighing at the merest glimpse of her. Rupie and I have found it amusing. He likes Holly himself, of course."

"Whatever amuses him," I said, letting my anger show.

Vera raised her fine, penciled eyebrows, like upside-down smiles on her forehead. "Everyone is too cynical these days," she said.

"Around here, that's true."

"Everywhere," she said. "The intractable point is, Holly and Rupert have an arrangement, and it's between them. That's what arrangements are. If you should wish to make your own arrangement with Holly, that's your business. But you mustn't expect Rupert to admire your entrepreneurial skills." Her voice lowered now. "I should lie back, were I you."

Lie back? And let Holly drift away from me, as she certainly would? I had already seen this happening. A week or more had passed since the episode at Paestum, and she had shown no signs of wishing to pursue our relationship in any conventional sense. I had stupidly hoped that she would acknowledge me as her lover. I wanted her to move into the cottage with me and expected Grant to give in, possibly to acquire a new "research assistant." But it was obvious my wishing and assuming would have no effect on the reality before me. I was powerless to change anything at the Villa Clio. After my fashion, I was just another servant—one who could type and translate Latin and supply reasonably civilized conversation at the table. I was also an entertaining subject for Grant and

Vera, one they could chuckle over in bed. But to imagine myself a genuine player on this great stage was simply hubris.

"I must warn you," Vera said, a raspy voice betraying years of smoking. "Rupert is like certain wild animals. When threatened, they don't understand the meaning of restraint." She took a sip of wine, searching for my reaction. "Knock, knock? Have I got through, darling? Have you heard what Mother Vera has been saying?" Her eyebrows maintained an interrogative arch.

I understood, but I didn't assent, unwilling to let Holly go so easily. Unfortunately, the course of true love only grew bumpier. I attempted to speak with Holly alone on several occasions, nabbing her outside Grant's study or in the garden, but she brushed me off, pretending that her duties preoccupied her. One afternoon I found her at the poolside and lured her into my cottage for a drink. Sitting at the three-legged table, I explained that I had not slept since getting back to Capri, that I felt desperate. I told her, once again, that I loved her.

"You mustn't carry on," she said, with the no-nonsense undertones of a British schoolmarm.

"Mustn't?" I repeated.

Holly looked sternly at me, her lips tight. I thought she might slap me.

"I don't understand," I said. "We had such a good time in Paestum."

"We had good sex," she said.

"That counts for something?"

She stared at the table, running her finger along a crack. "One can always find a sexual partner."

"One can," I said, repeating her expression in a mocking way that I knew was ill-advised. But I couldn't help myself. It was no longer possible to repress my frustration and anger. "I thought we had," I said, hesitating, "a kind of sympathy for each other. We seemed—"

"I do like you," she said, looking up. "It's that you push rather hard. You insist, and that's boring. A man should not insist."

"But I love you," I said.

She looked away, and I realized this approach was not going to work with Holly Hampton. Somewhere in her life she had learned to suspect expressions of feeling. And I saw that one could not force affairs of the heart. Like rainwater coursing down a hillside, they had to carve their own runnels, taking a path that gravity and the terrain allowed.

"I'm sorry about what happened in Paestum," she said. "I should never have gone away with you. I was angry with Rupert."

"And you're not angry now?"

"Yes and no," she said.

I said she was mistaken if she believed she had a future with Rupert Grant. He was merely using her. Vera, too, was using her.

"And what about you, Alex? Are you not using me as well?"

I felt a hardness in the pit of my stomach. She was, of course, right. Nevertheless, I hoped to salvage whatever I could of the fragile relationship begun at Paestum. "Rupert doesn't care about you," I said.

"But I *do* care, actually," a voice called.

A look of fear crossed Holly's face.

Grant stood hugely in the doorway of the cottage, as if summoned by our conversation. Like a retired British colonel in the tropics, he wore khaki shorts and a military-style shirt, with epaulets. I couldn't remember the last time he'd come to my cottage.

"May I come in?" he asked, opening the screen door.

"Go away, Rupert," said Holly.

"This is my house, what?" he said, approaching. He hovered beside the table.

"I'm asking you to leave, Rupert," said Holly, with admirable calm.

Grant stared at me, as though peering down the barrel of a gun. His eyebrows stood out, white and bristling. The hair streamed upward and backward, electric. There was something wild about him—a throwback to the Stone Age. "I should watch my back, Lorenzo," he said.

"Don't be melodramatic," said Holly.

I rose to my feet.

"I say," he said, "you're a brave man, aren't you? A warrior, like your brother." After a hideous moment during which I thought he might take a swing at me, he turned and left the cottage.

Holly's cheeks glistened. I had never seen her weep before, and this unsettled me. Ignorantly, I had imagined her a creature of absolute self-confidence and balance, beyond the usual petty reactions. I stood behind her, putting my hands on her neck, kneading the muscles at the point where her neck and shoulders joined. She appeared to relax into the motion, tipping her head toward one shoulder, then the other.

"We're friends, Alex," she said. "Not lovers. Can you accept that?"

I didn't want to accept it, but had no choice. "What about Paestum?" I wondered.

"A mistake. I wasn't thinking."

"I see," I said.

After giving me a chaste kiss on the cheek, Holly left the cottage. I listened to her footsteps dissolving on the path, and assumed that she was hurrying to catch up with Grant, needing to reassure him that I meant nothing to her. But how could I be sure of this? How could I be sure of anything?

*two*

_____

I returned *Love's Body* to Toni at the Villa Vecchia on the afternoon before her departure, for America, the next morning. Her term at Bryn Mawr began in three days, she explained, while busily packing. I sat on the edge of her bed as she folded items of clothing and put them, like bits of a puzzle, into a candy-red Samsonite suitcase. The door to her balcony was open, and a dry breeze puffed the curtains and felt cool on my face.

"It's a peculiar book," I said, "but brilliant."

Toni nodded, studying a box of loose jewelry, trying to determine what she could afford to leave behind and what must go back to college with her. A number of skirts and blouses were lined up on the sofa.

"Brown pulls so many ideas together," I added, trying to win her attention.

"So many quotes," she said, distracted.

"Yes. But he somehow makes everything sound like his own voice."

"Isn't that what writers do?" She sat beside me now, as if suddenly aware of my presence in the room. "What's wrong, Alex?"

"What do you mean?"

"You're still upset about Marisa," she said. "I don't blame Rupert Grant entirely, but I almost do."

Marisa was not the issue, but I played along. It seemed easier than raising the specter of Holly. "It's true that he asked her to leave," I said. "That was a blow."

Toni shook her head. "Look at the situation with some critical distance, huh? He wanted to turn her into one of his muses, and that's ridiculous. It's sick, even."

"That's a strong word."

Toni was flushed with purpose. "It's the right word. He never saw Marisa as a human being. The same is true of Holly. These girls are—were—so naive. I don't know who to kill—them or Grant."

"Holly sees through him," I said.

Toni scowled. "Give me a break. She's still there, isn't she?"

I guessed that Holly would soon be gone, but wasn't sure. One could never be quite sure about Holly.

"What about you?" she asked. "Gonna hunker down? Find yourself a little Capresi bride?"

"I'm going," I said.

"Really?"

I nodded.

"Does Grant know?"

"No, but he'll be glad to get rid of me. I'm just waiting for the moment."

"Where will you go?"

I realized how much I liked Toni Bonano now, telling her about my lack of plans. Her kindly presence was reassuring.

"Here's my address," she said, scribbling on a pad beside her bed. "I've got an apartment this year. You can stay there anytime." As though the inducement would help, she noted that Philadelphia was a brief ride away.

I put the address in my pocket, assuring her that I'd visit—probably sooner than later. Seeing that she was too busy to sit around chatting with me, I said good-bye, kissing her on either cheek.

"Take care now," she said, gravely, as though I were going into battle.

The idea of returning to the Villa Clio did terrify me, and I wondered if I shouldn't hop on the next ferry, leaving everything of Capri behind in a locked trunk, memories and all. But that would have been immature, I told myself sharply. I must not, under any circumstances, behave immaturely.

*three*

---

After my mother's illness, my father assumed the role of family correspondent. His mode was upbeat. My mother looked "pretty good, for a lady whose health is rotten," he said. On most days, she was "like her old self—minus the vitality." The doctors had given her a handful of pills, "every color of the rainbow," and she gobbled them at intervals throughout the day. Her appetite—no small thing—had fully returned. He and she often talked about me, remembering my superior work at Scranton Prep and Columbia. "When it comes to brains," he wrote, "you got the goods." My mother thought I would make an excellent teacher, but he still thought I was going to be an asset to the business one day. My grandfather in particular hoped I would eventually work for Massolini Construction. He was, of course, pleased that I had found the Old Country an interesting place. But what exactly did I like so much? Wasn't the standard of living in Italy below what you could find anywhere in America?

I wrote home faithfully, ignoring all hints about returning to Pennsylvania, taking care to frame my experience on Capri in ways that would make sense in Luzerne County. In one letter, I casually mentioned to my father that I'd been to Salerno, and had stood on the beach where he landed. That news had provoked a single line of response: "As far as I'm concerned, you can keep Salerno."

The unspoken request in every letter was, "Alex, come home." But Pittston no longer felt like home. Nowhere did, though the Villa Clio had at first felt like a place I'd been looking for unsuccessfully all of my life. I refused to criticize it, taking for granted its small guilts and large assumptions. I bought greedily into Grant's view of things, and did my best to make him believe I shared his opinions. Yet now I found our conversations painful. I continued to type manuscripts for *il maestro*, but there was no emotional payoff anywhere. He would merely grunt whenever I appeared at his study with a pile of typescript, barely acknowledging my presence. The possibility of taking another poem to him for criticism had withered.

Once, as I sat taking dictation in my slow fashion (which annoyed him), he lifted the dagger from his desk and flung it toward me, missing my head by two feet or so. The blade whizzed past, sticking in the wallboard with a menacing twang.

I gaped at Grant, barely able to believe that had happened.

"Sorry, old man," he said, "but I needed to wake you up."

"I'm perfectly awake," I said.

He continued the dictation as though nothing had happened, and I tried to resume writing, but my hand shook so badly I could not grip the pen. He wanted to kill me, I thought. And perhaps he would.

Another time, when I had stopped to admire a bed of belladonna lilies, newly flowered, in the lower garden, he came up to me from behind, putting his hands on my shoulders and squeezing. I froze, thinking he might snap my collarbones, then turned to face him.

"Not to worry," he said, with fumes of whiskey on his breath. "I do like you, Lorenzo, my dear boy. But I did have something to say—rather sotto voce, what?"

I waited attentively.

"Were I you," he said, "I should forget about Holly. Put her out of your bloody head."

"That's not possible," I said.

"Anything is possible."

I looked away from him.

"You've got the beginnings of a talent," he said, shifting the subject onto ground where he felt certain of his position. "A glimmer of something in the poems, perhaps. Your prose is tolerable." From him, these were mighty compliments. "I should think about travel. A young man must travel, what? Find something to write about."

We had talked of this before. His own youthful travels in distant lands had been famously crucial to his development. In his writing, he often referred to places he had, quite literally, touched. I recalled another occasion where he said, "It was your man, Hemingway, who suggested one should seek out experience. Quite right, that. Otherwise, one is condemned to write novels about adultery in suburbia. Americans like them, of course."

"The English do as well," I replied, more to annoy him than to make a genuine point. That he didn't press for examples relieved me.

We stood face to face, him swaying like a blown rose on its stem. The fragility of his presence struck me: the dry, rough skin that grew more translucent every day, the blue veins in his cheeks, the bad teeth and thinning hair. I was too young to see that, in mere decades, I could find myself similarly worn.

"I should recommend Tangiers," Grant said. "I have an old friend there, Bowles. American chap. Not a bad writer. He will see you."

"You're asking me to go?"

"Nonsense," he said.

I would not back away. "You must tell me if I'm no longer welcome."

"Dear fellow," he said, reaching his hands around my neck, "you're absolutely mad." He leaned close to my ear. "I should miss you terribly if you abandoned our little nest. I should be forlorn."

To my relief, he drew back. After a puzzled look at me, as though trying without success to remember my identity, he turned toward a path that led to the sea and stumbled into the shadows of the cyprus allée. And no bird sang.

ooooo

I began to plot my exit, convinced that the time to leave Capri had come. Vera was increasingly erratic, saying odd things, making innuendoes, clipping my verbal wings with scissoring asides. I felt unwelcome in her kitchen, and avoided what had been a place of warmth and diversion. My Italian culinary education skidded abruptly to a halt. With Toni Bonano gone, I had Patrice alone for friendship, though his agonies with Giovanni made him a less than jolly companion. He could not understand how a perfectly healthy, red-blooded queer like Giovanni could prefer a pink-cheeked, bosomy girl of no particular charms to him, a spiritual heir of the *philosophes*. He must somehow get Giovanni off the island, he said, but he knew that was impossible. "These Capresi," he said, "they have no other place in mind. There is Capri for them—nothing else."

Holly simply ignored me, although one Sunday afternoon in mid-September, she suggested that we have a picnic together at the Villa Jovis. Rupert and Vera were having a rare meal away from the Villa Clio with Mona and Eddie von Bismarck, whose guest of honor was W. H. Auden. That my favorite poet should have landed on Capri was both thrilling and frustrating. In fact, there seemed a touch of malice in Vera's voice when she told me about the dinner I'd be missing. "He's such an amusing chap," she said, as she left.

It was a steep climb to the Villa Jovis, often eased for day-trippers by donkeys, whom they engaged in front of the Quisisana. (The sex lives of these pathetic beasts amused guests of the hotel in the late afternoons, as they sipped cocktails on its *terrazza elegante*.) Holly and I approached from the south, coming through dense eucalyptus and oak woods above the Tragara to the villa's manicured grounds. This principal residence of Tiberius was built into the northeastern peak of Capri—placed strategically to survey the island as a whole, the Sorrentine Peninsula beyond, and the Gulf of Naples.

One had to imagine what the villa might have been in its heyday, since only a honeycomb of stone cisterns, reticulated walls, and uneven floors remained. Grassy pathways led from terrace to terrace. The actual living quarters of the emperor had been built close to the edge of the cliff, giving way to imperial baths and a spectacular terrace, with a view to the mainland. We walked through the loggia onto the broad *ambulatio*, with its pocked columns still in place beside ilex and umbrella pines. Tiberius would pace there, in the early evening, contemplating the fate of Rome. (A nearby lighthouse, restored in recent years, communicated with the mainland; it apparently crumbled only a few days before the emperor's death.)

It was here, on the *ambulatio*, that the emperor once spoke in hushed tones with his supposed friend and political favorite, Sejanus. In a bizarre and brilliant move, he sent his adjutant back to Rome with a sealed letter, which he asked to be read in the presence of all senators. Sejanus and his followers—a potent faction within the Roman government—believed that he was about to be honored with newly created powers. With Tiberius living so far from the center of power, he would act as the emperor's vicar in Rome, his chosen deputy. He listened with horror as the letter, which contained a warrant for his arrest and immediate execution, was read.

Since Holly had not heard this story, I relayed it in some detail, having read the original version in Tacitus. I embellished the tale myself, describing Sejanus as a "fawning young man who secretly believed himself at least the intellectual equal of the emperor."

"Oh, I meant to tell you," said Holly, slyly. "Rupert has a letter for you."

"For me?"

"What a nit you are!"

"You're wicked."

"Really, Alex—you are such a silly man."

I drew close to her, nose to nose. "You think I'm a fawning young man, don't you? I'm Sejanus."

"On the contrary," she said, "you've stood up nicely to Rupert in the past few weeks. He's quite beside himself." She backed away from me and peered over the cliff, which dropped to the green sea below. It was there that so many of the emperor's enemies—or supposed enemies—were dashed. In a terrifying flash, I could see Marisa tumbling through the air, her body end over end. The rocks below seemed to reach for her, but the moment of the crash never came. She just tumbled and tumbled.

"Are you all right, Alex?"

I refocused my eyes and saw Holly before me. "Rupert tried to kill me the other day," I said.

"What?"

"That dagger on his desk," I said. "He threw it across the room, missing my goddamn head by a couple of feet."

"Why do I know you're not kidding?"

"He's a bastard," I said.

"Marisa told me he'd done the same to her," she said, coolly, "only a few days before she died."

I could believe almost anything about Grant, but this stretched credulity. Marisa was utterly compliant: hardly a threat to him. He had clearly made a calculated assault on her from many angles, physical and mental, in the weeks leading up to her death. He had not, I hoped, wished her to kill herself, but he tried his best to drive her away.

Holly said, wistfully, "He can be so considerate at times."

"Now you're the nit," I said. "He's a monster. A brilliant writer, maybe, but a monster."

"I suppose," she said.

"Do you love him?"

"I don't think so," she said.

"We've got to get away."

"I don't know."

"I do," I said.

Below us, the sun glittered on the sea, driving a path toward Naples and a whole world that was not Capri. To my eye, it beckoned brightly.

*four*

_____

I woke up early the next day, eager to leave the island. Already the whole scene on Capri felt like a dream: remote and insubstantial, phantasmagoric.

I loved walking to the piazzetta for breakfast, lingering over coffee and pastries, writing poetry. I could write in the morning, before the tasks of the day consumed me, when my mind felt clear and large, awake. I'd been filling a notebook with rough drafts of poems in the past weeks, and considered this my secret hoard. I planned to raid those pages for months to come, finding fragments of verse that might, with a little coaxing, become poems. It was a lesson I'd learned from Grant, who often sat in the garden under his favorite lemon tree with a notebook in hand, scribbling odd lines, images, unusual words, names for characters in future fictions, titles that might one day find a poem or novel attached to them.

It was a brilliant morning, the sea on fire below as I made my way toward the piazzetta along the familiar path. I felt keenly alert as I followed the Tragara above the Unghia Marina, while sunlight sharpened its edges on the tumbling dolomitic shelves of Mount Solaro. The rooftop of the Certosa di San Giacomo—an obvious landmark above the Marina Piccola—glistened, as if made of tinfoil. I deeply enjoyed the Camerelle in early morning, with its cloistered aura, the distinctive smell of dung, cat piss, and laundry soap permeating the air as shirts and bedsheets flapped on balconies. The paving stones below were a rich amber color, bordered by late summer flowers. It struck me that Capri never disappointed the senses, rushing at every organ full blast, with variety and texture. I felt a pang, and knew I would miss the island. I might never again recapture this world of light and sound, of smell and taste. Covetously, I ran my fingers along the walls, prizing the chalky stone with its rough and porous grain.

Emerging into the piazzetta from the shadows of the via Vittorio Emanuele, I temporarily lost my vision. The sun was too bright to absorb, so I waited for my eyes to adjust in the shade of a candy-striped awning, taking a whole table to myself at the Bar Alfonso. The Capresi never used these tables, since they charged a little more for the drinks and food in the open air. But I didn't care, having spent very little of my grandfather's money in the past months.

I settled in, opening my notebook to a blank page. The waiter, a young, smooth-cheeked fellow in a white jacket, knew me well by now; he didn't have to ask what I wanted but simply brought an espresso with an almond-encrusted cornetto, still warm from the oven. It was a sign that I'd been accepted as a regular. Contented, I stared ahead, vaguely watching the local traffic in the piazzetta, and vaguely waiting for that elusive thing called inspiration. I was trying (without success) to keep my immediate problems as far from my conscious mind as possible.

With a disorienting rush, I realized that the man sitting at the next table was W. H. Auden. One could hardly mistake the famously grooved face, the lidded eyes with pouches below them, or the hair combed straight to one side like an English schoolboy en route to chapel. His rumpled linen jacket needed laundering, and there were ashes on his gray trousers. On the table before him was last Friday's edition of the *Daily Telegraph*, and he was reading the sports pages. (Grant had told me about Auden's obsession with games, and we'd often talked about his notion of poetry as "a game of knowledge.")

Though I wanted to introduce myself, it seemed gauche and rude to disturb him while he was having breakfast, taking a break from his life as "W. H. Auden." It would, in fact, have annoyed me that morning had someone unexpectedly appeared at my side demanding attention. I savored the solitude in company one finds in a public café—an atmosphere cherished by writers. On the other hand, I had only one life, and Auden meant a lot to me. I might never have another chance to meet him, to hear the voice, to look into his eyes. The encounter would probably strike him as a mild irritation, a petty disturbance in an otherwise uneventful day; but it would matter to me. I would think of it for decades to come, cursing myself to the grave if I didn't make the move.

While still debating whether or not to interrupt him, I found myself standing by his table. The decision seemed to have been made for me.

He looked up and, to my relief, smiled—his teeth were brown, uneven. "You're not Italian," he said. "I can always tell by the jeans. You bought those in America, didn't you?"

"I'm Alex Massolini," I said. "I work for Rupert Grant—as his secretary."

"Ah, my old chum! Please, sit." He offered me a cigarette, but I refused.

"Americans despise smokers," he said. "But it's a foul habit, this not smoking." A white scum gathered in the corners of his lips.

"I've got nothing against smoking," I said, taking a seat.

"Good chap!" He sucked at the cigarette, inhaling with gusto. The smoke disappeared into his lungs forever as a quiet satisfaction flooded his face. His fingers were tobacco-stained, the nails bitten.

"I'm very glad to meet you," I said.

He studied my features. "Let me guess: you're a poet," he said.

"How did you know?"

"I've a sixth sense for such things, my dear. Tell me about your poems. I'm all ears."

"I've written very little. It's more that I'm trying to write poems."

"Well done," he said, irrelevantly. His mind seemed to wander, then he snapped back into focus. "Whom do you read?"

This was easy. "I've been reading your poems for a long time," I said.

"That's not possible," he responded, wiping fresh ashes from the sleeve of his jacket. "You haven't been alive long enough for that to be the case."

"Let's say that as long as I've been interested in poetry, I've admired yours."

He seemed embarrassed by this, taking a sip of coffee.

"'Musée des Beaux Arts' is almost a perfect poem," I said.

Auden smiled. "Almost? Whenever anyone tells me they like a particular poem, I feel as though I've been pickpocketed," he said. "No matter. I like that poem as well as you do. I should like it just as well if someone else had written it."

"It's inspired," I said.

"Oh, dear," he said, with a worried look. "I'm not very keen on that notion. Inspiration. What's that? A passing feeling, with no real connection to any present reality. I place very little weight on how I felt about a certain poem whilst writing it. One must be careful not to overestimate such things. A poem is a verbal machine. Nothing more. One tinkers. There are decent mechanics and poor ones."

"You seem to prefer formal poetry."

"One does whatever appears to work. I like it when gifts come in neat boxes, don't you?" He twisted the cigarette into an ashtray. "I often tell young friends who want to be poets that they should learn everything they can about rhymes, meters, stanza forms, and so on. A poet who writes free verse has to invent the world afresh in every poem, and only the greatest—or luckiest—pull it off. Whitman could manage, or Eliot. For the most part, free verse is sloppy. One doesn't like squalor on the page."

Since he was in a chatty mood, I decided to risk something. "Some of your poems are obscure," I said. "Does it bother you when critics say that?"

"They're not obscure to me," he said. "I'm writing for myself, after all. My readers are just eavesdropping, would you say?"

"I suppose."

"Look, dear. I pay no attention to critics. In a way, I wish poets would be judged only by their peers, like physicists. Nobody ever said, 'But I didn't understand your formula, Dr. Einstein.' Notice that bad physicists are usually not applauded. But what of bad poets? Do you read the reviews in the Sunday papers? Shocking. And the prizes! I'm always appalled by the shortlists, and offended by the winners."

"I don't think about that," I said, and it was true. That sort of professional envy would come later, when I actually had something to compare with others.

Auden was delighted, however. "Try to remain obscure as long as you can," he said. "It's much safer. And forget about this word 'inspiration.' A young poet has to court his own muse, but Dame Philology should become his mistress. Go deeply into words. And don't be concerned with originality."

"So far, that hasn't been a problem," I said. "I'm an imitator."

"I'm sure Rupert would approve," he said. "He's been imitating me for decades." There was an artful pause. "And what do you make of Rupert? Tell the truth now. I won't tattle."

"He's very disciplined," I said.

"Of course," Auden said. "Discipline, in a man of intelligence, is a sign of ambition."

"His best work is probably in the novels."

"Alas, I've never read one."

"Really?"

"I prefer detective stories, that sort of thing."

"You've written prose."

"Quite a lot, I should say. Had to make a living. Mostly book reviews, lectures. It's all a bit scrappy."

Scrappy, indeed. I had, with excitement, read and admired *The Dyer's Hand*, a volume of aphoristic essays and reviews. But I understood that he'd focused on poetry with a unique vengeance. Few poets had written with such variety, in so many forms, many invented for the occasion. The range of his voice, from colloquial to formal modes, dazzled me. The problem was, the audience for such virtuosity was surely dying.

"Do you have anyone in mind, when you write a poem?" I wondered.

"What a funny question," he said. "Do you know, sometimes, when I read a book and adore it, it seems to have been written for my eyes only. I don't want anyone else in the world to know about it, so I keep mum. As a poet, I should like to imagine that thousands of chaps—or ladies—are out there feeling like that about my poems. They've all got a tremendous and wonderful secret which they are loath to share."

What he said made such astonishing good sense, and he clearly enjoyed saying things he'd probably said a thousand times before. He would make, I thought, a marvelous teacher.

"Tell me something of yourself, Alan."

"Alex," I said.

"Yes, yes. So you are happy at the Villa Clio? It's a lovely spot."

"Not really," I said.

"Oh, dear. I suspect the worst, so tell me the truth."

"It's not so bad," I said. "I'm in love."

He drew back, feigning disbelief. "In love? Not very wise, dear," he said. "Who is she? Or he?" He lowered his voice. "Not Rupert, I should hope? He doesn't deserve it."

"An English girl," I said. "Rupert's research assistant."

"He's very keen on his research, isn't he? I've heard about this obsession—from Vera, the poor darling."

"I don't know what to do," I said.

"Make a complete fool of yourself," he said. "It's your right and your duty. You're a young man. Do what follows naturally—as the night the day."

"I'm going to leave Capri," I said, "as soon as possible. And with Holly, if she'll come."

"Oh, she'll come," Auden said. "Abduct her, if she won't. The Italian police are hopeless. You have absolutely nothing to worry about."

I laughed, saying I would take his advice, and this cheered him inordinately. For whatever reason, I had the feeling that he needed my cheer that morning. His bright, healthy spirit seemed uncomfortably trapped in a flabby, unwholesome body that had never willingly been found on a squash court. His complexion—the skin papery and sulfurous—reflected a life of booze and cigarettes. ("His apartment in New York always looked like an ashtray that no one bothered to empty," Grant once told me.) It didn't surprise me when, only a couple of years later, he died—a man in his early sixties, but one whose flesh had long since become irrelevant.

After a few further minutes of chatter, I sensed that Auden wished to regain his solitude. The fleshy eyes kept glancing away from me, toward the sports pages. His fingers began to drum the table.

"I've taken enough of your time, Mr. Auden," I said, rising.

"How nice to meet you," he said, putting forward a hand to shake, a habit perhaps acquired in New York.

I returned to my table and began to write—a true story about an old man called Gus who lived in my neighborhood in Pittston. He occupied an otherwise abandoned Bricktex building on the corner of our block, and children tended to taunt him. Mothers warned against speaking to him at all. The grandmother of a friend informed me that Gus "ate children for breakfast." One day, I caught up to him as he limped along the street, starting a conversation. He seemed glad for my company, and invited me to his filthy apartment (old newspapers were stacked waist-high in every corner). He offered me cookies and a glass of Coke, served in a coffee-stained cup, and—with some reservations—I ate and drank. Gus was supposedly retarded, but I found our conversation delightful— he talked of nothing but the Yankees and their current season. "Mickey Mantle," he said, "very good. He hits so many homers!" He grinned at me, toothlessly. "And you," he said, "what is your name and do you play baseball?" I told him about my Little League team and my dream of pitching for the Braves like Warren Spahn. I also confessed to problems with throwing a curve. "It's hard," I said, and he nodded aggressively. Curve balls are hard to throw, he agreed, extracting a baseball from the pocket of his sweatshirt. "Put your fingers like this," he said, showing me how to place my fingers on the seams of the ball in a particular way. "Try it," he said, handing me the ball. "I think you will throw a curve today."

I left him that day with a feeling of peculiar exhilaration. I was not Gus, and I was not retarded, and I would never, ever live in such a peculiar apartment. And if, by some rotten twist, I found myself in parallel circumstances, I would open my heart to every child on the street.

When I glanced at the table beside me, I noticed that Auden was already gone.

*five*
———

"He's quite hysterical," said Holly, whom I met on my way to the cottage. "I don't know what you've said to him about us." Annoyance wrinkled her brow.

"Who?"

"Rupert!" She seemed quite hysterical herself, her eyes moist and red.

"You've been crying. What's wrong?"

"I must get away. You're right."

"Did he hurt you?"

She looked at me as though I were mad. "He's too savvy for that. And too British."

Mimo was glaring at us, crouching in the garden with a trowel, so I insisted that she come into my cottage.

"What did he say exactly?" I asked, putting a mug of tea before her.

"He said I had disappointed him."

"That's all?"

I suspected she was not telling the whole truth. Grant was capable of immense scorn. I had seen it, and wondered when it might turn in my direction. I never guessed, however, that Holly could be abused by him in this way. He had, toward her, been almost solicitous.

"It was the tone," she said. "And the expression on his face. I've never seen him like that."

"He knows how I feel about you," I said.

"Please, Alex. We mustn't go there."

I shrank inwardly, aware that I would not further my cause by making such remarks. "We may actually be in some danger here," I said.

Holly smirked—one of her patented expressions. "What a lovely streak of melodrama."

"Thanks."

"We're not in any danger," she said, "but we should leave. This place is too uncomfortable."

"You'll go with me?"

"I've packed," she said. "We might even go this evening, on the last ferry."

I agreed at once.

"I've got only two cases," she said. "Rather large ones, I'm afraid."

I had only one suitcase and a backpack, but it would not be easy to slip away from the Villa Clio without attracting attention. I wondered if, indeed, it was even advisable to leave in such a manner, as though we'd stolen the silverware. "Maybe we should tell them," I said. "We owe them something."

"I don't think so," she said. "I can't face him." She smiled through tears now. "I'm rather a coward, as you see."

I'd been going through my options for several days, and concurred with Holly that under the present circumstances it would be wise to abandon the island without further notice. Grant was behaving perversely, and Vera played along. They had, effectively, terminated my position. On top of which, I felt angry with them both, and wanted to demonstrate that my existence didn't depend on theirs. I could go wherever I pleased. I could write my own books, rather than type Grant's. I could cook my own elaborate dinners, in my own kitchen, without their sufferance.

So I spent the afternoon making arrangements for departure. We'd take the last ferry, at nine, though that meant having to abandon the dinner table rather precipitously. The Grants would, perhaps, suspect that something was amiss; but they would never guess we were leaving, and without notice.

I stopped by the Quisisana to tell Patrice about my plans. "I am not wanting this," he said, standing on the cool, marble floor of the vestibule outside the dining room in a white jacket. "Now I am alone here, on Capri, when you go. Maybe I will go, too. With you, Alexi. There is no point to stay."

That was the last thing I wanted. "You can follow," I said. "I'll send my address, when I have one. Probably in Rome." I explained that Holly and I were going together.

"This is love!"

"Not exactly," I said, "but I'm hoping."

"I am hoping, too," he responded. "I am feeling that Giovanni, he doesn't believe this marriage is love. It does never work. He will love me, when he realize . . ." His eyes widened. "We can join you, in Roma! I have loved Roma, no?" For an awful moment, I thought he might break into song.

"We may go to England," I said. "I'm not really sure."

"Go to Roma, Alexi," he advised in a hushed tone. "The English are very cold. I have told you this many time. England is a country of the head. They have no physical senses. You can examine this in their food, in the ugly clothes. The newlywed, they come to Capri, and they don't hold hands or kiss. They say, 'Isn't the hotel jolly nice, poppins?' This is their only pleasure!"

I hoped that Patrice, when he turned to philosophy, had greater sophistication, but I doubted it. He was no Jean-Paul Sartre, but I would miss him badly. He had lightened my days on Capri, giving me solace and companionship.

"I am coming to see you away," he said, kissing me on either cheek, solemnly, before shuffling back to the grand dining hall. The slump in his shoulders spoke volumes. I guessed that his time on Capri had come to an end as well.

Before dinner, I packed my few belongings, cleaned the cottage, finished a last assignment from Grant (typing a batch of letters to his London agent and publishers), then paused to read again a letter from Eddie Sloane, my brother's army friend. It had been waiting for me upon my return from Salerno, having been forwarded by my father. It was postmarked from Iowa, written in a carefully scripted hand—the letters all tipping to one side.

*Dear Alex,*

*You don't know me, but I was in your brother's platoon in Nam. I was with him when he got killed. We were good friends, and this was hard for me but I'm sure harder for you and your family. My condolences to you and them.*

*Once he said that if anything happened to him—that sort of thing was on your mind there—that I should write you. He wanted you to know he did have a good friend through his tour. We looked out for each other. Talked a lot, late at night. Nothing else to do sometimes but sit around and slap mosquitoes and talk, and I learned a lot from Nick.*

*He said you were damn smart, and was always bragging about your college and stuff you accomplished. He didn't know how you could read so many books and not lose your vision! That's what he said, and he was mighty proud.*

*Nick was smart himself, as you know. I never saw a guy like him, so concerned to get things right. And he talked about you all the time. That's all I really wanted to say. I don't know exactly what goes on between brothers, since I don't have one, but he said he really missed you over there, and he said it was nice that he had somebody to write to. And Jesus, he spent time on those letters!*

*I am trying to put this in the right words because it seems important. I wanted to explain—you probably know it anyway—that Nick cared about what happened to you, and he said he was looking forward more than anything to getting back. But you know, he's still thinking about you. I got to believe he's somewhere.*

*After I came back, it was hard to adjust, for me. After all that mess, the war, and the guys who didn't make it, like Nicky. Sometimes I try to push it away, like a dream, and I say it didn't even happen. The world couldn't be like that.*

*So, that's all. If you ever get to Davenport, this address is where you can reach me. We can go for some beers, and I'll tell you stuff you never heard in your life before.*

The letter was signed, "Sincerely, Edward Sloane." I found it strangely comforting that my brother had spent his last months near Eddie. It told me something about Nicky that he would find such a friend. He'd come a long way in a short time, had discovered and amplified a fine, intelligent, and wise part of himself, one that—had he been luckier—he'd have carried back from Vietnam.

Now I put Grant's letters in a neat pile on the table, and wrote a note to him and Vera. It would have to suffice:

*Dear Rupert and Vera,*

*I'm leaving in a stack here what has become my final assignment from Rupert. You will know by now that I have left Capri, for good, with Holly. I can't speak for her—her motives are probably different from mine. But I will say that I felt my time at the Villa Clio had come to a natural end. Unfortunately, I did not feel comfortable with saying good-bye. I'm sorry about this. The past week—the past month—has been, for me, a difficult time. I'm leaving, but I'll be in touch again by letter. Let me say I regret my stay on Capri didn't end more happily, and that I will always remain grateful for the many things I learned in your company. I think I will never forget the Villa Clio, or either of you.*

It surprised me when, instinctively, I wrote "Love, Alex," at the bottom. That was a false note, but I could not help it. I still feared Rupert Grant, and continued to admire him; but I didn't "love" him. Vera was, perhaps, another matter. I had made a genuine connection there, and many things she had said to me would reverberate for years to come. I also dashed off good-byes to various friends and acquaintances, such as Peter Duncan-Jones, the Bonanos, and Father Aurelio. Each had offered forms of consolation and encouragement, and I would miss them.

It would have been more pleasant to leave Capri under better circumstances, but I felt an urgency that could not be quashed. I had to go, immediately and without further notice.

Holly came to the door, breathless. "I've asked Mimo to take my bags to the ferry," she said.

"Won't he tell Rupert?"

"Have you ever heard him speak?"

I saw there was no turning back. We would leave that night on the ferry, after dinner, slipping away into the dusk. Exactly where that journey would end I couldn't imagine.

*six*

_____

Before dinner, I carried my suitcase and knapsack to the Bar Vittoria, in the Marina Grande. They would keep my things there, with Holly's. I wanted as smooth a getaway as possible, and could visualize an incensed Rupert Grant bearing down on us, a bull with flaring horns, trying to prevent our departure. I'd had a sequence of nightmares about that dagger of his, envisioning it stuck in my back as I walked the metal gangway onto the ferry—a scene from one of Graham Greene's thrillers.

To my horror, the Grants had invited Auden to dinner at the Villa Clio that night without telling either me or Holly. I discovered this when entering the long sitting room, where Auden—or the ghost of the poet— sat alone in a faded linen suit on the white sofa beneath the whitewashed walls and high vaulted ceiling. His pale hands were awkwardly folded before him—like unwelcome pets that had crawled into his lap and made themselves comfortable. Above his head loomed a painting by Peter Duncan-Jones, the one where an androgynous creature with three eyes and two navels was being fondled by several grotesque, smaller figures of indeterminate sex.

"Hello, Mr. Auden," I said.

He raised his eyebrows when he saw me, as if to say, "What? You again?"

I wondered what Grant had in mind. Was he trying to make up to me, having guessed that I felt dejected about not meeting him the day before? Was this a conciliatory gesture from Vera? I began to question the whole business of departure. Perhaps I should tell Holly I had changed my mind, and we must proceed in some orderly fashion? We might give a month's or a week's notice. Or resolve to stay on Capri indefinitely: Grant was already talking about a new assistant, another Italian girl (recommended by his Italian publisher, Mondadori) who would replace Marisa, and she would surely consume his erotic imagination for a while. I no longer knew what made sense, though I'd begun to question so much of what I'd appropriated from the Grants. Their way in the world was not mine.

Vera entered with a tray of drinks. Vodka for Auden, with ice. No mixers. Wine for the rest of us.

"Let me introduce Wystan," she said.

"We've met," he said.

"Really?"

"In the piazzetta this morning," he said, looking at me coolly. "We had a little seminar, didn't we?"

Vera looked at me strangely, as if aware for the first time that I had a life apart from her and Rupert. I didn't only exist while lounging in their presence. I was, indeed, a whole forest of falling trees with nobody but myself to hear them crashing to the ground.

Grant himself entered from the kitchen with a glass of whiskey, Holly trailing. She had obviously been crying, but I saw she was dressed for our journey: jeans, leather shoes, a sturdy cotton sweater—one I'd seen her wearing in Salerno and Paestum. I tried to catch her eyes, but she turned away.

"Alex has already met Wystan," Vera said.

Grant ignored the remark. "How can you drink that bloody stuff, Wystan. Tastes of motor oil."

"I prefer *good* vodka, to be sure," he said.

We pulled up chairs, forming a semicircle around the visiting poet, listening as he continued a conversation with Grant that had been underway for some time. He had left New York, he said, forever. It was "too much like Calcutta, only without the amenities." He didn't like Richard Nixon, nor did he trust Henry Kissinger. Christ Church, his old college in Oxford, had made him an honorary fellow, offering the use of a college house in the garden behind the Senior Common Room—a tiny cottage, where Anglican clergy were often housed.

"Ah, the Anglicans," said Vera. "Many are cold, but few are frozen."

Auden had doubtless heard this before, but smiled politely.

"You're the archbishop of poetry, what?" Grant said, barely concealing his irony. "Stephen will be killing himself."

"Stephen has become a bore," said Auden. "Spenders his time trotting about America."

"Giving poetry a bad name," Grant added.

"The fees are grand," Auden said. "I don't think anyone actually reads Stephen now, do you?"

"They never did," said Grant.

They referred, I knew, to Stephen Spender. Grant always made fun of the line, "I think continually of those who are truly great." "Nobody ever thinks continually of anything," he said. "Do you, Lorenzo?"

He and Auden kept the conversation mainly to gossip about old friends and associations—a gambit that naturally excluded me and Holly. I realized how uncomfortable this name-dropping made me. Even Vera looked at a loss, hearing that blizzard of names torn from the contents of an out-of-date anthology: Edgell Rickword, Bernard Spencer, Peter Hewitt, Roy Campbell, E. J. Pratt. A whole generation had sunk like Atlantis into the wine-dark sea of literary history, from which few names are ever recovered.

At seven—very early by Italian standards but typical of the Grants— we went into the dining room, aware that Vera would have prepared a feast for Auden, beginning with scrippelle 'im busse—lovely crepes in beef broth, a speciality of Abruzzo. She had promised to teach me how to make them, but that never happened. There was, as usual, a small pasta dish, followed by succulent pork rolls: cotechino in galera. They were wrapped in prosciutto, browned in sautéed onions, then baked. The dessert was among my favorites: almond cake (torta di mandorle). I had smelled the almond aroma as soon as I entered the house that evening. It felt like a signal from Vera, a sign of truce.

I listened intently to the conversation, my palms sweaty, watching the

black-handed Neapolitan clock on the mantel as it swallowed the minutes. Each fat tick reminded me that my time at the villa was coming to
an end. The wine that night was a white Trebbiano—Vera had heard me
compliment it one evening—and I found myself drinking more heavily
than usual, with Maria Pia's cousin, young Alfredo, filling my glass almost
compulsively. Barely through the main course, the room seemed to
enlarge and contract. I saw Auden's massively wrinkled face (which he
described as looking "like a wedding cake left out in the rain overnight")
through alcohol-distorted vision. But the wine also gave me the courage
to inject my own opinions into the conversation, as when Auden referred
to Kissinger again and I began a monologue about Cambodia, suggesting
that it was insane to attack that hapless nation. There would only be dis-
ruptions and reprisals.

"You don't know what you're talking about, Lorenzo," Grant said,
sternly, when I stopped for breath.

"I do," I said.

"Nonsense," he said. Blue veins were bulging in his temples, and his
lips stretched thin. "You're like most young Americans. They know nothing of history, but they're full of opinions—ignorant and childish opinions."

"Better than the English young," said Vera, rising to my defense.
"What a gormless lot they are!"

Holly dipped her eyes to the table, gormlessly.

I felt confused, and wanted to pound my fist on the table and shout
something terribly incisive, but could think of nothing appropriate. I did
not at all want to pursue this subject. I'd been sucked into a whirlpool,
and it was time I extricated myself.

"I should relax, Rupert," said Auden. "One doesn't want a coronary at
our age."

Auden, bless him, assumed control of the conversation now. He began
to lecture us on his favorite detective novels, saying it made one feel so
"cozy and complete" to lie in a warm bath and read them. He told Grant
he should consider writing something along the lines of Dorothy L. Say-
ers, whom he described as one of the best novelists of the century.

Grant, with a lofty sigh, said, "Wystan, you're such a schoolmaster."

Auden demurred. "Please, dear. School*mistress*."

I laughed sharply, but realized as I leaned back in my chair that it was nearly eight-fifteen. It would take at least twenty minutes, probably more, to get to the Marina Grande. I glanced at Holly, leading her eyes to the clock.

"I must go," I said. "I'm afraid I have a headache."

Vera looked at me in a puzzled way.

"By all means," said Grant, delighted to see me go.

I passed through the kitchen and stepped into the violet shade of the garden to wait for Holly, who emerged some minutes later. She had apparently contracted the same headache.

"The last ferry is often late," I said, trying to reassure her as we hurried toward the gate.

The last thing I recalled of the Villa Clio was the smell of wild cyclamen, soft and mournful, more like the memory of a smell than the thing itself.

## *seven*

─────────

The serpentine descent to the harbor by taxi was a blur, bringing us into the Marina Grande at ten minutes past the hour. We fetched our things from the bar and lumbered toward the docks. I had Holly's cumbersome bags in either hand. Unease flowed through my body, making me queasy.

Patrice came running toward us, waving. "She have gone," he said.

"Who?"

"This ferry to Napoli. She has disappear without you. The time is passed, and you have missed her."

I shook my head. It was impossible to return to the Villa Clio now, heaving our suitcases, tails between our legs. We'd have to wait in the Marina Grande until morning, staying at a hotel. "Fucking hell," I said.

"Not to worry, Alexi. I have Giovanni to help," Patrice said, fluttering his wings, beckoning. "Please, come this way."

Rather dazed, we followed him to the western part of the harbor, where yachts and local fishing boats were tied up for the evening, hip to hip. Giovanni's ungainly vessel idled at the dock, deep-throated, ready to board. The water had turned deeply sanguine in the harbor, and a yellow moon hung in the sky like some improbable lantern, lighting the way to Naples.

"Giovanni and I will take you," he said. "He has no problem. I have engage the boat for you."

I looked quizzically at Giovanni.

"*Napoli, no?*" he inquired, with a sweet smile.

"*Napoli, sì,*" I said.

"*Andiamo, subito,*" he called, matter-of-factly, revving the engines in neutral as Patrice helped Holly onto the deck. I lowered our suitcases in, then leaped aboard as Patrice untied the lines.

There was a click as the gears engaged, followed by a low groaning sound of the engine. The familiar marine smell of diesel mingled with salty air, the boat yawing from side to side, lifted by currents. We followed a bright yellow swath of moonlight on the water, making our way across the Bay of Naples toward what, for me, seemed like the greatest mystery of all, my life to come.

"I am sad for this," Patrice said, quietly, with a hand on my thigh. "You are my best of friend, Alexi," he said.

"And you're mine," I said, my thoughts turning to Nicky. *Funny how good you can feel,* he'd written, *when you hear certain things, which is probably why we say them. To cheer ourselves up. To make it possible to put one foot in front of the other without losing it.*

I glanced briefly at Holly, who watched Capri dwindle in the dusk behind us, sinking from view. But I refused to look back myself. I had looked back enough for a man of my age, and from now on, my direction was forward. That was my only resolution, and one I knew I could never keep.

*epilogue*

I left Capri under cover of darkness, not thinking that thirty years would elapse before I set foot on the island again.

After landing in Naples with Holly that night, we found a cheap *pensione* near the harbor, then traveled the next morning by train to Rome, where an English uncle of hers owned a gloomy modern apartment overlooking the river on the Lungo Tevere della Vittoria. (He preferred Florence, where he also kept an apartment. We saw him only once, for dinner, in a restaurant near the Pantheon.) Our relationship, such as it was, hobbled along for several weeks. We made each other miserable until, near the middle of October, she asked me to find another place to live. By that time, I was more than ready.

I traveled for two months, in France and England, then returned home for Christmas. Columbia welcomed me back for the spring semester, and I graduated only a year behind my class. The next three decades were—how could they not be?—eventful. My mother died in her early fifties, her heart in tatters, but my father lived on until 1997, by which time Massolini Construction had dwindled to a mini-version of its former self. Needless to say, I never went into business with my father and grandfather.

In a desultory way, I managed to write four books of poetry and three novels—a modest production, although I like what I accomplished, as did a modest gathering of readers. I taught here and there, eventually landing a permanent job at Bowdoin, in Maine. Recently, in the *Atlantic Monthly*, I published an essay on Rupert Grant, drawing on those months at the Villa Clio for atmosphere. For the most part, I focused on his verse, which I've increasingly come to respect. I referred to him as "one of the last English poets whose work one actually memorized" and said that I'd learned the essentials of my craft from him.

I didn't say, of course, that I'd come to despise him, and that his way of gobbling up those around him had left a sour taste in my mouth. I never mentioned Marisa or Holly, or the problems faced daily by Vera. I never mentioned his narcissism and spite for other writers. As a negative model, Grant had powerfully affected me, and long ago I decided it was better to live my life honestly and lovingly, with respect for those around me, than go to my grave with a trunkload of literary honors.

Some months after the essay appeared, I received a note from Capri. The Grants and I had not been in communication since my rude departure, even though I'd promised to write. Even after three decades, I recognized Vera's meticulously formed letters in black India ink—familiar because she had written several recipes by hand into my notebook, and I still used them. She wrote:

> *My dear Alex,*
>
> *Your piece on Rupert was sent by a friend in New York. It was quite charming. I do hope this finds you well, old thing. Do visit the Villa Clio again if you discover yourself in these parts. We're a long way from anywhere, of course.*

It was signed, "Affectionately, Vera." I found it puzzling that she had said so little, after all this time, and that she had signed it with affection. Yet the note eased old and deeply rooted feelings of guilt. I'd left like a thief, not even bothering to thank my hosts, however difficult they had been. They had taken me into their lives at a time when I could not have been an easy guest: wearing my troubles on my shirtsleeves, moving uncertainly among various propositional selves—many of which I gladly abandoned as soon as I found my footing in the adult world.

An invitation to a literary conference in Naples put Capri within easy reach only a few months later, and I took this as a sign. Arriving in that dilapidated city a day early, I thought of trying to find Marisa's grave, but the logistics of that made it seem impossible. I realized now how often I thought of her, and—most vividly—her terrible death. I had been writing poems about that event for many years, yet I still didn't understand what happened, or whose fault it was, or why she had gone to such an extreme length. That kind of thing moves beyond the realm of understanding.

I boarded a crowded hydrofoil for the island on a clear morning in late September, unsure of what exactly I would find at the Villa Clio. What I knew about Grant in the past decade was sketchy enough. Until the mid-1990s, he had occasionally published poems in places like *The New Yorker* and the *Times Literary Supplement*. They were wistful verses, mostly about the persistence of desire in old age—a theme borrowed from Yeats but embodied with an unmistakably Grantian inflection. His last full collection, *Love and Lemons,* had won a prize in Britain in 1989, prompting a number of lengthy reconsiderations of his career. There had been no new novels for two decades, but a fairly recent television adaptation of *Siren Call* had kept interest in his fiction alive. He would have just passed his ninety-third birthday a few months before.

Despite the lateness of the season, the ferry teemed with day-trippers, mostly Europeans. Capri had, if anything, grown in popularity since I had lived there. Disembarking at the Marina Grande, I felt dismayed by the profusion of hotels, restaurants, and tourist shops that lined the quays. The yachts in the harbor appeared more numerous and larger than those I'd remembered, most of them flying international flags. I had to wait for nearly half an hour to get a taxi to the piazzetta.

A certain dread mingled with curiosity as I retraced the path to the Villa Clio, although the decades had done less damage to the surroundings than I'd have guessed. The piazzetta absorbed its tumult of visitors with dignity, as ever, and the Camerelle still smelled of laundry soap and cat piss. The sun was brilliant along the Tragara, and I found the view of the Marina Piccola and Mount Solaro as dazzling as before. Apparently the lack of roads on Capri and its steep terrain had prevented the kind of

development that had ruined much of the Amalfi coast. Rich people preferred to drive up to their holiday villas in Land Rovers nowadays, even
in Italy.

I was let into the Villa Clio by Maria Pia, who had changed in the usual
ways. She was plumper now, with ankles like tree stumps. Her silvery
hair was oddly unkempt, unwashed, and the hair on her arms was
coarsely matted, thick, swirling from wrist to elbow. I remembered the
mustache, but the unsightly birthmark on her cheek surprised me. Had
I somehow not noticed that before? She dipped her head toward me, in
recognition and respect, but there was an element of contempt in her
expression, as if she still resented the manner of my departure.

"*Venga qui, professore,*" she said, as she had before I had genuinely earned
that title. I was led into the kitchen, where Vera stood at the counter with
her hands deep in a bowl of flour. I couldn't help but smile. It was as if
she'd been standing there for the past thirty years, waiting for me.

"Hello," she said, wiping her hands on her apron. I had sent a note
ahead, so she expected me.

"Hello, Vera," I said, kissing her on either cheek. "Nothing seems to
change around here."

"I have," she said, wiping sweat from her forehead with the back of
one hand. "I'm rather a wreck."

"Not true," I said, "you look wonderful."

"What complete bosh," she said.

But she did. She was smaller than I remembered her, but just as lively.
Her gray eyes glinted, flecked with green. Her hair had gone whitish
gray, but it shimmered, cut straight above her forehead. Her face seemed
remarkably free of wrinkles for a woman over seventy, and she had never
added an ounce of fat. If anything, she had grown thinner.

"I need a drink," she said, reaching for a bottle of sherry. "We'll have
lunch in an hour. You will stay, of course."

"Of course," I said.

I sat for a while with her in the alcove, answering a flurry of questions
about my life. I had a wife now, yes, and two children—twins, now seventeen. I was a professor, and had written numerous books. She seemed
genuinely pleased for me, and wished I had brought my wife, Alice,

whom I met while doing graduate studies in comparative literature at Yale, having switched from classics after Columbia.

"Next time," I said.

I asked about Grant with hesitation.

"He's not been well," she said, confirming what I'd heard. "It's his memory, you see. I don't know what to call it. Senility? Dementia? He hasn't recognized anyone in four or five years."

I asked to see him, and she directed me to the garden. "He sleeps there most of the day, under his tree," she said.

I remembered that lemon tree, where I had sometimes gone myself to sit in imitation of the master. Going into the garden, I discovered a shrunken version of Rupert Grant, now asleep in a canvas chair, barefooted. He wore ragged trousers and a shirt that looked like a painter's palette, stained with a variety of meals past. A straw hat shaded his face, and his chin slumped on his chest. There was no fruit on the tree behind him.

"Hello, Rupert," I said, hovering.

He sniffed several times, then snorted. Looking up, his eyelids quivered, then opened; the eyes themselves appeared cloudy, full of mucus. The lines on his face had become deep rivulets of perspiration, and his hair had grown long and white, resting on his shoulders behind the hat. His feet were knobby and lobster-red, the toenails brownish yellow.

"I'm sorry to wake you, Rupert," I said. (It occurred to me that I had never felt comfortable using his first name when I lived at the Villa Clio.)

His eyes cleared suddenly, and he leaned forward, studying my face like a text from another era, deciphering, translating. Then he rose, drawing himself up to something of his old height, seizing my wrist with two hands.

"Do you remember me, Rupert?"

He smiled, with a crooked row of tobacco-stained teeth flashing briefly. Then he let go, and sat, and I knew I had not managed to get through to him, not in any important way, and that somehow this was exactly what I should have expected.

*acknowledgments*

---

My deepest thanks to Charles Baker, Ann Beattie, Chris Bohjalian, and Ron Powers, who read this novel in some earlier version and offered suggestions. Thanks to my wife, Devon Jersild, and to Terry Karten, my editor, for their meticulous attention to my revisions. Finally, thanks to Gore Vidal for countless suggestions along the way. I should note that the translations from Rilke are my own.